Performing Palimpsest Bodies

Performing Palimpsest Bodies: Postmemory Theatre Experiments in Mexico

Ruth Hellier-Tinoco

intellect Bristol, UK / Chicago, USA

First published in the UK in 2019 by
Intellect, The Mill, Parnall Road, Fishponds, Bristol, BS16 3JG, UK

First published in the USA in 2019 by
Intellect, The University of Chicago Press, 1427 E. 60th Street,
Chicago, IL 60637, USA

A catalogue record for this book is available from the
British Library.

Front cover image: Roldán Ramírez in *Mexican Trilogy
(Trilogía Mexicana): Malinche / Malinches* by La Máquina de Teatro,
directed by Juliana Faesler and Clarissa Malheiros, Mexico City, 2010.
Photo credit: La Máquina de Teatro and Christa Cowrie.

Back cover image: Ruth Hellier-Tinoco in *pre / now / post: una
trilogía* by Ruth Hellier-Tinoco, USA, 2013 (with image of Ruth Hellier
in *Aztec* by Leicestershire Theatre in Education Company, 1991).
Photo credit: Timothy Cooley.

Copy-editor: MPS Technologies
Cover designer: Aleksandra Szumlas
Production manager: Faith Newcombe
Typesetting: Contentra Technologies

Print ISBN: 978-1-84150-466-7
ePDF ISBN: 978-1-78938-010-1
ePUB ISBN: 978-1-78938-009-5

Printed and bound by CPI / Antony Rowe, UK.

In memory of

my mum Margaret and my dad Ken

*(my dear mum died in the Royal London Hospital on 25 June 1987,
and my dear dad died in my arms on 16 February 2016)*

and
my brother-in-law David
*(who died surrounded by Joy,
Jon, Steph, Tamsin and Kevin on 17 February 2016).*

Dedicated to

*Jesusa Rodríguez, feminist performance artist,
theatre director, activist and now senator.*

Contents

List of illustrations

The majority of the photos portray four specific performance projects of La Máquina de Teatro. I am deeply grateful to the artists of La Máquina for sharing these photos.

Photos for each project are mainly included within the corresponding analytical chapter (Section Two, Chapters 3, 4, 5 and 6). Repetitions and juxtapositions of illustrations are also included in Section One and the Epilogue. To simplify the labelling I reference the four projects with the following abbreviations:

Trilogy   *Mexican Trilogy* (see Chapter 3 for analysis).
La Máquina de Teatro.
Photo credit: La Máquina de Teatro (including photos by Christa Cowrie).

Zapata   *Zapata, Death Without End* (see Chapter 4 for analysis).
La Máquina de Teatro, A la Deriva Teatro, Teatro de la Rendija, Colectivo Escénico Oaxaca and A-tar.
Photo credit: La Máquina de Teatro (including photos by Andy Castro, J. Martin, ensemble participants, R. Hellier-Tinoco).

War   *War in Paradise* (see Chapter 5 for analysis).
La Máquina de Teatro.
Photo credit: La Máquina de Teatro (including photos by Andy Castro and J. Martin).

Time   *Time of the Devil* (see Chapter 6 for analysis).
La Máquina de Teatro.
Photo credit: La Máquina de Teatro (including photos by Andy Castro).

Acknowledgements

As I reflect on what remains, through the traces, glimmers, specks and ephemera, I cherish and value all the diverse inspirations and interactions of so many people—friends, family, teachers, students, artists, scholars and other travellers—who have shaped my journeys over the passing years and have influenced this book.

For their specific interactions in creating this book, I particularly thank: Juliana Faesler and Clarissa Malheiros, the two extraordinary directors of La Máquina de Teatro, for all their stimulating, profound and playful contributions; the many performers and creative artists involved with *Trilogía Mexicana, Zapata, Muerte Sin Fin, Guerra en el Paraíso* and *La Hora del Diablo,* including Diana Fidelia, Natyeli Flores, Roldán Ramírez, Horacio González García Rojas, Sandra Garibaldi, Edyta Rzewuska, José Juan Cabello, Elizabeth Muñoz and the practitioners of A la Deriva Teatro, Teatro de la Rendija, Colectivo Escénico Oaxaca and A-tar; Mariana Gándara, a director at el Museo Universitario del Chopo during the residency of La Máquina de Teatro; and Antonio Prieto Stambaugh, for his astute and insightful feedback on this manuscript.

For broader professional, intellectual and creative contributions, I thank: the inventive undergraduate and graduate students at the University of California Santa Barbara who have taken my classes on "Creating Experimental Performance: memories/histories, processes/practices," "Theatre and Performance in Mexico: Embodying, Resisting and Subverting Stereotypes," and "Performance Studies"; the students who acted as research assistants, particularly Luis Mendoza, Daisy León and Kimberly Valenzuela; faculty and staff at UCSB who have supported me since my migration to the United States in 2011; colleagues and students involved with contemporary performance, theatre and dance at the University of Winchester, 2002–11; colleagues in the fields of performance studies, theatre, dance and music, particularly in the Dance Studies Association (formerly Congress on Research in Dance and Society for Dance History Scholars), Performance Studies International, the Society for Ethnomusicology, the British Forum for Ethnomusicology, the Association for Theatre in Higher Education and the American Society for Theatre Research; teachers and fellow students at the Guildhall School of Music and Drama, London (1973–79); Birmingham University, Departments of Music, Drama, Dance (1980–83), City of Birmingham University (PGCE Drama in Education); Birmingham Conservatoire (Ph.D.), especially Mark Lockett and Peter Johnson; teachers and students at St Thomas

Aquinas, Bishop Challoner and Camp Hill schools; friends and family on the islands of Lake Pátzcuaro, in Morelia and elsewhere in Mexico; collaborators in *Mexican Studies/Estudios Mexicanos* at UNAM; and many performers and artists with whom I worked in the acting world in Britain in the 1980s and 90s.

I am deeply indebted to the editorial team at Intellect for their professionalism and patience, especially Jessica Mitchell, Amy Damutz and Faith Newcombe.

Finally, I thank my family and my friends (especially in Britain, Mexico and the United States), Griffin the cat and my dear husband Tim Cooley for his unwavering love and sustenance.

Section One

Outlines

Figure 1.

Introduction

Creating theatre through remains of bodies of history

How do we share our lives with what remains?
—Juliana Faesler & Clarissa Malheiros, artistic directors, La Máquina de Teatro, Mexico

How does one come to inhabit and envision one's body as coextensive with one's environment and one's past, emphasizing the porous nature of skin rather than its boundedness?
—Diana Taylor, *The Archive and The Repertoire*

If the past is never over, or never completed, "remains" might be understood not solely as object or document material, but also as the immaterial labor of bodies engaged in and with that incomplete past: bodies striking poses, making gestures, voicing calls, reading words, singing songs, or standing witness.
—Rebecca Schneider, *Performing Remains*

[S]cenic works can articulate a relation between the body as a holder of collective memory and as an unfolding of poetic presences.
—Gabriel Yépez [1] [2]

Figure 2.

Transdisciplinary experimentation

experiment: *a course of action tentatively adopted without being sure of the eventual outcome [noun]; try out new concepts or ways of doing things [verb].*

As humans, we are deeply aware of our bodies as containers and transmitters of memories and histories through trans-temporalities. We become conscious of alterations and transformations over time; of accumulated layers, sediments and iterations; of multi-temporal connections; of discontinuities, repetitions and juxtapositions; of remains and traces. We experience trans-temporal relationships with our predecessors, our prior selves, our environments and our pasts. We connect with collective memories and bodies of history through myriad remains in diverse forms: literary texts, oral stories and linguistic codes; photographs, images and objects; embodied archival repertoires of movements, gestures, voices and sounds; smells and tastes; architectures and spaces; ephemera and barely tangible existences. As creators, performers, spectators, participants, teatristas, practitioners and witnesses, we make use of these connections to explore complex pasts within complicated presents to generate possible futures.[3] In performance projects and creative theatre workshops, we can reactivate bodies of history through playful and rigorous transdisciplinary experimentation, performing powerful re-visions that provoke and challenge. Through these performance practices, we can "activate and open the past within the present."[4] We can "imagine other 'potential historical realities' and thereby 'open up a different future.'"[5] Articulating "a relation between the body as a holder of collective memory and as an unfolding of poetic presences," we can use these creative processes to work through productive tensions of trans-temporal traces by performing palimpsest bodies.

Bodies of history

This book presents a study of four theatre projects that provocatively experiment with bodies of history. All were created by La Máquina de Teatro, one of Mexico's most renowned performance and scenic arts companies, founded and directed by two remarkable women artists, Juliana Faesler and Clarissa Malheiros (Figure 25). These performance projects start with an individual (dead or mythical) body who continues to impact contemporary lives and who remains as a presence in collective memories. In workshops and performances the creative artists translate from myriad traces to generate a plurality of possibilities through bodies as archives and embodied archival repertoires.[6] As they play with time through simultaneity, coexistence, multiplicity and juxtaposition, they merge and accumulate iterations of numerous stories, histories, journeys and lives. Through liminal performance and postdramatic theatre strategies they perform layered, plural and trans identities. They examine questions of power relations, discrimination and memory itself through re-activating scenarios of material already worked on. Seeking to confront and transform stereotypes, they offer feminist and queer re-visions of official histories and collective memories.

Through the creation of this book, by sharing some remains of these performances of La Máquina, I seek to gesture to possible futures by inspiring potential practice and creating community. In her seminal discussions of archives, repertoires and performing cultural memory in the Americas, Diana Taylor describes a "collaborative production of knowledge [in which] writing and embodied performance

Figure 3.

4

have often worked together to layer the historical memories that constitute community."[7] George Lipsitz suggests that communities can be called into being through performance, particularly connecting past and present.[8] Together, the embodied performances of La Máquina and these writings (and photographs) are palimpsest archival-repertoires layering global memories to constitute community.

In this introduction, I offer some basic frameworks that set the scene for the chapters that follow. These outlines comprise: 1) descriptions of palimpsest bodies; of postmemory and rememory; of re-vision of scenarios; and performing remains; 2) a summary of La Máquina de Teatro and the four case studies; 3) an overview of my research methods and experiences of performing palimpsest bodies in Britain, Mexico and the USA; and 4) a discussion of translating remains of performances into words.

1. Outline of interpretive and creative trans-temporal frameworks

Performing palimpsest bodies

Palimpsests are inherently trans-temporal, containing traces and remains of previous existences even as they are experienced in a present moment. Palimpsests are formed through movements over time, through layering and sedimentation, through complex arrangements and through shifts and accumulations of iterations. Palimpsests contain a plurality of fragments and ephemera, existing through simultaneity and juxtaposition. Palimpsests provide evidence of multiple journeys, stories and environments through a temporal narrative that is often ambiguous. Palimpsests involve strategies of re-using and re-forming, where traces endure, sometimes scarcely palpable, sometimes ghostly, yet always remaining.

All these qualities and processes are useful for interpreting, and indeed creating, experimental theatre and performance dealing with bodies of history and collective memories. Performing palimpsest bodies always contain trans-temporal plurality. Performing palimpsest bodies can "literally touch time through the residue of the gesture of the cross-temporality of the pose" through performing remains.[9] Re-activating remains of bodies of history from images, texts, embodied repertoires and barely tangible traces connects personal lives with collective memories in composite environments. Through layering, accumulations and iterations, palimpsest bodies perform complex trans-temporal provocations and re-visions.

Postmemory and rememory

Postmemory describes an overt temporal relationship between a present generation and past actions and histories, to draw on Marianne Hirsch.[10] The relation with the past is active and generative, mediated by imaginative investment, projection and creation. Hirsch's concept of postmemory is eminently useful for this study: these performance projects deal with past actions as bodies of history through relationships of postmemory. These bodies of history exist as multiple remains and as scenarios of material already worked on, which are re-imagined through theatre experiments. As these relationships of postmemory contain overt trans-temporal tensions and duality, the participants are inherently performing palimpsest bodies.

Rememory indicates embodied experiences of individual and collective stories. Rememory is a continued presence of something forgotten that returns through a body in the form of visceral experiences, as evocatively depicted by Toni Morrison.[11] Rememory embodies an experiential doubleness of "my memory" and "not my memory" through presences, remaining as traces, that are concealed and suddenly revealed. Rememory comprises an overt temporal relationship between past histories/memories and present experiences. As with postmemory, Morrison's concept of rememory is invaluable for considering core practices of La Máquina at the heart of the theatre projects in this book. The artists use experiences of rememory for their body-based creative strategies, opening up questions of tensions between individual and collective memories and histories. By inhabiting bodies of history through deeply embodied experiences of rememory they are performing palimpsest bodies.

Re-vision (re-membering) of scenarios

Re-vision (re-membering) involves re-doing and producing new from and with old texts, specifically with the aim of challenging and transforming inherited values, stereotypes and oppressive norms, as proposed by Adrienne Rich.[12] These "texts" are scenarios of materials that have already been worked on.[13] In the theatre projects of La Máquina, these "texts" are remains of bodies of history, existing in multiple forms as visual, literary, oral, embodied, sonic, spatial and sensory material traces. These remains of bodies of history are re-membered, re-formed and performed through practices of assembling and re-assembling by performing palimpsest bodies.

A scenario "makes visible, yet again, what is already there: the ghosts, the images, the stereotypes [...] [and also] haunts our present, a form of hauntology that resuscitates and reactivates old dramas," as Taylor has described.[14] As scenarios work through reactivation rather than duplication, these recognizable and familiar texts provide rich material for trans-temporal corporeal theatre experiments. For La Máquina, these are scenarios of power struggles, discrimination, fragility, leadership and domesticity, existing as relationships of postmemory and experiences of rememory. Through a doing with the done, these artists generate productive tensions and playful re-visions by performing palimpsest bodies.[15]

Performance remains: Performing remains/performing the archive/performing cultural memory

For this study on palimpsest bodies and performing remains, I am inspired by the discussions of many scholars and artists who explore the potency of live collective

Figure 4.

performance practices in ethical processes of corporeal inquiry.[16] In particular I turn repeatedly to the compelling and complex writings of Taylor, specifically relating to embodied repertoires, archives, performance, environments and pasts. Given that Taylor explicitly analyses contexts in Mexico, both in relation to theatre and performance and also to complex histories of racialization and colonization, her ideas are profoundly pertinent.[17] I also draw on Rebecca Schneider's significant work on performing remains/performance remains and performing the archive. Schneider has described the "citational quality of performance," which encompasses "citing other work, co-opting other work, creating an action by acting or reacting, enacting or re-enacting, [and] making of the single body a stage across which whole histories […] are brought to bear."[18] She notes that "Any action, here, is already a palimpsest of other actions, a motion set in motion by precedent motion or anticipating future motion or lateral motion."[19] Schneider's words describe the processes of the artists in my study and also my processes of critique (as creation) as I cite Schneider's ideas to analyse the work of La Máquina. Working from the generative embodied question of La Máquina—"How do we share our lives with what remains?"— I relate this to Schneider's evocative depiction of performing remains:

> If the past is never over, or never completed, "remains" might be understood not solely as object or document material, but also as the immaterial labor of bodies engaged in and with that incomplete past: bodies striking poses, making gestures, voicing calls, reading words, singing songs, or standing witness.[20]

2. La Máquina de Teatro and four performance projects

La Máquina de Teatro—the Theatre Machine—is one of Mexico's leading contemporary scenic arts companies. The work of directors Faesler and Malheiros has been described as "without a doubt, one of the most brilliant demonstrations of theatrical vanguard of our time."[21] The artists of La Máquina develop appropriate aesthetics through explorations in theatre labs, working with body-based and transdisciplinary devising processes.[22] Their imperative is to ethically, playfully and rigorously create scenic arts events that provoke and engage. As reflective practitioners they use ensemble practices to work through collective creation. For processes of devising, Malheiros engages creative play strategies developed through her training with Jacques Lecoq and her long career as a theatre performer, teacher and director. Faesler draws on the methodology Viewpoints, returning to the same questions again and again from different perspectives, always through understandings of history as experience. Without adhering to any particular system, they encompass transdisciplinary practices, strategies and elements that cohere with the "experimental performative types" of liminal performance and postdramatic theatre.[23] Through multi-corporeality, they work through diversity, complexity, simultaneity, contradiction and density. Through transversality, they develop overt crossings. They combine experimentation and challenges through aesthetics of *convivio*—a close sharing with the audience—and *relajo*—provocative playfulness. Their strategies and approaches explicitly engage feminist cultural positionings and frameworks, incorporating concepts of trans-ness, multiple identities, fluidity and queer sensibilities, always with a seriously rigorous playful critique.

Four outlines

For this book, I have selected four performance projects that explore matters of temporalities, memories and histories, and which use individual iconic bodies of history as the core provocation for creative practice. As Faesler explains: "The company has the goal of creating bridges between the present and the past, between the real and the fictional. We search for relations between symbols of the contemporary world, of history, of different systems of articulation of memory and the scenic arts [...] We wanted to work with cultural fictions and historical realities—to see where these paths cross."[24]

These projects are not concerned with mimetically reproducing and re-enacting received official histories; rather, they playfully and provocatively enable re-visions of scenarios of personal and collective memories and histories. The artists play with and through iconic bodies who have shaped shared histories and memories, and who continue to resonate in present-day cultural contexts. They deliberately challenge notions of chronological time by crossing and merging temporal boundaries. They investigate pressing issues of the present to re-imagine possible futures. By deliberately seeking to cross and blur boundaries, they experiment with practices of liminality, in-betweenness, both/and states and ambiguities to offer provocative, feminist and queer interpretations through performing palimpsest bodies.

1. *Mexican Trilogy* comprises three full-length works that were created over three years by a small team of artists, and that continue to be performed by an ensemble of five actors. In this multifaceted, transdisciplinary stage piece, through remains of three bodies of history from the fifteenth-and-sixteenth century, the ensemble reactivates scenarios of conquest, violation, memory and complicity. Through Emperor Nezahualcóyotl, Moctezuma II and slave girl turned translator La Malinche they generate deeply complex performances of trans-temporal crossings that provokingly and playfully explore issues of discrimination, truth and relationships (Figures 4 and 10).

2. *Zapata, Death Without End* was a yearlong multi-ensemble project connecting five collectives from as many regions. Through remains of the body of history of Emiliano Zapata, one of the most iconic leaders in the Mexican Revolution (1910–20), the ensembles reactivated scenarios of heroes, land and liberty. With their localised understandings of "home" the five groups brought deeply personal experiences to these shared explorations. Collaborating with La Máquina were A la Deriva Teatro (Guadalajara), Teatro de la Rendija (Mérida), Colectivo Escénico Oaxaca (Oaxaca), and A-tar (Tampico). In the final theatricalized event in Mexico City, performers and spectators joined together on stage for a compelling three-hour co-participatory performance of diversity and inter-dependency (Figure 5).

Figure 5.

Figure 6.

3. *War in Paradise* was a three-week intensive workshop project in which twenty-five artists generated a powerful unfinished performance of work-in-progress through remains of the body of history of 1960s resistance leader Lucio Cabañas. Through corporeal and spatial practices, the practitioners reactivated scenarios of repression and fragility to perform ethical embodiments of resistance and care (Figure 6).

4. *Time of the Devil* is a full-length solo work in which Malheiros performs a corporeal philosophical inquiry into existential questions of life and death, inspired by Fernando Pessoa's eponymous novel. Through remains of the spectral no-body of the Devil, the artist reactivates scenarios of precariousness, liminality and performativity, playing with perspectives, body parts and death masks (Figure 7).[25]

Figure 7.

3. My palimpsest bodies in performance and life

Research methods and experiences

For these discussions of transdisciplinary, devising projects in Mexico I draw on extensive long-term experiences, combined with specific material-gathering processes. To assemble the detailed research materials on La Máquina I have used six interconnecting methods:

1. Presence at and participation in live workshops and performances, providing first-hand experience of, and an intimacy with, the practices and practitioners;
2. Multiple viewings of performances (live and recorded), providing an immersion in minute-by-minute performance aesthetics, energies, dramaturgies and structures;
3. Interviews with artists and company members, providing insights into individual experiences. The unstructured interviews were open and free flowing, so the interviewees merged a wealth of knowledge and experiences about experimental theatre-making practices, processes and aesthetics, with personal understandings of contexts and histories of Mexico;[26]
4. Analysis of documentation produced by La Máquina (including blogs, Facebook postings and material provided for audiences), enabling me to delve into the provocations and processes undertaken by the company;
5. Analysis of published performance reviews in major media press outlets, allowing me to consider reception by critics and audiences;
6. Creation and performance of my own live theatre performance, *pre/now/post: una trilogía*, using a practice-as-research-in-performance (PARIP) methodology, enabling me to investigate their practices corporeally, and to experientially understand the palimpsest bodily characteristics of their work (Figures 11 and 12). [27]

More broadly, I bring into play my professional and life experiences over the last thirty or so years. As a creative artist, performer, teacher and facilitator of performing arts, music, theatre and dance for more than three decades, I draw on a wide range of practices as a reflective practitioner.[28] As a researcher of performance my work engages in diverse debates and discourses in fields including performance, dance, theatre and music studies. As a scholar of performance and cultural practices in Mexico, I draw on over two decades of studying and living in and with Mexican contexts, enmeshed in histories, politics and ideological perspectives.[29] As the current editor-in-chief of the bilingual, binational and multidisciplinary journal *Mexican Studies/Estudios Mexicanos*, I am in the position of engaging with cutting-edge scholarship in multiple fields on a daily basis.[30]

Together, these experiences and practices provide me with different forms of understandings which are necessary for this research project. I am particularly reminded of the observation by Eugenio Barba, recently re-iterated by Marco De Marinis, that "Often […] theatre historians come face to face with testimonies without themselves having sufficient experience of the craft and process of theatre making. [...] Historical understanding of theatre and dance is often blocked or rendered superficial because of neglect of the logic of the creative process, because of misunderstandings of the performer's empirical way of thinking, and because of an inability to overcome the confines established for the spectator..."[31]

In "Situating the Critical Discourse," theatre scholar Juan Villegas noted that "[t]he description or interpretation of a specific culture is always mediated by the historian's social imaginary, her/his system of values and degree of cultural competence in reading the signs and the context in which the signs were produced. [...] [It is] a discursive practice mediated by the cultural historian's ideological and cultural position."[32] Similarly, in *Performing Mexicanidad*, Laura Gutiérrez discusses "the implications embedded in the network of translations in relationship to differences: national, cultural, gender, and sexual," describing how "my project and I, as a bilingual and bicultural critic, are both part of that network of *trans*-lations, that is, part of the movement of words, concepts, theories, and products across 'borders.'"[33] In framing this project on performing palimpsest bodies, I am conscious of my own criss-crossing, interweaving and multi-contextual experiences. I am a migratory crosser of boundaries (artistic, academic, geopolitical, national), with co-existing presences in Britain, Mexico and most recently the United States of America. In Santa Barbara, I am embedded in multiple entangled dialogues and practices, not least with undergraduate students in my classes, where I engage the very provocations used by La Máquina in their creative processes. I inhabit in-between and liminal spaces of plurality and potentiality.

Scenario of power relations and encounters of difference

My experiences of Mexican histories were initiated through a devised theatre project in Britain in 1991. Those theatre practices connect directly with my experiences of witnessing performances of La Máquina de Teatro in the new millennium, leading to my own performance practices of *pre/now/post: una trilogía* and the writing of this book. As an artist,

creator, performer, spectator, witness, scholar and receiver I am therefore aware of my own body as a container and transmitter of memories and histories. Here, I locate myself in this study through these three inter-connected theatre experiences.

1. *Britain:* In the 1980s and 1990s, as a professional artist, I performed in and created many theatre and performance works exploring scenarios of power relations and encounters of difference.[34] In 1991, I was engaged as an actor and creator to devise a theatre work for children titled *Aztec* (Figures 8 and 9).[35] The core material was a "scenario of encounter," investigating

Figure 8.

Figure 9.

relationships of power and domination. Our aims were to challenge our audiences to come face-to-face with stereotypes of discrimination, and to consider questions of history, knowledge and truth. The three bodies of history were Emperor Moctezuma II (ruler of the Mexica civilization), Hernán Cortés (Spanish conquester) and the Indigenous woman known as La Malinche (who acted as translator for Cortés). We used familiar processes of devising to create the theatre piece over the course of some weeks. Although these histories seemed distant both geographically and temporally—taking place in the sixteenth century in a landmass palpably far away in the Americas—we explored scenarios of power relations, domination and discrimination that were very present in twentieth-century Britain. We worked with relationships of postmemory of power and colonization.[36] For remains of the bodies of history of Moctezuma, Cortés and La Malinche we read contemporary histories extensively and exhaustively. We viewed images of codices (painted books) and we scrutinized photos of Aztec-Mexica sculptures and ceremonial structures. Working through experiences of rememory of personal fear and control, we played with trans-temporal crossings through our own "selves" in twentieth-century Britain. From these remains and traces we improvised and crafted scenes. We used strategies of liminal performance and postdramatic theatre. Through a simultaneous dramaturgical structure we crossed temporalities by layering and juxtaposing fragments of stories and narratives.

We generated re-visions of histories narrated in books and represented in media sources, which presented Mexico as "foreign" and "unknowable."[37] We performed multiple identities, merging narrators, Spanish conquistadores, Aztec-Mexica rulers and priests, Indigenous city dwellers and our-selves (my-self "Ruth") debating with our fellow creators about the writing of History. We put on and removed items of clothing as layers of identities—a helmet, long-braided hair, a tunic, a feather, a string of beads—assembling, disassembling and reassembling our "selves," yet with traces remaining. We carried objects as significant items of peoples and places—a map, a doll, a codex with footprints and a sword. In the environment of the transversal space two traces of two "worlds" were re-constructed: a stone-coloured Aztec-Mexica pyramid at one end and a large grey, overbearing, metalized Christian cross at the other. In one brief moment, "I," Xochitl, an Indigenous girl gripping a little doll, was knocked to the floor and trampled by "Cortés" and the "European invaders"—a helmet-wearing performer holding a schematic horse-head on a pole. In my body I still experience that little girl's body, clutching the tiny doll's body, looking up at "Cortés" as he trampled me to the ground.

2. *Mexico City:* In new millennium, I experienced the provocative and complex performances of *Trilogía Mexicana* (*Mexican Trilogy*) by La Máquina. I was struck by a sense of performing palimpsest bodies. Combining and juxtaposing multiple linguistic texts, movement vocabularies, costumes, skin-coverings, objects and spatialities, the five actors simultaneously performed layers of histories with obvious explorations of contemporary politics. Here were five professional performers using liminal performance and postdramatic theatre strategies to provocatively critique the "scenario of encounter," investigating relationships of difference, power struggles and domination. The bodies of history were Emperor Moctezuma II, Hernán Cortés and La Malinche. The temporal frame

Figure 10.

was extended to incorporate fifteenth-century Emperor Nezahualcóyotl. Through complex, multi-corporeal and transdisciplinary practices the artists challenged their audiences to come face-to-face with stereotypes of discrimination and to consider questions of history and truth. As I experienced the unfolding performance works, I witnessed and felt so many connections with my own experiences of creating and performing *Aztec* in 1991 in Britain. Yet, these artists created and were performing the theatre pieces in the very location and environments in which the lives were lived; where the destruction, transformation and colonization took place; and where the consequences and legacy exist as experiences in daily lives (Figures 1, 2, 3, 4, 10 and 13).

3. *United States of America:* In the second decade of the new millennium in my (new) home of Santa Barbara, California, as a creator-scholar I create from remains of *Mexican Trilogy.*[38] I sit and stand for hours on end, endeavouring to translate bodies, voices,

Figure 11.

Figure 12.

spatialities, emotions and ephemera into words. This book is part of what remains. In a dark theatre studio at the University of California, Santa Barbara, I generate re-imaginings through practice-as-research-in-performance, seeking to incorporate the complex practices of La Máquina into my body, getting them under my skin, through my muscles, into my voice and breath, and to connect through my own palimpsest body.

In a scenario of breathing through time, I move a conch shell to my lips, breathing deeply and exhaling into the trans-temporal iconic sonic object to generate waves of sound and embodied connections, as books lie strewn around the space (including my own book *Embodying Mexico*). In a scenario of truth/knowledge/memory, I wear a grey masculine formal business suit (a trace of five Malinches in *Malinche/Malinches*). I stand in front of a photograph of a [former] self, performing Xochitl—the Indigenous girl gripping her doll in *Aztec* in Britain—as I hold two tiny body-objects of directors Malheiros and Faesler. We—"Malheiros," "Faesler" and a spectral light-form of my performing self—gaze toward a book (containing writing on embodiment, memory and creativity). Through this accumulation of layers, bodies, lives, histories and memories interweave and accrue through performing palimpsest bodies (Figures 11 and 12).

4. Translations of remains: Remains of translations

Mexican Trilogy is a provocation to create three performances drawing on a reflection of our present history and the relationship that we sustain day by day with our prehispanic past…three pieces, remnants, or snippets, three endeavours or processes of memory. Our undertaking is to tell stories/histories of the daily relationship that all we Mexicans have with stones, with books, with languages, food, and our traditions.

How do we share our lives with what remains?
—Clarissa Malheiros & Juliana Faesler

Translations carry risks and challenges

"How do we share our lives with what remains?" indicates two interconnecting processes: 1) creating live performance from traces (images, objects, texts, sounds, movements, sensory ephemera and experiences); and 2) translating from live performance into words. Both are palimpsest processes and both are part of this study. The question was originally posed by the artists of La Máquina: firstly, as a provocation for themselves as they created performances through experimental devising processes; and secondly, for their audiences experiencing the live theatre events. The inquiry is charged with notions of collective memories, lived experiences, shared histories and tangled temporalities. It opens up ideas of palimpsests as performance, postmemory, rememory, scenarios and re-vision.

"How do we share our lives with what remains?" is a pragmatic question that is grounded in action. I make use of this question as an on-going trace in this book as I sift through the remains of four creative processes and performances. I translate, interpret, and transform moving bodies, sounds, sensorial forms and spatialities into words. Acts of translation are acts of transfer. They involve processes of carrying across, of moving from one place to another, of converting to and of expressing in another language. These acts of translation are always fraught with risks and challenges, with precarious consequences.[39] Acts of translation formed the core of the life of La Malinche, the woman who acted as translator and interpreter for the Spanish conquistador Hernán Cortés. Her performances of translation assisted the colonization and devastation of a civilization. Interpretations of her acts of translation resulted in La Malinche, and women more broadly, being branded "traitor." In their *Mexican Trilogy, Malinche/Malinches*, the artists of La Máquina reactivate scenarios of translation to perform deep re-visions of gendered and racial discrimination (see Chapter 3 for analysis). With this writing I perform three translations and interpretations: from postdramatic, liminal performances and workshop processes into words; from Spanish language to English; and from performance deeply embedded in Mexican contexts into performance ideas that readers unfamiliar with these environments and histories may connect with. Performing palimpsest bodies are always bodies in translation.

Performance into words as extreme palimpsests

Peggy Phelan has asked: "What are the forms of writing that will allow us to hold the moving body?"[40] Susan Foster has depicted "the conversion of movement into words," explaining how "I scrutinize this movement and then feel my torso lift and strain as I search for the words that would describe most accurately this gesture's ability and intent. [...] I am a body yearning toward a translation. Am I pinning the movement down, trapping it, through this search for words to attach to it?"[41] Discussing processes of viewing, experiencing and writing about dance, André Lepecki proposes that "the body's presence is always predicated by absence."[42] There are complications in expressing experiences of creative processes. As Keith Negus and Michael Pickering explain: "Any effort to articulate the experience of the creative process pushes us to the edge of what words can say. It inevitably involves having to bridge the gap between the sensational experience of creating [...] and the necessity of translating an understanding of that experience into language that can be communicated to others."[43]

In "The Performance of Translation," Patrick Primavesi discusses relations between text, performance and gesture, drawing on Walter Benjamin—"The Task of the Translator"—and Bertolt Brecht. He observes:

> Benjamin reflects the provisional nature of translation and its irreducible violence, a necessity of interruption and choice and the obligation to perform a loss of parts and details. Against the similarity to the original, he describes the structure of a temporary and only fragmentary displacement by which a translation represents translatability in all other languages: [...] Benjamin defines translation as a process of destruction and transformation. [...] From a pragmatic point of view, translators always have to decide what to keep and what to lose.[44]

Given the density and complexity of these live transdisciplinary performance projects of La Máquina, my processes of translation have necessarily involved selecting brief elements for discussion. I have made decisions about what to keep and what to lose. For each project I have made selections of fleeting scenes and tiny elements through which I can present aspects of performing palimpsest bodies as postmemory, rememory, scenarios and revisions. I incorporate repetitions of words and concepts as I shift from past tense to present tense, from then to now, from passive to active. I fluctuate between long sentences with multiple clauses, and short collections of words that form barely grammatical phrases. As I attempt to reflect the aesthetic and political performance practices of La Máquina—positing that life is not straightforward and that meaning is not evident—I utilize writerly writing.[45] My descriptive and interpretive analyses are therefore intensely provisional and fragmentary. They are in themselves extreme palimpsests, where the remains, traces and footprints of live bodies moving, speaking and interacting in time and space in specific historical, cultural, social and political contexts exist in and as words on these pages.[46] Together with the words, a few photos of each project provide split-second fragments of complex embodied, spatial, moving, sonic, sensorial and interactive practices. I have curated these photos to present sequences, juxtapositions and repetitions and to offer some visual forms of these deeply experiential practices.

Valorization and paradox: Writing and embodied performance

Translating from embodied practice into words is not only challenging but also encompasses the inherent paradox of using writing to examine and valorise embodied practices. Notably, within her discussions of cultural memory, archives and repertoires, Taylor considers the valorization and perpetuation of certain kinds of materials: "The dominance of language and writing has come to stand for *meaning* itself. Live, embodied practices not based in linguistic or literary codes, we must assume, have no claims on meaning. [...] Part of what performance and performance studies allows us to do, then, is take seriously the repertoire of embodied practices as an important system of knowing and transmitting knowledge."[47] In a seemingly contradictory move—but one apposite for a study of theatre work enmeshed in incongruity—I therefore take seriously the embodied repertoire of La Máquina and, by translating the moving performing bodies into writing, I aim to valorise their work and contribute to a constitution of community. To repeat Taylor's words: "writing and embodied performance have often worked together to layer the historical memories that constitute community." This study, then, is part of the documentation, a "collaborative production of knowledge"—part of the trace.[48]

Knowledge and global interconnections through performance

This book encompasses two elements of "knowledge" that tend to be marginalized: body-based performance and Mexican scenic arts. I have noted that there are challenges in translating live body-based performance, leading to a very different presence than that of script-centred theatre, rendering these practices less visible and less documented. Over two decades ago Villegas observed that "traditional studies on theatre—Latin American or Chicano/Latino—tend to neglect the 'theatrical' and 'performance' side of 'theatre' and privilege 'dramatic texts.'"[49] Although there are "scripts" for the theatre works presented in this book, they are not plays, but multi-aesthetic projects that use a multiplicity of fragmented and juxtaposed written texts spanning many centuries (and combined in devising workshops). Given my focus on body-based, transdisciplinary aesthetics, I include only the very briefest extracts of these.

Taylor also reflected on global power relations in terms of knowledge:

The West has forgotten about many parts of world that elude its explanatory grasp. Yet, it remembers the need to cement the centrality of its position as the West by creating and freezing the non-West as always other, 'foreign,' and unknowable. Domination by culture, by 'definition,' claims to originality and authenticity have functioned in tandem with military and economic supremacy.[50]

Villegas has raised many questions concerning the relative absence of Latin American theatrical discourses from histories of western theatre.[51] Too often, Mexican theatre and performing arts practices are allotted an "other" role, deemed foreign and unknowable. With this book, I aim to address a paucity of English-language studies on contemporary, experimental performance and theatre in Mexico and to present a framework that makes this pertinent for all creative artists, scholars and students interested in contemporary theatre and performance. This is contemporary [Mexican] theatre, by contemporary [women] practitioners.[52]

I am inspired by Roselyn Costantino's forward-looking, ethical framing of critical performance analysis. In her significant studies on Mexican performance she observes:

> [o]ur work as critics has required the same kind of rethinking and reinterpretation that [Astrid] Hadad proposes (recycling and reinterpreting the very images, forms, and spaces that have constructed the categories of female and, by extension, national identity). Implicit in that process is the task of locating what traces of the past linger in the present and devising strategies to move more humanely toward the future.[53]

Similarly, as Marco De Marinis has perceptively described, "theatre can be made not only by *producing* performances (performative works) but also by *looking* at them or studying them, writing about them, passing on their memories, writing their history, or researching their processes."[54] Through the traces of this book, I seek to transmit memories and to write histories by making theatre from the performances of La Máquina. Through these processes I reconstruct and create, for "critique is itself a *poiesis*, a making."[55]

I first became aware of the stimulating and deeply poetic creations of La Máquina through The Magdalena Project, an international network of women in contemporary theatre and performance.[56] This global community of artists and scholars seeks to generate connections, regardless of national, cultural and political borders. At a moment in time during which heightened tensions in global relations are rife with antagonistic stances of wall-building and war, I offer the playfully-rigorous and provocative performance processes of La Máquina and the community-building work of Malheiros and Faesler as a counter to these divisionary positions.[57] I seek to draw attention to part of the extraordinary richness and diversity of contemporary performance, theatre, dance and scenic arts in Mexico. As The Magdalena Project artists aim to generate networks, my hope is that this study may contribute to collective global interconnections through performance.

Structure

This study is structured in two sections followed by a reflective Epilogue.[58]

Section One: Outlines, comprises three chapters that provide the framework and contexts for the four performance projects in Section Two.

In this Introduction I have outlined ideas of performing palimpsest bodies, postmemory, rememory, re-vision and scenarios; presented a brief introduction to La Máquina and the four performance projects; and discussed frameworks of research methods and translation.

In Chapter 1, I repeat and expand on the creative-interpretative ideas, discussing the concepts in more detail, drawing on recent scholarship in performance, theatre and dance studies.

In Chapter 2, I turn to the working practices of La Máquina and contexts in Mexico, specifically, experimental theatre and performance, and concepts of temporalities, bodies, histories and environments as palimpsests.

Section Two, "Four Performance Projects," presents discussions of the performances: Chapter 3, *Mexican Trilogy*; Chapter 4, *Zapata, Death Without End*; Chapter 5, *War in Paradise*; and Chapter 6, *Time of the Devil*.

The book closes with the Epilogue, in which I offer some reflections on the four projects and return to the core ideas of performing palimpsest bodies as ethical and creative forms for generating re-visions.

Figure 13.

Chapter 1

Performing re-visions: Palimpsests, postmemory, rememory and remains

Palimpsest is concerned with the essential ambiguity of bodies and of location. Both of these, like a palimpsest, have the surprising capacity to be home to more than one story at any given time. The surface of things resonates with the secrets of the unknown possibilities.

— Shobana Jeyasingh, *Palimpsest*

Mexico City today is a palimpsest of histories and temporalities...

How does one come to inhabit and envision one's body as coextensive with one's environment and one's past, emphasizing the porous nature of skin rather than its boundedness?

— Diana Taylor, *The Archive and the Repertoire*

La Malinche as Palimpsest

— Sandra Cypress

Seen from the point of view of a rationalist, European "order," or even from the US, the Mexican "order" often appears as a "disorder" or "non-order." It is precisely in this disorder or "non-order" that I believe lies the crux of the Mexican imaginary. [...] This confrontation of orders corresponds to what some consider the encounter, for others the "mis-encounter," of two worlds, as the conquest, colonization, and neocolonization processes have come to be known, processes which have been extended over a period of five hundred years and about which so much has been said.

— Maris Bustamante

... history is made by bodies...

— Susan Foster, *Choreographing History*[1]

History as experience and body-to-body transmission

Experimental performance practices are particularly effective for reactivating bodies of history in order to explore collective memories and contemporary lives. In creative workshops and live theatre, transdisciplinary processes open up fascinating opportunities for generating connections between pasts and presents to re-imagine possible futures. Strategies of simultaneity, juxtaposition, mixing and reiteration using multiple movements, vocalizations, linguistic texts, objects, clothes, spatialities and sensory phenomenon are all constructive for performing remains. Fundamentally, these practices incorporate a "phenomenological sense of history as experience, as active involvement and awareness (all necessarily corporeal)."[2] These processes emphasise "the ultimate importance of experience as a privileged way of accessing and generating knowledge [which] differentiates a performative approach to history from a literary and a scientific one."[3] This model values "the site of any knowing of history as body-to-body transmission," as Rebecca Schneider argues in her discussions around performing remains and performance remains.[4] Through labs and performances, performers and witnesses can experience "the bodily articulation of fragments of history, [which are] absorbed and metabolized through various moments of consciousness and temporality."[5]

These corporeal and experiential understandings of history and knowledge are key to the theatre practices of La Máquina de Teatro, and in particular, to the four performance projects presented in this book. The artists initiated each of the four projects with a body of history. Using multifarious forms of "remains" in collective devising experiments, they sought to work across temporal borders, examining contemporary contexts through the question: "How do we share our lives with what remains?" By explicitly seeking trans-temporal crossings, the

Figure 14.

Figure 15.

practitioners deal with bodies as layers and entangled networks of histories, using concepts of bodies as plural, mixed, both/and, in-between and liminal. Through activating scenarios of material already worked on they incorporate traces and remains through coexistence, accumulation and involution to perform challenging re-visions.

As outlined in the Introduction, to interpret the trans-temporal, body-based performance practices I have proposed the concept of performing palimpsest bodies. I combine this with postmemory, rememory, scenarios and re-vision as analytical frameworks. In this chapter, I describe these interpretive and creative frameworks in more detail, specifically addressing elements that apply to the four projects in Section Two and drawing on recent discourse in performance, theatre and dance studies. I have structured these overlapping explanations in three parts: 1) palimpsests and performance; 2) postmemory and rememory; and 3) re-vision (re-membering) of scenarios. In the final section I describe the key elements of performing palimpsest bodies.

1. Palimpsests and performance

Home to more than one story

I first came across the idea of palimpsest as performance in 1996 in Britain, through a sophisticated and explorative dance work titled simply *Palimpsest*.[6] With moving bodies, the choreographer Shobana Jeyasingh sought to investigate embodied questions of personal and collective memories, histories, migrations and journeys, by layering and interweaving traces of multi-temporalities through bodies in movement. To create her complex performance, she drew on her corporeal archival-repertorial experiences, reinterpreting and re-imagining her personal embodied knowledge of transmitted traditions. Ever since my experiences of that performance over twenty years ago I have been intrigued by the concept of palimpsest, particularly in relation to generating live performance through moving bodies and environments. Jeyasingh describes how "palimpsest is concerned with the essential ambiguity of bodies and of location. Both of these, like a palimpsest, have the surprising capacity to be home to more than one story at any given time. The surface of things resonates with the secrets of the unknown possibilities."[7] These qualities of plurality, ambiguity, juxtapositions and coexistence are all deeply constructive for performing remains of bodies of history. Being "home to more than one story" indicates personal narratives and lives. An embodied state in which the surface of things resonates with the secrets of the unknown possibilities offers a generative description of bodies in performance as complex sites/sights of great potential, comprised of layers, sediments and accumulations. In transdisciplinary performance, this palimpsest aesthetic encompasses any potential performative elements, including spoken texts, vocalizations, gestures, clothing, objects, sonics and spatialities.

For Jeyasingh, palimpsest is not only concerned with the essential ambiguity of bodies, but also the ambiguity of location. Locations contain many stories where the surface of things resonates with the secrets of the unknown possibilities. Bodies inhabit locations as physical and sensory environments. Over time, they are places, spaces and "homes," containing entangled and intertwining traces of collective memories and histories. In trans-temporal performance, a stage and workshop space becomes a palimpsest location, containing multifarious stories performed as fragments, traces and remains of lives.

Connecting with Jeyasingh's account of palimpsest, encompassing bodies, locations and stories, Diana Taylor invokes this concept to evocatively portray Mexico City as "a palimpsest of histories and temporalities."[8] This depiction is obviously significant for my analysis of theatre works that were created and performed in Mexico City and which seek to respond to and reactivate bodies of history deeply embedded in this environment. Within her discussions of performing cultural memory Taylor describes forms of memory interconnecting buildings, architectural layout, material space and mental space as a framework for individual and collective memory.[9] She asks: "How does one come to inhabit and envision one's body as coextensive with one's environment and one's past, emphasizing the porous nature of skin rather than its boundedness?"[10] She describes a body performing a mixed (*mestiza*) cultural identity that is a product of history: a body that is both/and.[11] These characterizations and inquiries open up ideas of trans-temporal interconnections through remains of bodies of history reactivated by experiencing bodies.[12]

In another important application of the concept of palimpsest, and as cited in the Introduction, Rebecca Schneider has engaged the term "palimpsest" to describe the citational quality of performance, explaining: "Any action […] is already a palimpsest of other actions, a motion set in motion by precedent motion or anticipating future motion or lateral motion."[13] Usefully, her description incorporates multi-temporal and multi-spatial/movement elements that apply to the performance projects of La Máquina. Schneider refers to the idea of "beginning again and again. But this beginning, by virtue of its 'again-ness,' is never for the first time and never for the only time—beginning again and again in an entirely haunted domain of repetition."[14] This notion of "again-ness" and the haunted domain of repetition offer connections with postmemory (re-imagined fragments of past traumas) and rememory (experiences returning through the body). Here, in performance, palimpsests obviously encompass repetitions (and re-visions) of other elements (poses, words, objects, movements), which therefore set up productive tensions through the trans-temporal relationships.

Connecting memory with corporeality, author Thomas De Quincey has offered another poetic description of palimpsest, specifically in terms of disparate fragments. In "A meditation upon the deeper layers of human consciousness and memory" he refers to the palimpsest structure of the brain as an "involuted" phenomenon.[15] Otherwise unrelated texts are interwoven, competing with and infiltrating each other. These understandings of layers and interweaving, particularly in terms of involution—involved and intricate—are particularly useful for considering trans-temporal and juxtaposed experiences, traces and remains which are contained within a performance frame.

Multiple stories, lives and subjectivities

These distinct yet overlapping notions of palimpsest, characterised by Jeyasingh, Taylor, De Quincey and Schneider, are valuable for interpreting the performative bodies and experimental strategies of La Máquina as they explore memories and histories through performing palimpsest bodies. In their theatre processes, the practitioners use sensory material to experience pasts through living bodies, inhabiting locations and environments, and incorporating manifold stories, lives and subjectivities through body-based, transdisciplinary practices that repeat and transform prior actions. They reflect and perform experiences of Mexico City: where "remains" and "traces" of many peoples and times are simultaneously present; where bodies are understood as always multiple; where mestizo/a bodies are mixed bodies, containing a compound sense of both/and that is always double (or triple) coded; where histories comprise layers, accumulations and superimpositions; and where landscapes and urbanscapes contain structures from previous uses.[16]

Figure 16.

Re-forming

Palimpsest incorporates the physical actions of re-forming and re-shaping while still bearing tangible traces of earlier and other forms.[17] In Spanish, palimpsest is often described as sustaining or preserving the footprints of previous writing—*conserva huellas de otra escritura anterior*. Footprints are traces and ephemeral indicators of corporeal physical presences, movements and journeys, offering relations and connections between pasts and presents. The footprints are not a body, yet they persist as remains and evidence of a body.[18]

Together with the qualities and characteristics of palimpsest already described, I also draw on other explanations from disparate fields that are particularly useful for interpreting the performance projects of La Máquina. So, palimpsests are:

- accumulated iterations of a design or site caused whenever spaces are rebuilt or remodelled, where evidence of former uses remains (*architecture*);
- dust lines remaining visible after an object or appliance is relocated (*history of design*);
- layers of archaeological remains, accumulated iterations, and sites of remains presenting a mixture of layers which prevent knowing which is the "superior" and which is the "inferior" (*archaeology*);
- alterations of landscapes of ancestors by generations of dwellers (*landscape archaeology*);
- landscapes composed of a mosaic of active and inactive landforms of different ages (*physical geography*);
- riverbeds whose path of flow has been slowly modified—in relation to geological time—, revealing evidence of both paths (*geology*);
- contradicting glacial flow indicators consisting of smaller indicators overprinted upon larger features (*glaciology*);
- ancient craters on icy moons of the outer Solar System whose relief has mostly disappeared, leaving behind only an albedo feature—caused by light reflected by a planet or moon—, or a trace of a rim, known as ghost craters (*planetary astronomy*);
- objects placed one over another to establish the sequence of events at the scene of an accident or crime (*forensic science and engineering*);
- plaques that have been turned around and engraved on what was originally the back (*antiquarianism*);
- augmented realities brought about by melding layers of material places and their virtual representations (*technology and artificial intelligence*);
- disk utilities used for looking at details of different storage devices (*computing*).[19]

Characteristics of performing palimpsest bodies

From these varied descriptions and applications I have generated an interpretive-creative collection of characteristics of performing palimpsest bodies which I present in full at the end of this chapter. Briefly, each body in performance is plural, performing relationships that are trans-temporal. These relationships are evident through the performance and reactivation of remains of bodies of history, which exist in multiple forms and modes (including, but not limited to, visual images, written historical accounts, spoken phrases, sculptures, objects, architectural forms, locations, embodied archival repertoires of dances, songs, gestures and poses, foods, smells, tastes and many forms of specks, glimmers and ephemera). Within theatre labs and performances, these remains are performed through strategies of coexistence, simultaneity, plurality, multiplicity, sedimentation, interweaving and layering, re-using fragments to create accumulated iterations. Encompassing movements over and through the same space and place, and playing with notions of visibility, ephemerality, ghosts and spectres, there is always a sense of stories that are caught in the middle. As investigative experiments of collective creation, performing palimpsests involves performing uncertainties, ambiguities and contradictions; valuing plurality, multiplicity, liminality and in-betweenness; and questioning clear-cut notions of truth/fiction and reality/history.

Trans-temporality, simultaneity, liminality and futurity

Most obviously, the idea of palimpsest is inherently concerned with trans-temporality, mingled with the understanding of past/present not as successive but as simultaneously produced. In other words, a palimpsest contains past/present as co-existing entities, and also signals notions of across and through time. In his much-cited study of temporality (specifically dealing with inner experiences of time, memory and movement), Henri Bergson describes how each past is contemporaneous with the present that it was, so that all of the past coexists with the new present in relation to which it is now past.[20] I use Bergson's notion of creativity, repetition and doing/acting to conceptualize palimpsest bodies in performance, specifically in terms of postmemory experiments and rememory experiences:

> If matter does not remember the past, it is because it repeats the past unceasingly, because, subject to necessity, it unfolds a series of moments which each is the equivalent of the proceeding moment and may be deduced from it: thus its past is truly given in its present. But a being which evolves more or less freely creates something new every moment: in vain then should we seek to read its past in its present unless its past were deposited within it in the form of memory. Thus, to use again a metaphor [...] it is necessary [...] that the past should be *acted* by matter, *imagined* by mind.[21]

Pasts are deposited within bodies as forms of corporeal memories. These pasts are reactivated through moving, speaking and interacting bodies. These theatre practices take "time itself as a subject and malleable phenomenon [...] transforming the experience of time," and "unfolding time" through "tangled temporalities."[22] The explanation of interdisciplinary performance artist Maris Bustamante (cited above) is particularly useful as a characterisation of ordering time.[23] The "confrontation of orders" that she depicts is a form of palimpsest, created through interweaving, intertextuality and involution.

A palimpsest contains traces of another time through the notion of liminality. Liminality relates to the subjunctive mood of culture indicating potentiality and futurity. As a key component of the Spanish language, the subjunctive is embedded in Mexican ways of being and doing.[24] Performances of liminality involve "a striving after new forms and structures," founded in corporeal processes of transition and transformation."[25] Ileana Diéguez, one of Mexico's most renowned scholars of performance, discusses the liminal as a metaphorical condition that engenders "unexpected, interstitial and precarious states," generating practices of inversion, which "parody and overthrow conventions" and which "subvert relations and destabilize them."[26] Liminality also incorporates a state of in-betweenness: in other words, a temporal palimpsest plurality, as I describe presently.

Multiple bodies

As temporality is understood through coexistence, simultaneity, multiplicity, mixing and unfolding, so these ideas are applicable to bodies, including bodies in performance. To draw on Peggy Phelan: "We have multiple bodies in the way we now speak of multiple identities."[27] Stuart Hall's seminal description of multiple identities is pertinent to bodies, thus: bodies are "fragmented and fractured; never singular but multiply constructed across different, often intersecting and antagonistic, discourses, practices, and positions. They are subject to a radical historicization, and are constantly in the process of change and transformation."[28] A mixed body (formed through mestizaje) always contains the plurality of both/and. Bodies also contain plurality through haunting and absence. As Lepecki described: "The body's presence is always predicated by absence," remaining as "a conglomerate of traces."[29] In theatre, performing bodies inherently contain a plurality, for "the body is 'always already' in representation."[30] Therefore, when live performing bodies reactivate and play with remains of bodies of history, they are performing palimpsest bodies through multiple traces, codes and remains.

2. Postmemory and rememory

Concepts of postmemory and rememory both incorporate trans-temporal relationships through an understanding of bodies as transmitters and holders of memories and histories. Bodies connect traces of collective and personal memories, as "the past" is experienced in the present through remains, fragments and ephemera.[31]

Figure 17.

Postmemory: Creation, projection and imaginative investment

For my understanding of postmemory I draw specifically on Marianne Hirsch:

> "Postmemory" describes the relationship that the "generation after" bears to the personal, collective, and cultural trauma of those who came before—to experiences they "remember" only by means of the stories, images, and behaviors among which they grew up. But these experiences were transmitted to them so deeply and affectively as to seem to constitute memories in their own right. Postmemory's connection to the past is thus actually mediated not by recall but by imaginative investment, projection, and creation. To grow up with overwhelming inherited memories, to be dominated by narratives that preceded one's birth or one's consciousness, is to risk having one's own life stories displaced, even evacuated, by our ancestors. It is to be shaped, however indirectly, by traumatic fragments of events that still defy narrative reconstruction and exceed comprehension. These events happened in the past, but their effects continue into the present.[32]

Core elements of Hirsch's idea are particularly germane for considering key aspects of the performance experiments in this book.[33] Crucially, postmemory realises "the past" in terms of generative and imaginative processes, incorporating creation and projection into the future. At the heart of postmemory is the idea of "post" as an ongoing, trans-temporal relationship, not a simple coming after but a procedure in "ana-" indicating "back" and "again."[34] Postmemory, therefore, incorporates characteristics of coexistence and simultaneity. Postmemory encompasses personal and collective experiences and pasts, and connects through relationships of personal and collective notions of "history" and "our ancestors." Although Hirsch applies the time element of postmemory to one generation, I extend the temporal frame from "the generation after" to multiple generations over many centuries, where the inherited memories/histories encompass collective and personal traumas of impositions, exclusions, resistance and violations. The theatre projects of La Máquina specifically encompass over six hundred years of multiple accumulations of power struggles. They create theatre experiments through relationships of postmemory by reactivating remains of bodies of history and performing palimpsest bodies.

For my creative-interpretive model of performing palimpsest bodies, postmemory encompasses key elements:

- understanding "the past" as experiences transmitted through stories, images and behaviours using remains of oral texts, written documents, visual images, objects and embodied archival repertoires;
- creating through "the past" experienced in the present as traumatic fragments of events that are translated into an equally fragmented dramaturgical structure;
- using fragments of stories, images and behaviours not to generate narrative reconstructions, but as re-imaginings and new creations;
- playing with cultural fictions and historical realities and combining fragments of remains in unexpected ways to generate contradictions, ambiguity, complexity and in-betweenness;
- opening up questions of truth, history and memory to generate re-visions for possible futures.

Figure 18.

Rememory: Experiencing through bodies

Rememory incorporates experiences through and with human bodies and also encompasses many aspects of postmemory. Toni Morrison's deeply poetic and evocative use of rememory is wholly corporeal, connecting intimate personal experiences with collective histories. In her extraordinary novel *Beloved*, Morrison describes and portrays manifold bodies: living, dead, aging, broken and spectral. She is writing about remains and ghosts of the US Civil War, involving oppressed, racialized and gendered lives. In Morrison's story, Sethe, a mother, black woman and former slave, is "remembering something she had forgotten she knew."[35] Her rememory returns through her body: it is experiential, sensory and involuntary. It is also fragmentary and ephemeral, returning as traces. Key to Morrison's concept of rememory is a spectral body: the body of Sethe's (dead) daughter Beloved. Morrison describes the embodied presence of Sethe's daughter living among them and growing older.

Invoking my notion of palimpsest bodies, the spectral body of Beloved exists as a palimpsest body—simultaneously material, immaterial, phantasmagorical, aging, multi-temporal, disappeared, present and absent. At the heart of Morrison's novel are narratives and scenarios of ancestors who dominate the post-Civil War generation of former slaves. As "former" slaves, the deeply embodied enslavement of their bodies is, of course, wholly present. Rememory, therefore, also fundamentally incorporates postmemory. Rememory is very individual yet the scenario is collective. Sethe's body and Beloved's spectral body are part of long and profound histories of racialized, gendered bodies, of struggles for justice and of relations of power.

As a form of memory, rememory is embodied knowledge, concealed, covered, but present. The living body is a storehouse and repository, a form of archival body and body as archive.[36] Taylor has described how "memory is embodied and sensual [...] conjured through the senses; it links the deeply private with social, even official, practices."[37] In "Theatre of Witness," playwright Karen Malpede discusses notions of embodied memory in terms of traumatic bodily experience, writing of "taking into the body the sensations of another's struggle."[38] Roselyn Costantino, in her extensive analyses of Mexican theatre and performance artists, asks: "How do bodies remember and what traces exist of the body written across by the dominant? How are these traces inscribed and hidden in our interior and exterior universes? Precisely where upon or in the body and psyche do those memories reside?"[39] Choreographer Alonzo Lines has spoken of excavating movement from bodies, as a single body offers up networks and layers, skin and flesh, networks of organs, bones, muscle and tissue.[40] Indira Pensado describes "bodies as containers of experiences in which bones record more than skin."[41] Rememory encompasses ever-present matters of haunting, of the materiality of the body and of material existence. The body of Beloved is evident to Sethe as a tangible presence that is experienced, felt and sensed. Others witness the effects of the actions of her body, though her body is unseen. This is particularly apt for dealing with performing traces of remains of dead bodies of history. These bodies incorporate absence, presence and disappearance where "live" is not antonymic to "dead."[42] They exist as simultaneous elements and as palimpsest bodies of rememory.

In the four theatre experiments of La Máquina analysed in this book, remains of bodies of history are reactivated through relationships of rememory. These experiential and corporeal practices offer deeply affective embodied memories, connecting personal experiences with collective histories. In performance, these are palimpsest bodies that reveal and unfold traces of embodied memories. Trans-temporal connections, however ephemeral, are always present as each body contains traces of dead, dying and absent bodies.

For my creative-interpretive model of performing palimpsest bodies, rememory incorporates key elements:

- valuing experiential and embodied performance practices as forms of inquiry to probe collective and personal histories and memories;
- using practices and aesthetics of deeply sensorial participation;
- understanding bodies as archives and as containers and transmitters of memories;
- engaging a sense of doubleness (my memory and not my memory) connecting individual and collective memories and individual and collective histories through processes of body-to-body transmission;
- embodying questions of death, of dying, of the materiality of bodies and of haunting.

Figure 19.

3. Re-vision (re-membering) of scenarios

Feminist transformations

The artists of La Máquina explicitly seek to perform re-visions by reactivating and experimenting with remains of bodies of history. At heart, re-vision incorporates generative relationships with the "past" to create re-imaginings and possibilities. Through performing palimpsest bodies, the practitioners strive to destabilize stereotypical narratives, transforming them into projections for the future. Through relations of postmemory and rememory, they re-member pre-existing texts as scenarios of material already worked on.

Adrienne Rich's concept of re-vision involves an overt temporal, political and ethical relationship performed through acts of going back and entering texts from new critical directions, not in order to know the texts better, but to transform them and to "live – afresh."[43] Within a distinctly feminist framework, Rich developed her ideas in a piece evocatively titled *On Lies, Secrets and Silence*, describing how re-vision "is for women more than a chapter in cultural history; it is an act of survival."[44] Re-vision involves a deeply ethical stance: "We need to know the writing of the past, and know it differently than we have ever known it; not to pass on a tradition but to break its hold over us."[45]

Such re-visioning is a common thread in feminist performance practices. In the context of Latin American performing arts, Laurietz Seda discusses how "it is necessary to (re)think, (re)create, and (re)articulate the interstitial spaces that permit an interrogation of limits and absolute, reductionist definitions."[46] Issues of historicity concern the truth-value of knowledge and claims about the past, so that official versions of national narratives can be challenged. In their deeply insightful research on theatre and performance in Mexico and Latin America, Patricia Ybarra and Beatriz Rizk have described theatre as a "site of historiographical revision" that is useful "for problematizing history" and for "destabilizing historical myths known to its public."[47] In her seminal study of memory-theatre, Jeanette Malkin describes how performance can be used to "renegotiate the traumas, oppressions, and exclusions of the past" and "evoke erased memories of national pasts, to recontextualize, reopen canonized memory-'narratives,' rethink taboo discourses, intervene in the politics of memory and repression, and to engage (and occasionally enrage) the memoried consciousness of its audience."[48]

In postmemory theatre experiments with remains of bodies of histories, the "texts" encompass multiple forms. They include accounts of official histories inscribed with words and visual images. They comprise archival-repertorial forms performed through speech acts, gestures, movements, spatial relationships and sensorial expressions. As Schneider described, "Rich was writing about *texts*, but the same sense of 're-vision' [...] might be applicable to performances or enactments of what Judith Butler has termed 'sedimented acts.'"[49] As all "human experience in general is necessarily a re-enactment," understood as twice-behaved behaviour, so there is "a reiterative reenactment across time of meaning [...] through embodied gestures."[50] These experiences and enactments are scenarios of "'material which has already been worked on.'"[51] They are forms of "embodied history," "the institution made flesh" and the performance of "institution, social class and social difference."[52] They are texturalized traces, ephemera, and "traces, glimmers, residues and specks of things," understood through relationships of postmemory and rememory.[53]

Reactivation and multiplication

Within the processes of theatre experiments these multiple remains, texts and scenarios offer the potential for stimulating re-visions through performing palimpsests. They become vital elements to be translated into a plethora of performative forms. As Taylor has described, a scenario "usually works through reactivation rather than duplication."[54] A scenario "makes visible, yet again, what is already there: the ghosts, the images, the stereotypes."[55]

These stereotypes "can be changed by writing *the body* differently, rewriting the body, and *re-membering* the body, to effect social change."[56] These processes incorporate "a re-membering (deconstruction) of the elements of which they were made in the first place," as feminist scholar Terry Threadgold describes.[57] In workshops and performances these performative processes involve strategies of fragmentation, simultaneity, juxtaposition and involution. They incorporate decontextualization, re-contextualization, assembly and reassembly.

Re-vision through performing palimpsest bodies involves deliberately seeking to work across and through binarized divides, experimenting with forms of liminality and in-betweenness, through crossings and multiplication.[58] These crossings are dynamic processes that are "open to possibilities of mediation, transformation, or transgression within, across, and beyond the absolutist limits and definitions that attempt to control subjectivities."[59] These performing palimpsest bodies demonstrate "the politically radical potentialities of the live body in action; […] [they] function 'as complicated sites where subjectivity challenges subjection, where resistance initiates its moves.'"[60] These processes incorporate overt relationships with past bodies of history and with ancestors, as forms of in-betweenness. In-betweenness is a condition, an ontology, a process of living, not a temporary state or phase that is being passed through.[61] These are forms of "nepantla," encompassing in-betweenness as plurality and connecting with embodied acts of resistance, intersections and borderlands.[62] Nepantla is a "liminal" space where multiple forms of reality are viewed at the same time. Nepantla involves living in the borderlands and being at literal or metaphorical crossroads, as Gloria Anzaldúa has so evocatively explained.[63] Being in the middle and containing parts of more than one culture are obvious palimpsests: trans-temporal containers of traces. Such crossings and crossroads are the very intersections of La Máquina's embodied explorations through remains. These are the "viewpoints" engaged by the artists of La Máquina to generate re-visions as possibilities, potentials and pluralities through productive tensions of cultural fictions and historical realities. Reactivating scenarios of material already worked on through performing palimpsest bodies enables ethical relationships of convivio. These are performances *with* audiences not only for audiences.[64] As "the scenario forces us to situate ourselves in relationship to it, as participants, spectators, or witnesses" these practices propose inclusive and participatory experiences through performing remains.[65]

Figure 20.

Figure 21.

Performing palimpsest bodies

Palimpsest bodies are…

- trans-temporal bodies, performing and transmitting remains and traces through coexistence, simultaneity, superimposition, sedimentation, intertwinement and entanglement;
- connective and community-making bodies, conjoining collective and personal memories and histories;
- archival-repertorial bodies, revealing and concealing evidence of multiple lives and stories and existing as sites and sights of remains and ephemera;
- citational and repetitious bodies, performing accumulations of iterations and again-ness yet creating difference with each repetition;
- dynamic bodies, re-forming and transmitting re-visions, re-memberings and re-imaginings for presents and futures;
- trans, liminal, both/and, nepantla and in-between bodies, crossing borders, blurring boundaries and incorporating multiple viewpoints;
- provisional, contingent, potential, subjunctive and if-I-were-you-bodies, performing inversions, re-visions and revolutions;
- multi-layered and sensorial bodies, mixing private hidden memories with public manifest histories;
- intertextual, intertextural, involuted, ambiguous, contradictory, decontextualizing and unfixing bodies, juxtaposing multiple fragments;
- co-extensive and intersecting bodies, inhabiting and envisioning pasts and environments through profoundly sensorial corporealities;
- moving and shifting bodies, forming footprints, depositing ephemera, marking transitions, tracing journeys and materializing temporal paths;
- playful, inquiring, translating and experiential bodies, seeking to transgress and transform;
- witnessing, inquisitive, radical, convivial and participating bodies.

Figure 22.

Palimpsest bodies…

- embody history and knowledge through body-to-body transmission, crossing cultural fictions and historical realities;
- experiment with postmemory, re-imagining fragments of shared ordeals and traumas to generate future projections;
- experience rememory, re-forming deeply embodied, half-forgotten personal and collective physical occurrences;
- reactivate scenarios of material already worked on, translating complex histories-memories and performing re-visions of remains;
- intertwine imagination, memory, sensorial perception and actuality through which the past is a becoming;
- generate productive tensions through trans-temporal traces and ephemera;
- unfold poetic presences to suggest other ways of being;
- unsettle memories and resist amnesia;
- breathe across and through time;
- remain differently.[66]

Figure 23.

Chapter 2

La Máquina de Teatro: Trans-temporal theatres, bodies and environments in Mexico

We wanted to work with cultural fictions and historical realities—to see where these paths cross.

Mexican Trilogy is a provocation to create three performances drawing on a reflection of our present history and the relationship that we sustain day by day with our prehispanic past…three pieces, remnants, or snippets, three endeavours or processes of memory. Our undertaking is to tell stories/histories of the daily relationship that all we Mexicans have with stones, with books, with languages, food, and our traditions.

How do we share our lives with what remains?

— Juliana Faesler & Clarissa Malheiros, La Máquina de Teatro

Figure 24.

Creating within environments and pasts

From the abundance and diversity of theatre, performance and scenic arts in Mexico I have opted to focus on one company: La Máquina de Teatro. From the multiplicity of performances of La Máquina I place the spotlight on four distinct projects, all of which use transdisciplinary collective creation strategies to explore issues of shared histories and memories. As with all performance-makers, the practitioners engage with their environments and sensibilities as they generate provocative performance projects. These artistic and cultural practices are deeply enfolded and embedded in local and national perceptions and experiences of temporalities, bodies, histories and spatialities as multiple and entangled. All these are veritable palimpsests.

I return again to Diana Taylor's probing inquiry: "How does one come to inhabit and envision one's body as coextensive with one's environment and one's past, emphasizing the porous nature of skin rather than its boundedness?"[1] This complex question encompasses many intersecting elements that are useful for discussing the performance projects of La Máquina, opening up interconnected yet distinct arenas of theatre strategies and of state politics and contexts. Bodies are overtly at the core of the inquiries. Bodies are understood and conceptualized in terms of living experiences and embedded subjectivities (forms of rememory) and projections and possibilities in relation to past traumas (forms of postmemory). Bodies are in relationship with environments, offering connections to temporal, architectural, physical, artistic, cultural, political and sensory settings. Bodies are in relationship with pasts, generating ties with official histories and memories remaining as traces in multiple forms. When the artists of La Máquina utilize the question "How do we share our lives with what remains?" as a provocation for generating theatre experiments, they are specifically exploring matters of bodies as coextensive with environments and pasts, seeking to investigate aspects of inhabiting and envisioning bodies through sensory and corporeal practices. Through relationships of postmemory and experiences of rememory— as breath and voices emanate from deep inside skin—they generate vibrant performances with beating hearts, pulsating blood and muscular frictions. Through reactivating scenarios of material already worked on, they reconstruct remains of bodies of history as collective memories. As bodies strike poses, move bricks, sing songs and tap flesh they are performing palimpsest bodies with multiple trans-temporal traces.

In preparation for my discussions of the four performance projects in Section Two, in this chapter I set out some key features of the practices, strategies and performance aesthetics of La Máquina. For readers familiar with Mexican contexts, these understandings will already be unmistakable. For other readers who may be less familiar with such contexts, these outline explanations offer important touchstones. It is important to point out that many of the theatre strategies and performance aesthetics used by the artists of La Máquina will be recognizable as practices of postdramatic theatre, liminal performance, body-based theatre and total theatre. Equally, their methods of collective creation and devising, particularly using Lecoq techniques and Viewpoints, will also be broadly familiar to theatre and performance scholars and practitioners. So my aim here is to outline how key elements of the four projects are fundamentally entangled in sensibilities of Mexico, rather than explicate these theatre practices and processes in more general terms. Although my main focus is on La Máquina, I also give some very brief contextual references to other theatre and performance trajectories and artists in Mexico as pertinent to the four performance works.

Mexico has extensive and profuse theatre and performance trajectories, particularly in terms of experimentation, body-based and transdisciplinary scenic arts, so the references here are fragments of very complex arts scenes. I have included some suggestions for further reading.[2] This chapter is divided into three sections: in the first part, I present a summary of La Máquina in relation to their ensemble methods, range of projects, experimentation, transdisciplinary and body-based practices; in the second part I briefly describe the four performance projects; in the final part I turn to issues of entangled temporalities, bodies, histories and spatialities, ending with an outline of key processes and practices.

La Máquina de Teatro—the Theatre Machine

Two extraordinary women

For over twenty years, the company La Máquina has consistently worked at the cutting edge of contemporary performance, theatre and scenic arts. Juliana Faesler and Clarissa Malheiros, the two founders and artistic directors, have created and facilitated a wide array of theatre works, laboratories and projects, with performances in major theatre spaces, at prestigious events in Mexico and beyond, in multiple community-based contexts and for many different audiences.[3] Their creative work is always politically and aesthetically stimulating and deeply playful, and has been described as "without a doubt, one of the most brilliant demonstrations of theatrical vanguard of our time."[4] Faesler and Malheiros are prolific artists, whose multi-tasking processes include roles as creators, performers, facilitators, entrepreneurs, teachers and producers. Mexican dance scholar Margarita Tortajada Quiroz has remarked on "the strength often required by women to make creative works."[5] She observes that women creative artists must transgress dominant frameworks to construct their own corporeal traces, drawing attention to "the challenges that women artists have faced in order to gain legitimation and construct their own creative spaces."[6] This portrayal aptly depicts Malheiros and Faesler as they continually seek to generate original and stimulating performance projects, labs and seminars, aiming to be responsive as activists in changing political contexts. La Máquina describe themselves as "a body (un cuerpo)—a collection of parts and an organic system," a metaphor that is frequently used to portray ensembles using body-based practices.[7] Faesler and Malheiros direct La Máquina as a company with a changing participation. As their work is project-based, so they engage actors, dancers, musicians, composers, designers and other creative artists for each specific undertaking. Their theatre projects encompass a wide range of

Figure 25.

forms, including devised work, tradaptations of classic plays and novels, opera, theatre works specifically for children (incorporating exquisite puppetry) and community labs.[8]

Palimpsest studio: An empty space filled with remains

The studio of La Máquina is located at the back of a large house in the south of Mexico City, in the neighbourhood of Coyoacán, a few blocks from where Frida Kahlo painted her now-iconic images of her own body.[9] A slightly raised wooden platform is framed on two sides by freestanding lines of interconnected red velvet theatre seats, dislocated from their former place within well-ordered rows inside a theatre building. The seats re-form a trace of performing and witnessing bodies. A mirrored wall and a half-wall form two other sides of the frame. A bookcase in a corner contains ephemera and fragments from multiple projects. Large pieces of paper taped to the wall are covered in scribbled words, interconnected with lines and arrows, forming dramaturgical structuring maps. This creative palimpsest studio of La Máquina—this empty space—is infused and saturated with multiple crossings of archival repertorial bodies containing networks and layers of histories, memories and temporalities. Experimental performance labs necessarily encompass palimpsest processes of re-using traces and fragments through doing and re-doing. Forms are generated through bodies, voices, objects and ephemera, which, in the nitty-gritty of the minute-to-minute, hour-to-hour and day-to-day activities, are assembled and reassembled. Within an improvisatory framework, gestures, movements and voicings are fixed and unfixed through the repetitions of corporeal fragments incorporating practices of liminality and in-betweenness (Figures 26 and 75).

Experimentation and transdisciplinary practices

Malheiros and Faesler bring a multiplicity and complexity of disciplinary expertise, combined with an urgency of political passion, to their creative projects, performing provocations that connect global politics with intimate relationships. They experiment with theatre practices to explore on-going socio-political-philosophical inquiries. The aesthetics, strategies and forms of La Máquina are not easily compartmentalized or labelled. One reviewer has described how, "since the company's creation, Faesler and Malheiros have generated a space of interchange and exchange between different artistic expressions within the world of stage arts, with a concern to reconcile disciplinary boundaries, while moving forwards in creating their own distinctive and rich universe."[10] Their processes, aesthetics and forms connect with many practices and movements from many global contexts and within Mexico, including physical theatre and total theatre, theatre of the body (el teatro del cuerpo), corporeal techniques (técnicas corporales), transversal performance (la escena transversal), transdisciplinary and experimental theatre arts, laboratory (laboratorio), teatro de búsqueda ("seeking" theatre) and personal theatre (teatro personal).

Many of the strategies and aesthetics of postdramatic theatre, as delineated by Hans Thies Lehmann, are pertinent, predominantly that no one element is necessarily primary, requiring audiences (and practitioners) to engage forms of synaesthetic perception and hovering attention, simultaneously and variously taking in visual, spatial, movement, sonic and linguistic elements.[11] Likewise, the "experimental performative types" of liminal performance, as described by Susan Broadhurst, are all applicable. Drawing on a particularly

Figure 26.

useful summative description of Broadhurst's liminal aesthetics, the artists of La Máquina engage:

> a certain "shift-shape" style...a stylistic promiscuity favouring eclecticism and the mixing of codes...cynicism, irony, playfulness...self-consciousness and reflexiveness, montage and collage, an exploration of the paradoxical, ambiguous and open-ended nature of reality.[12]

In their wide-ranging projects, Malheiros and Faesler incorporate "processes of experimentation and sets of creative strategies."[13] The terms "experimental," "experimentation" and "experiments" are particularly apposite for indicating the exploratory, investigative, open and seeking processes that the practitioners (and in some projects, spectators) undertake.[14] As experiments are courses of action tentatively adopted without being sure of the eventual outcome and procedures undertaken to make a discovery, so these terms offer a useful framework for these projects. To draw on Collins' description of experimental and devised performance, this is theatre that is embedded in "innovation and risk-taking."[15] Yet their performances are not new for the sake of new.[16] Rather, the artists develop aesthetic innovations that are apposite for the specific material being worked on. Their approaches engage ideas of multiple identities, fluidity and trans-ness, challenging binaries through queer sensibilities and encompassing feminist cultural positionings. They deliberately seek to engage transdisciplinary practices to cross and complicate boundaries and borders.[17] Their explorations of theatre and performance aesthetics are fundamentally interwoven into explorations of thematic inquiries and questions. For Faesler, generating creative practices through questions "comes from having read Handke and many others—all these types of texts that are closer to a strategy of asking questions."[18] These questions are most obviously forms of material already worked on—they are recognizable scenarios ready for reactivation. They are scenarios of power relations, of encounters and difference, of constructed identities, of gender and sexuality, of master narratives, of truth, prejudice and resistance, and of life, death and existence itself.

Feminist questions and rigorous playfulness

The creative projects of Malheiros and Faesler are responses to their *inquietudes*—their preoccupations and concerns—where the political is personal and the personal is political. Drawing on theatre scholars Elaine Aston and Geraldine Harris, in their discussions of feminist performance makers, I characterise the creative work of Malheiros and Faesler as "politically resistant," as they seek to re-vision and complicate stereotypes and norms.[19] At core, their experimental, investigatory theatre practices "question the very nature of our accepted ideas and belief systems," producing "new ways of knowing and new ways of being."[20] Jaime Chabaud, renowned Mexican playwright and director, has written of "the anger that lives with us [causing us] to ask ourselves again about the function of culture and the arts in this context of extreme violence, impunity and social inequality."[21] Although a form of anger does indeed inspire the artists of La Máquina, their work is politically resistant through the sensibility of rigorous play and playful rigorousness. Despite, or because of, the deep traumas with which their projects engage (relationships of postmemory and rememory), they aim to empower, motivate and open up possibilities for future actions, rather than work with expressions of "feel[ing] good about feeling bad."[22]

Serious play is key both to the creative processes and also to the aesthetics of performances. As Faesler describes: "You can see this in all the works by La Máquina—we always have this bittersweet flavour. We've always worked in this area of humour and tragedy—it alters the mood. The performances are transformed into other things and we return." Their strategies encompass elements of the ludic—spontaneous and playful—as they deal irreverently with difficult material. They incorporate a playfully disruptive attitude of "*relajo*," aiming to mock the established order of things with comedy, shock and surprise.[23] Drawing on Jesusa Rodríguez, one of Mexico's most prolific and influential feminist cabaret-performance artists, (and long-time collaborator with Malheiros and Faesler), they use humour, "as a manner in which to see the world from distinct angles, [...] permit[ting] us to see it in all its ambiguity and its ridiculousness."[24]

Figure 27.

Figure 28.

Mexico: Long trajectories of experimentation

To put these practices into perspective, the artists of La Máquina engage with and draw on exceptionally rich trajectories in Mexico. Mexico is one of the most diverse countries in the world in terms of engaged, politically resistant, inspirational and challenging scenic arts, with a plethora of performance, theatre, dance, music and visual arts practices. As Chabaud has observed: "Contemporary Mexican theatre cannot be regarded as a homogenous block [...] There is not one big entity that defines us as a whole [...] [it is] a phenomenon that is very complex."[25] Over the last hundred years, since the end of the Revolution (1910–20), experimental ensembles, companies, collectives and artists have proliferated. In the decades after the Revolution, as a new nation and a sense of Mexicanness (*mexicanidad*) was generated through state-driven processes, diverse forms of experimentation materialized with the avant-garde evident through multiple movements. Artistic practices overtly brought together ideology and politics in a search for aesthetic forms corresponding with content. Scenic, visual and literary arts movements were many and varied, exploring a range of aesthetic practices.[26]

In the second half of the twentieth century there was an acceleration of radicalization, as contemporary theatre encompassed practices that were more hybrid through the larger presence of visual arts, media and performative actions. Experimental university theatre and multidisciplinary events were prevalent. Strategies of postmodern experimentation were widely applied, particularly engaging plurality and overt temporal juxtapositions. Alternative forms in playwriting, conceptual art, performance art, contemporary dance, ensemble-based companies, collective creation practices, laboratories and workshops proliferated.[27]

In the twenty-first century there is a profusion of artists and ensembles integrating diverse disciplines as expressive formats for transdisciplinary scenic creation. Many are using corporeal techniques, theatre of the body and transversal performance, generating live performances through collective creation.[28] Long-term ensembles, companies and collectives are particularly significant. A deep-rooted sense of exploration through live arts has continued, encompassing both institutional and national incentives that facilitate and encourage new work and also performance-based resistance movements seeking institutional change.[29]

Embodied inquiries

Body-based practices and strategies are fundamental to the creative projects of La Máquina. As Faesler describes: "The way in which La Máquina works has always been very corporeal and body-based—a *physical* theatre." Through their projects these artists demonstrate "the politically radical potentialities of the live body in action."[30] They especially incorporate the play-based strategies of Jacques Lecoq and the improvisational Viewpoints processes of Anne Bogart.[31] Since her intensive training with Lecoq in Paris, Malheiros has developed her expertise over three decades, using a methodology where creativity through body-play forms the core. Following Lecoq, and engaging strategies for making work in an ensemble, she generates performance languages that emphasize the physical playing of the actor-creator in a state of play (*jeu*). Within a framework of constant stimulation of creative work, and the development of a shared language built on observation and analysis, her practices involve constantly creating in and through the body.[32] Malheiros also draws on her scenic arts and acting training in Brazil (her country of origin), and her performance experiences in Europe and the Americas, including working with major figures in New York (such as Jerzy Grotowski and John Townsend). Complementing Malheiros's expertise, Faesler particularly engages Viewpoints as a productive methodology. She describes this as "really doing not acting," noting that "using this system generates unexpected things that are very interesting."[33] With a strong foundation in visual, spatial, architectonic and body-based dynamics, Faesler draws on her studies and expertise in scenography, costume design, acting and directing in Britain and Mexico.[34]

Mexico: Long trajectories of body-based performance

For their corporeal work, the practitioners of La Máquina draw on and connect with long and rich trajectories of performance and theatre artists in Mexico. These artists overtly work through and with their bodies as a core site and sight for exploration. While pointing up the dangers of essentialization, many of these artists encompass a diverse range of practices that resist classification but which incorporate aesthetics and strategies including cabaret, performance art, popular theatre and revue. English-language readers may be particularly familiar with performers such as Jesusa Rodríguez, Liliana Felipe, Astrid Hadad and Tito Vasconcelos.[35] Writing of Rodríguez, Roselyn Costantino describes how "the body is never taken as value free" and "is a primary signifier; a site for meaning, a location and sign itself."[36] Notably, Rodríguez and Felipe have both collaborated with Faesler and Malheiros on various projects.

Over the last few decades, conceptual performance artists have worked through radical corporeal investigation to engage the totality of performance elements using strategies of bodies in *extremis*.[37] As Antonio Prieto Stambaugh describes, they aim "not only to expose the construction of the body in culture, but also the metaphorical and physical destruction of bodies in society."[38] Many of these performance artists, such as Lorena Wolffer, deliberately explore thresholds of hyperreality. Although La Máquina does not usually engage strategies of hyperreality, their work is nevertheless in dialogue with these artists in terms of socio-political aims. Indeed, Wolffer has been invited by La Máquina to contribute to their workshops, laboratories and seminars.[39]

Outline: Four performance projects

Collective creation: Theatrical experiments with remains of bodies of history

The four projects presented in this book engage widely differing models of practice in terms of project duration and number of participants, yet all are connected through their ethical intentions to create transformative experiences. Each uses collective creation strategies working through body-based processes.

1. *Mexican Trilogy* comprises three staged works and an ensemble of five performers. Over the course of three years, the ensemble and other creative artists generated the full trilogy, devising and performing Part 1—*Nezahualcóyotl/A Scenic Correlation of Memory and Times*—before moving to Part 2—*Moctezuma II/The Dirty War*—and then Part 3—*Malinche/Malinches*. At the heart of the project are three bodies of history (two state rulers and a slave girl turned translator) all of whom lived in the fifteenth and sixteenth centuries and all of whom are deeply embedded in twenty-first century contexts as forms of collective memories. Through relationships of postmemory the project re-imagines issues of loss, violation and a search for identity and hope. Through experiences of rememory the project explores personal and collective manifestations of fear, forgetting and discrimination.

By reactivating scenarios of material already worked on the artists perform re-visions that value "knowledge" as questions, as personal stories and as ancestral wisdom. Through crossings with twenty-first century humans and atemporal beings, five performers embody liminal plurality. This complicated set of pieces encompasses multiple accumulated iterations

Figure 29.

of literary texts, gestures, costumes, vocalizations, objects and spatialities contained within an evocative and evolving scenographic environmental stage-space (Figures 4, 10, 14, 15 and 29).

2. *Zapata, Death Without End* incorporated five theatre collectives from diverse states in the Mexican republic. The performers collaborated over the course of a year, through shared and individual devising workshops, ultimately generating co-participatory public performances. The participants experimented with remains of the body of history of Emiliano Zapata, one of Mexico's most troped and iconic revolutionary figures of the 1910 Revolution. Generating trans-temporal crossings from the Revolution to the dirty war of the 1960s and 70s, to pre-Hispanic lives, to the Spanish invasion and to present-day experiences, the practitioners reactivated scenarios of resistance and control. Through relationships of postmemory the project re-imagined traumas of loss, hope, institutional power and impunity. Through experiences of rememory the project explored embodied games of childhood and joys of everyday eating. Through shared questions—What is the value of land? What is freedom? What is a hero?—the ensembles experimented with soil, stones,

Figure 30.

writings, songs, food, drink and stories, engaging multiple performance aesthetics from hyper-physicalization to quotidian walking. In the final event, performers and spectators mingled on stage for a co-participatory performance, gesturing, speaking, singing, writing, listening, eating and drinking in a collaboration of embodied diversity.

3. *War in Paradise* brought together twenty-five creative artists and students of varying ages to collaborate for three weeks on a small studio theatre stage in Mexico City. The practitioners experimented with remains of the body of history of Lucio Cabañas, a rural teacher turned resistance leader in the 1960s rights movements, who was assassinated in 1974 on government orders. Drawing on the eponymous literary work by Carlos Montemayor for traces of corporeal remains, the short-term project specifically focused on investigating the potential of creative processes and theatre strategies. Trans-temporal crossings connected traces of the 1960s and 70s to the 1910 Revolution, to the Spanish conquest and to the "now" of twenty-first century movements for social justice. Using iconic gestures (raised fists), objects (subverted national flags) and spatialities (linear confrontation), the practitioners worked through postmemory traumas of repression, defiance and material fragility, reactivating scenarios of power struggles and corporeal destabilization. Through rememory the artists reconstructed embodied experiences

Figure 31.

of school, fiestas and militaristic exercises. Performative fragments generated in workshops were woven together to form an hour-long unrehearsed, non-finalized public performance of work-in-progress, performing re-visions of power relations and resistance to official amnesia.

4. *Time of the Devil* is a solo theatre work performed by Malheiros and created by Malheiros and Faesler. The artists experimented with remains of a body of history who is a conceptual no-body, yet whose form is deeply incorporated in collective memories and histories of power struggles, of religious control and of fear—the Devil. The Devil is inherently connected with remains of dead bodies of history and with daily living. Each person exists with perceptions of their own after-life. Drawing on the dialogical configuration of Fernando Pessoa's novel (the inspiration for this project), Malheiros leads herselves and her spectators on a trans-temporal, corporeal philosophical journey. She reactivates scenarios of material already worked on as existential embodied questions of life, of death and of the materiality of bodies. Postmemory is configured as the trauma of death and not-knowing, which Malheiros re-imagines by inviting her audiences to read their futures on tiny pieces of paper inside fortune cookies. Through experiences of rememory she balances precariously, changing perspectives and unfolding new problems. Through explicit performativity and constructedness, she layers and juxtaposes clothes, spoken texts and gestures as re-visions of concepts of truth, fixity and knowledge. She plays with remains of bodies, carrying a headless body and moving with body-less death masks. Finally, she ends in a corporeal attitude of in-betweenness, discontinuity and potentiality.[40]

Figure 32.

53

Palimpsests: Bodies, histories and spatialities

Through these four projects, the artists play through entangled trans-temporal traces, overtly combining remains in multiple forms from many centuries as they experiment with juxtapositions and simultaneity. Diverse fragments of movements, gestures, spoken texts, vocal sounds, spatialities, sonics, objects and costumes are performed concurrently or successively. Each body performs a plurality of identities, as the stage space becomes a container of liminal possibilities, de-contextualizing and re-contextualizing multifarious remains. Each of the four projects specifically engages perceptions of trans-temporalities as experienced through bodies, histories and spatialities.

Palimpsest bodies: Plural, both/and, mixed and trans-temporal

The concept of bodies as plural, both/and, mixed and trans-temporal (palimpsests) is one of the most obvious performative elements in these projects. This sense of corporeal plurality connects with one of the most foundational concepts of identities in Mexico. Overt corporeal mixings remain as evidence of multiple relationships of invasion, violence, violation, domination and power struggles. Taylor has described mestizaje (mixing/miscegenation) as both/and bodies, such that multiplication and simultaneity are forms of transmission.[41] In the four projects, the artists of La Máquina generate various mixings, crossings, multiplications and simultaneities. At any one moment, a performer's body is performing trans-temporal plurality. In *Mexican Trilogy* Nezahualcóyotl is crossed with city dwellers of twenty-first century Neza City and atemporal deities; in Part 2, a massacre of Indigenous peoples in 1520 and of demonstrating students in 1968 are merged and performed simultaneously, as five bodies speak and move together on a single platform of bricks; and in Part 3, La Malinche is many Malinches.

Perceptions of bodies as "mixed" have the "origin" in two specific bodies: La Malinche—the Indigenous translator and intermediary for Cortés; and Cortés—the European invader and colonizer. Two individual bodies (cuerpo) embody the conjoining and transformation of two bodies of peoples (corpus) to create a new mixed (mestizo) body. Together they produced a son, their conjoining generating a mixture: a form of palimpsest containing traces and evidence of other pasts, places, peoples, environments and bodies. Together, colonized and colonizing bodies generate multiple intertwining layers.

The woman known as La Malinche is one of the most complex and reiterated figures in Mexico. Her body stands in for intersections between national identity and gender identity. Through La Malinche, Woman is regarded as problematic, associated with subordination, shame and slavery.[42] Provocatively referencing the trauma of mestizaje, Octavio Paz

Figure 33.

(in)famously described Mexico as "a country whose mixed heritage has left the inhabitants as inheritors of traditions of conquesters or conquested. That is why in every moment a Mexican must choose between 'fucking or being fucked.'"[43] As so many artists have done before, the practitioners of La Máquina specifically use this scenario of postmemory (and experience of rememory) to experiment with remains of the woman known as La Malinche, performing deeply corporeal fragments of acts of exploitation, abuse, translation and complicity.

Significantly for my study, scholar Sandra Cypess has specifically portrayed La Malinche as a palimpsest, interpreting her through notions of intertextuality. For Cypess, "'La Malinche' functions as a continually enlarging palimpsest of Mexican cultural identity whose layers of meaning have accrued through the years. With each generation the sign 'La Malinche' has added diverse interpretations of her identity, role, and significance for individuals and for Mexico."[44] In the transdisciplinary experiments of La Máquina (in *Mexican Trilogy*, *Malinche/Malinches*), La Malinche is created from a multiplicity of stories of present-day lives interwoven with a few known "facts" about the woman known as La Malinche. She is performed through five business-suited bodies of liminal plurality, containing and unfolding complex layers of remains. As a plurality of Malinches, these bodies are veritable tapestries of subjectivities who vocalize and challenge Paz's words and who act as hyper-communicating silent witness. As they wring the body of Cortés and gesture at happy families, they perform re-visions of history, knowledge and truth through strategies of performing palimpsest bodies (Figures 29 and 34).

Figure 34.

Palimpsest histories: Invasions, both/and, in-betweenness and superimpositions

Perceptions of Mexican histories as entangled, sedimented and multiple are key to these performance projects of La Máquina. I repeat here the evocative depiction of Mexican interdisciplinary feminist performance artist Maris Bustamante:

> Seen from the point of view of a rationalist, European "order," or even from the US, the Mexican "order" often appears as a "disorder" or "non-order." It is precisely in this disorder or "non-order" that I believe lies the crux of the Mexican imaginary. [...] This confrontation of orders corresponds to what some consider the encounter, for others the "mis-encounter," of two worlds, as the conquest, colonization, and neocolonization processes have come to be known, processes which have been extended over a period of five hundred years and about which so much has been said.[45]

Bustamante encompasses two crucial elements that the artists of La Máquina explore through experimental theatre strategies: 1) the understanding of temporal arrangements as non-linear; and 2) histories—of conquest, colonization and neocolonization—as processes. Temporalities and histories are perceived through notions of movements, ruptures, transformations, superimpositions, reforms, revolutions and accumulations. These include: sixteenth-century Spanish invasion and colonization; nineteenth-century wars of Independence, invasions, impositions and territorial loss involving France and the US and internal reforms; twentieth-century Revolution, 1960s and 70s countercultural movements and the dirty war, and increasing neoliberal capitalism; and twenty-first century challenges and governmental impunity.[46]

Multiple iterations of prehispanic, colonial, independent, revolutionary and countercultural pasts and peoples mingle and merge with globalized, postmodern and capitalist presents. Indeed, in his discussions of construction and representation of cultural identity in Mexico, Daniel Cooper Alarcón has usefully described Mexicanness as a palimpsest of competing yet interwoven narratives that have arisen through a process of erasure and superimposition.[47] There is a persistent sense of "before" the Spanish invasion and imposed traumatic transformation, colonization and founding of New Spain.[48] The concept of nepantla (as noted in the previous chapter) encapsulates a living experience of palimpsest plurality. Nepantla, a Nahuatl word meaning "in the middle of it," was used five hundred years ago by Mexica as they were being colonized by the Spaniards.[49] Postmemory therefore encompasses relationships with traumas from many generations, felt in the present as processes of living with invasions, superimpositions, rifts, disappearances, liminality, in-betweenness and reforms.[50] Senses of "loss" of former civilizations and cosmogonies of Mesoamerica are present in many forms: in embodied archival repertoires of linguistic codes, dances, gestures and musical forms; in stones and sculptures; in belief systems; in foods and cultural practices; and, most profoundly, in human bodies. Questions of "Who am I?" and "Where do I come from?" are ever present, with a sense of an on-going search for self and collective identity, through notions of collective histories and memories.

Figure 35.

Crossing historical realities and cultural fictions

In these performance projects, the practitioners of La Máquina specifically engage questions of history, not as re-enactment but as an exploratory re-imagining and reconstruction, deliberately interweaving multiple temporalities.[51] Faesler approaches questions of history through multiplicity, engaging Walter Benjamin's notion: "'To articulate the past historically does not mean to recognize it 'the way it really was.' It means to seize hold of a memory as it flashes up at a moment of danger.'"[52] As Faesler portrays: "The thing about history is that it's not one, it's many, it repeats itself, it alters, it continues happening." This idea of repetition is a way of thinking about history as scenarios of material already worked on that are therefore open for reactivation and re-vision. Relating to ideas of liminality, Faesler describes her own perceptions of history both as a portal and as passing through and across a threshold. She again draws on Benjamin: "'Are we not touched by the same breath of air which was among that which came before? Is there not an echo of those who have been silenced in the voices to which we lend our ears today? [...] [T]here is a secret appointment between the generations of the past and that of our own.'"[53]

In order to play with and through history the practitioners engage concepts of "real" and "fictitious" as "crossing" or "trans." Faesler explains: "We wanted to work with cultural fictions and historical realities—to see where these paths cross." Repeating a strategy used

Figure 36.

many times before by multiple scenic artists in Mexico, this approach draws on the notion of "fiction" as itself as already multiple.[54] By using ideas of cultural fictions and historical realities, the artists explore the "ambiguity of opposition of real and fictitious."[55] Although the projects are initiated with "real" individual people (or entities, in the case of the Devil), the framework of crossings opens up many possibilities. These are correlations of postmemory, where relations with the past are active and generative, mediated by imaginative investment, projection and creation. Faesler discusses how "the word fiction doesn't worry me in the theatre, because I assume that fiction is something recovered. For me nothing is invented. It's an exercise in memory. [...] What we do in the scenic arts is reconstruction. So you are reconstructing things from yourself." In these experiments, the "self" (or selves) of each performer and participant are inherently part of the creative processes. Questions of "Who am I?" and "Do you remember?" are posed in relation to bodies of history from many prior centuries and decades. Here, the self and autobiography are forms of postmemory and rememory. In discussions of performance-making, Emma Govan and colleagues describe "the production of autobiography [...] [as] a result of a reflection upon personal experience that is subjected to the filters of memory and personal editing [...] 'We might say, then, that autobiography is neither fictive nor nonfictive, not even a mixture of the two. We might view it instead as a unique, self-defining mode of self-referential expression'...a creative space in-between."[56] When this creative space in-between is combined with plural in-betweenness of bodies of histories, these many layers and traces offer great potential for re-imaginings. By creating through entangled histories, the artists of La Máquina therefore perform palimpsest bodies as multiple intersectional identities that are fluid and compound, liminal and plural.

History as scenarios in the making

For La Máquina, audiences are specifically included in these scenarios of history through relationships and strategies of convivio.[57] History is not "done" and for viewing, but in the making. The over-riding aesthetic is therefore one of directness and of being still in-the-moment.[58] By creating structures of convivio, these projects involve an encounter

Figure 37.

of presences, dialogical audience-performer relationships and performance *with* the audience not for audience.[59] An understanding of trans-temporality opens up possibilities, inviting audiences to be co-participants. In *Mexican Trilogy*, the interrogative phrase "Do you remember?" is directed at spectators as an invitation and a provocation to consider specific events that took place in multiple centuries for re-imagining future actions. For the duration of *Zapata, Death Without End*, the entire audience is on stage with the performers, participating by drawing, writing, smelling, drinking and eating. In *War in Paradise*, as the twenty-five performers sit across the front of the stage the spectators are placed in the role of senator for a brief and unexpected moment. Throughout *Time of the Devil*, the solo performer dialogues with the audience and circulates in the auditorium, offering a bag of fortune cookies and inviting each person to contemplate their own futures.

Iconic bodies and modes of being

The artists of La Máquina turn to iconic bodies of history in order to open up possibilities and perform re-visions. As B. Christine Arce has described: "Specific historical bodies [...] have been appropriated in Mexico by different cultural genres [...] [and] their bodies become metaphors for the tensions within the spaces they occupy. [...] More than a 'mode of thought' which governs the expectations that are held of certain people these are modes of being through bodies."[60] In a country as diverse as Mexico, performances of power are enacted through troped iconic bodies, where the micro of the individual body (cuerpo) creates the macro of the united, collective, national body (corpus), through processes of imagined communities.[61] These bodies are re-formed as statues, as names of streets and towns, as icons to identify metro stations and through myriad other appearances, with notable national performative commemorations and memorializations.[62] Familiarity, therefore, presents day-to-day connections with these iconic bodies of history as material already worked on. In the performance projects of La Máquina, these bodies are deconstructed and reconstructed as trans-temporal palimpsest bodies for re- and un-imagined communities.

Mexico: Long trajectories of theatre and performance decontextualizing history

For these creative projects inquiring into bodies of history, La Máquina connects with rich trajectories of theatre and scenic works that strive to problematize official narratives, particularly presenting re-visions of historic myths of archetypal heroes and gendered historical narratives.[63] Over the course of many decades multiple playwrights have utilized strategies of decontextualization and deconstruction as they "seek to reconstruct the past and provide another reading of episodes included in the official history […] [offering] another interpretation of 'historic facts/acts,'" using "the past to illuminate the present."[64] These theatre artists have aimed to "disrupt the narrative on stage, and challenge the audience's own desire to create tidy and closed narratives."[65] Such works often engage playful, non-narrative, fragmented structures, combining fact and fiction, movement in time, temporal shifts, coexistence and juxtapositions, simultaneous dramaturgy, collage, narraturgy, reality and hyperreality and documentary.[66] Equally powerfully, performance artists have used their own bodies as both site and sight of historical, feminist re-visions. Through strategies of hybridity, simultaneity and liminality, artists such as Rodríguez and Hadad perform corporeal, vocal, and visual iterations of iconic bodies of history.[67] Similarly, many ensembles and collectives (such as el Teatro de Ciertos Habitantes, Teatro Ojo, Teatro Línea de Sombra, La Rueca, La Rendija, La Comedia Humana and Lagartijas tiradas al sol) have generated complex performative works that provocatively re-vision historical narratives and stereotypes through transdisciplinary practices and strategies.

Palimpsest spatialities: Coexistence, transformations and environments

In these four projects of La Máquina, perceptions of spaces as plural, both/and, mixed and trans-temporal are a core aesthetic. Through architectonics the stages and workshops are containers of diversity and of transformations; they are archival palimpsests of multiple lives. For Faesler, architectonics involves both "the architecture of the space and [also] the forms and the organic-ness of the space in relation to the human being who inhabits it." This speaks to Taylor's inquiry: "How does one come to inhabit and envision one's body as coextensive with one's environment and one's past…?" Without representing one obvious place, location or time, the performance spaces encompass remains of, references to and re-visions of many environments and pasts.

In the twenty-first century, the metropolis that is Mexico City stands on an island in a lake—home of Mexica migration. The Valley of Mexico contains traces of the drained

Lake Texcoco, now home to the City of Nezahualcóyotl. Taylor's portrayal of Mexico City as "a palimpsest of histories and temporalities" is obviously significant.[68] She describes how the city "functions as the mental and material space providing a framework for individual and collective memory," explaining that "the buildings and architectural layout remind even the most distracted passerby that this is a violently practiced place."[69] Sites and sights of pre-invasion civilizations remain as stones and artefacts above and below the surface and as physical landscapes that have been altered through human interventions.[70] In the aftermath of the Spanish conquest, the central pyramid was deconstructed and the stones re-formed into the central Roman Catholic cathedral. There is a deep awareness that the huge central plaza (el Zócalo) covers up remains of the vast Mexica ceremonial site, where structures and artefacts exist just below the surface. From time to time, remains are suddenly discovered and uncovered. In 1978, electrical workers encountered a huge Mexica carving, which led to the excavation of the site of the Great Temple.[71]

Through centuries of invasions, reforms and revolutions, traces of prior ways of living are visible, despite attempts to erase one way of life to make way for another.[72] The city is therefore comprised of multiple remains existing in the form of layers, fragments, accumulations, constructions, deconstructions and reconstructions. One location stands out as perhaps the most profound site and sight of postmemory and rememory, and as an explicit, overtly visible palimpsest of tangled temporalities, histories, and peoples—the Plaza of the Three Cultures, Tlatelolco. Here, stones of structures of the pre-invasion Mexica civilization stand alongside a colonial church, constructed in early 1600s, surrounded by a large utopian housing complex completed in 1966.[73] Here, on 2 October 1968, ten days before the start of the Olympic Games, this plaza became the scene of one of Mexico's worst acts of terror, and one of the acutest events of postmemory, as hundreds of peacefully-demonstrating students were massacred in cold blood by military and police under official government orders (Figure 38).

These perceptions and understandings of spatialities are evident in all four projects discussed in this book. Most overtly, through the tripartite palimpsest structure of *Mexican Trilogy*, the

Figure 38.

artists play with accumulations and transformations in the Valley of Mexico across six hundred years (Figure 39). In Part 1 (*Nezahualcóyotl/Scenic Correlation of Memory and Times*), the high inclined panels that are positioned around a red rhomboid platform present narrow entrances through which sharp paths of light produce geometric shapes. Bodies appear as shadows and spectres moving in and out of sculptural poses, mixing contemporary lives and atemporal deities. Throughout Part 2 (*Moctezuma II/The Dirty War*), the stage space is exposed and open to the side walls, presenting a raw and public place within which the performers assemble and reassemble a hundred grey bricks into formations of pyramids, plazas and pedestals. As they sift through remains of history with vocal texts, embodied gestures, costume overlays and iconic objects, they generate a visual and aural performance of construction, deconstruction and reconstruction, specifically reactivating the Tlatelolco massacre on an open layer of bricks (Figure 38). In Part 3 (*Malinche/Malinches*), the homely space is strewn with recognizable furniture and objects of everyday Mexico City life, intermingled with re-used iconic artefacts of conquest. Gradually, these items are moved around and re-ordered, only to be cleared away for the eventual spatial infusion of life-size maize plants, connecting origins of life with everyday lives and with genetic modification (Figure 39).

In the multi-ensemble project *Zapata, Death Without End*, for the duration of the three hour performance, the stage becomes home for the five distinct groups of performers and all the spectators, who co-mingle and co-participate. With piles of stones, mounds of earth, egg-box constructions, trailing electrical wires and lights, paper-layers of newly drawn faces of Zapata and a table covered with cooking ingredients, the environment is formed and re-formed, generating multiple connections through disparate traces. For the three-week project *War in Paradise*, the absence of scenery, furniture and specific lighting generates a sharp focus on the twenty-five bodies, proposing deep connections to recent (and continuing) traumas of bodies that are tortured and disappeared. Through *Time of the Devil* the shimmering blue beams of light highlight the disconnected struts of wood that proffer possible pathways and steps. In this playful investigation into the materiality of bodies and after-lives, the stage floor is progressively littered with front-facing tiny red devil-bodies and staring white death masks, modelling an environment of trans-temporal bits and pieces.

Experiments with remains: Strategies, aesthetics, processes and practices

To bring this chapter to an end and to transition to the four performance projects in Section Two, I conclude with a brief summary of the core elements at the heart of these practices of La Máquina. Directors Faesler and Malheiros are reflective practitioners and engaged artist-citizens, who playfully and rigorously facilitate inventive and investigative processes. As they create experiments through relationships of postmemory and experiences of rememory, they reactivate remains of bodies of history by asking: "How do we share our lives with what remains?" Their processes are broad and inclusive seeking "remains" in many forms: visual images, objects, speech, linguistic codes, writing, embodied archival-repertoires, sensory experiences, spatialities, colours, light-forms, -scapes (land, urban), architectures and barely tangible ephemera. In collaborative workshops they enable practitioners to experiment with these traces and remains, playing with and through multiple crossings and personal experiences, and reactivating scenarios of material already worked on. The range of remains is translated into an equally expansive and inclusive range of performance practices encompassing a plethora of movements, gestures, poses, spoken texts, linguistic codes, vocalizations, costume designs, spatial dramaturgy, lighting, sonic forms, scenographic elements, objects and sensory elements. These are transdisciplinary forms that require audiences to engage synaesthetic perception and hovering attention, simultaneously and variously taking in visual, spatial, movement, sonic, linguistic and sensory elements.

Movements, gestures and poses range from everyday walking to explicit hyper-physicalization. Vocal forms range from everyday speaking to explicit hyper-vocalization. Speaking is performed as speech acts and as utterances of vocality through citational practices of narration, colloquial banter, formal dialogue, poetic recitation and political oration.[74] Words do not "belong" to the speaker but are performed as fragments with many interpretations. Official scholarly accounts and rememory experiences are amalgamated and mixed, blurring notions of real and fictional, and challenging embedded hierarchies, stereotypes and status. Costumes and body-coverings are chosen and designed for their intertextual resonances, specifically invoking multiplicity and trans-temporality. Objects are selected carefully for their familiar resonances, then used and re-used to complicate and transform. Spaces and lighting generate suggestions of trans-temporal environments, acting as containers for the inquiries and reconfigurations. Each body in performance is plural, connecting shared bodies of history with bodies in present environments. The artists perform expressions of identities, not characters, with senses of "selves" always present. Dramaturgical structures are created as collages and sequences, interweaving and juxtaposing scenarios of material through overlays and accumulations. Through these practices the practitioners complicate and contest received histories and everyday prejudices. Through performing palimpsest bodies, multiple remains become opportunities for present lives offering possibilities for abundant re-visions.[75]

Figure 39.

Figure 40.

Section Two

Four Performance Projects

Chapter 3

Mexican Trilogy: Scenic correlation of memory and times

Five performers, three years, three entangled parts:

1. *Nezahualcóyotl / Scenic Correlation of Memory and Times*;
2. *Moctezuma II / The Dirty War*;
3. *Malinche / Malinches*

> *Mexican Trilogy* is a provocation to create three performances drawing on a reflection of our present history and the relationship that we sustain day by day with our prehispanic past…three pieces, remnants, or snippets, three endeavours or processes of memory. Our undertaking is to tell stories/histories of the daily relationship that all we Mexicans have with stones, with books, with languages, food, and our traditions. How do we share our lives with what remains?
> — Juliana Faesler and Clarissa Malheiros, La Máquina de Teatro[1]

Translating and ordering remains

Mexican Trilogy comprises three theatre works, performed by an ensemble of five actors and devised by a small creative team.[2] In this complex set of composite and transdisciplinary pieces, five bodies perform multiple trans-temporal remains as plural and layered identities, crossing and merging over six centuries of lives. They inhabit and envision pasts and environments, challenging divisions between private and public, truth and fiction, collective and personal. As the performers inquire of themselves and of the audience "Do you remember?" they make gestures, carry bricks, sit and embroider, voice florid poetry, chant lists of names and tell intimate I-stories. They reiterate movements and vocalizations, transforming them to generate an accumulation of remains, sedimentations, iterations and ephemera.

In order to present and discuss aspects of this trilogy in relation to concepts of palimpsest bodies, postmemory experiments and rememory experiences I have selected a few brief moments and elements from what is a remarkably complex set of theatre pieces. I start by giving a general overview, then move to each part in turn, before finally reflecting on key strategies of the trilogy as a whole. For each part, I describe some essential aspects, followed by fragments of scenes as performance examples. I have created my own interpretive titles for these scenarios. The examples are structured in two parts: a writerly description (in italics) and an interpretation. Rather than include names, I have identified performers by a single letter. Reflecting the accumulation of iterations, my explanations for each part are increasingly longer.[3]

Impetus, heart and outlines

At the heart of this project are three bodies of history: two state rulers and a slave girl-turned translator. All lived in the fifteenth and sixteenth centuries and all three are thoroughly entangled in twenty-first century lives as forms of collective and personal memories and histories. Relationships of postmemory connect with scenarios of loss, violation, migration and power struggles. Experiences of rememory incorporate fear, forgetting, abuse and discrimination. By generating obvious "crossings" to twentieth- and twenty-first-century humans and atemporal beings the project reactivates scenarios of material already worked on to perform numerous re-visions.

Figure 41.

For directors Faesler and Malheiros, the impetus for the project in 2006 came from a sense of collective anxiety and the need for a just and sensitive political leader. As Faesler describes: "There was the huge political fraud. It was a very difficult moment. We were a very depressed country. We were looking to see if there was an inspiring figure in Mexico's past who could be the hope for a ruler who cares about his people. So that's where the idea of Nezahualcóyotl came from. He is a hugely important figure to study. As a vision and a presence, Nezahualcóyotl is a poet, a statesman, a skilful politician and the first ecologist of the Americas."[4]

If this name is unfamiliar to you, I invite you speak his name, moving your tongue, lips, vocal chords and breath: Ne-za-wal-koy-ot. You are reactivating remains of Nezahualcóyotl.

So, for Part 1 of the trilogy, this body of history provided a rich source of remains for inquiries into present predicaments and into pressing societal and political questions. Nezahualcóyotl exists as a man who is deeply part of twenty-first-century Mexico. He is inherently symbolic of perceptions of "loss" of Mesoamerican ways of being—practices that were altered irrevocably after the Spanish invasion. Generating theatre experiments through remains of the body of Nezahualcóyotl therefore offered the potential for reactivating scenarios of leadership, migrations and hope.

For Parts 2 and 3, the artists looked to Mexico's deepest traumas: invasion, violation, domination and conquest, focusing on two interfacing people—Moctezuma II and La Malinche. Moctezuma II acceded to the demands of the invading Spanish forces, leading to his death and the ruin of his city and peoples. The tragedy and mystery of why he consented continue to remain, provoking questions of power, control, complicity and destruction. La Malinche was hired as the translator for the Spanish conquester Cortés, after being sold into slavery as a girl. She acted as the "tongue" for Cortés and bore a child with him. Her name is used as a slur and a pejorative, ("malinchista"), provoking questions around gender, discriminations and stereotypes.

Transdisciplinary and trans-temporal aesthetics

Through remains of these three bodies of history the ensemble generated *Mexican Trilogy: Nezahualcóyotl*; *Moctezuma II*; and *Malinche*, creating complex responses to and re-visions of official histories. A small team of creative artists, directed by Faesler and Malheiros, created the trilogy over three years, devising and performing one part before moving to the next. Each part is distinct, with multiple connections through all three, performed through reiterations and juxtapositions of scenarios. For each part, the core body of history is mixed with others to generate obvious trans-temporal crossings. These crossings encompass twenty-first-century urbanites, Mesoamerican deities, twentieth-century resistance leaders and the selves of performers and audiences. This trans-temporal plurality is contained in one place and one space through 600 years—the Valley of Mexico.

The artists used forms from multiple time periods (thirteenth to twenty-first century) existing in myriad modes (stones, sculptures, painted images, writing, poems, oral stories, e-mails, everyday items, clothing, food, songs, dances, breathing, smells and barely tangible ephemera). The trans-temporality and multiplicity of "remains" were transformed and translated into equally plural transdisciplinary and theatrical aesthetics, involving movements, vocalizations, spoken texts, costumes, objects, dramaturgy and scenography:

- *Movements:* physicalization and choreography ranges from the familiar and everyday to extreme movement vocabularies; from walking, eating and embroidering, to gestures and poses reactivating still images of bodies in sixteenth-century codices;
- *Vocalization:* speaking and vocalizing engages a multiplicity of vocal aesthetics, shifting through many modes, including everyday talking, declamatory speaking, narration, story-telling, recitation, personal musing and extended vocalization;
- *Verbal texts:* linguistic texts from multiple centuries are spoken by five voices simultaneously and successively, generating a palimpsest fabric of coexistence and intertextuality;
- *Costumes:* garments reference familiar twenty-first-century clothes, transformed through inversions and layerings to generate plurality and liminal in-betweenness;
- *Objects:* artefacts are used as iconic signs and re-contextualized in later scenes;
- *Dramaturgy:* dramaturgically, one scene contains multiple layers as it overlaps with and merges into another to create crossings and intersections, as an accumulation of stories caught in the middle;
- *Scenography:* spatially and architectonically, the three "spaces" are distinct: high red panels leaning inwards with tiny portals; an open stage littered with grey bricks; and a cluttered, (dis-)ordered apartment.

For the duration of the trilogy, the stage is a palimpsest site and sight, crossed and transformed by the people who inhabit it, through multiple and connected articulations and definitions of same space. Each of the three parts engages distinct aesthetics, moods and scenographies, generating a sense of journeys through transforming environments, even as they are all located in the "same" Valley of Mexico, existing in the present, offering re-imaginings for future lives. Through performing palimpsest bodies, *Mexican Trilogy* is an archival-repertorial container of many traces and remains: multiple temporal spaces exist in one moment and one temporal space contains multiple existences.

Figure 42.

I

To think "Nezahualcóyotl" is to talk with history, with books, with the "Roji Guide" for Mexico City; to converse with what was lost, with the unceasing conquest. To think "Nezahualcóyotl" is to regain one's self; it is also the strategy of interchange between the stage and the street, between history, myths and the divine; between living and life. Close your eyes, think of the word, speak it: "Nezahualcóyotl." Are we him and his contemporaries and are they us? Yes and no; Yes, because the passions, the human emotions, the richness and the poverty are the same, the terrain is the same. No, because we do not perceive of the universe and our environment in the same way; no, because we have utterly transformed this region. And yet we are them and they are us; we are simply people moving through/in history.

II

Walk through the Historic Centre of Mexico City. Feel the stones, the cries, the always-existing souls of the dead. Lean down to each culvert and hear the voices of the depths. Glance sideways at the yellow plastic shoe, the smiles of the people. At heart, what remains: the Great Temple. I hear the insistent rhythm of the drum and the sigh of a flute. Someone comes close, holding out their hand with coins in a tin. The feather and flag undulate.

I

Pensar "Nezahualcóyotl" es platicar con la historia, con la monografía, con "La Guía Roji" de la Ciudad de México. Conversar con lo que se perdió, con la incesante conquista. Pensar "Nezahualcóyotl" es reconquistarse, es también estrategia de intercambio entre el escenario y la calle, entre la historia, la fábula y lo divino; entre lo vivo y la vida. Cerrar los ojos, pensar en la palabra, pronunciarla: "Nezahualcóyotl." ¿Somos él y sus contemporáneos y ellos son nosotros? Sí y no: Sí, porque las pasiones, las emociones humanas, , la riqueza y la pobreza son las mismas, el territorio es el mismo. No, porque no percibimos el universo y nuestro entorno de la misma manera; no, porque hemos transformado hasta el extrañamiento esta región. Y sin embargo somos ellos y ellos son nosotros: somos simplemente gente transitando por la historia.

II

Caminar por el Centro Histórico de la ciudad de México. Sentir la piedra, el griterío, el siempre estar de las ánimas. Inclinarse en cada alcantarilla y escuchar las voces de lo profundo. Ver de soslayo el zapato amarillo de plástico, las sonrisas de la gente. En el fondo lo que queda: El templo mayor. Oigo el ritmo insistente del tambor y el suspiro de una flauta. Alguien se acerca, extiende en su mano una lata con monedas. Ondean la pluma y la bandera.

Nezahualcóyotl (printed programme)
La Máquina de Teatro, Mexico City, Mexico, 2007
Juliana Faesler and Clarissa Malheiros.

Part 1: *Nezahualcóyotl / Scenic Correlation of Memory and Times*

Trans-temporal crossings

As one of Mexico's most replicated and troped figures, Nezahualcóyotl exists through a sense of collective memory that is tangibly maintained in twenty-first-century Mexican lives: his name, body-form and poetic words are recurring presences. Known as the Poet-King, a visual imagining of his body is replicated on the 100-peso note, passing hands each day in countless transactions as he looks out from these tiny pieces of paper. His name is given to many streets, to a metro station and to a whole city neighbouring Mexico City (Nezahualcóyotl City—Ciudad Nezahualcóyotl), so countless people speak his name day after day.[5] All these presences offered potential to generate trans-temporal crossings. These crossings involve two distinct "bodies" and "times":

- *crossing 1* incorporates contemporary lives and the environment of Nezahualcóyotl City, encompassing five named individual humans (a young man, a young woman, a girl, a transgender person and an older woman with Alzheimer's);[6]
- *crossing 2* extends to five atemporal and immortal deities of the Mexica cosmogony, who are non-human forms yet who inform humans of their own characteristics.[7]

All temporalities are performed as coexisting palimpsest bodies.

Remains

To generate Nezahualcóyotl (from here on shortened to Neza), the ensemble worked with many remains: codices (painted documents created by the Mexica, depicting human bodies undertaking a multitude of actions and comprising glyphs and symbols); stone objects, pyramids, sculptures, colours, spatialities and textures (experienced by visiting Teotihuacán, the Great Temple and the National Museum of Anthropology and History); poems by or attributed to Neza, translated from Nahuatl into Spanish (these poems display a great transcendental seeking and contain dialogues expressing doubts and dilemmas); books and scholarly texts (including biographies of Neza); "history" taught through live classes as part of the devising sessions by a major scholar; a Mexica dance form; and a Mexica ball-game.[8]

To generate crossing 1 (five individual humans living in Neza City in the twenty-first century), the ensemble worked with experiences of local residents of Neza City and personal life experiences.

To generate crossing 2 (deities of the Mexica cosmogony), the ensemble worked with stone sculptures, painted images and orally transmitted myths.[9]

Scenarios, postmemory and rememory

As scenarios of material already worked on, the practitioners focused on matters of home, migrations, power struggles, compassion, diversity and death. Experiments with postmemory encompassed questions of complicity and impunity, using experiences of rememory to explore fears of forgetting where home is and participation in violence.

Performance structure and dramaturgical flow

Over the course of many weeks of devising processes the artists generated, crafted and shaped the performance material. Using the three crossings, the ensemble created a dramaturgy interweaving and overlaying four distinct traces of narratives:

1. a chronological life-journey of the man Neza, from his father's death, through his accession to become ruler and ultimately to his death;
2. brief episodes of trauma in the lives of the five twenty-first-century Neza City inhabitants;
3. presences of the five Mesoamerican gods;
4. lives of the performers and audience as "themselves," engaged in real-time Mexico City.

These are structured as one continuous dramaturgical flow to perform a veritable multi-temporal palimpsest of juxtaposed and involuted lives, stories, experiences, memories and histories.

Textured costumes and painted skins

Through costumes and body paint, each of the five performers' bodies is an obvious trans-temporal palimpsest—liminal, both/and, ambiguous and yet familiar. Each performer covers their body with a layer of paint to create a distinct and individual marking. By painting on the skin, each body is fully visible, yet altered and transformed through a simple process of layering: yellowy-brown body and yellow face painted with brown curvy lines (the traces of wisdom/old age); blue body and blue face painted with a yellow stripe down the centre; obsidian black feet and hands, black face with yellow ovals around the eyes (skull-like), and hair braided over her head in a traditional pan-Indigenous style; red body and face; and white body with white facial markings.[10]

Over their painted body, each performer wears recognizable clothes—trousers, skirt and tunic. These are distanced through two processes of transformation: knitting and painted texturing. The familiarity is transmuted through processes that Faesler refers to as "materialization, [in other words,] made with material that gives a sense of distance. Everything needed to be knitted with organic materials, with different types of natural fibres, so there are things knitted from maguey rope, then there's wool, and some are hybrid."

The performers are barefoot, drawing attention to the multiple criss-crossing journeys along paths of light, re-forming remains of footprints in codices, indicating human lives and migrations (Figure 43).[11]

Figure 43.

Identities and objects

As the painted bodies covered with knitted-then-painted clothes add or remove a headdress or object, they merge between and morph into new identities, setting up juxtapositions through layering and accumulations. Neza is rendered as multiple and performed throughout by all five performers—sometimes for a scene or sometimes for a fleeting moment. Strategies include repeating a movement phrase, voicing a poetic text and speaking as "I, Neza." Neza is transferred from one performer to another, leaving traces among all five performers. The audience are also addressed by the performers as "Nezahualcóyotl," incorporating them all into the question: "Are we him or is he us?"[12]

In contrast, the twenty-first-century Neza City inhabitants are performed as individual identities, each with a distinctive object or article of clothing: a school backpack, an apron, a blonde wig, a rag and a plastic bag. Each object acts as a trace that adds a layer, rather than visually transforming the body into somebody else.

The deities are performed with transferable headpieces and clothing that are removed and placed on another performer.[13] Each deity moves with a distinct physicalization, connecting recognizable everyday movements with deeply sculptural forms. Through these shifts and transfers, deities encompass forms of embodied transmission and knowledge.

Criss-crossing paths

As a form of enclosed container, the stage is covered with a wooden platform formed of a red rhomboid with the apex facing down stage pointing towards the audience, surrounded by high red panels leaning inwards with small gaps in-between the panels. The five bodies emerge and disappear through these crevices, as lights shine to form criss-crossing paths generating a multiplicity of journeys (Figure 42).

A multiplicity of aesthetics

The multiplicity of remains is translated into a multiplicity of movement vocabularies, spoken texts, vocalizations, spatialities and gestures. Movements comprise sculptural poses, everyday gestures of politicians and heightened physicalizations of battle created from iterations of Danza Azteca choreographies. Bodies appear in the entranceways and disappear. They run across the space and exit as quickly as they come, offering fleeting glimpses. In brief freeze-frame tableaux, the bodies are temporarily fixed. Sharp lighting produces multiple shadows and ephemera. Speaking encompasses myths and legends, colloquial everyday speech, twenty-first-century political declarations, poems by Neza and other fifteenth-century authors, and poetic descriptions of the ideology of Mexica bodies. Vocalizations encompass deep-throated cries, soundscapes and wailing.

Performance examples

Scenario of materiality of memory and time (1.1)

C appears at the back opening, in the dimly lit enclosed red space. Wearing a long knitted tunic with yellow-painted skin, she holds a large brazier-headdress, which she places on her head. A crisp beam of white light marks a path.
She walks very slowly in a direct, straight line towards the audience. She vocalizes a throaty sound, telling of the origins of the universe, a story of time out of time and her own memory.

As she walks, two other perfectly formed crisp dark bodies appear in profile on the panels, facing away from her, moving with her and increasing in size as she progresses—shadow bodies. All three bodies move together in real time. (Figures 1 and 44).

At the opening of *Mexican Trilogy*, C performs as origins and time. Her headdress is a reiteration of a familiar stone sculpture of the elder god of gods and of fire Huehuetéotl. Her body takes a sculptural form, and, as she places one foot slowly but decisively in front of the other, there is a deliberate connection to the earth. Her unfolding hands are weaving through space as she speaks stories as myths, her oral transmission passed down through generations of bodies since time immemorial. Her body generates and is joined by ephemeral and spectral bodies who journey with her. These bodies are formed of reflected light—a phantasmagorical reality. Through the body of the deity and myth, through the deeply poetic vocality and stories of creation, these multi-textural moving bodies are remains of Neza and of every body, unfolding questions of postmemory—"where do I come from?"—"what is time?"—"who am I?"—"what is memory?"

Scenario of materiality of memory and time (1.2)

C performs a scene pairing with the opening scene to generate a palimpsest:

C wanders into the space, wearing a simple apron over her knitted tunic. She walks around, taking a meandering path as she looks about her. She speaks to herself and to everybody, talking in a rambling way about her life and asking "Do you know where my home is? Where is my home?" (Figure 44).

C performs Cuca, a resident of twenty-first century Neza City with Alzheimer's. The apron is a familiar gendered household object of domesticity and class. It is layered over the knitted

Figure 44.

tunic and painted face, which persist as traces of the elder god of gods. Her recognizably colloquial speech and her apron place her in the present, as she wanders around, unsure of where her home is.

= Together, through the body of C, the two scenes form a productive tension as the second overlays the first to generate contrasting and accruing traces. Through the spatial paths, direct and meandering; through movements of unfolding and wandering; through speaking of elaborate narratives and asking where home is; through shadows and ghosts; through rememory of the trauma of forgetting and losing one's memory, through postmemory of mortality, one body re-imagines possibilities through trans-temporality.

Scenario of fragility (1.1)

N half crawls and half falls into the space. She wears a short pleated skirt and carries a brown leather schoolbag. Her body and face are painted obsidian black and her hair is in braids over her head. She drags and hobbles her body to the front of the platform. She takes paper out of her bag and tries to bandage her ankle.
She stands up, in the path of sharp, white light, facing the audience, drawing her arms up to her chest, as she contracts her abdomen, and pushes her hands forward.
She cries out: "Help me. He raped me. I killed him." *She sobs and cries.*

N performs schoolgirl Xochitl of twenty-first century Neza City, marked through the school bag as an object of now, together with the school uniform and the colloquial and familiar speaking. Her painted body and face locate her as a deity and as death itself through trans-temporal remains. From her recognizable speech and movements, her body twists into an extreme physical form. She physicalizes her internal anguish through her hyper-choreographed movements, crossing from the everyday forms of contemporary urban life into traces of violation through time.

Scenario of fragility (1.2)

N stands centre stage wearing the brown schoolbag. She speaks directly to the audience, reciting a florid fifteenth-century poem, Song of War:
"Jade, gold, your flowers, oh God, only your treasures, oh Life Giver.… For who does one live? Death at the edge of obsidian knife, death in war.… Dust from a shield spreads itself, fog from darts spreads itself. Perhaps, truly, it is an opportunity to come to know the site of the mystery? Only the fame, the power dies in war. A little is carried toward the site of the disembodied."

Through the recitation of the poem, N overtly performs remains of Neza, speaking of materiality, time and value, and asking many questions about war, death and life, through a form that is heightened, mystical and elaborate.

Figure 45.

Together, through the body of N, these two scenes form a productive tension, as the body of the young contemporary schoolgirl merges with the philosophical body of the leader of the Mexica peoples, who merges with the deity, to perform a complex palimpsest body. Her body performs an unsettling of internalized pain and a re-vision of vulnerability and complicity. An eloquent, sensitive, decision-making leader stands strong, through the body of a violated and conflicted young human (Figure 45).

Scenario of unifying diversity

All five performers stand face-to-face, arguing and shouting at each other. With flowing movements, the five discrete bodies move together to create a pose, forming the iconic sculptural body of Coatlicue, Mexica Mother of Gods. (Figure 46).

Five distinctly different trans-temporal bodies merge to produce one body of plurality. As five bodies breathe together as one, just for a few moments in time, the ancient deity Coatlicue is reactivated and re-visioned as a container of multiplicity, of in-betweenness and of liminality, with intertextual and intertextural traces. Through a radical dissolution of binaries, these trans-temporal bodies combine to generate one nurturing body through remains of Neza.[14]

Figure 46.

Foreshadowing: Significantly, in this momentary scenario, N's body forms the tongue. This foreshadows her palimpsest body as La Malinche, *la lengua*—the tongue/translator—in Part 3 *Malinche/Malinches*.[15]

Scenario of afterlife

Each performer superimposes a simple skull (calaca) mask over their face. They all face the audience. With a loose, swinging physicalization they move across the space, from side-to-side, talking about how they each died, as they point and wave at the audience. (Figure 47).

As a scenario of human ephemerality, this playful scene re-imagines postmemory traumas of death and dying. The skull is perhaps the most potent, ubiquitous and familiar corporeal signifier of death.[16] These are bodies dealing with their own deaths and their souls. Each mask is a simple cartoon-like black-and-white cardboard cut out which the performers push over their own nose, rendering the "living" nose visible. Under the facial skin of each performer is a "real" skull, generating a triple-layered palimpsest face of life/death. The face is "dead" while the body remains unchanged, even as the layering and haunting of doubleness

Figure 47.

creates a tension between materiality and immateriality. As they integrate the audience into their musings, they provocatively play with existential questions.

Scenario of power

A path of white light shines from the back to front of the platform. Four performers walk gently along the shaft. They carry between them a small figurine-body, which they carefully locate at the front of the platform, close to and facing the audience. They dress the miniature body in a royal blue cloak and place a tiny headpiece on his head, with the audience as witnesses to this celebration. They speak to the body-object as they list their demands and exhortations, imploring him and advising him on how to govern:

Figure 48.

"Do not waste the savings of your people.—Do not use the army to hurt your people.—
Don't build mega-libraries for personal ostentation.—Don't privatize the petroleum
industry.—Don't privilege the monopolies.—Don't bow down to those who have
money—they rarely see the good of your people." (Figure 48).

Neza's remains are re-imagined from the recognizable body depicted on the 100-peso
note—but formed with a small body-object. As the performers speak to him with profoundly
contemporary words that are deeply familiar through the specific references to current
actions of the president, they merge the presence of the wise fifteenth-century leader with a
twenty-first century president, performed as hope and pleading for future lives.

Scenario of death and remains

*D wears a necklace of bright orange marigold (cempasuchil) flowers around her neck. She
speaks as "I, Neza" and speaks of Neza's death. She kneels on the ground as she embraces the
little body-figure. She recites a poem attributed to Neza:*
  "Like a painting we will be erased. Like a flower we will dry up here on earth. Like
  plumed vestments of the precious bird…we will come to an end…though you be of jade,
  though you be of gold, you also will go there, to the place of the fleshless. We will have to
  disappear, no one can remain."

*The four performers envelope her body in a large cloth. D's doubled-up body is folded into the
cloth, gently lifted off the ground and carried away on the back on R, in a line of bodies walking
barefoot slowly along a pathway of light.* (Figure 49).
Through this unfolding scene, D performs Neza's death as potential life through her trans-
temporal entangled palimpsest body. She performs traces of four coexisting identities:

Figure 49.

Emperor Neza, the Mexica guide god (Huitzilopochtli), a twenty-first-century girl Juana and herself, Diana. One body merges public, private, living, dead, human and mythical. Her poetic vocalizing transitions perspectives that move from being Neza—"I"—to speaking about Neza—"he"—, even as she holds the body-object of Neza within the garland of live flowers—flowers which are a powerfully evocative symbol of communal celebrations of death and ancestors, marking collective and personal acts of remembering. As she enfolds the body inside the flowers, and as her body is then enfolded inside the cloth, these layered bodies appear as a bundle containing the remains of lives and memories, folded into each other and transported on a journey.[17]

Scenario of trans-temporal compassion and support

Shafts of white light criss-cross the platform, forming a multiplicity of pathways and journeys. In pairs, performers traverse the platform, entering through an opening, and disappearing through another, as one deity leads one twenty-first-century Neza City dweller. Each time they appear and re-appear, they add or remove an object or piece of clothing to perform another identity, transforming from deity to contemporary inhabitant in a fleeting moment, even as they perform plurality.
C wanders backwards through a tiny gap between two panels. She wears her apron. D steps in and extends her hand. She wears her headdress of balloons performing the guide god Huitzilopochtli. C asks: "Are you going to take me to my house? Do you know where it is?" *D takes her hand and leads her gently through a portal.* (Figure 50).

Through this pairing of bodies, C performs traces of the woman with memory loss who has forgotten where her home is. She is led by D who performs as the atemporal deity of guidance.

A moment later, C returns through another opening. She has removed her apron, and returns with her brazier-headdress marking the elder god Huehue. C is carrying N on her chest. N's legs are wrapped around C's body and they are face to face. N wears her brown schoolbag on her back. N asks: "So, everything moves?" C walks slowly and deliberately, reiterating her opening walking movement. Now she traverses the space from one side to other, speaking slowly and poetically: "Yes, the above and below, the centre and around, the day and the night, the here and the there..."
N's body, a traumatized, raped child's body of rememory, speaking existential poetic words of Neza, is enfolded in an atemporal body of wisdom, offering a complex corporeal intertwinement of hope and futurity.

This final scene incorporates multiple trans-temporal layers and amalgamations through reiterated movement phrases, gestures, spoken texts, costume layers, objects and spatial forms. Each body is a trans-temporal palimpsest, and each pair combines to generate a dense accumulation of layers and traces. The connections between Neza, twenty-first-century inhabitants and the Mexica cosmogony are performed as inherently interconnected and coexistent. As the five bodies rapidly transform and re-emerge, they appear as flickers of tangled temporalities and always as plural bodies. The many reiterations of traces connect myths of time with questions of justice, governance, support and memory. All these lives are connected and contained through the body of history of Neza, performed as re-visions to offer potential and hope, through poetic and philosophical wisdom.

Figure 50.

86

Part 2: *Moctezuma II/The Dirty War*

Trans-temporal crossings

Moctezuma II exists as a major presence of postmemory in the twenty-first century. His actions of submission continue to cause incomprehension, even as the consequences of his actions continue to permeate countless aspects of daily life. He endures through multiple remains, from naming of streets and buildings, to body-replications in statues and visual artworks.[18] Moctezuma's role in one of the weightiest face-to-face meetings in world history has been replayed countless times. As scenarios of encounter, violation and conquest, these are materials that have been worked on again and again.[19] Part 2 involves two trans-temporal crossings:

- *crossing 1* incorporates the 1960s and 1970s and the dirty war, when social justice movements were violently suppressed by state forces.[20] One scene specifically reactivates the 1968 Tlatelolco massacre;
- *crossing 2* incorporates the "now" of living with questions of the past within an overt framework of collective reflection and consternation.

Remains

To generate Moctezuma, the ensemble worked with many forms of remains: accounts written by Spanish conquistadores and missionaries; recently translated Nahuatl accounts; codices and other visual images; and with stone structures above and below the surface in Mexico City.[21]

To generate crossing 1 (the dirty war of the 1960s and 70s), the ensemble worked with remains as oral testimony accounts of the 1968 massacre and other narratives of insurgency and guerrilla movements; and experiences of locations and environments of Mexico City, including Tlatelolco.[22]

To generate crossing 2 (present lives and resistance movements), the ensemble worked with remains as names of Indigenous languages; personal experiences; and the manifesto of the Zapatista Army of Nacional Liberation.[23]

Figure 51.

Scenarios, postmemory and rememory

As scenarios of material already worked on, the practitioners focused on matters of constructions of history, encounter, conquest, violation and relationships of power.

Experiments with postmemory encompassed questions of violent repression and human cruelty, using experiences of rememory to explore uncertainties of truth and fear.

Performance structure and fragmented dramaturgy

For *Moctezuma II* the ensemble created a fragmented structure comprising self-contained scenes that are juxtaposed and superimposed. These encompass:

1. the meeting of Moctezuma and Cortés, Moctezuma's death and the Spanish overthrow;
2. incidents of rebellion and insurgency in the 1960s and 1970s;
3. questions of living with remains in the "now" of Mexico.

These scenarios are constructed then deconstructed, time and again.

Costumes as dust, labourers and codex bodies

The five performers' bodies suggest construction-deconstruction, archival objects and buried remains through complex costume designs (Figure 52).

Dust: The five performers wear recognizable contemporary clothes: shirt, skirt and jeans. They are distanced with a white-ish mottled colouring, as if covered in dust, appearing as buried, archival bodies that have been unearthed from their resting place; and simultaneously appearing as bodies of labourers who are constructing or reconstructing a structure—a pyramid and a historiographic narrative—totally covered in the dust of the earth/archives. These ambiguous bodies (dust-bodies) appear to be visible ephemera, in a state of fragility

Figure 52.

and alteration, referencing disappearance and presence, archives and cultural history, something remaining after something has been moved, the material transformation of a body at death, and concealed bodies retrieved from under the surface (Figures 53 and 59).[24]

Codex both/and nepantla bodies: To generate the presences of sixteenth-century Indigenous bodies, the performers overlay their dust-clothes with painted object-costumes, reconstructing visual forms from painted codices. They place a 2D in-profile head-face in front of their face. Each head-face is a literal outline trace, painted on one side only, with only one eye. The head-face does not mask and cover the live face, yet, when a performer stands in profile, the Indigenous head dominates, though the living face behind is visible. This offers a perspective of looking through one face to another face—two heads, one body. These moments of both/and are fleeting, captured in brief instances of stillness. At all other times the Indigenous head is always transforming as the performer moves, in a liminal state of in-betweenness and subjunctivity. Each face appears more or less substantial depending on the perspective, generating multiple viewpoints. Each head has its own life and embodies a haunting presence that can be looked through to a "living" face beyond. Fabric flows from the head-face to generate a sense of layering, merging one identity with another. As the performers stand in-profile, they reactivate poses and gestures from codices, speaking from multiple perspectives, inside and outside the action, present and past. "History" is viewed and heard through these haunting presences. "History" is destabilized, questioned, reconstructed and re-visioned through these nepantla bodies (Figure 52).[25]

"Moctezuma" is embodied as a 2D face in-profile, marked by a headdress and cloak. "He" is transferred from one performer to another, "removed," disembodied and dragged away (Figures 51, 54–56).

"Cortés" is present as the principal non-Indigenous sixteenth-century body, performed with a layered and painted body reactivated from codex images. A live performing body wears painted armour that is superimposed over a skirt to generate an obvious juxtaposition (see below for description) (Figures 54–56).

"Cortés" is also embodied with the use of single and iconic object: a helmet. This helmet is also used and re-used through Part 3 *Malinche/Malinches* as an artefact of power, domination, abuse and concealment (Figures 59 and 67).

Constructing movements: 2D gestures and violent poses

In contrast to the fleeting bodies in Part 1, movement vocabularies in Part 2 encompass 2D in-profile gestures and poses, juxtaposed with walking and moving bricks. Reactivating remains of the codex bodies, the performers stand and hold pictographic frames. Through the archive of the codices, these bodies have been contained in these familiar poses for centuries. Now, the moving-then-still bodies—layered with painted clothes—perform liminal and both/and bodies. They offer audiences time to look and to see how the bodies moved there—evoking the question, "how did we get here?" (Figure 52).

Constructing "home" with bricks

The moments of slow and heightened contemplation through sixteenth-century bodies are contrasted with bodies moving bricks. Approximately one hundred building bricks are littered on the stage. These grey bricks are a ubiquitous building material, providing a tangible and familiar sight of everyday transformations and "home." Over and over again the five performers move the bricks around the stage, repositioning them in different configurations. They appear to be like children playing with toy bricks, assembling and reassembling; and they seem to be labourers, undertaking their arduous physical work. They place the bricks together to create a moment of finality, then deconstruct and move them again, literally constructing, deconstructing and reconstructing formations.[26]

As they move the bricks they are working through difficult questions of history using multiple linguistic texts and codes, speaking remains of historical records and eye-witness accounts, all framed by the reiterated question: "Do you remember?" They sift through historiographical narratives and collective memories, constructing, presenting, then deconstructing a scene to perform structural, textural and scenographic palimpsests. They are moving through histories, speaking and gesturing with words of sixteenth-, twentieth- and twenty-first-century witnesses (Figures 26, 42 and 53).

Stark and open spatialities

In contrast to the closed, dark-red, spectral and container-like space for *Nezahualcóyotl*, the stage for *Moctezuma II* is non-specific, meta-theatrical and ambiguous. The walls of the stage are visible, indicating that nothing is hidden and everything is out in the open. The grey bricks are the raw materials for the labour of these both/and bodies as they inhabit and construct their traumatic and searching environment.[27] In the Scenario of massacre, five bodies stand and fall on a single layer of bricks. In the extensive openness five bodies reactivate two massacres, separated by four hundred years, which were perpetrated in enclosed plazas trapping their victims inside the inescapable space (Figure 58).

Shifting perspectives, language and speaking: I/you, now/then

Throughout *Moctezuma II*, several vocalizations and speaking strategies are used to generate complex, intertextual and trans-temporal networks. The palimpsest bodies enunciate linguistic texts that create a dense accumulation of involuted and interconnected traces of textural bodies. These are bodies that are speaking about bodies and giving voice to bodies. Five voices layer, juxtapose and interweave fragments of texts (written and oral) spanning 500 years, to generate productive tensions through temporal and aesthetic juxtapositions. All these texts implicate bodies. Some explicitly describe human bodies, broken and killed by the Spaniards in the sixteenth century and by the government in the twentieth century.

Tenses and pronouns: Vocalization incorporates different forms of linguistic codes, including everyday conversational speaking, declamation, narration, poetic oration and political declaration. Texts cut between and merge eyewitness accounts, reporting and story telling. Fluid uses of linguistic tense and personal pronouns shift the perspective time and time again:

—speaking in present tense, first person "I" suddenly changes to past tense, third person "they"
—as they reconstruct the 1968 and 1520 massacres they speak in the present tense "I"
—they speak as "*I, Moctezuma*" and "*I, Cortés,*" then "*he, Moctezuma*" and "*he, Cortés,*" placing themselves inside and outside the frame and the moment, through techniques of a double-frame, present-tense narration.

The performers do not identify as contemporary individuals or "themselves." A question of who "they" are remains throughout, as the five actors perform fluid, open and unsettling palimpsest bodies.

Reiteration: Vocal textual reiteration creates a complex intertextural and intertextual linguistic strategy, using accumulation and transformation as a form of palimpsest textualization.[28] As rhetorical strategies, these frequently take the form of questions.

Layering and overlapping: Multiple forms of linguistic texts are spoken alternately by one performer, contrasted by all five performers speaking short fragments sequentially, overlapping, doubling up and in unison. These techniques open up historical accounts to processes of deconstruction and reconstruction, performing notions of truth and history in flux as they destabilize fixity.

Questions: As the performers speak to each other and to the audience directly, everybody is overtly included in re-membering and reflecting. With an increased sense of uncertainty, repeated questions punctuate otherwise seemingly fixed historical accounts—"*How did it happen?*"—"*Are we a cowardly peoples?*"—"*That's how it was, wasn't it?*" One persistent question is repeated throughout: "*Do you remember?*" It is an open question that hangs in the air, a question of postmemory, and a question of "now," as scenarios violation and domination are reactivated.

Lists: Another reiterative vocal strategy involves speaking lists, including names of Indigenous languages; contemporary movements for Indigenous rights; contemporary foods; and treasured commodities of pre-conquest Mexica.[29] The lists are spoken by all five performers as a rhythmic and unfolding vocalization. They are overtly fragmented, yet the vocalizing interweaves a texture of connectedness, simultaneously attesting to the contemporary multiplicity that is Mexico and marking presences of Indigenous languages and peoples in the now, while recognizing the traumatic concept of "loss."

Figure 53.

Performance examples

Scenario of breathing through time

D stands in a pool of light on a platform of bricks. On her head she wears the multi-coloured balloon headdress. She wears a contemporary skirt and shirt, mottled with dust-like whiteness. She holds a conch shell to her lips. She tilts her head backwards and visibly inhales as her ribcage moves outwards and upwards. She exhales, blowing hard into the shell, generating a resonant, vibrant sound. (Figure 41).

In this opening scene, D performs multiple trans-temporal traces connecting Nezahualcóyotl with Moctezuma II and with twenty-first-century environments. As remains of Nezahualcóyotl and Mesoamerica, she wears the headdress of fragile balloons marking the deity Huitzilopochtli, and performing four temporal traces.

As remains of Moctezuma, the conch shell is an evocative and haunting iconic sonic object: the embodied action of blowing into the shell connects with myriad bodies across many centuries performing the same movements (breathing across time); the sound is an ephemeral sonic trace across centuries (both body-movement and sound are forms of embodied archival repertoires); and the shell, as object formed in an ocean, remains. As D stands on the brick structure, she connects with grey contemporary building materials in symbolic architectural form. Wearing the dust-body costume, she appears to have been recently discovered, uncovered and pulled from under the surface, even as her clothes indicate twenty-first century city life.[30]

Scenario of a face-to-face encounter

D enters from one side of the stage wearing an elaborate 2D in-profile head and feathered headdress, with a long cloak and train on one side, superimposed over her skirt, but only partially covering it, creating an overt doubleness and layering. She performs as Moctezuma. C enters from the opposite side wearing a 2D in-profile helmet and painted full-length, metal body armour down one side of her body. She pulls behind her a small, toy antique wooden horse-tricycle, in a seemingly childlike gesture. Her skirt is clearly visible under the painted, overlaid armour, creating an obvious intertextual and intertextural juxtaposition and tension. She performs as Cortés.
The two performers stand on two separate low piles of grey bricks, in-profile facing each other.

C: "He spoke the following words..."
D: "Finally, they were face to face..."
C: "Can it be you? Is it you? Is it true that it is you, Moctezuma?"
D: "Yes. It is me..."

In an unfolding scene, two performers re-vision the face-to-face meeting of Emperor Moctezuma and conquester Hernán Cortés in 1519. This in-profile scenario of encounter reactivates an iconic visual image from painted codices with obvious visual doubleness throughout, and with multiple layers generated through speech and linguistic codes.

Moctezuma's texts are direct quotations from *The General History of the Things of New Spain*, an account written in the sixteenth century by Franciscan friar, Bernardino de Sahagún.[31] "History" is therefore spoken as an authoritative text, voiced through a trace of a head. The words of Moctezuma and Cortés are voiced in the first-person present tense, yet the in-profile mouths of "Moctezuma" and "Cortés" do not move. The narration is spoken through and with the same bodies, and therefore given a meta-theatrical and double-temporal framing. Through the layering of costumes and texts, the two live bodies of the performers are both part of, and separate from, the historical painted and cut-out humans, generating tension between the doing and the done, between the actions as contained in archival words and painted images, and the bodies of reactivation.

D and C step off their brick piles and walk towards each other. Slowly and with great gentleness C moves her hand to touch the face of "Moctezuma," as D moves her hand to touch the face of "Cortés."

Two women queer time and touch history, as they caress each other's cheeks, through traces of two bodies of history whose face-to-face encounter changed the face of history.

D speaks as she slowly detaches the head, feather headdress and cloak, disassembling "Moctezuma." D holds the in-profile head and body of "Moctezuma" so that it is fully present as a complete body.

By speaking and removing "Moctezuma," she poetically separates and disconnects the live body, the spoken words and the head of "Moctezuma." The juxtapositions of voice and body unfold questions of identity, materiality and body.

C turns to face the audience:

"So, Moctezuma led me through the street to a large and beautiful palace…He came back with many varied jewels of gold and silver…"

Facing the audience, the body of Cortés is barely visible as C voices Cortés in the first person.

C removes the in-profile head of Cortés and turns to face Moctezuma.

The two iconic men are face-to-face and present, but they no longer have a human body supporting them. Spoken words and bodies are connected and disconnected.

D stands with the cloak of Moctezuma draped on the ground. C places "Cortés" on the cloak of Moctezuma.
Two other performers remove their in-profile heads and place their heads onto the cloak. D folds the head of "Moctezuma" into the cloak, which now appears to be the dismembered no-body of Moctezuma.
D drags the cloak along floor, heavy with material wealth and removed heads. The tiny body of the toy horse remains as a trace of "Cortés." (Figures 54–56).

Experimenting with postmemory and rememory, this scenario of encounter is a dense, intertextual and intertextural unfolding of provocative poetic presences, performed with slowness and deliberation, through reconstruction and deconstruction. These performing palimpsest bodies offer experiences of contemplation and reflection, with no attempt to provide any answers. Poses and gestures are performed as remains of painted codices, and voiced words are remains of literary documents. By speaking "through" bodies of history, with these gestures, poses and movements, these performers generate obvious doubleness and haunting. These are complex, both/and bodies, offering and containing many viewpoints and perspectives. These dust-bodies of history hint at questions of archives and repertories: they are bodies as archives and archival bodies remaining differently. As they move, speak, pose and gesture they unfix matters of truth, historicity, power relations, betrayal, material worth and trust.

Foreshadowing: This "Scenario of encounter" forms a palimpsest scenario with the "Scenario of violation" in Part 3 *Malinche/Malinches*, incorporating Cortés and La Malinche. Here, Moctezuma and Cortés stand face to face. In Part 3, La Malinche is violated by Cortés. Layered together as a palimpsest performance they form the relationship of macro body (corpus – two civilizations) and micro body (cuerpo – two humans).

Figure 54.

Figure 55.

Figure 56.

Scenario of fragility (2)

N stands atop a small pyramid of bricks facing forward. She speaks calmly, officially, and authoritatively:

"It is I, your Lord Moctezuma who speak to you. I come to tell you not to fight, Mexicans—"
Suddenly, she contracts her abdomen, drops her head, contorts her body, draws her arms up in front of her body, and pushes her arms forward.
She straightens herself up, releases her tightened torso and continues to speak calmly and authoritatively, accepting the takeover. (Figure 57).

As N speaks words as Moctezuma, she is accepting Cortés and welcoming him. Her body suddenly twists into a contorted physicalization as she reiterates remains from Part 1: a trace of the schoolgirl who was raped and who killed her rapist; and a trace of Neza as state leader, contemplating human fragility through poetic voicing of the Song of War. With the accumulated traces from a scenario of rape and a scenario of human fragility, as she voices the words of Moctezuma, her body accrues remains of sixteenth-century submission, passivity and complicity. She connects fifteenth, sixteenth and twenty-first-century bodily traces of girl, man, powerful, weak, violator and violated. Her body evidences the internalized experience of anguish and deep trauma, intermingled with the pressure of imposed conformity, through rememory of collective and personal trauma.

Figure 57.

Scenario of massacre

At front centre stage the performers construct a single layer of bricks to create a platform. Standing side by side behind the square of bricks, the performers leap into the air in unison, gesturing upward. Together they take a step onto the brick stage, gazing out into the darkness of the auditorium, staring directly at the audience, as penetrating bright lights shine in their faces, illuminating expressions of fear and terror. Pressed together they form a tight cluster of bodies.

One after another they speak fragments of text:

"It was the day of the fiesta of our lord Huitzilopochtli. We were celebrating in the temple…The plaza was full of people…—There were snipers on the roofs.—Those who were going to kill us covered one hand with a white glove."

The performers point and look directly at the audience and speak short fragments of past-tense narration and present-tense action in quick succession, creating a dense cross-temporal intertwining.

"Do you remember?—
—Suddenly there was a gunshot in the distance. We didn't know where it came from.—'Get down!' someone shouted. 'They're going to kill us!'—They closed the eagle entrance in the smaller palace…and when it was closed, they all took their positions.—The plaza was a mousetrap.—I remember perfectly the blood running down the forehead of someone who was by my side.—I had blood in the sides of my shoes, in the hem of my dress.—'Everyone against the wall! Everyone on the ground, and whoever raises their head will go to hell!' they said to us."

Standing huddled, the bodies push, touch, crouch and lean sideways, falling…falling as one body, in slow motion, bodies contorted, awkward, one on top of the other, heads falling slowly down to the ground.

N removes a red kerchief from her pocket and stares at it as she speaks.

"In the plaza the following day there was rubbish, clothes, bloodstains covered with newspaper, blood that was still fresh mixed with water.—The people cried for their dead, our dead, and prepared them for incineration.—They said, 'They are just bodies.'—Do you remember?…—Today, the liars know the truth.—In an instant they were stabbed, with deep slashes…—"

As the lighting state changes, washing the stage with a subtle muted hue, the performers step off the brick plaza, moving to pick up more grey bricks that are strewn around the stage, and slowly placing them one on top of another as they begin constructing a pyramid. (Figure 58).

Reactivating remains of two massacres separated temporally by 448 years to perform them as one tangled event through five bodies, the performers generate one of the most compelling scenarios of postmemory.

Figure 58.

In 1520, thousands of Indigenous nobles were massacred by the Spanish invaders in México-Tenochtitlan, trapped inside an enclosed plaza during a fiesta; on 2 October 1968 students and citizens were massacred by state soldiers under the highest state orders, in Mexico City's Plaza of the Three Cultures, Tlatelolco, trapped by the surrounding structures. Locationally, the two events occurred within a mile of each other. In both instances those killed were unarmed and unsuspecting of the violence that was meted out to them. Both massacres happened in enclosed plazas, with no possibility of escape.[32]

Throughout this scene, the five performers speak phrases and questions from first-hand narrative accounts of both massacres: for the 1520 slaughter these are translations of Nahuatl-language accounts from the Indigenous perspective; for the 1968 massacre, these are testimonies of oral history, gathered and published by renowned author Elena Poniatowska. The distance of time is performed in the "now" through a present-tense voice—"Get down!"—as the five bodies cower and huddle. The anonymity of a crowd is personalized with only five bodies, each an individual, yet also moving as one. They are bodies in the process of being executed under official orders, trapped by the architectural limitations of an enclosed plaza, which is reconstructed in performance as an open stage with no visible limitations. Only the boundary of the single platform of bricks demarcates the spatial containment. The body-movements are non-mimetic choreographies, forming poetic contrasts to the directness of the bodily violence in the speaking voices. The performers speak words as the remains of survivors and witnesses, as they simultaneously perform dying and death. The witnessing public are incorporated into the unfolding events: the insistent repetition—"Do you remember?"—is a provocation to reflect. This scene of entrapment and massacre is a complex network of embodied multi-temporal residues in which five bodies perform a scenario of official control and violence, through doubleness, haunting and corporeal remains.

Scenario of truth/fiction

The performers build a small pyramid with the bricks. Four performers sit at the front of the stage close to the audience, speaking directly to and with them:

    — "There are various versions of the death of Moctezuma…"
    — "Perhaps what is certain is that four days after the massacre, we found the bodies of Moctezuma and Itzcuauhtzin thrown from the royal palaces…"
    — "Those who found them immediately took them in their arms…and put them on top of the bonfire. The fire crackled and the body of Moctezuma smelt of burnt flesh."
    — "…that's how it was, wasn't it?"

In almost total darkness, pierced by an intense blue light on the pyramid in the centre of the stage, one performer carries a heavy fire-burner, with a flickering and crackling flame, and carefully places it on top of the pyramid.
All five performers crouch around the base of the pyramid.
For two minutes everybody remains motionless, staring into the flame, as it sizzles, sputters, sparks and flickers.

Through this intensely still and sombre aesthetic of communal ritual and questioning, the performers facilitate an inclusive, embodied and sensory trans-temporal experience. The performers shift between speaking with historical distance and speaking as contemporary witnesses—witnesses of the death and dead body of Moctezuma. They speak directly to the audience, asking them to question historical accounts by describing different versions of the death of Moctezuma, moving between present and past tense, complicating issues of presence and truth. The words from sixteenth-century texts evoke deep sensory experiences through descriptions of the smell of burning flesh, combined with the visceral experience of the crackling and flickering blue flame,

    The provocation—"*That's how it was, wasn't it?*"—is an invitation to the public to collectively share in probing official accounts and narratives. In a real-time collective mediation and shared communion on death, the performers and audience sit in stillness, memorialization and contemplation. The absence of the body of the aggressor "Cortés" is palpable.

Scenario of power plays

The intense stillness of the meditation on death around the pyramid erupts in an explosion of noise and movement, as the performers chatter away noisily and bring bits of furniture and objects into the space: a bright pink plastic tablecloth, picnic cups, empty food bags, a map, binoculars, a metal trunk, an ornate antique wooden chair, the toy antique tricycle-horse, the conch shell, a white alabaster bust of a bearded man and a book titled "Before Cortés" (in English). As they sit on the pyramid, moving bricks to make themselves comfortable, the performers talk in colloquial dialogue and banter of twenty-first-century Mexico City.

Through the spatial, movement and vocal contrast, the shift from the scenario of the weight and consequences of Moctezuma's death and actions of Cortés, to the "now" of everyday lives creates a haunting juxtaposition. As the five performers break into a frenetic and playful scenario of contamination and transformation, they are living consequences through different forms of remains: a conch shell and the tiny horse; a large antique wooden chair and a metal trunk (which are re-used in Part 3); numerous objects of twenty-first-century

Figure 59.

living—a plastic tablecloth, cups, bottles and candy wrappers; and subtle vocal expressions and body positions which reference complex lives.

N takes a helmet out of the metal trunk. She puts it on her head as if playing dressing up. She sits casually in the large, opulent wooden chair, with one foot on the plush seat. She holds the lid of a metal trashcan as if it were a shield, excitedly shouting—"Look! Who am I? Who am I?" *Speaking with a caricatured and exaggerated accent from Spain, with her leg hooked over the arm of the chair, she declaims—*"I am Hernán Cortés, comfortably installed in my new kingdom." (Figure 59).

N plays at being Cortés. In contrast to the previous first-person accounts of "I, Cortés," and the overt layered painted codex-body, now "being Cortés" has become a game, as history is enacted through child's play of dressing up and pretending to be Cortés. The question *"Who am I?"* is playful and childlike, and a real provocation about the man Cortés. At this moment, N's body contains traces of Moctezuma standing on the pyramid, contracting her body with internalized anguish, acceding to the demands of the aggressor.

As she puts on the helmet, she performs remains of the conquest of Moctezuma and initiates a performance trace that re-appears throughout Part 3, *Malinche/Malinche*. Her playfulness acts as a foreshadowing palimpsest body when her body will become "the woman known as La Malinche," about whom little is "known," and who will be raped front and centre stage by Cortés.

Scenario of broken bones and song of sorrow

The performers sit on the pyramid and speak poetic words:
   —"But they defeated us…
  Do you remember?
  They killed us with hunger, thirst, illness and dirty war. […] And all this happened to us.
  We saw it, we wondered at it. With this terrible and sad fate, we were anguished.
  Broken bones lie upon the roads, hair is scattered everywhere …
  The walls are with spattered with brains.
  The waters are red, as if stained with dye,
  and when we drink from them it is as if we were drinking salt water…"—

In this final scene, a sense of tragedy returns after the noisy and contemporary scenarios of playing at being Cortés. The performers articulate a Nahuatl poem describing the bodily destruction of the conquest of Mexico-Tenochtitlán as experienced in 1521.[33] Asking "Do you remember? and speaking as "us" creates a trans-temporal form of inclusivity. As the performers speak through overlapping and repeating words and phrases, they create an intertextural and intertextual weaving. Bodies, archived as words, are re-membered as sonic utterances through breath and vibrations, moving again through time and space.

Part 3: *Malinche/Malinches*

Trans-temporal crossings

La Malinche exists in twenty-first-century Mexico as a pervasive presence. Unlike Nezahualcóyotl and Moctezuma, she is not known for her body-form and she does not have (m)any streets, concert halls, a metro station or a city named after her. Yet, she is ever-present through her name—malinchista and malinchismo. Both are pejorative labels characterizing women as the source of betrayal and nefarious behaviour. La Malinche's individual body is a collective corporeal icon of great complexity and contradiction: the embodiment of treachery, the original perpetrator of contamination through miscegenation, and the traitor who bore a child with the foreign invader. She embodies the classic mythic archetypal trilogy of mother/whore/virgin: symbolic mother of the Mexican people; whore of foreign invader Hernan Cortés; and virgin as quintessential victim (a young girl sold into slavery and abused in every way by those who exploited and dominated her). La

Figure 60.

Malinche was hired by Cortés as his translator, his interpreter, his tongue—*la lengua*. Her body forms the ultimate liminal and in-between body: a corporeal intermediary moving between two powerful leaders, transferring power through speech; and the genealogical body of reproduction, carrying and transmitting new life merging two world powers.

La Malinche's body is a supreme body of postmemory—of violation, rape, procreation and profound loss—; and of rememory—for her corporeal experiences of violation and sexual penetration. Although all the projects of La Máquina engage feminist cultural positioning and strategies, Part 3 explores scenarios of gender, sexuality, power relations, womanhood, motherhood, truth, writing History and embodied subjectivities more overtly through the body of history of La Malinche.

La Malinche juxtaposes the two powerful and governing men of Parts 1 and 2. In contrast to Parts 1 and 2, the trans-temporal crossings in Part 3 are more entangled. They incorporate multiple named people (mostly women) in the twenty-first century and deities of the Mesoamerican cosmogony. As an accumulation of remains from Parts 1 and 2, Part 3 incorporates all the previous crossings, which reappear and are re-formed as fragments of scenarios in the form of vocal texts, poses, objects, costumes, vocalizations and movements.

Remains

To generate La Malinche the ensemble again worked with *The True History of the Conquest of New Spain* and scrutinized visual depictions of La Malinche in codices.[34] But virtually nothing is known about the life and death of the woman known as La Malinche. As Faesler explained: "How can you begin to have a conversation? [...] There's a lot you can say about the conquest. But La Malinche—we don't know anything about her. So we could fill the house with books about La Malinche and it's all fiction—we would read and read and then we'd say: 'Well, it could be.' [...] But how can you dare say that it *was* like that? There are three hard facts we know about her. We know that as a nine-year old girl she was sold in a market, she was abused and raped until she was captured by the Spaniards. We know that she must have been able to speak at least six languages to be able to undertake business in the different cities, but that's all we know. But there are fundamental questions: Where are her bones? Where did she die? When did she die? Where was she born? When was she born?"[35]

From this "absence" Faesler and Malheiros generated the body of history of La Malinche from multiple and specific lives. They made a decision "to construct history from real histories. It's all supposition. So she might have been divorced; had children; owned a truck. [...] We sent a general email to our friends saying, 'We are doing *La Malinche*. Send us your stories.' When we began receiving the stories [...] we started to discover that there was a sort of structure, which helped us find a way through the life of La Malinche."

These short stories of personal life experiences—stories of rememory—became the core of the performance. These I-stories are roughly chronological—there is a life-journey path, from birth, young life, rape, violation, to old age. As Malheiros describes: "It is the story of La Malinche: La Malinche as a little girl, La Malinche who gets sold at the market, La Malinche who later arrives with Cortés, La Malinche who is given to Jaramillo, and La Malinche who dies and nobody knows where her bones are....It's like a small spine or skeleton. The first texts are more or less all childhood stories: *'I was born face down...'; 'I dreamt my father...';* *'My father died when...'* After that it moves to the harsher stories: *'he raped me.'* There's something more hurtful there—abuse. Then it goes on to relationships, and then it goes on to that sort of cross-over through the encounter of worlds."

Throughout Part 3, these I-stories are spoken using a similar format: the telling starts with a first-person "I," and concludes with the speaking of a name: "*—Ermita,*" "*—Clarissa's mum,*" "*—La Malinche.*" Each I-story is performed as a rememory of personal experiences, spoken out into the space and shared with everybody present. These form the dramaturgical and vocalized thread that weaves through the whole performance, generating a complex intertextual and intertextural fabric of memories and subjectivities. A sixteenth-century body merges with twenty-first-century bodies, as an individual life of the woman known as La Malinche is given subjectivities, and as multiple individual experiences of many women are translated into her subjectivity.

Not speaking as hyper-communication

La Malinche is often characterized as *la lengua*—language and tongue. The intersection of her tongue as language and language as her tongue represents a form of betrayal, which is extended to all women. She stands accused of speaking translated words that caused the destruction of a civilization.[36] In this performance, the tension of speaking as betrayal is performed through a non-speaking body. Embodying the potency of La Malinche's body-part of the tongue Faesler does not speak. She is dressed identically to the other four performers, and participates fully in all the scenarios, but her embodied presence moves in stark contrast to the other four performers who all speak as "I, Malinche." There is a sense of always waiting for her to speak—yet she does not. She is an un-speaking La Malinche, a body of tremendous potency, combative and resistant.[37] Hers is a performance through silence and hyper-communication: a subversive, hyper-present presence—not an absence—a witness, and a corporeal challenge to and re-vision of official narratives damning La Malinche's gendered, speaking and reproductive body (Figures 25 and 70).

A plethora of vocalizations and I-stories

The core of speaking throughout Part 3 is formed with multiple I-stories. Other forms of vocal strategies are also incorporated including, colloquial bartering familiar from local markets; recitation of genealogical trajectories; a children's game of grandmother's footsteps, playing with the word "chingar"; quotations from renowned authors Margo Glantz, Gloria Anzaldúa, Octavio Paz and Juan Miralles; and meta-dialogues from the devising workshops, incorporating questions about history.

Inserting violence into familiar and familial movements

Throughout Part 3, there is a predominance of everyday and familiar movements: sitting at the kitchen table, embroidering, fighting with cushions and playing a game of grandmother's footsteps. But the everyday is constantly interrupted by moments of still-image poses and gestures of codex reconstructions. One scene incorporates a brief hyper-real physicalization of rape, as Cortés and La Malinche fight and struggle, and as Cortés overpowers La Malinche. In the final scene, as the deities return from Part 1, they wander through maize plants holding gestural poses.

Shop-bought conformity and masculinity

La Malinche is performed as trans-temporal plurality, queered and multiplied through obvious twenty-first-century clothing. All five performers are dressed identically in men's shop-bought, formal, grey business suits comprising jacket, trousers, waistcoat, white shirt, necktie and black shoes. The alikeness and multiplication of the ubiquitous masculine clothing suggest generic, compound and bought-in-a-store identities. They are figures of

Figure 61.

urban city life, conforming and fitting in. These suits form a conspicuous palimpsest with another iconic Mexican woman known for constructing her own sense of womanhood in relation to betrayal and reproduction: Frida Kahlo.[38]

These grey business suits are forms of archival body-containers with expectations of gendered and social performativity. Throughout the performance, these expectations are challenged and subverted by playing with components of the suit. The performers wear and use the jacket to create playful and powerful re-visions: it is worn back-to-front to form a straightjacket; it is tied around the waist to create an apron; it is wrapped around the head to form a towel; and it is carried in arms to form a baby's body (Figures 61, 66 and 67).

Partway through Part 3, C appears wearing the apron from Part 1, as a trace of the woman with Alzheimer's. She then she returns with her long knitted tunic, inserting obvious remains of Nezahualcóyotl, of pre-Hispanic civilizations and life-ways, with traces of scenarios of origins and forgetting (Figure 62).

In the final scene, three other performers appear wearing their painted-knitted covering from Part 1, symbolically returning to questions of origins and futures as they inhabit an environment filled with maize plants (Figure 70).

A chaotic and ordered living environment

At the opening of *Malinche/Malinches* the stage is strewn with objects and furniture, giving the impression of a chaotic yet lived-in contemporary apartment. Towards the back, high and intricate geometric latticework screens allow light to shine through, providing an entrance into this familial living space, and simultaneously casting deep shadows.[39] Objects from Part 2 are evident: the large wooden antique chair, the pink plastic table cloth covered in plastic cups, the metal travel trunk, a pile of grey bricks, a white alabaster bust of bearded man and a helmet. Other objects and pieces of furniture are new: a table, chairs, metal stools, cushions, a rocking chair, an upended sofa, cups, cooking equipment, an ironing board. These pieces of furniture and objects are moved around over the course of 50 minutes, as the performers gradually transform and alter the living space.

Suddenly, and without warning, the performers frantically remove furniture and articles from the space. A few objects remain: the antique chair, the white head, the trunk, bricks and the helmet. In this plaza-like space they play a game of grandmother's footsteps, tracing and re-tracing their steps as they play with and through the concept of "la chingada"— "fucking or being fucked."[40]

In the final scenario, the performers gradually fill the empty space with life-size maize plants. Evocatively trans-temporal, these plants cross traces of human origins with contemporary daily food with transnational biotechnologies of genetically modified maize (Figures 42, 63 and 70).

Figure 62.

Threads of I-stories connecting involuted scenes

Part 3 is structured through a series of scenes that start and end unexpectedly, creating abrupt shifts in material. All these juxtapositions are woven together with an almost continuous thread of vocalized I-stories.

All five performers perform La Malinche simultaneously and shift in and out of other identities. In contrast to the constant exchanges for performing Nezahualcóyotl and Moctezuma in Parts 1 and 2, now two specific performers enact extended scenes as "La Malinche" and "Cortés." For my descriptive analysis below I particularly focus on this pairing. R mostly performs as Cortés and N as La Malinche. However, for one scenario this is reversed to generate a complexity of contradictions and accumulations of traces.

Performance examples

Scenarios of gendered domesticity

The five performers sit scattered around the stage at different levels and positions, in different types of chairs. Each performer is intensely focused on embroidering.
One performer stops embroidering, looks up and speaks out into the space, as if recalling a memory:

"On a summer morning I was given life…—Adriana."

As they listen the other performers continue embroidering. After speaking the name of the I-story, the performer resumes embroidering.
Another performer stops embroidering, looks up and speaks an I-story… Then continues embroidering. (Figures 63, 65 and 116).

This opening scene generates a dramaturgical fabric by interweaving multiple fragments of I-stories. One after another four business-suited bodies stop embroidering to recall and share experiences. They speak as if they are reminiscing for themselves and simultaneously talking to everyone around them. Each person exists in their own space of personal intimacy, undertaking an action of domesticity. With a sense of quiet and reflective sharing, they create a rhythm of their everyday lives, incorporating performers and audience alike.[41] As they sew and listen, their palimpsest bodies are home to many stories, revealing secrets and subjectivities. Through their voiced threads of rememory they generate an intertextural and intertextual vocal palimpsest. Here, La Malinche exists through the trans-temporal traces of I-stories. Stereotypical expectations of "office," "man" and "work" coexist with "home," "woman" and "pastime" performing a provocative juxtaposition.

Figure 63.

Scenario of breathing through time (3)

The performers sit, embroider, verbalize I-stories and listen.
Together, they stop embroidering. Each person reaches down into a bag by the side of their chair and takes out a conch shell.
Together, they tilt their heads back, place the conch to their lips, inhale, exhale and blow together, generating a breathy, multi-tonal but resonant timbre. (Figures 23 and 64).

Through this brief and seemingly simple action, the five business-suited bodies hold and blow into conch shells to perform complex trans-temporal traces. They generate connections through breath, physical movement, sound and an iconic object. There is an accumulation of traces connecting present lives with La Malinche, Moctezuma, Nezahualcóyotl and Mesoamerican deities.[42]

Figure 64.

Figure 65.

Scenario of transgressive and tongue tied

R sits in the opulent antique chair and embroiders. He stops embroidering and speaks an I-story, concluding with "—La Malinche."
He opens his mouth, sticks out his tongue and lifts his tie to his tongue to form an extension of his tongue. (Figure 65).

R speaks as "I, Malinche" as he sits in the chair used by N playing at "being Cortés" at the end of *Moctezuma*. R plays with concepts of the tie and tongue, transforming his tie in a beguilingly simple action. The tongue represents La Malinche's skilful power and everlasting scourge as translator. A tie is a tiny strip of fabric, yet it is a ubiquitous sign of masculine formality and conformity and a mark of masculine power, "civilization" and "correctness."

Scenario of fragility (3)

N is pushed and pulled around the stage, being bartered and sold for low-value objects (a vase, eggs, cushions), through familiar and colloquial market-speak. She wears the brown leather schoolbag.
She suddenly contracts her abdomen, pushes her arms forward and lets out a piercing roaring sound as she enunciates her name. (Figures 10 and 72).

N embodies the young girl La Malinche in the process of being sold. The schoolbag from *Nezahualcóyotl* repeats a trace of the twenty-first-century schoolgirl. With this familiarity of a market scene, N reiterates a hyperphysical movement and vocalization from Part 1 and Part 2. In this accumulation, her palimpsest body contains traces of the twenty-first-century schoolgirl (who was raped and who killed her rapist); fifteenth-century Emperor Nezahualcóyotl (poetically contemplating human fragility); sixteenth-century Moctezuma (as submission, passivity and complicity); and now La Malinche and other trans-temporal humans who are de-valued, spoken for and violated.

Scenario of materiality of memory and time (3)

C enters wearing her knitted over-painted tunic, superimposed with her grey business-suit waistcoat, which she wears back to front.
She is carrying the bright pink plastic tablecloth, which she unfolds, shakes out and places on the table.
She pulls the cloth off the table, folds it up, shakes it out, places it on the table, pulls it off the table, folds it, shakes it out, places it on the table...
As she folds and unfolds, she speaks I-stories and names:
   "Your children: Catlina Pizarro, Luis de Arellano, Leonor Cortés Moctezuma...My children: Martín Cortés, María Jaramillo. I didn't know them. They took them from me." (Figures 13, 66 and 115).

C performs a simple, private and familiar ritual of everyday gendered domesticity as she places a cloth on the table, seemingly in readiness for eating. But she disrupts her completed

Figure 66.

action by starting again, slowly removing the cloth and folding it. She repeats her actions of placing and removing over and over again, as if suspended in time, but deeply embedded in the moment of repetition.

She wears the knitted tunic as remains of Part 1, performing traces of a twenty-first-century woman with Alzheimer's, unsure of where her home is; an elder god of time, holder of the origins of time and life; and a fifteenth-century poet-ruler; now coexisting with the woman known as La Malinche and contemporary lives.

Each time she removes and re-places the tablecloth an absence of memory is physicalized and de-constructed, unfolding questions about the fallibility of memory. The unknown-ness of La Malinche's life as History merges with an emptiness of identity as memory (what is a body without memory? what is memory without a body?). As she articulates I-stories, she generates a fabric of inter-connected subjectivities, constructing La Malinches' life through multiple lives. C speaks as La Malinche, naming the children of Cortés as "your children," and the children of La Malinche as "my children," naming children that she did not know as she voices the violence of removal. As La Malinche/woman, C's body is marked by material traces of texts that damn her as subservient—the inverted masculine business-suit waistcoat over her chest and heart (the Mexica organ of memory), performing a re-vision and resistance to containment and stereotypes. As a trans-temporal body, C performs multiple intertextural traces, resisting fixity through her actions of folding and unfolding.[43]

Scenarios of violation: One, two, three

A pairing of N and R embodying La Malinche and Cortés is reiterated three times, presenting three explorations as palimpsests encompassing intertextual layering and accumulations.

Scenario of violation (1)
Four performers stand in line side-by-side facing front. They maintain static body-poses replicating 2D painted images from a sixteenth-century codex of Tlaxcala, depicting scenarios of La Malinche and Cortés.
R wears the helmet as "Cortés" and poses with his hand raised in the gesture of Christian piety (two fingers together raised, two closed held over the palm with the thumb).
With their bodies inert, holding this archival sixteenth-century pose, the performers begin moving their tongues and mouths as they speak out into the space, uttering racial and gendered insults about bodies, invoking body parts and skin colour.
The scene suddenly explodes into full physical violence—N turns and hits R. She hits him again and again, grabbing a broom and hitting him again and again. They grapple together, moving fast around the living space. R grabs a stool and holds it to his face to defend himself. N grabs R's hair. With explosive and ferocious sustained energy, R grabs N's whole body, dragging her centre stage facing the audience, and throwing her forcefully on the floor face down. He pins her down with his body, pulls down his trousers and underwear and forces himself on her, revealing his penis and simulating penetration. (Figure 67).

Through this unfolding scene, the fast-moving grey-suited bodies of N and R physicalize an almost-real violation as La Malinche and Cortés, voicing violence and trauma. This scene forms a palimpsest with the "Scenario of a face-to-face encounter" in Part 2. In *Moctezuma*, the live bodies are superimposed with painted forms and fabric. Words of violence are spoken through the outline head-faces of 2D codex images. Now, in Part 3, the live bodies of the codex image begin as unmoving still images. But the tongues articulate words: words of racialized and corporeal insults, words transmitted across the centuries and words prevalent in the twenty-first century; words of collective violence against women and private violence between two people in intimate relationships; words connecting violences of sixteenth-century acts of conquest and violation with contemporary violence against Indigenous peoples meted out by governments and individuals. From the archive of the codex, the rape begins: the violence contained in the painted bodies emerges, as moving tongues and mouths re-form words of insult: the violence of insults increases in dynamics and ferocity, eventually exploding into ferocious physical violence. Everyday household objects are used as weapons of attack and defence.

As material already worked on, the scenario incorporates traces of a real and metaphorical meeting of two worlds, embodying the collective rape of one peoples by another, and of one human by another. Connecting intimate family relations with military, religious and institutional power and control, the two bodies of R and N reactivate multiple remains. They physicalize struggles for power, domination and control as R overpowers N, forcing her to submit to his aggressions.

R stands front centre stage: his upper body is covered in his formal white shirt, tie and waistcoat; his lower body is naked, exposing a limp penis and bare legs, with his trousers and underpants around his ankles. His hand is raised in the Catholic gesture of piety. He wears the helmet, and speaks as Cortés under his breath:

—"I stood before him; Moctezuma. I looked in his eyes—he looked at me for a while in silence. I looked into the eyes of the one whom no-one could look into the eyes of.…I whispered to him not to struggle, not to fight. I convinced him. So he didn't struggle. He kept himself in his palace. He was already dead."

He takes the helmet off his head and places it over his limp penis. (Figures 67 and 71).

After the extreme movement of the physical rape, the stillness and static pose generates a formidable tension. The words of "Cortés," spoken by R who has just raped N, form a provocative palimpsest with the words of "Moctezuma," spoken by N in Part 2 as she stood atop the pyramid (externalizing her anguish of rape, passivity and complicity). R's words to the violated ruler invoke multiple forms of violences. R's body is duplicitous: the potent body-part of conquest, violation, reproduction and masculinity is exposed and then concealed. R stands in a palimpsest pose: the helmet—an archival-repertorial object of immense power and masculine military might—overlays his penis.

The unspeaking body of J watches, partially visible, yet partially obscured. She acts as a silent, hyper-present witness to the violence. The spectators witness her witnessing the actions.[44]

Figure 67.

Scenario of violation (2)

N and R enter, chatting in a friendly and colloquial way. Each holds a conch shell in one hand. N now wears the helmet on her head. She sits on the tiny child's tricycle-horse.

N speaks as Cortés—" I went down in history as the 'Inventor of Mexico' and you, well, the 'chingada' 'the fucked one.'"

R speaks as La Malinche—"…it could be, but the truth is you were a son of a bitch."[45]

Together they inhale, tilt their heads backwards, lift the conch shell to their lips and blow in unison.

N pedals the tiny tricycle-horse across the stage with her knees to her chest, riding awkwardly. She settles in one spot and goes round and round in tiny circles, holding the conch shell high with her upstretched arm.

R squats on the lid of the metal trunk, clutching the conch shell and speaking directly out to the audience. As he speaks he grasps at his chest, as if trying to tear open his body, as he holds out his tie:

> —"'The Chingada is passive. Her passivity is abject; she does not resist violence, but is an inert heap of bones, blood and dust. Her stain is constitution and resides, as has been said, higher in her sex. This passivity, open to the outside world, causes her to lose her identity; to lose her name; she is no one; she disappears into nothingness; she is Nothingness. And yet she is the cruel incarnation of the feminine condition.' That's what Octavio Paz said.
> —La Malinche." (Figures 2, 18, 68 and 71).

In this second scenario of violation N and R perform an entanglement of trans-temporal traces through scholarly texts, iconic objects, meta-moments from the devising workshops and reiterations from Part 2.

N's helmet-wearing body creates two obvious palimpsests: 1) she joins with a childlike moment at the end of Part 2, as she placed the helmet on her head, sat cockily in the large chair and uttered the words "I, Cortés" as she played at "being Cortés"; 2) she joins with the previous Scenario of violation in which her own body was violated by the helmet-wearing body of R, performing "Cortés," in which the helmet was finally used to obscure the "tool of violation" (R's penis).

Through their utterances, N and R create two complex re-visions:

1. In the first voiced pairing, N articulates "Cortés," combining two intertexts as one sentence. Both are scholarly fragments of words written by renowned authors whose concepts have shaped perceptions of La Malinche and Cortés.[46] R voices "La Malinche" and responds to the two authors. He also reconstructs a reiterated episode from the creative processes of *Malinche/Malinches*: each time the artists asked for the "historical truth" from historian Dr Berenice Alcántara she simply responded: "It could be."

2. In the second voicing, R again voices La Malinche, who now speaks Paz's essentializing and damning words. Paz presented La Malinche as a violated woman, part victim, part traitor

Figure 68.

to her nation, using the concept of La Chingada ("the fucked one"). R's body joins with his previous iteration performing the violent violation of La Malinche's body (N). N, as Cortés, is now sitting awkwardly on the tiny child's toy, riding round and round in little circles.

The conch shell is present as reiterated remains of Mesoamerican indigeneity. The helmet and the tricycle-horse are reiterated remains of aggression, violation and suppression. As N and R breathe together through the conch shells they express deeply embodied trans-temporal waves of connection. As they combine and re-frame well-known words through their clawing and cycling reiterating bodies, they unfix and transform familiar racialized and gendered histories and narratives.

Scenario of violation (3)

R enters holding an action-man doll and thrusts it into N's hand with the order "Bathe me."
R removes his shirt and climbs into the open metal trunk (on top of which he had squatted as
"La Malinche" reciting Paz's damnation of women). C, wearing her knitted tunic and apron,
wets, shampoos and towels R's hair.
Simultaneously, N kneels on the floor in front of a small metal tub of water and begins to play
with the doll: she undresses the doll, taking off his trousers and shirt, and bathing him in a
small bowl of water. As she bathes him she speaks to him.

   —"I bathe you with herbal water, spring water. I bathe you, I scrub your back…You became Captain La Malinche. You were my voice, my presence. You were me and you didn't even realize. I conquered this land. I conquered this land…"

As she speaks, her anger builds. She bends the tiny body backwards, distorting it almost out of his recognizable body-form; she slaps him with the back of her hand, she squeezes, twists and wrings his body. (Figure 69).

For this third scenario of violation, N and R return to their previous roles performing La Malinche and Cortés. Cortés' body is duplicated as a tiny, plastic action-man type doll. The scene is one of dense hyper-gendered daily domesticity.

   As N plays with her doll, she connects with traces of "playing at being Cortés" (Part 2) and the raped girl who killed her violator (Part 1). She speaks as the woman La Malinche, voicing thoughts that might be formed by countless wronged people. From the innocence of the childhood game (a rememory), N transforms her playing experiences into physicalized anger as she speaks of unacknowledged capabilities, disrespect and affront. As N was forced to the ground by the powerful body of R as Cortés, so now she controls the oppressive body of the conquester, through a transformed action-man body-object.[47] Containing an accumulation of traces, her body is simultaneously mother, child, violator and violated. The live body of R as Cortés forms a visible doubleness. As C attends to Cortés, washing and drying his hair, her body also performs an accumulation

Figure 69.

of traces of domesticity (the woman with Alzheimer's) and wisdom and support (the elder deity of time carrying the body of N on her chest across the space at the end of Part 1).

Scenario of knowledge as questions

In an unlit stage, the performers vocalize terse questions in the darkness, like ephemera moving through time and space:

— "Did you ever think of killing him?" — "Did it hurt to see your people die?" — "Did you ever shoot anyone?" — "What is the Holy Spirit?" — "What is on the other side of the sea?" — "Did it hurt when they took your children away?" — "What is the meaning of soul?" — "What are they looking for?" — "Are we prisoners of our own words?" — "Why did they like gold so much?" — "Were you ambitious?" — "Which side were you on?" — "Is there maize in your land?" — "Why did they come?" — "Why did they only have one god?" — "Where do your bones rest, Malinche?" —

The performers slowly and carefully carry large maize plants onto the stage. They make repeated journeys in and out of the space. Four performers are now wearing their knitted-painted costumes from Part 1, Nezahualcóyotl.
C carries her headpiece of the elder god of gods and her face is covered with lines of age. She treads very slowly through the maize to the front of the stage, speaking the names of the genealogical descendants of Cortés. (Figure 70).

This final evolving and transforming scene presents an environment of in-betweenness and liminality, not as a threshold for moving across, but as an inhabited palimpsest of plurality. Knowledge of La Malinche's death and La Malinche's dead body are formed through questions, spoken as tiny shards in the "now" of the live performance. La Malinche's corporeal remains are assembled and scattered through vocal traces, connecting with the myriad I-stories of contemporary women, created through five palimpsest bodies containing trans-temporal accumulated remains of multiple subjectivities. In the dimness and shadows, bodies pass almost silently through and around the maize, posing questions about knowledge, history, truth and experiences.

The gradual filling of the stage with maize plants offers trans-temporal connections to origins, presence, regeneration and futurity: maize is symbolic of the origin-myth, the staple everyday food for life, and now tied to the politics of genetic modification. These plants inhabit the stage like human bodies that are also growing, propagating, giving life and dying. As the performers return to embody their bodies of *Nezahualcóyotl*, this final accumulation generates further tensions, performing an environment of coexistence with time immemorial, with wisdom of ancestral knowledge and with individual humans in the maelstrom of contemporary living. Only F's body remains clothed in remains of the masculine business suit. At the back of the space, two piles of grey bricks and one tie remain, as traces of human constructions and translations.

Figure 70.

Reflections on remains: Performing palimpsest bodies

1 plus 2 plus 3 equals a plurality of potentials

Through an unfolding of poetic presences and an accumulation of traces, this trilogy of contrasting yet interconnected works is an intensely powerful and visceral piece of theatre. Familiar scenarios of "history" and "home" are reactivated and re-imagined. Matters of knowledge, history, memory and truth are posed and re-posed through embodied questions. Subjectivities and identities are always multiple and plural, assembled and disassembled, constructed and deconstructed, with accretions and layers.

As palimpsests are experienced through concurrences of trans-temporal traces, so *Mexican Trilogy* works through the performative flow of the theatre event. The five bodies are contiguously and simultaneously fifteenth-, sixteenth-, twentieth- and twenty-first-century humans and atemporal immortals, all interfacing and coexisting in one space and place—the Valley of Mexico. Through an understanding of Mexico City as a palimpsest of histories and temporalities these bodies inhabit and envision their collective and individual memories through their sensorial, archival, repertorial and ephemeral bodies.

Part 1: Five differently-painted bodies and faces, covered with knitted-painted clothes, seem otherworldly, ethereal and familiar. In fleeting moments, they strike sculptural poses, recite florid poems, narrate myths of time and plead with the president of "now." Through the shadows and dimness, Nezahualcóyotl's poems of philosophical leadership offer models for twenty-first century lives. A woman forgets where home and is guided by Indigenous deities. As these bodies run in and out of the intense, bounded red space, where precise criss-crossing pathways of light provide transitory glimpses, they connect public and private, outside and in. The minimal objects and the sharp lines and geometric shapes produce an environment of presence as texture, full of energy and potential.[48] For a brief moment, five bodies come together to form one body of trans-diversity.

+ Part 2: Five dust-covered, archival, labouring bodies—bodies of "now"—move bricks again and again. They work in an environment of ruins and future structures in the public space of the bright and starkly open stage. They seem unsure of themselves as they construct, deconstruct, reconstruct, assemble, disassemble and reassemble, attempting to make sense of brutal actions and accounts of history connecting events of five decades ago and five hundred years ago—and now. They speak lists of names of present-day Indigenous languages, inserting them into "history" as resistance to official amnesia. They reconstruct painted images of bodies contained in codices, layering painted remains onto slowly moving bodies, speaking as "I, see" and "they, saw," performing states of in-betweenness, plurality and liminality.

A head peers through a trace of a head, performing presence and absence as coexistent and transforming. Two women superimposed with archival body-forms of military might and power stand face-to-face on tiny brick structures. They stretch out a hand, queering and re-membering through trans-temporality, reactivating the scenario

Figure 71.

of encounter worked on so many times before. Standing together on a single layer of bricks, enclosed inside an inescapable plaza, five bodies articulate words of witnesses and murdered at the massacres in 1520 and 1968. They fall together in the process of being killed, performing brutality and fragility. With a helmet, a toy horse-tricycle, a conch shell, an antique chair and a plastic tablecloth, they ask questions, again and again, attempting to excavate remains of cultural fictions and historical realities. Sombre, open, slow, unsettling, ambiguous and raw, they invite real-time meditation on tragic scenarios of control and transformation.

+ Part 3: Five ubiquitous and conforming business-suited bodies sit and embroider in a (dis-)ordered environment of everyday interiority and familial privacy. They sew threads of everyday lives, interweaving an unfolding fabric of subjectivities, in a palimpsest vocalization of I-stories, performing the absence of "knowledge" and "historical accounts" as lives and experiences. Re-visioning the gendered traitor-tongue of La Malinche, one body speaks truth to power, embroidering but not speaking in an act of unspeakable hyper-communication. They all embody La Malinche, playfully and seriously queering, multiplying and re-fabricating her life in the domestic environment of "home." Five business-suited bodies raise conch shells to their lips. As they inhale and expand rib cages; as they exhale and breathe into the shells; as they generate reverberating waves of sound, they reiterate trans-temporal traces of corporeal movements, breath, vibrations and objects crossing multiple generations.

The space is permeated with recognizably contemporary furniture and objects, mixed with remains of Moctezuma: a helmet, a toy horse-tricycle, a conch shell, an antique chair and a plastic tablecloth. In this private, frenzied, familiar and unsettling atmosphere, five bodies reactivate scenarios of conquest and violation, and of rape and control. With words, gestures and movements they reiterate remains of *The True History*, of codices, of scholarly accounts, of poses of piety and of the multivalent word "chingar" ("to fuck"). A woman returns with her painted-knitted tunic of time and memory, overlaid with an inverted masculine business waistcoat. She stands at the table, unfolding-folding-unfolding the tablecloth, as she speaks I-stories and names the children of La Malinche and of Cortés, performing traces of loss, reproduction, betrayal, home and forgetting. Five bodies stand in a line re-forming an archival-repertorial sixteenth-century pose contained in a painted image. Two unmoving bodies move out of the pose expressing words of everyday violence of racial and gendered discrimination. In a rage of hyper-real actions, two bodies struggle viciously, culminating in a simulation of rape. Repeatedly, the five bodies insert the "now" of familial and governmental violence and complicity into experiences of the exploitation and rape of La Malinche. These bodies re-pose embodied questions of "encounter" and "difference." La Malinche speaks Paz's damning critique of her and twists the tiny inert body of the action-man Cortés. Her actions of rememory connect individual and collective traumas, containing trans-temporal traces of abused/abusing child, betrayed/betraying adult and violated/violating human.

Accumulations, repetitions and difference: "How do we share our lives with what remains?"

A trilogy offers the potential to return again and again, with each return offering difference and new perspectives.[49] Reactivating scenarios of material already worked through repeated remains presents the possibility of opening up diverse viewpoints. In *Mexican Trilogy*, three iconic bodies of history offer great potential for repeated returns. Scenarios are explored each time through the remains of a different body of history. Parts 2 and 3 reactivate scenarios of violation and conquest from oppositional spaces of public and private. Each contains obvious traces of the other without one being the "original." Together, they generate productive tensions to destabilize and re-contextualize recognizable encounters. They juxtapose the violation of individual and collective Indigenous lives in the sixteenth century with individual and collective lives in the twenty-first century. Cortés—the aggressor, conqueror, violator and father of two of La Malinche's children—is embodied in both parts, yet is core of neither (Figure 71). Through repeats and accumulations, the five bodies accrue more complications with the increase of remains and sedimentation. Each body seems less fixed, more defiant, more radical and multi-layered, producing an intensity of playfulness and depth. In Part 3, with one repeated gesture, N's body generates deep trans-temporal reverberations. As she contracts her abdomen and presses her arms forward, she re-imagines historical traumas of postmemory and reveals deeply embodied experiences of rememory. She performs complex and conflicted traumas of violence and complicity through trans-temporal traces (Figure 72).

Each body of history is re-imagined with distinctive strategies, forming the performativity of identities and subjectivities as complex and changing. Nezahualcóyotl is transferred from performer to performer through speaking words of poetic texts and named as "I." Moctezuma is assembled onto the body of a performer, as an outline head-face and cloak and voiced through official documented accounts. La Malinche's presence is always plural,

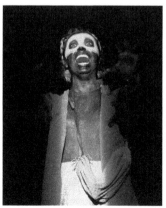

Figure 72.

through the grey business suits and the I-stories. Nezahualcóyotl's death is performed as a double body, with the little plastic body-object enfolded in a trans-temporal embrace. Moctezuma's death is performed as a description of the smell of burning flesh and real-time contemplation. La Malinche's death is performed as questions vocalized in the darkness of a dynamic trans-temporal environment.

The spectators are invited to share in the scenic explorations through the open and communal question: "How do we share our lives with what remains?" With specific performative strategies, the performers incorporate the public into an environment of convivio. When they ask "Do you remember?" the question is posed as a provocation to share in challenges about "truth," to resist official narratives and to unsettle memories. When they return again and again to familiar scenarios they invite their spectators to scrutinize each repetition from differing standpoints. When they face their audience with masks of death and sit in silence around the base of the pyramid, they ask them share in the communal reflection and contemplation. When the five performers reactivate the pose of "Happy Family," they invite the spectators to laugh at the absurdities of constructed norms (Figure 63).

At heart, *Mexican Trilogy* is a palimpsest holder (a corporeal archive) of trans-temporal embodied experiments. Through a passionate sense of playfulness, combined with a genuine convivial exploration of contemporary issues, these poetically-political and politically-poetic postmemory experiments encompass artistic forms of great potential. The sheer range and diversity of remains both saturates the performance aesthetic and creates an atmosphere of connection, as these performers re-imagine potential ways of being through performing palimpsest bodies. They perform trans-temporal bodies as sites and sights of possibilities; they construct "knowledge" and "history" as experiences; they embody a leader who is poetic and just; they challenge constraints of gendered knowledge and they disrupt stereotypes; they counter institutional forgetting of state violence; they offer models of justice, compassion and support; and they share the deep and playful wisdom of everyday lives.

Figure 73.

Chapter 4

Zapata, Death Without End

Five collectives, one year, co-participatory performance

For the duration of the yearlong project *Zapata, Death Without End*, five theatre collectives from various regions of Mexico collaborated to generate a dynamic and multifaceted exploration of shared histories of revolutions and resistance. The project engaged an inclusive structure for diverse yet combined collective creation processes. Over the course of the year, the many participants devised performative work through multi-ensemble workshops and group-specific devising sessions in their hometowns. By creating embodied experiments through remains of a body of history, the five groups explored experiences of postmemory and rememory in their localised environments. Bringing their own objectives and expertise to the practices, the five collectives generated a multiplicity of political and poetic performance responses with many trans-temporal crossings.

As a culmination of these extended inventive processes the five ensembles gathered in Mexico City in March 2015 for a final week of workshops. Together, they structured their devised material to generate public performances, embracing widely contrasting performance styles and aesthetics, yet utterly interconnected through a core body of history. Extending the inclusiveness to the spectators, the final performances incorporated not only the many performers on stage, but also the public audience. For the duration of the three-hour performances the spectators were on stage with the twenty-five or so performers in an unfolding co-participatory and immersive theatrical event. Using a flexible and multi-layered dramaturgical structure, comprised of fully rehearsed and semi-improvisational scenes, everybody was integrated into the experience. With an explicit sense of openness, playfulness and community these dynamic performances facilitated deep convivio through shared yet disparate understandings of living.

Figure 74.

Reiterated body of history

One body of history formed the heart of these creative inquiries: Emiliano Zapata. He is one of Mexico's most troped and iconic revolutionary figures, known as a hero for his role in fighting for the land and rights of marginalized peoples in the 1910 Mexican Revolution. In this project, the purpose was not to re-enact biographical moments of Zapata's life, but to work through remains of Zapata in order to generate embodied inquiries into present lives, with the potential for transformation. Matters of land, freedom and heroes were translated into questions:—"What is the value of land?"—"What is liberty?"—"What is a hero?" In these postmemory theatre experiments these questions formed shared scenarios of material already worked on, open for multiple explorations in creative workshops. Using soil, food, songs, childhood games and stones, the participants investigated issues of land rights, food cultivation, domestic labour, gendered expectations and urban transformations. They worked through corporeal experiences of rememory connecting highly public awareness of assassination and resistance to deeply private sensations of guilt and hope.

Within the transforming environment of the stage space, inhabited by bodies being moved and moving bodies, the co-participatory live event offered a performance of possibilities and re-visions. In the powerful penultimate scenario of everyday living, three performers prepared and cooked a meal in real-time, as they told stories of their daily lives, living with stresses of localized yet transnational drug violence. As a final act of provisionality—and embodying remains of Zapata as death without end—they invited everybody to gather around the cooking table to share in an everyday action of eating (Figures 85 and 86).

Selections and translations

In this chapter my focus is on the final staged performances in Mexico City. As the performances were complex forms of multiplicity, with performers and spectators co-participating on stage throughout, I have selected small sections for my translations into writerly descriptions. My aim through this descriptive analysis is to interpret some of the strategies and aesthetics as performing palimpsest bodies. Even though these events are in the past, I use the present tense for my descriptions. In order to facilitate identification, I refer to the ensembles by their home-location and refer to individuals by the first name. I have also distinguished between sections generated by each collective (collective) and sections that include the public as co-participants (co-participatory). I have also added my own brief titles for the descriptive fragments.

A container of involuted plurality

Five diverse collectives

The project was conceived of and directed by Juliana Faesler, who invited four other theatre ensembles to collaborate in the project. Through the duration of the project, about twenty-five participants were involved, although this number fluctuated as people came and went. The five collectives were: La Máquina (Mexico City); A la Deriva Teatro (Guadalajara, Jalisco), a long-established professional community and schools' theatre company; Teatro de la Rendija (Mérida, Yucatán), a professional experimental, body-based and conceptual company; Colectivo Escénico Oaxaca (Oaxaca City), a community-based collective working with teachers and professors and engaging with Indigenous communities in the surrounding regions; and A-tar (Tampico, Tamaulipas), a loose ensemble of a theatre director and collaborators.[1]

Together and at-distance: Creative processes

Over the course of the year the project involved four main types of processes: multi-ensemble intensive workshops; ensemble-specific workshops; sharing at-distance through virtual technologies; and finally public performances. The composition of some collectives remained fairly stable and others varied, even during the four final performances.

- *Multi-ensemble intensive workshops:* After the initial setting up of the project through virtual technologies (Internet and WhatsApp), the five collectives met together in Mérida, Yucatán, hosted by Raquel Araujo, director of La Rendija. Over the course of a week, the participants used devising processes to generate performance ideas.

Figure 75.

129

- *Ensemble-specific workshops:* The five groups returned to their communities where they continued to generate and shape material through live workshops in their home cities.

- *Virtual collective creation:* The ensembles maintained a network of creative practice using virtual technologies to share their ongoing ideas.

- *Multi-ensemble workshop:* In January 2015, the five collectives again gathered together for a week of shared devising processes in the studio of La Máquina in Mexico City (Figure 75).

- *Ensemble-specific workshops and virtual collective creation:* For two more months, each ensemble continued to devise and share material.

- *Multi-ensemble workshop:* In March 2015, the five ensembles gathered for a final week on the stage of the studio theatre el Foro del Dinosaurio of el Museo Universitario del Chopo, Mexico City.

- *Performances:* For four nights, the five collectives collaboratively performed a three-hour performance on the stage in el Chopo (Figures 28 and 76).

Creating crossings through remains of a body of history

Remains: Body, hero, land, liberty, death…and horses!

Zapata is known as an archetypal hero and iconic revolutionary, embodying activism for human rights and struggles for land and freedom.[2] He was assassinated by an opponent in

Figure 76.

1919 and his dead body was photographed as tangible proof of his death.[3] In the twenty-first century the emotive photograph of his dead body and iconic photos of his living body are reproduced and disseminated as graphic representations (Figure 81). T-shirts, posters and other paraphernalia portray him with his broad moustache, large *charro* hat and suit (used specifically for horse-riding). In the Mexico City metro system a visual pictorial icon of an eyeless face, large moustache, shirt collar, single bullet-strap and large hat signifies the station "Zapata."[4] His body has been replicated on the 10-peso bill, with his hands cradling ears of maize—the iconic foodstuff of everyday sustenance; of Indigenous and peasant rights; and of human creation.

Throughout Mexico, numerous institutions, movements, streets and organizations take Zapata's name. Since the formation of the Zapatista Army of National Liberation in 1994, his name has become familiar globally, connected with justice and rights for Indigenous and oppressed peoples, and associated with land and education.[5] His body is a palimpsest body, standing in for and holding traces of multiple historical moments, connecting the injustices done to native Indigenous peoples by the Spanish conquesters in the sixteenth century with twenty-first century movements for rights.

All these remains of Zapata offered productive sources for postmemory theatre experiments. All form scenarios of material already worked on, connecting official histories with collective and personal memories, interfacing private lives with public politics. To create a focus for shared yet diverse inquiries, the participants used five key ideas: the material body of Zapata; the axiom "Land and Liberty"; Zapata as hero; the phrase "Death without end"; and horses. Each was translated into multiple forms, encompassing objects, gestures, spatialities, clothes, linguistic texts and sensory experiences. The material body of Zapata involved experiments with his outline body-form, photographs of his living and dead body and representations of his iconic clothing. "Land and Liberty" was transformed into two penetrating questions—"What is the value of land?" and "What is liberty?"—facilitating processes with earth, soil, food, drink and matters of home.[6] Zapata as hero was translated into a searching question—"What is a hero?" "Death without end" offered poetic inquiries into permanence and materiality through rememory experiences of survival, resistance and fear.[7] The notion of "horses" activated explorations of domination and freedom, crossing sixteenth-century Spanish conquest with twentieth-century revolutionary struggles for land and liberty.[8]

Through these remains the participants generated trans-temporal crossings connecting the struggles of the Revolution with the dirty war of 1960s and 1970s, with Spanish subjugation and destruction, with the "now" of rights movements and resistance to transnational drug-traffickers and neo-liberal capitalism. Each collective used their localized experiences in devising workshops in their home locations to generate a plethora of corporeal performative ideas. In the shared multi-ensemble sessions, they shared and structured their diverse experiments to create a scenic embodied palimpsest through remains of the body of Zapata.

Figure 77.

Everybody on stage: Inclusive performances in Mexico City

Spatial and dramaturgical palimpsest inside a studio theatre

For the final week of the project, the five ensembles gather in the theatre space el Foro del Dinosaurio in Mexico City. The theatre is located inside a large contemporary arts building, el Museo Universitario del Chopo. This sizeable metal-framed building just to the north of Mexico City is home to exhibitions and performances of contemporary visual and performative art.[9] Inside el Foro fixed rows of theatre seats face forward to a proscenium arch stage. The stage is small, with a solid back wall and small wings. Two short flights of steps connect the auditorium with the stage.

On the stage of the studio theatre the five ensembles create a spatial and dramaturgical environment of inclusion. Their overriding aim is to facilitate diversity and participation through shared remains. Spatially, the audience are on stage for the duration of the event. They enter the auditorium through doors at the back and are invited to walk down through the auditorium and onto the stage, where they remain, mixing and mingling with the five ensembles. Only minimal objects and furniture are used. The space is a dynamic environment through the presence of diverse bodies. These bodies are moving and being moved. At one moment they are still, quiet, listening and watching and in the next moment they are dancing, laughing and eating together. Dramaturgically, the three-hour event is a multi-layered, involuted palimpsest of stories, journeys, lives and experiences. Through fully-rehearsed scenes, semi-improvisational scenes and scenes with the public as overt co-participants, each section is distinct yet intersecting, generating accumulations and sedimentations of traces.

Inclusion and diversity through clothes/costumes

Establishing an environment of embodied plurality, the five ensembles wear many different forms of clothing, ranging from casual everyday clothes, to nationalistic and regional outfits, to T-shirts displaying the face of Zapata:

Mexico City: Juliana wears a charro suit of black jacket and trousers (with silver buttons down the sides) and a large charro hat. This costume is an iconic and gendered body-covering, deeply embedded in constructs of national unity. Used by Zapata and thousands of other horse-riding men during the Revolution, it was appropriated for postrevolutionary institutional constructions of authentic Mexicanness and nationalistic folkloric music and dance repertoires.[10] Carmen wears casual jeans, shirt and a charro hat, and affixes a moustache to her face;[11] Isaac wears black shirt, jeans and black folklórico dance shoes, specifically used for performing nationalistic repertoires of rhythmic footwork known as *zapateado*; Sandra wears casual black shirt and leggings (Figures 19 and 80).

Guadalajara: all performers wear matching crisp white shirts and neat ties, recognizable as the regional clothes of Jalisco. Susana wears a *rebozo* (shawl), at times using it to carry her daughter on her back, chest or hip (Figures 36 and 81).

Mérida: two performers wear casual workshop clothes (sweat pants and T-shirt) and Katenka wears a traditional embroidered blouse (Figure 82).

Oaxaca: all performers wear jeans and T-shirts of varying colours. Their T-shirts are printed with the iconic face of Zapata and the words "Oaxaca Colectivo—Zapata, Muerte Sin Fin." The reproduced face of Zapata forms a literal palimpsest body with his face layering over the body parts (hearts, lungs and other vital organs) of all the performers. The face of Zapata is transformed by the contours of the differing body-shapes of the wearers, as the accumulated iterations of remains of Zapata are reactivated over the beating hearts and breathing lungs of living people. Itandehui wears a rebozo and carries her child on her back or hips (Figures 76 and 84).

Tampico: the three performers wear familiar and casual everyday clothes of jeans and T-shirts. Sandra wears a traditional embroidered blouse (Figures 85 and 86).

Co-participatory: Transformation

Even before the spectators enter the auditorium they experience remains of Zapata as a palimpsest body on the sidewalk outside the building. Zapata's face is formed as an ephemeral trace of chalk-dust. To enter the building, each person must walk on remains of Zapata's iconic body. Each footstep and each moving body alters the corporeal outline, as these footprints and journeys gradually transform his reiterated, spectral body-form. The stencils are a form of reverse face or inside out face: the holes where the face should be allow the chalk dust to accumulate. Zapata's face appears ghostly—a haunting—comprising an accumulation of millions of tiny specks—remains of minute marine organisms, generated through millennia of transformations. The sidewalk is a public space, so these fragile traces of a familiar face are open to any passers-by, offering embodied connections to Zapata's political project of inclusion (Figure 78).

Figure 78.

Co-participatory: Coexistence

Once inside the building, the spectators enter the back of the auditorium, moving to sit in the rows of seats. The performers approach them, inviting and encouraging them to walk up the five steps and onto the stage, as bright stage lights shine down on the gathering assembly. On stage, people walk around and chatter. Before long, the stage contains about one hundred people, as audience and performers circulate and mingle. It is not clear who is who. All seem to be in a liminal and palimpsest state of subjunctivity, waiting and ready for possibilities. Boundaries are blurred and crossed as spectators are invited to become co-participants.

Co-participatory: Re-writing history and heroes

A man's body lies in the centre of the stage. His arms are crossed over his chest and his eyes are closed. Stones are scattered around his body, creating a sense of a graveside. As the public walks around the body, looking down at the body, some performers approach the public individually, offering each one a pen and two stones, asking the question: "Who is your hero?" Each time the performer explains that the individual should write the name of their hero on the stones—first name on one stone, surnames on another—concluding: "When you are done, please place the stone by the body." In a short while everybody is writing names on stones and placing them around the corpse-like body.

In an atmosphere of communal and hushed calm, the stones offer trans-temporal connections to transformations and re-use. The stones are palimpsest objects that have been removed from a landscape and repurposed for writing within performance. The actions of writing and then placing the stones are acts of re-membering and re-visioning of "Zapata as history." Now, "writing of history" is transformed from bodies of children in a school into writing of personal memories and stories. As the stones are accumulated around the body, the words on the stones create an interweaving and multi-layered texture of people as heroes.

Sandra, from Tampico, invites everybody to sit around the body. She picks up her two stones and begins to speak in a casual and improvised manner. She tells of her youth theatre work in Tampico, of the upsurge in violence in the city due to the organized crime of the drug traffickers, of her plans to cancel a theatre workshop and of the actions of an adolescent named Oliver, who urged her to go ahead with the workshop as planned, saying

Figure 79.

135

that cancelling would be giving in to the criminals. As she names Oliver as her hero, she holds her stones and looks around, with the rememory of recent traumatic experiences revealed through her gestures, facial movements and muscles. Through remains of Zapata, she creates re-visions and performs resistance through her hero, the teenage boy Oliver.

Sandra turns to a member of the public, inviting them to pick up their stones and share their story of their hero. After some hesitation, one person begins their story, with an obvious embodied rememory of their mother, who struggled to provide food for daily living...; Sandra then invites another person, who tells of an iconic woman of Mexican history...; and another...; and another. As soon as one person finishes and re-places their stones, another person starts. These traces of lives and of collective and individual memories are accompanied by moments of laughter, stillness and hesitation. The embodied speaking voices draw listeners deep into personal and collective experiences. The "heroes" are trans-temporal, encompassing close family still living—especially mothers and sisters—and "famous" women who are known for their acts as scientists, intellectuals, religious leaders and artists.

As a shared performative gathering of convivio, the witnessing processes are important to the layering of memories. The scene around the "dead" body is an act of communal ritual; a memento mori—"remember that you have to die"; and a rememory of sitting around gravesides for the collective celebration of day of the dead. The newly arrived spectators are invited to be co-participants, sharing in an act of personal and collective re-vision, engaging rememory through processes of writing, speaking and listening, and re-membering of Zapata. Already, remains of the body of Zapata become a palimpsest that is home to many stories (Figure 79).

Co-participatory: Death without end

The "dead" body lies centre stage, enclosed within an accumulation of names of heroes documented on stones, and surrounded by the sitting performers and co-participatory spectators. Suddenly, he lifts up his head, sits up, stands up and walks away from his resting place. On the floor where his body had been lying, an outline of a body remains—the iconic image of Zapata drawn on paper. The chalked outline marks a death, a spectre or ghost of the living body, and a palimpsest of a recently removed body. The stones remain—a trace of distant pasts, shaped through transformations over millennia. Zapata's body has generated a multiplicity of other heroes as the stones form an accumulated trace of Zapata's body.

Collective one—Mexico City: Truth and lies

Four Mexico City performers generate a three-part progressive and overlapping dramaturgy: (1) Fragility—Sandra tells stories of her grandfather and her own body; (2) Construction— Juliana, Sandra and Isaac construct a city of egg-boxes, while Carmen reads from her i-pad; (3) Assassin—Juliana tells of her experiences as a 6-year-old girl held in the arms of the president.

Figure 80.

1. *Fragility:* Sandra places a chair centre stage as everybody creates a circle around her. As she begins to tell stories of her grandfather who fought in the Revolution, her words form traces of Zapata, transmitted through oral telling. Sandra's body forms a palimpsest body connecting her own self to her grandfather's actions and experiences 100 years before. Through shifts in her narration, she moves from looking back to present tense, speaking as if present in the Revolution; then changes again, speaking as if in the years after the Revolution when her grandfather needed government support for his health. In a sudden shift, Sandra's body is very present, as she tells stories of her own body, lifting her shirt and revealing a scar. As she briefly uncovers parts of her skin to reveal scars, she speaks of her battle with cancer and her survival. Revealing her scarred body is her witness to survival: a scar is the remains of cutting and

removing.[12] Through remains of Zapata, Sandra's body is trans-temporal, connecting her genealogical blood ties to her grandfather's life and experiences. She holds traces of collective postmemory and rememory of trauma, as the individual lives of Sandra's grandfather and herself coexist with the collectivity of fragility and injustices.

2. *Construction:* In near darkness, Isaac, Juliana and Sandra begin to transform the space, walking in, out and around the space, carrying and placing square, cardboard egg-box trays on the floor in structures and in towers. The towers sway precariously. Juliana places stage lights with trailing cables on the ground. She carefully locates tiny self-contained lights atop the structures and towers. The stage space is altered as audience and performers stand and/or sit around, witnessing the transformation. The stage seems to be a form of city-scape: the egg-boxes are themselves empty containers, which usually hold items of great fragility. This cityscape is being constructed from everyday objects; the stage lights and wires are theatrical elements that are usually unseen.

   Sandra has placed a cardboard horse-head over her own head. Isaac wears a horse-head. Both perform rhythmic footwork of zapateado, stamping and swishing their feet. These are sonic and movement traces of traditional embodied dance forms, used for social and religious celebrations, and an embodied repertorial trace of folkloric nationalism after the Revolution.[13]

   Throughout the construction, and in the semi-darkness, Carmen has been standing reading from her iPad. She supports a cardboard horse-head on her back and wears a moustache as iconic traces of Zapata. Her iPad glows in the dark and is an obvious object of the twenty-first century. She reads evocative prose, asking questions about bodies, memory, the Revolution, land distribution, commemoration and corruption. She repeats two questions: "…and the body?," "…and memory?" Her steady voice and stillness stand in contrast to the chaos and movement of the spatial transformation around her.

3. *Assassin:* As Carmen closes her iPad and Juliana begins to speak. She wears an awkwardly-fitting charro suit and holds a large hat —"When I was six years old, in 1971, I was a representative of my primary school for the Independence celebration, dressed in a charro outfit." —She puts the hat on her head —"I remember standing in a line at the National Palace. I was very nervous, waiting for President Luis Echeverría Álvarez. As he walked past the line, he picked me out and took me with him." —

   Isaac picks up Juliana, lifting her awkwardly off the ground, one arm under her legs, one under her back, taking the full weight of her body, as if carrying a child.—"This was 10 September 1971, just three months after the Halconazo. I was in the arms of an assassin." A photo of Echeverría is passed around from hand to hand, offering experiences of rememory.

   In this brief moment, Juliana's rememory of experiences as a 6-year-old girl is performed as one of Mexico's most terrible events of postmemory.[14] As Juliana's feet dangle, and as her heavy and uncomfortable 50-year-old body is held up inelegantly, her 6-year-old child-self is interwoven, layered and sedimented in her adult body. Her child-adult body and her individual rememory connect with the enormity of collective memory: one live body holds traces of the dead and broken bodies of 1968 and 1971, and of the individual whose violence suppressed the movements for social justice. Through the charro suit, Juliana's body connects to the postrevolutionary unification movement to generate a united national body. In this trans-temporal pose, Juliana's body resists official history, containing and performing an "unsettled memory."[15] Her body holds collective traces of death and creates a tension through truth and lies. Her held-high body seems to be a "host" (hostia) and a sacrificed body, given in remembrance, a body offered up for witness.[16] After all, this same body was held in the arms of the assassin.

The scene ends as the four Mexican City performers frantically dash around the stage destroying the egg-box structures in a frenzy of kicking and stomping, re-forming the space, seemingly like children playing a game. The other performers assist by carrying bits of egg-boxes and lights, by moving chairs and preparing the space for the next transformation. As an exploration of the complicated constructed urban environment and seat of institutional power that is Mexico City, this unfolding dramaturgy interweaves an accumulation of remains of Zapata, coexisting in this fabricated and fragmented space. The four bodies are distinctly different as they co-inhabit the evolving territory. Their bodies offer fluctuating viewpoints and perspectives, existing as nepantla bodies of both/ and. They seem to be children playing with egg-boxes and horseheads, re-forming stories through the past. The rhythmic footwork of zapateado inserts a sonic embodied repertoire of performed nationalistic power. In the dimness, there is a tangle of electric cables and the glimmer of tiny lights. Inserting a luminous glow of "now" into the shadowy environment, Carmen reads from her iPad by wireless technological connectivity. The spectators and other performers witness the constructions from the periphery, yet, all share the collective experiences in these corporeal palimpsests of involuted stories. Sandra incorporates a personal rememory of revolution as she re-members her own grandfather who fought for land and rights. She lives her own resistance and survival, revealing scars on the surface of her skin as sights/sites of corporeal fragility. As Juliana re-members her self in the arms of the president-assassin, she speaks truth to power through her palimpsest body (Figures 19 and 80).

Collective two—Guadalajara: Producing home

The Guadalajara ensemble plays with remains of Zapata through a dramaturgy of three interconnected, sequential and overlapping sections: (1) a carnivalesque and transgressive game of darts; (2) an impossible domestic task of grinding earth; and (3) a re-vision of a children's action-song.

1. *Darts:* Everybody mingles around as two performers place a board covered in inflated black balloons on stage. The black colour of the balloons sets up an obvious contradiction

with notions of multi-coloured party balloons. Acting as fairground callers, Horacio and Alejandro shout out to the crowd to gather around, asking for someone to step up and throw three darts. They explain that the aim is to burst three balloons, and that each burst balloon will result in either a prize or a forfeit. A woman volunteer steps forward, takes the three darts and takes aim at the balloons. In a familiar atmosphere of a local fair (feria), everyone shouts, cheers and claps, actively participating in the collaborative action. A burst balloon reveals a tiny piece of paper. One of the callers takes the piece of paper and reads: the words form political questions about local land use; or the words reward with a prize of mezcal. The mood shifts rapidly from celebratory to grave as deeply challenging provocations of injustice are inserted into the festive environment. A little communal shot glass containing mezcal is offered around the gathered crowd, replicating a common ritual in local ferias. The familiar taste of the drink provides moments of sensory experience. Volunteers continue to accept three darts and take their chances with the dartboard.

One by one the balloons are burst and the image is gradually revealed. As a weighty palimpsest body, it is the iconic photo of the dead Zapata, seemingly spattered with red blood spots. The trace of the man who fought for the ideals of liberty and land had been obscured by the frivolity of a game. Through the dart throwing and the witnessing, everybody has become complicit in an underhand betrayal of trust.

2. *Repetitions:* Susana kneels on the ground with a wooden tortilla press and a pile of earth. She takes a handful of earth, puts it into the press, presses down, opens the press and pushes the earth out the other side. She narrates a story of owning land, of land removed and of an infertile plot of land that is useless for cultivation.

    Her kneeling pose and repetitive movements are trans-temporal corporeal traces that connect with millions of women. The tortilla press is a gendered object of domesticity used in daily life to prepare the staple food. Maize is the iconic and mythical food of origins and native peoples, a deeply powerful signifier of human life. Her kneeling body is an archival-repertorial container of countless traces of women as she takes the iconic corporeal pose of "Indigenous woman," disseminated in the postrevolutionary era of constructing "Mexicanness."[17] Her working actions—opening, pressing, opening, pressing—are repetitions of everyday lives. In place of the soft dough of masa is a fistful of stony earth. Each fistful is impossible to crush in the press; the earth is pushed out as stony as when it started. The action is repetitive, but unproductive.

3. *Home:* Ana quietly sings a familiar children's song as she moves her hands through tiny gestures of "home":
    I have a little house that is like this and like this
    [hold hands vertically to form walls, then touch finger tips to form a roof];
    And from the chimney smoke goes up like this and like this
    [rotate index finger and spiral upwards];

And when I want to enter I knock like this and this
        [close hand to form a fist, flex forward and back from the wrist twice];
And I clean my shoes like this and like this
        [pull one foot back, replace, pull the other foot back, then replace].
She performs the well-known actions with diminutive movements in the space. With fingertips touching she creates a tiny roof as she gestures above her head. Each gesture traces parts of a house, as the words describe a personal home in the present: "I have a little house." She sings softly, slowly and contemplatively. The usually loud, uncontained and boisterous children's action game is now a gentle ritual of reflection. Gradually

Figure 81.

everybody joins in, singing quietly and gently, tracing and multiplying tiny walls, roofs and smoke puffs, each performing their own palimpsest bodies from childhood.

In this immersive and involuted yet deeply interconnected dramaturgy, "real" remains of Zapata's body—the reproduced photographic image of his corpse on the dart board—seem to act as a trans-temporal witness. "He" is witness to scenarios of home and familial sharing. Within the charged and festive environment of bustling feria, everybody repeats vocalized shouts of encouragement as a single body aims at dart the board. In this hit and miss situation, the consequences of each repeat unfold narratives of seized land or a glass of mezcal.

With the familiar object of the tortilla press, a body who is kneeling and working through repetitive everyday gestures offers a deep connection to gendered domesticity. The repetitions of this embodied archival repertoire, combined with vocal articulations about unfair distribution of land and of food rights, presents a compelling provocation. As everybody unites to sing and form tiny houses, the stage becomes a container of dynamic and contemplative traces (Figure 81).

Collective three—Mérida: Regenerations and dominations

Three trained physical theatre performers generate a simultaneous dramaturgy of three juxtaposed bodies, each moving in their own environment of freshly decanted earth.
Katenka, Rafael and Alejo each haul a heavy sack to the front of stage and stand with their backs to the empty auditorium. The spectators and performers gather to look towards them and out into the darkness.
Each performer stands a pool of light as they tip their sack upside down, out of which falls fresh earth, generating three small mounds. Particles rise into the light beams. The fresh dirt has a pungent smell that pervades the air. Throughout the scene, Katenka, Rafael and Alejo each remain in their own mound of earth, moving within the earth and gradually transforming it.

- *Procreation:* Katenka wears a delicately embroidered traditional blouse, under which she has a seemingly pregnant belly. She kneels in the earth and she raises the front of her blouse to reveal a finely woven shawl—a *rebozo*— around her belly. A rebozo is a quintessential and ubiquitous body-covering of "woman," virtue, motherliness and maternity. It is used to carry babies and to hold fresh produce. In the postrevolutionary era, a rebozo was used as an icon of pan-Indigenous woman. In this performative context, Katenka carefully removes her rebozo, plays with and swings it, as if swinging a little baby. She sings a gentle lullaby, voicing an archival-repertoire of reproduction. As she opens the rebozo, she reveals a body of earth in place of a body of a baby. In this exposing action, the expectations of fertility and reproduction, through human-body as mother and earth-body as mother, combine and merge. She empties the earth into her mound, generating a further accumulation. With fluid movements, she sits in the earth, creating patterns with her bare feet, twisting, standing and revolving her rebozo around her. She lays the rebozo in the earth, fills it again, then with her bare hands, drags earth over it, again and again, until it is eventually completely obscured, seemingly burying earth inside earth.

• *Exhaustion:* Rafael shifts his body to form a horse-like pose—arms forward, torso bent, head high and shaking. He begins a steady galloping movement, with bare feet pounding in the earth, repeating this rhythmic action over and over. His feet are returning to the same place again, and again, and again, undertaking a journey to nowhere. His face stares forward in gritty persistence. Through his galloping movements his body seems human-animal, and in a perpetual liminal state. He is pushing his body to the extreme, with

Figure 82.

sweat mingling, and with the rising dirt particles, he becomes more and more exhausted. In the hushed space, the sound of his heavy breathing is very present as he seems to struggle for air. His pounding movements are felt by everybody as embodied vibrations through the stage-floor. His individual body connects viscerally to the collective body. He performs traces of Zapata as struggling and persistent revolutionary bodies, through his horse-human movements, connecting destruction of Indigenous bodies in the sixteenth century with fighting revolutionaries in the 1910s.

- *Bones:* Alejo stands in his earth-pile holding a jaw-bone of a horse. This object is the literal remains of a body and ephemera of "death."[18] He twists and turns, manipulating the body-remains and generating a beating sound. He kneels and places his own head where the head of the horse had been, generating a visual palimpsest of coexisting life-death, horse-human and freedom-slavery.

Through the three mounds of earth and the three differently moving bodies, this scene offers a unfolding of poetic presences with immeasurable trans-temporal particles rising into the air. Each body is a palimpsest body performing traces of cycles of life. As they inhabit their environments of gradually transforming earth, they are also transformed by the earth. They alter the earth through their movements as their bodies are marked and overlaid with earth. One body works with repetition and exhaustion; one with revelation and concealment; one with regeneration and reproduction. Katenka's body recreates from deep inside her self, offering a visceral experience of procreation with the earth inside her rebozo. Rafael's body is exposed to reveal the workings of his contracting muscles and his expanding ribcage. His vocalized breath exposes the workings of his lungs under his skin. Alejo's body unites with bones of an animal, as he rotates and circles in the space. Everybody is witness to these sensory transformations (Figure 82).

Co-participatory: Re-forming

Large pieces of blank paper and pieces of charcoal are quickly distributed to everybody on stage with the instruction to draw a picture of Zapata. Kneeling on the ground, the assembled performers and co-participants begin to sketch and draw. In an atmosphere combining

Figure 83.

laughter and studied concentration, multiple bodies move hands across paper to form numerous body parts—recreating Zapata. The stage floor is covered with an accumulation of Zapata's face, body, moustache, eyes and hat. The numerous body-forms overlap and juxtapose each other, generating a collective re-vision of Zapata and a foundational layer for the personal stories of the Oaxaca performers (Figure 83).

Collective four—Oaxaca: Rituals of everyday life

Eleven performers create a ritualized space of repeated embodied actions, as one after another each performer tells a life-experience story. Through one continuous dramaturgical flow, one fragment connects to another and another, through a repeated ritual of speaking and marking the body with earth.
The floor is covered with a layer of overlapping and juxtaposed papers displaying the re-created faces of Zapata.
Adding to this palimpsest of Zapata's faces, the Oaxaca performers display remains of the face of Zapata on their T-shirts. Everyone gathers around and is standing or seated in a circle.

Rosario begins to speak softly, holding a small vessel containing soil. As she speaks, she turns her head to look at each person, connecting her very personal and intimate life experiences with those around her. She narrates her experiences of her land, of soil, of home. Her experiences return through her body as gestures, facial expressions and vocal articulations. The trauma of fear, disappointment and the guilt of struggle to put food on the table for her daughter are visceral. She stops speaking. She wets her hands with water from another pot and dampens the soil in the vessel. Then with three fingers draws the dampened earth across her face, marking her skin. Her face is transformed and layered by the earth, incorporating atemporal remains of the earth, coexisting with Zapata and her own daily struggles. She gently passes the vessel containing the earth to another person in the circle, in a small transaction of transmission, care and connection…

Olga holds the vessel of earth, recounting her story, marking her face with earth and passing the vessel to another…

Palemón cups the vessel in his hands and walks around the space, speaking gently in his native Mixtec language. His embodied vocalizations are welcoming, even though the words may be unfamiliar to most on the theatre stage. Palemón speaks the embodied archival repertoire of pre-invasion peoples, one of over sixty native languages spoken in Mexico in the twenty-first century. His passionate vocalization connects with Zapata, with struggles for Indigenous rights, with the EZLN and with many contemporary movements for human rights. He takes a fistful of soil and walks over to a spectator, offering them the soil. They hold out their cupped hands as Palemón opens his hands and lets the earth fall, with the receiving hands trying desperately to contain every grain. With this transmission from one body to another—hands to hands—the sharing of earth and the sharing of responsibility is offered as a visceral and tangible performance…

Itandehui moves into the centre, carrying her daughter Luna on her hip, holding her in place with her rebozo (an obvious embodiment of generational reproduction). Itandehui speaks her story of hope and rubs earth on her own face and that of her child—mother and daughter marked together…

Jesús holds the vessel of earth, gently telling of his connections to land and migration, in Mexico and the United States…

Marycarmen continues, speaking of her experiences and carrying a handful of earth, which she transfers to another person…

then Manuel…

then Ángeles…

then Omar…

then Federico…

In this ritualistic scene, the many performers of the Oaxaca Collective generate an intensely personal environment of intimate life experiences and earth, wholly interconnected through shared histories, and performed on a foundational yet fragile layer of multiple iterations of Zapata. Each person performs within the structure of the ritual—speaking and marking— but each is distinct. Marking bodies with wet earth seems at once ritualistic and sacred— repetitions since time immemorial. Yet the deeply personal life experiences seem familiar and recognizable. These stories reveal intensely personal struggles and emotions and deep connections to land and home. Each story and life exists through links with all the other lives, creating an involuted multi-textural atmosphere of subjunctivity. Each time and with each story, everybody on stage listens to one voice, creating an environment of hushed and sensory embodied listening. As palimpsest bodies, these listening bodies are actively incorporated into the community of sharing.

When a handful of earth is transferred from hand to hand—from person to .person—these bodies generate a profound sense of interconnection by giving and receiving. In these actions there is an evitable degree of loss: tiny particles slip through infinitesimal cracks between fingers. Even though each body seems to be desperately trying to hold on to each precious fragment, inexorably these transformations happen (Figure 84).

Co-participatory: Transformation

From the intensity, stillness and hush of the ritualistic daily-life I-stories, the performers transform the environment again. As the sound of a familiar song fills the space, everybody moves around. As mezcal is passed around, the stage becomes a convivial and raucous setting for laughing, chattering and swirling bodies.

Figure 84.

Collective five—Tampico: Resistance through everyday cooking

The three Tampico participants perform a continuous dramaturgy interweaving three elements: cooking a meal, inviting spectators to smell petrol and offering spectators mangoes to eat.

Sandra, Víctor and Sergio set up a table at the very back of the stage against the wall. Sandra puts on her apron and begins to organize cooking equipment: a stove top, a large pot, a chopping board, knives, a bag of potatoes, onions and shrimp. Mangoes, candles, herbs and condiments are lined up in preparation on the table.
Everyone brings chairs into a semi-circle facing the table and the back wall, with their backs to the auditorium.

1. *Cooking*: Sandra starts to prepare shrimp stew, a specialty of Tampico. She puts a pot of water onto the stovetop and begins to chop onions. As she chops she chats informally, telling stories of her daily life in Tampico. She talks about the violence on the streets, of meeting up with her friends Víctor and Sergio, of not knowing whether it is safe to walk the streets because of the control of territory by rival drug-traffickers. She focuses her eyes on her sharp cutting knife, but looks up now and again to connect with her listeners. As she cuts the onions her eyes weep tears. Her rememory of fear is tangible. Her body offers traces of countless daily (gendered) bodies preparing everyday sustenance, performing her daily repetitive actions as she prepares a meal. The scene intermingles everyday domesticity and a sense of getting on with life, with the performativity of a demonstration cooking show.[19]

   Sandra reiterates her story of her hero: a teenage boy, Oliver, who had challenged her not to cancel a scheduled theatre workshop, despite the presence of danger and violence. In the opening section of this performance event, Sandra had held her stones and told her story in the hushed kneeling of rememory around remains of the body of Zapata. As a transformed repetition, this re-telling of the same story holds traces of Zapata as an activist, offering another re-vision of "hero," performed through the everyday normalcy of preparing food, yet within the dangerous environment of high-stakes territorial battles.

2. *Petrol*: Víctor picks up a clear glass bottle filled with liquid and removes the lid. He walks from person to person around the semi-circle, holding the bottle to each person's nose. The bottle contains oil (petrol). As each person sniffs there are many visceral reactions—experiences of rememory through smelling. This is an uncommon olfactory experience, smelling and seeing liquid that usually transfers unseen from pump to car. As he walks, Víctor talks of the oil industry in Tampico, of foreign companies, of appropriation and expropriation, of huge profits, of this liquid that is so iconic and deeply embedded in questions of exploitation, control and mobility, extracted from far below the earth's surface. As a trace of distant eras, it is intimately part of the transformations of Tampico. As a commodity of twentieth- and

Figure 85.

twenty-first-century Mexico, nationalized in the 1930s, oil is a trace of remains of Zapata through struggles for justice, and resistance to monopolizing wealth.

3. *Mangoes*: Sergio picks up some mangoes, walks from person to person around the semi-circle, offering mangoes to everybody. As people bite into their mango, sticky juice oozes from the fruit and flows down the sides of their mouths. As he walks, Sergio talks of this quintessential food of Tampico. As fruits of the earth that are so symbolic of capitalism and consumerism, the mangoes offer a trace of Zapata.

    As Víctor and Sergio both talk of their everyday lives, they embody a passion for their city, through two inter-related and juxtaposed objects of oil and mangoes; through hyper-locality and transnational business; and through the earth as container and producer.

    As Sandra continues to cook, the smells of frying onions saturate the space. She stirs the potatoes, shrimp and onions together in the pan as she speaks of the intense violence and danger in her life. As Sergio walks around the space, he speaks with fervent urgency about the need to continue with life "as normal" as a way of resisting violence.

This scene reactivates scenarios of everyday life in a kitchen. Scenarios of normalcy and freedom are performed as cutting onions and preparing potatoes and as eating mangoes. Through rememory experiences of fear, the disrupted lives of Sandra, Víctor and Sergio are re-contextualized and transformed through everyday meal preparations. Everybody on stage is invited to share their intimate space, sitting with their backs to the empty auditorium and facing the back wall. They are in the private and convivial environment of "home." As Sandra, Víctor and Sergio chat and chop, stir and smell, they perform their resistance to the daily violence of drug-traffickers and to institutional collusion and complicity (Figure 85).

Co-participatory: Transformation

As Sandra announces that the stew is ready, and as Sergio continues to speak, his voice is gradually drowned out by the sounds of a familiar song that grows louder and louder. Everybody begins to sing along, pushing back the chairs and moving into a celebratory swirl of dancing and talking. Soon, everybody gathers around the table and joins in the act of eating. In this final transformation the stage has become a site and sight of everyday normalcy and conviviality. On the dartboard, the bloodied face of Zapata remains (Figure 86).

But this is a "performance without end," presenting no finality or conclusion. There is no decisive end scene or applause. The liveness of the performance transitions into daily life, maintaining plural liminality and the possibility of other re-makings. Slowly, people walk off the stage, down the steps and through the auditorium. They walk out of building into the night air, stepping on what remains of the dust-traces of Zapata on the sidewalk as they move towards their futures.

Reflections on remains: Performing palimpsest bodies

Over the course of the year and in the final co-mingling staged performances, this complicated and invitational project enabled multiple performers and spectators to participate in deeply convivial postmemory theatre experiments, within a framework of serious and exploratory playfulness. From the core provocation of re-membering Zapata, the unfolding project encompassed an extraordinary range of collective and personal responses. As a palimpsest provides evidence of multiple journeys, stories and environments with criss-crossing temporal narratives, so through multiple forms of remains this project generated deep connections between public and private understandings of the Revolution, of the 1960s and 70s resistance movements, of Indigenous repressions, of transnational organized drug crime, of procreation, of survival, of territorial struggles and of daily living and home-making.

By reactivating shared scenarios of freedom, land, heroes and "death without end," each ensemble explored the collective material within their local environments. The sheer diversity of outcomes is a demonstration of the significant potential for such a multi-ensemble project to be a container of plurality and multiplicity:

- The Mexico City participants create an environment of precarious constructions, rhythmic footwork, poetic recitation, trailing electric cables and twinkling lights. They ask their fellow performers and spectators to be witnesses to the scars of a cancer survivor and to a body re-membering being held in the arms of an assassin.

- The Guadalajara participants generate an interactive, familial and complicit environment of a jostling popular fair. They invite everybody to enjoy a game of darts and to drink mezcal, as they insert penetrating facts of territorial injustices into the convivial atmosphere in order to challenge and provoke their co-participants. As the face of the dead Zapata is gradually uncovered with each burst of a balloon and as a kneeling women tries to crush stones in a tortilla press, everybody re-forms their childhood selves through a simple song of home-making.

- The three Mérida performers produce a stimulating olfactory and visceral environment with three fresh mounds of earth. As particles of dust rise into the beams of the lights, the three bodies kneel, twist and gallop within their territories, poetically and evocatively confronting the participant-spectators with embodied questions of human control and consequences.

- The many participants of the Oaxaca Collective create an open environment of individual personal stories, performed on the foundational layer of overlapping pieces of paper, newly covered with faces of Zapata drawn from collective memory. As one by one they stand and kneel on the traces of Zapata, they personally invite everybody to listen carefully to their story. As they mark their faces with wet earth and transfer fistfuls of soil from one body to another, they reveal traces of home, land, freedom and fragility.

- The Tampico performers generate an intimate and personal home environment by re-creating Sandra's kitchen. Spectators and performers are invited to make a semi-circle of chairs around the table laden with food and cooking equipment, as Sandra chops and chats away. Through the everyday preparation of food, the three practitioners perform deep resistance to the violence of their city.

From the outset of the event, the public spectators were encouraged and invited to be co-participants, actively engaged in embodied processes and practices of re-membering Zapata. As they wrote on stones, threw darts, sang a childhood song, drank mezcal, traced Zapata's face, smelled petrol, witnessed scars, listened to personal stories and ate mangoes they were intimately incorporated into performing remains of Zapata through communal "doing." Within the first ten minutes of the performance, as they gathered around Zapata's reiterated prone (seemingly dead) body-form, every one inscribed names of personal heroes on stones, resisting militarized and gendered stereotypes and generating an accumulation of heroes of everyday life. In the final ten minutes of the performance, everybody is invited to eat the freshly cooked meal together as an action of conviviality and potentiality.

In this vibrant and visceral space, through provocations offered by remains of the body of Zapata, each body is a palimpsest body, containing and transmitting archival repertoires connecting personal and collective experiences. Each body is performing remains by striking poses, making gestures, voicing calls, reading words, singing songs and standing witness. By activating and opening the past within the present, through the community engagement of difference in the "now" of the live performance, these experiments enabled diverse participatory experiences with unexpected outcomes. Incorporating shifts and juxtapositions, the performers and spectators moved through deep personal memories to shared celebrations, and through moments of meditative stillness to raucous laughter. For three hours, these interdependent yet different bodies formed an ecological yet transitory community. Merging stories of daily life struggles and survival with celebrations of hopes and expectations, and with regeneration and futurity, remains of Zapata were performed as challenges and as projections in a dense and involuted accumulation of traces. The multifarious actions became re-imaginings of acts of revolution, performed in a scenic environment of complicated yet supportive multiplicity and possibility.

Figure 86.

Chapter 5

War in Paradise

Twenty-five performers, three weeks, work-in-progress

Documentary workshop

For three weeks, twenty-five creative artists of varying ages collaborated on a small studio theatre stage in Mexico City to experiment through embodied practices. As a culmination of the project they performed an unfinished dramaturgical showing of work-in-progress. Within the starkly dynamic theatre space, twenty-five bodies offer unfolding poetic re-imaginings as they generate evocative and ethical responses to scenarios of resistance and control of the 1960s and 70s. Bodies stand witness as a single inverted body balances and voices political words of struggle. Bodies gesture with raised fists as they make calls of defiance in a collective trans-temporal performance of resistance. Bodies tap bare flesh as they make multiple meandering journeys around the stage space, transforming violent acts into tender sounds and movements. Multiple bodies speak as "I, Lucio," performing myriad stories and lives as coexistence.

At the heart of the project was Lucio Cabañas, a man who was assassinated in 1974 on government orders. In the turbulent countercultural era of the 1960s, Cabañas had transformed himself from a poor, rural schoolteacher into an activist for social justice, becoming a resistance leader and revolutionary who fought for collective rights.

Brief translations of remains

In this brief chapter I discuss some key elements of the practices and work-in-progress performance. As with the previous chapter, even though this event took place in 2015, I engage the present tense for my descriptive-analysis.

Figure 87.

Figure 88.

Pragmatics and poetics

As directors of La Máquina de Teatro, Juliana Faesler and Clarissa Malheiros regularly facilitate workshops and train artist-creators through their ensemble practices. The *War in Paradise* project was initiated and facilitated by Faesler, who acted as skilled instructor and also active participant, using a model of ethically involved praxis.[1] Given the brief time period and number of participants in this project, Faesler selected one literary text as a core source: the novel *War in Paradise* by renowned author Carlos Montemayor.[2] The aim of the project was to explore creative processes and strategies, specifically incorporating intertextual and trans-temporal body-based practices in a documentary workshop—"laboratorio documental." All the participants applied to be part of the workshop and committed to being present for four hours a day for three weeks. Participants ranged from already-working theatre and dance artists to those with minimal previous experience, therefore embracing a radical, hybrid, time-pressed and transitory community of twenty-five creator-participants.

Remains

Creating through a body of history

With Cabañas at the heart of this performance project, postmemory encompassed a deep sense of collective disturbance. Although Cabañas is not a body of history whose body-form and name are widely known in the twenty-first century (unlike Zapata), his actions are embedded in recent relationships of postmemory. Reverberations of the violent governmental acts of the dirty war of 1960s and 1970s are still very present in contemporary Mexico.[3] They are experienced as traumatic fragments of events that still defy narrative reconstruction and exceed comprehension. Some participants in the theatre project were alive during the period and all had family and friends who experienced those events. This project therefore involved a deep sense of inhabiting and envisioning these recent pasts and environments.

Cabañas lived in an era of intense governmental oppression and control, when social justice movements and student protests were repressed through military agents working under state orders. Government tactics involved military brutality and disappearances. In an environment of increased suppression, Cabañas created the Party of the Poor as an action against poverty, and for peasant and Indigenous rights, education and land, overtly reiterating the aims of the Mexican Revolution. From his role as an "unknown" schoolteacher, he defied a sense of powerlessness to become a force to be reckoned with. Even the CIA classified him as "Mexico's best known guerrilla."[4] When he was just 35 years old, on 2 December 1974, Cabañas was killed by government agents in a shoot-out with soldiers. In the twenty-first century, the "absence" of Cabañas as an official troped and iconic body of history is significant—he is not celebrated through state institutional contexts because he embodies opposition to official governmental politics, even as social justice activists celebrate him.[5]

For director Faesler and these postmemory theatre experiments, Cabañas offered great potential for reactivating scenarios of material already worked on. Scenarios included: power struggles and resistance; militarization and discipline; school and family gatherings; and human fragility and precariousness. Through Cabañas, the practitioners created trans-temporal crossings connecting with the Mexican Revolution (through traces of Zapata); with sixteenth-century acts of colonization and conquest; and with present day lives in contemporary acts of resistance.

Translating from a palimpsest literary text

As a source for translating remains of Cabañas into embodied theatre practices, the text of Montemayor offered three key strategies:

- Montemayor engages a framework of postmemory and palimpsests. He uses fragments to re-imagine events, to examine questions of an official and truthful "history," and to analyse oppressed and militarized bodies. He generates layers of "truths" about bodies through an obvious plurality, generating juxtapositions between accounts of history. He does not reproduce well-documented official versions (it is not a "fact-based" account) but offers insights into repression suffered by activists, journalists and citizens, encompassing scenarios of power struggles, militarization and resistance. His performative writing strategies and aesthetics therefore enact textual re-visions of official narratives and versions of history.

- Montemayor interweaves two distinct dialogues: the "voices" of Cabañas and poor citizens and the "voices" of the Army and the State. Most significantly for theatre processes exploring cultural fictions and historical realities, these are not "real" dialogues re-produced from documented accounts, but interpretations and reconstructions crafted by the author. The literary text is already a translation of remains incorporating a dialogical and questioning strategy.

- Montemayor writes explicitly about bodies, describing the actions of Cabañas and the guerrillas, and the abuses and tortures perpetrated against the Indigenous people of Guerrero.

Figure 89.

Embodied archival-repertoires of rememory

In the environment of the theatre workshops these linguistic strategies and structures were translated into live body-based practices. The practitioners explored multiple viewpoints crossing cultural fictions and historical realities. They embodied concepts of duality and plurality and translated textual traces and remains of bodies into movements, gestures, spatialities and sonics. The participants particularly worked through familiar forms of embodied archival-repertoires, each with their own environments and contexts: marching: salsa-dancing and singing; protest chanting and fist-raising; and skipping. All these were experienced as forms of rememory connecting private and public experiences.

- *Marching* is a powerful trans-temporal and personal trace, connecting militarization (performing governmental counterinsurgency strategies) and school environments (in which children march and salute the national flag);
- *Salsa-dancing and singing* are ubiquitous actions repeated through popular and familial environments of communal sharing;
- *Protest chanting and fist-raising* offers a universal trace of vocal and gestural resistance; [6]
- *Skipping* evokes contexts of children who are playing with fun and abandon.

Archival objects

Using another familiar improvisational theatre strategy, two evocative objects were also used to stimulate re-imaginings and re-visions: the national flag and a balaclava:

National flag: As a profoundly weighty object, the national flag engages deeply embodied acts of control, power and conformity to state rules. The flag connects civic ceremonies with choreographed rituals of patriotism. It is used to generate embodied respect through a corporeal repertoire of movements and gestures, reiterated in schools and plazas each day, binding individuals to the united collective.

In workshops, the practitioners re-activated these scenarios. They improvised with national flags, drawing on rememory experiences of schools and civic ceremonies, seeking to perform re-visions of official uses. In one scenario they kneel on the floor cleaning the surface with the scrunched up flag. Even the flag itself was subverted, replacing the usual tricolour red, white and green with black and white, making obvious connections to the flag of anarchy (Figures 90 and 95).[7]

Balaclava: A balaclava—*un pasamontañas*—is a deeply evocative object. This distinctly multivalent and trans-temporal article has connotations of subversion and rebellion, covering heads of guerrillas and revolutionaries who stand up against oppressive state governmental structures.[8] As a form of dis-embodied archival object and powerful signifier, in twenty-first century Mexico it connects corporeal remains of Cabañas and his resistance to state oppression with contemporary movements for Indigenous and peasant rights. It is most specifically known as the face-camouflaging used by the Zapatista Army of National Liberation, creating an obvious trans-temporal connection to the Mexican Revolution and the (assassinated) body of Zapata. In the Zapatista Army, the knitted hood unifies women and men in their acts of struggle.[9]

In the theatre workshops, practitioners used this haunting and simple object to generate improvisations. They explored multiple viewpoints, experimenting with movement repertoires, gestures, poses, vocalizations and spatialities to perform fragile, youthful and defiant bodies (Figure 90).

Figure 90.

Performance of work-in-progress

Outline

Over the course of the three weeks the artists generated numerous fragments of individual and collective scenes. These were structured to create a dramaturgical collage for the final showing of work-in-progress. Throughout the performance, all the participants are clearly visible, offering a shared environment of inclusion. They wear easy-to-move-in workshop clothes (T-shirts, tracksuits and jogging pants) drawing attention to their reiterated gestures and movements. The audience, seated in rows facing the stage in the proscenium arch theatre space, are incorporated into the theatre piece through overt interactive strategies.

Performance examples

Scenario of discipline

A voice shouts a command, and twenty-five bodies form a circle, one-behind-another, facing clockwise around the stage. The limitations of the space constrain them. On another command they all start to jog forwards in unison at a steady pace in the circle—one two, one two, one two (left-forward, right-forward, left-forward, right-forward). Their bodies are in a tight formation, disciplined and in unity.

With another shouted command the pace quickens, as the twenty-five bodies jog faster, still in tight formation in the circle. With another shouted command—"backwards!"—the circle comes to a momentary pause, before continuing the one two, one two, one two, now moving backwards (left-back, right-back, left-back, right-back), in the same circular formation, awkwardly knocking into each other.

A voice shouts a command—"formation!"—and five people run to take up positions at the front of the stage, equidistant from each other, and the twenty remaining bodies form lines behind. Panting and exhausted, they begin to march—one two, one two, one two. Facing forward, bodies in parallel, straight and upright, with straightforward pelvises, they chant as they march.

Another shouted command, and the pelvises of twenty-five bodies shift from side to side, their feet stepping to the right side, centre, to the left side, centre, marking a salsa dance step, as the chanting merges into singing. They raise their right arm high, with a fist held in resistance. (Figures 88, 89 and 91).

In this unfolding scene, these seemingly simple movements, spatial formations, gestures and vocalizations perform multiple remains of Cabañas. Traces of disciplined, military, schooled, social and resisting bodies are juxtaposed, layered and merged. The simultaneity and accumulations transform easy interpretation into complexity and contradiction. The intertwining, intertextual and intertextural qualities create trans-temporal re-visions.

- *Marching bodies* perform a deeply trans-temporal form of embodied archival repertoire, reiterating movements of myriad scenarios of battles and wars. These are choreographies of allegiance to a state, performing homogeneity, discipline and compliance, and seeking to unify all individual bodies into a single confirming collective. Marching bodies are also childhood bodies, institutionalized in schools where children march and salute the flag. These movements are straight, forward and rigid.

- *Social dancing bodies* perform a familiar and multi-generational repertoire of fiestas and celebratory environments. These movements are twisting and flowing.

- *Resisting bodies with a raised fist* perform a simple hand-gesture as a reiterated trace of incalculable bodies resisting in the face of oppression. A raised fist of defiance connects bodies through centuries and through geographies. It is a corporeal gesture of solidarity, support, defiance and strength.

- *Running backwards* performs a symbolic movement of bodies that seem to be moving against the grain, struggling and re-tracing steps by moving in reverse rather than turning around. This choreographic deconstruction seems uncomfortable as "militarized" bodies quickly become struggling bodies.

Figure 91.

Through this scene, the movement and vocal forms are merged and layered, as one flows into another: a marching body transforms into a dancing body as the military lines are subverted, and the straightforward body is playfully queered. A solid pelvis and rigid parallel marching legs amalgamate with a hip swing, twist and a sexualized pelvis, to create plural intertexts and intertextures.[10]

Scenario of resistance

A tall man shuffles to the centre of the stage, bends and picks up the black knitted balaclava lying on the floor.
He pulls the knitted mask slowly over his head, covering his face and finding the tiny holes for his eyes and mouth.
He breathes heavily. With arms dangling, and legs gangly, he begins to slowly skip around inside the circle.
He skips round and round, faster and faster, moving closer then farther away. He skips round and round, round and round.
Suddenly he stops skipping and stands – motionless.
(Figures 6 and 92).

This skipping, masked body performs remains of Cabañas by incorporating traces of childhood and resistance. Skipping is an embodied repertorial archive of childhood and innocence: a "just because" movement for the delight and the sensation of living itself. The combination of intense and persistent almost threatening skipping

Figure 92.

performed by a tall adult body camouflaged and masked by a balaclava offers a complex palimpsest body that is simultaneously powerful, defiant, resistant and hopeful.

Scenario of revolution

A young woman strides to the centre of the stage with a schoolbag, from which she unpacks an apple, other food and a towel. She speaks, conversationally and dialogically, to herself and to everyone around. She speaks as "I, Lucio."
She positions the towel on the ground, she places the top of her head on the towel and pushes herself into a headstand, then a handstand. Her hands are now in the place of her feet. She continues speaking as "I, Lucio," as she holds her body erect yet inverted. (Figure 93).

Through this poetic solo scene, the balancing body of the young woman performs traces of Cabañas as a precarious, revolutionary, inverted, strong and risk-taking body. As she speaks the words of Cabañas in the first person—"I, Lucio"— she voices a call to action to stand up against the government. She performs a plurality of presences voicing "I" of Cabañas through her own balancing body. Through rememory of childhood games, the young woman merges Cabañas' body with her own, in a state of plurality, fragility and liminality, through balancing, destabilization and literal inversion.[11]

Figure 93.

Scenario of institutional duplicity

All twenty-five performers face the public directly. They walk straight forward purposefully in one line to the front of the stage. They sit with their legs over the edge, close to the front row of the audience. Each one looks at individuals in the audience, focusing their gaze. One by one, the performers begin to clap and applaud and shout "Bravo! Bravo!"
The lights go on in the auditorium and some of the public begin to join in the action of applause. Before long, everybody is clapping: the public are applauding the performers on stage, as the performers continue to applaud the audience, looking at them intently.
Suddenly, the performers speak to the audience: "Well done Senator!"
One by one the performers stand up, turn their backs on the audience and move back into the stage space. (Figure 94).

By incorporating the individuals of the audience in an action of duplicity and complicity, this scene performs traces of Cabañas, through experiences of deception and fraud. Everybody

Figure 94.

in the theatre becomes aware of the betrayal and trickery. The simplicity of walking, sitting and applauding seems to conform to the standard conventional protocol, signalling to the audience how they should respond. Yet, just at the moment when the public has been drawn in, they realize that they have been duped into becoming complicit. The simple phrase, "well done Senator" transforms the relationship. The public has unwittingly become "the Senator"—the body in and of power-making decisions. These movements of convention deconstruct and destabilize an embodied custom to perform an unfixing of truth and trust.

Scenario of transgression

A woman lies on the floor at the front of the stage. She wraps a flag around her face, covering her face entirely—the flag is the subverted national flag: black in place of green.
She begins to roll across the stage, her body rolling over and over and over.
She rolls to the front, coming perilously close to the edge…she rolls toward a row of feet of performers standing at the side of the stage…she rolls to the back of the stage reaching the solid wall.
Gradually she brings herself to her knees; then to a standing position.
Her hands are flattened against the back wall, feeling the hard surface, reaching and groping with the palms of her hands up the wall. (Figure 95).

In this intense scene, one rolling and reaching body performs an unsettling and precarious journey, re-membering Cabañas as a haunting of death and torture, and as seeking and searching for something. As the young woman covers her face with an altered national flag, she seems to be undertaking simultaneous actions of resistance, transgression, blinding and

Figure 95.

shrouding. The recognizable yet transformed national flag merges national heroes with radical resistance. The body does not salute or stand to attention, but rolls forwards, sideways and backwards around the space, almost falling, and eventually using the solidity of the wall to reach upwards. The body journeys across the floor making multiple crossings, yet no footprints and no visible traces remain. Through her movements, she is re-membering bodies of disappeared activists and performing profound re-visions of national narratives of forgetting.

Scenario of fragility

The twenty-five performers stroll, walk, amble and meander around the stage. They create wandering paths, some moving faster, some slower. Some cluster together, then move on. They detach items of clothing: a T-shirt is removed revealing a bare chest or breasts; a shirt is removed to reveal a bra; all clothes are removed to reveal a bare body. As they walk they gently slap their hands on their bodies, generating a light sonic of multi-rhythmic beats and pulses. (Figure 96).

Through these unfolding traces, these bodies combine poetic re-imaginings of postmemory trauma and deeply embodied experiences of rememory. Uncovering skin and tapping skin performs visual and sonic traces of the materiality of bodies. The exterior, outer layer of a body is made evident, and the interior layers beneath the skin are resonant with possibilities. The bearing of flesh offers expressions of innocence and birth, connecting human bodies through time. As adult bodies, they co-exist with traces of the broken bodies of the massacred, tortured and disappeared bodies and with remains of Cabañas. As the performers quietly walk around and touch the skin of their own body they are not re-enacting violences done to bodies, but performing a collective and ethical response and a re-imagining. Gentle touching and sounding of bare flesh performs an intense re-membering.

Reflections on remains: Performing palimpsest bodies

Through the framework of this intensive project, twenty-five practitioners performed multiple re-imaginings of collective and personal memories. In an atmosphere of a transitory creative community they worked with a difficult relationship of postmemory through the body of history of Cabañas, aware of their own daily lives in contexts of continued repressions and injustices. As a response to and re-vision of these pasts and environments, they generated powerfully poetic scenes, translating and transforming remains of Cabañas. Together, they experimented with scenarios of resistance, conviviality and power relations to create a complexity and density of traces.

Through these traces, Cabañas is re-visioned as plural and trans-temporal, crossing multiple boundaries and connecting individuals and collectives. The absence of scenery, furniture and specific lighting generates a sharp focus on the twenty-five bodies, proposing deep connections to recent (and continuing) traumas of bodies that are tortured and disappeared. In this dynamic environment, and through unfolding scenarios with marching, dancing, chanting, singing and running bodies, rigid narratives are destabilized and disciplined bodies are queered. Through experiences of rememory, these bodies perform expressions from deep within, half remembering and half forgetting. Childhood fears and joys emerge through bodies that balance, roll, laugh and skip. As an inverted and balancing body of childhood articulates political words and speaks as "I, Lucio," she precariously re-imagines possibilities. As a balaclava-wearing body skips around a circle, he connects childhood and resistance. As a rotating body rolls across the floor, her face covered by a subverted façade of democracy, she forms unpredictable yet transgressive journeys. As twenty-five bodies meander, meet and tenderly touch bare flesh, they confront institutional amnesia and offer their bodies as sights/sites for creating ethical and supportive communities.

Figure 96.

Chapter 6

Time of the Devil

Trans-solo, one body, many body parts

Deliberations

In the course of this solo theatre work, performer Clarissa Malheiros leads herselves and her audiences on an intensely corporeal and philosophical trans-temporal journey exploring existential questions of life.[1] The core body of history is inherently connected with death yet is not a dead body. The body is, in essence, a conceptual no-body, a spectral and mythical body, deeply embodied in collective memories and histories—the Devil. Frequently gendered as "masculine," but simultaneously phantasmagorical, the Devil is a spectral body of hauntology: neither absent nor present, neither dead nor alive, an anybody and a no body. Remains of the Devil exist as iconic corporeal forms and ephemeral ideas, invoking the question: "What remains of human bodies?"

Figure 97.

At the heart of *Time of the Devil* are embodied theatre experiments with postmemory. If postmemory is a traumatic relationship between present and past, mediated by imaginative creations for a future, then all humans encounter this relationship.[2] Postmemory incorporates the trauma of death and the ever-present presences of living with the "end of living"—a universal, inescapable quality of humanness. Rememory is performed as experiences of fear and unknowingness. Scenarios of material already worked on reactivate autopsies of life and shifts in perspectives.

Within a theatrical context of open dialogue and inquiry, Malheiros generates multiple traces of dead bodies and body parts. In this exquisite and playful trans performance, one live body on stage interacts with life-size death masks and a headless miniature body-form in an environment of bodily remains. She balances, twists and poses. She walks around the auditorium inviting her public to reflect on their futures with fortune cookies. She constructs her selves by layering her body with masculine formal wear, transfiguring her face with a beard and moustache. As she dialogues with herselves and her audience, she speaks a continual intertwining thread of multiple texts crossing two millennia, incorporating colloquial, scholarly and religious words.

From the density of this full-length work I have selected six fragments of scenarios for my brief discussion. I use my own descriptive titles for these scenarios and engage a fragmented poetic form.

Remains of the Devil

Selves, dialogue, duality

In twenty-first century Mexico forms of the Devil are very present, expressed in visual images, linguistic codes and ritual acts. This iconic no-body is depicted with a red, masculine human-mythical body, transmuted into a fantastical figure with wings and horns. This form appears on the card of "El Diablito" in the popular game of *loteria* and is theatricalized in street performances during passion plays.[3] Within sacred and corporeal rituals of Catholic mass, believers consume the body of Christ in wafer form to ensure their afterlife, performing duality with the presence of the Devil.[4]

In the theatre experiments of La Máquina, these "remains" are translated into theological words; into iconic wooden objects co-existing with death masks; and into the sharing of fortune cookies. Malheiros' original idea for this scenic experiment came from her fascination with the short novel *Time of the Devil* by Portuguese writer, philosopher and poet Fernando Pessoa.[5] In his work Pessoa uses two concepts that offer great potential for embodied practices connecting with dialogue and duality. Firstly, his novel is written as a dialogue between the Devil and Mary (mother of Jesus). The dialogical structure translates into the structure of the performance. In one long dramaturgical flow, Malheiros dialogues with herselves and her spectators in an obvious environment of convivio—*with* the audience. Through vocal texts, movements, gestures, spatialities and objects she sifts through viewpoints, perspectives and possibilities, as she assembles and reassembles concepts. She embraces both stage and auditorium, walking into and around the audience.

Secondly, in his novel, Pessoa conceives of the Devil as duality, as interstitial, between what life is and what life is not. Embodying these dual and interstitial forms, and reflecting Pessoa's own writing and sense of "selves," Malheiros generates multiple in-between and both/and forms. She performatively constructs her identities and interacts with body parts. She plays with death masks and carries a little double body-form. As the performance unfolds, her palimpsest body is always multiple and complex, containing repeats and reiterations of trans-temporal remains and traces.

Malheiros also draws on writing by three other authors spanning fifteen centuries. She speaks fragments of texts as she sets up complex linguistic juxtapositions and accumulations. She merges early Christian words of theologian and philosopher San Agustín of Hippo

(354–430 AD) with philosophical and journalistic ideas of Vilém Flusser (twentieth-century philosopher and journalist) and contemporary poetic forms of Mexican experimental dramaturge Cecilia Lemus.[6] As Malheiros speaks and combines traces of many literary texts, her body unfolds multiple movement traces, poses and gestures. She shifts from familiar everyday embodiments of walking to highly choreographed forms of physicality. She holds poses for reflection and contemplation before transforming into a dance with life-size death masks. In the dark space, large metallic containers emit intense blue shafts of light connecting floor and ceiling to create an architectonic environment of apparitions. The shifting illuminations offer experiences of waves of (in)tangible spectral presences. White paper bundles reveal traces of bodies. Simple wooden boards suggest shifting perspectives and little red devil-bodies inhabit the space in which Malheiros dances with death.

Performance examples

Scenario of constructing a material body

Malheiros walks onto the stage talking to the audience and to herselves simultaneously. She wears a crisp white men's formal shirt, seemingly of a previous century.

She walks off the stage as she continues talking about philosophical questions of life...

She walks onto the stage continuing to talk to the audience and herselves. Now, she wears a pair of men's black formal trousers, seemingly of a previous century.

She walks out of the space again...and then returns.

She sits on the floor facing the audience as she puts on black lace-up boots, continuing with her provocative musings...

She walks off the stage again...and then returns...she puts on a waistcoat...then a dinner jacket...then a tie...

She walks off the stage again...and returns with facial hair.[7] (Figure 98).

The everyday actions of dressing and arranging hair are very familiar. Yet, one by one, the layers of clothes and hair transform the body, opening up questions of bodies, identities and memories: What traces of the "original" remain? Who is this person? What is this body? What is identity? What is the truth? The performativity is obvious, through alterations of temporality and gendering: clothes shift her identity to a former time and a trans gender (is she Pessoa?). Despite the visual transformations, her voice remains unaltered.[8]

Together, her body and her voice perform fluidity, liminality and plurality, with interstitial and subversive elements. Two forms of reiteration and accumulation generate complex palimpsest traces through performative concepts. She physicalizes and vocalizes constructions of truth, identity, materiality, humanness and remains. As she walks in and out, in and out,

Figure 98.

she traces and retraces her journey: a journey that is exquisite in its normality and simplicity. As she talks about philosophical and ontological matters of life, her reiterated movements of walking and dressing produce an environment of shared normalcy. Looking directly at the seated audience, she creates an atmosphere of convivio and preparation, inviting everybody to begin a collective journey through life's most enduring corporeal uncertainties.

Scenario of perspectives

Malheiros carries a bundle of simple wooden sticks (bones?). As she talks, she places one stick on the ground. She takes a few steps and places another…then another…then another. All the time, she continues voicing philosophical questions and musings.

In a real-time action, Malheiros embodies concepts of connecting through time. In the dim light and shadows, the wooden sticks almost seem to be human bones. As she begins to place the first sticks on the ground, her task is unclear. There is no sense of order or form.

Then, little by little, one after another, the accumulation generates a pattern. She assembles a distinct pathway, created from small fragments. It seems that one piece is connected to another to generate one continuous, unbroken path. Yet, each piece is only connected to the others by the solidity of the floor and the flowing stream of vocalizing.

Walking on the stage floor, Malheiros retraces her steps to the first plank.

Slowly and very cautiously, she steps with great trepidation onto the first wooden plank, swaying as she tries to find her balance and sense of equilibrium. She has her back to the audience.

She then steps onto the next plank…and the next. She treads carefully away from audience on her constructed bridge-like route, on the flat and horizontal stage floor. Her body moves as if balancing, as if precarious, as if she might fall…into a precipice far below. (Figure 99).

Through this graceful choreography of straightforward walking, her body offers a challenge to perceptions and constructions of truth and perspectives. As she walks away from the audience, her body gradually transforms in position, so that the horizontal "bridge" seems to become a vertical "ladder." The plane seems to shift from horizontal to vertical, yet the

Figure 99.

only alteration is her corporeal movement of walking. [9] Her moving and speaking body performs both/and viewpoints that transform through the poetic unfolding of the scenario.

Scenario of fate

Malheiros walks off the stage into the auditorium. She carries a large bag full of fortune cookies.

She moves to the front row, inviting each person to take one of the little objects. She chats to the audience in a familiar way. The bag is passed around the audience and everybody reaches inside to extract a cookie. Some open their cookie and read the writing on the tiny piece of paper inside. One after another, Malheiros invites individuals to read their writing aloud and asks them if they believe it will happen. (Figure 100).

These collective actions perform re-visions of sacred and official narratives of guilt and fear in a performative environment of playful transgression. As Malheiros moves from the stage into the auditorium, her speaking shifts from intensely poetic to everyday colloquial. She performs the role of officiate, offering participation in a hallowed ritual. As she tenders the tiny objects, she subverts a sacrosanct ritual. These little edible objects become subversive iterations of the ritual of a Christian mass and the expectations of futurity, transforming the certainty of taking a

Figure 100.

"host" as the body of Christ to receive eternal life. The bag of fortune cookies contains multiple possibilities for future selves.[10] As each person takes a cookie and reads the words they are all incorporated into postmemory theatre experiments through the question of "what remains?"

Scenario of body parts (1) (body-less heads)

Malheiros carries a large, bulky bundle of "things" wrapped in white paper, which she deposits on the floor.

She gradually unfolds the paper.

She reveals and removes a life-size head, which she sets on the floor. The head is white with facial features and closed-eye indentations. The face seems to be staring out.

She returns to the bundle and removes another head, resting it on the floor.

Then another head…and another head…and another head.

As she voices ontological questions about life, death and materiality, Malheiros plays with the heads, carrying them around and placing them on the floor. She picks up heads, talks with them and walks with them.

She places one over her own face. (Figures 101 and 102).

Figure 101.

Figure 102.

As Malheiros poses and gestures with these death masks, she performs an unfolding and reiterative contemplation of remains. Death masks are "remains" of bodies and are body-less life-size heads. Each face is distinctive, made by encasing a face in a plaster cast following death. They are useful mementos of the dead, used to generate life-like artistic replications of the dead body. Now, in the theatre space, deposited on the stage floor, they appear as sculptural lifeless forms. These objects lead to questions: Whose faces are these? Are they death masks? Are they life masks of living bodies?[11]

As Malheiros places a death mask face over her own face she generates an obvious palimpsest, transforming her body and trying out death, generating an intense moment of corporeal plurality, in-betweenness and liminality.

Scenario of body parts (2) (headless bodies)

Malheiros carries a small grey headless body-form. She connects it to her own body and carries the body on her journey around the space.

She places her head where the head should be. She places the body's feet on the wooden planks and guides the body through the space. (Figure 103).

As a performance of obvious doubleness and haunting, this tiny body moves with Malheiros' body. She plays with this headless body, performing choreographies and vocalities of seeking; questioning; journeying; and balancing. The little body has solid form, yet needs to

174

Figure 103.

be supported and carried. It appears as a load and constant evocation of materiality: Is this what remains? Is this what we carry with us? Is this our burden?

Scenario of bodies as repertorial archives…in-between…caught in the middle

Malheiros picks up one of the scattered white paper sheets.

She places her face into it, covering her face completely.

She seems to move forward, yet her body is motionless and the paper is motionless—a sculptural form that seems to flow backward, as if blown by the winds of time…(Figure 104).

With this conclusion of postmemory theatre experiments exploring the ever-present presences of living with the "end of living," Malheiros's palimpsest body offers an appropriately complex performance. Her pose is one of a body caught in-between, in a moment of movement and transformation. Her body appears to be headless, yet the paper-form indicates movement. Her face is layered and superimposed by a paper mask as a shroud of death. Her body remains in an in-between state of subjunctivity, remaining with no fixed answers but multiple possibilities. The trans-temporal performative existential questions of life and death cease as Malheiros fixes herselves in a corporeal and vocal state of liminal contingency.

Reflections on remains: Performing palimpsest bodies

Time of the Devil is an intensely convivial work of stimulating performance. In an atmosphere of playful provocation, Malheiros enables audiences to engage with multiple viewpoints and to challenge their potential fears. With flowing choreographic and vocalized aesthetics, she positions ideas for everybody to consider. She performs re-visions of beliefs and knowledge to generate an accumulation of traces. Through relationships of postmemory, Malheiros re-imagines perspectives. Through relationships of rememory, she tentatively assembles her pathway and balances precariously. She reactivates scenarios of unknown after-life and of ritual beliefs. She poses questions time and again, inviting spectators to reflect on their potential futures contained inside a fortune cookie.

As she layers clothes onto her body and articulates metaphysical concepts, she constructs and transforms herselves in full view of the audience, queering time and her material body to generate plurality and liminality. As she speaks to and with herselves, she performs her own interstitial in-betweenness. As she places wooden sticks on the floor and alters her positionality, she plays with perception, generating possible conduits and stepladders. As she superimposes her own face with the faces of death masks she seems to rehearse her own death. As she organizes and re-organizes remains of dead bodies, she models possibilities and options within an environment of remains. In an environment of coexistence she seems to dance with death and vocalize life through her archival-repertorial body. Through these palimpsest bodies, Malheiros performs traces of an atemporal no-body and trans-temporal traces of every-body. These complex practices of Malheiros offer an interactive and spirited exploration of existential questions of life, translating and transforming collective anxieties and memories into a playful unfolding of poetic presences.

Figure 104.

Epilogue

Theatre for generating futures: Performing archives, remaining differently

> In a corporeal sense, the so-called past is neither gone nor actual, it is neither exactly accumulative nor does it simply vanish – the body intertwines imagination, memory, sensorial perception, and actuality in very sophisticated ways. The body itself moves according to these intertwinements while permanently producing new mnemonic, sensorial, actual, and imaginative connections that generate movement. In a corporeal sense, the past is a becoming.
> —Eleonora Fabião, "History and Precariousness"

> Our work as critics [...] [involves] the task of locating what traces of the past linger in the present and devising strategies to move more humanely toward the future.
> —Roselyn Costantino

> As the noted cognitive neuroscientist Michael Gazzaniga once said: "everything in life is memory, save for the thin edge of the present."
> —Joseph Jebelli, "We can cure Alzheimer's"[1]

experiment: try out new concepts or ways of doing things [verb]; a course of action tentatively adopted without being sure of the eventual outcome [noun].

Scenario of becoming

At the end of *Time of the Devil*, Malheiros strikes a pose of in-between potentialities. Her palimpsest body is an archival repertoire of remains, envisioning traces of myriad existential questions about the materiality life as she buries her face with the covering of death masks. At the beginning of *Mexican Trilogy*, Malheiros moves slowly forward, voicing myths of

Figure 105.

origins and time. Her unfolding palimpsest body is a repertorial archive of remains, revealing hidden fragments of stories as she is accompanied by two spectral shadow-bodies who journey with her (Figure 105). In these complex multifaceted works by La Máquina de Teatro, remains become opportunities for re-imaginings. Performing remains of bodies of history in live transdisciplinary theatre offers multiple possibilities. To draw on Gabriel Yépez, these are "works that articulate a relation between the body as a holder of collective memory and as an unfolding of poetic presences."[2] Through performing palimpsest bodies in postmemory theatre experiments the past is a becoming.[3]

In this brief Epilogue I retrace key elements of these performances as I gesture to the future. I return again to Diana Taylor's work on archives, repertoires and performing cultural memory, reiterating her depiction of a "collaborative production of knowledge [in which] writing and embodied performance have often worked together to layer the historical memories that constitute community."[4] Together, the embodied performances of La Máquina and these writings work to constitute community. Through these remains you are connected with traces of Faesler and Malheiros; with all with the many artists and audiences involved with their projects; and with the bodies of history incorporated into these projects. Your body is a palimpsest of collective memories and an unfolding of poetic presences.

Performing remains/performance remains[5]

For this study, I have engaged the notion of palimpsest bodies as a creative-interpretive idea for performing remains of bodies of history in postmemory theatre experiments. A palimpsest always contains trans-temporal traces, offering a form of plurality and dynamic tension. A palimpsest body re-members embodied gestures, vocalized calls and sensory experiences that resonate from deep within. Through these palimpsest bodies, matters of originals and copies are thrown into an intricate entanglement.[6] Through relationships of postmemory and through corporeal traces of rememory, these palimpsest bodies re-imagine other ways of being. Through experiments with disparate remains, these bodies perform productive tensions and missed encounters. Schneider has described how "theories of trauma and repetition [...] instruct us [that] it is not presence that appears in performance but precisely the missed encounter – the reverberations of the overlooked, the missed, the repressed, the seemingly forgotten."[7] In Hirsch's concept of postmemory, past traumas are understood as fragments of stories, repeated, projected and re-imagined. In Morrison's notion of rememory, past traumas of half-forgotten occurrences are experienced in corporeal traces. By reactivating scenarios through remains of bodies of history, these palimpsest bodies offer possibilities for forming reverberations of the overlooked, the missed, the repressed, and the seemingly forgotten.

In discussions of performing corporeality in Mexico, Antonio Prieto Stambaugh has considered how embodied performances resist amnesia and unsettle memories. He describes how "the memory of the creators, and in some cases also the spectators, is embodied in different ways indicating a staging of the intimate or secret subjectivity."[8] Reiterating Yépez, these works perform a relation between the body as a holder of collective memory and as an unfolding of poetic presences. At the heart of these performance projects of La Máquina, participants use personal and collective experiences of rememory to inquire into bodies of history, offering great potential to unsettle memories and stage intimate stories. It is through the trans-temporal crossings of multiple remains that these corporeal processes

Figure 106.

181

delve into difficult questions that confront official knowledge. As they reactivate scenarios of material already worked on they connect shared histories and personal subjectivities through palimpsest bodies. Returning to the words of choreographer Shobana Jeyasingh, a palimpsest has the "capacity to be home to more than one story at any given time. The surface of things resonates with the secrets of the unknown possibilities."[9] In workshops and performances, the practitioners of La Máquina play with time through simultaneity, co-existence, multiplicity and juxtaposition. They merge and accumulate iterations of numerous stories, histories, journeys and lives. Through liminal performance and postdramatic theatre strategies they perform layered, plural and trans identities. Through their rigorous and playful processes of collective creation, they cross cultural fictions and historical realities to generate unexpected tensions.

Analysing the potential of live performance, Peggy Phelan has explained that "Performance remains a compelling art because it contains the possibility of both the actor and the spectator becoming transformed during the event's unfolding."[10] Drawing on Jill Dolan's discussions of theatre and utopia, these performances "offer a place to scrutinize public meanings [and] also to embody and [...] enact the affective possibilities of 'doings' that gesture toward a much better world."[11] In the projects of La Máquina, through the pulsating sensory environment of live performance and within a social framework of collective memory, these multifaceted, provocative bodies invite and challenge spectators and participants to embrace an aesthetic of multiplicity and openness to dynamic relationships. Through an environment of convivio, they engage "a politics of invitation, [and] a politics of community."[12] From multi-year processes leading to finalized theatre performances, to ongoing processes of work-in-progress, to co-participatory performative events on stage, these projects facilitate poetic unfoldings with the potential to transform. Seeking to confront and transform stereotypes, they offer feminist and queer re-visions of official histories and collective memories. As bodies make gestures, read words, strike poses, sing songs and stand witness they are engaged in and with incomplete pasts, unfolding and folding time, performing unfixity and possibility.[13]

Figure 107.

Four reflections

1. *Mexican Trilogy / Scenic Correlation of Memory and Times*

La Malinche does not have time: the past and present are running simultaneously through our history. Yesterday's La Malinche is in today's women, not with the stigma of a traitor, but like a metaphor of multiplicity of Mexican women.
—Estela Leñero Franco, "Malinche/Malinches," *Revista Proceso*

With an ensemble of five performers and a small group of creative artists, this complex set of inter-connected theatre pieces was generated over three years working through three bodies of history. For Part 1, the Poet-King Nezahualcóyotl provided a rich source of remains for inquires into present predicaments of political leadership and sources of wisdom, offering the potential for reactivating scenarios of governance, of poetic responses, and of hope. For Parts 2 and 3 the artists looked to Mexico's deepest traumas: invasion, violation, domination, and conquest. Through remains of the bodies of history of Moctezuma II and La Malinche they reactivated scenarios of encounter, power, control, domesticity, complicity, knowledge, destruction, trust and compassion. Over the course of the trilogy, the stage space is transformed into an archival-repertorial container of texturalized traces, connecting individual and collective bodies and memories through multiple centuries. The five bodies are always performing plurality, co-existing in the transforming Valley of Mexico over six hundred years.

In Part 1, as a model of diversity, five differently painted bodies covered in knitted-painted clothes appear and disappear through tiny spaces, performing fragments of stories and lives. They speak of the origins of time, of losing memory, and of forgetting where home is; they voice philosophical poetic words of Nezahualcóyotl as a twenty-first century leader; they move together and unite for one brief moment, re-constructing the stone body of Coatlicue; and they guide, support and enfold one another as Mesoamerican wisdom carries contemporary uncertainties.

In Part 2, as a model of questioning truth and as resistance to institutional amnesia, five archival-dust-covered-labouring bodies assemble and reassemble constructions of accounts of history and formations of grey bricks, speaking fragments of "true history" as "I am/he was." Two layered bodies reactivate and queer the scenario of encounter: they stand face to face, reaching out hands to caress faces, their bodies superimposed with painted faces and body parts. Five bodies speak and fall together on a single layer of bricks containing massacred bodies 448 years apart.

In Part 3, as a hard-hitting, bitter-sweet confrontation of gendered violence and questions of "knowledge," five bodies sit and embroider, clothed in identical grey masculine shop-bought business suits. They vocalize personal I-stories of autobiographical subjectivities. They generate knowledge and history as La Malinche. One non-speaking, yet hyper-communicating body witnesses everybody. La Malinche speaks truth to power,

Figure 108.

uttering Nobel-prize-winning Paz's accusatory words. She plays with an action-man doll, wringing out his tiny plastic body. Through the sheer diversity of "remains" these five bodies incorporate myriad fragments of texts, gestures and vocalizations. They transform them into a complex accumulation of layers, sedimentations and iterations to provoke and challenge. As they gesture and speak florid poetry, as they chant lists of names and strike poses, as they embroider and tell intimate I-stories, these complex bodies perform the past as a becoming, re-imagining possibilities within a deeply convivial environment of shared inquiries (Figure 108).

2. *Zapata, Death Without End*

Over the course of a year, five diverse theatre collectives from disparate regions of Mexico collaborated, at distance and in person, to explore remains of one body of history—Emiliano Zapata, one of Mexico's most troped and iconic revolutionary figures. Three questions and a poetic phrase formed scenarios of material already worked on: —"What is the value of land?"—"What is liberty?"—"What is a hero?" — "Death without end." On a theatre stage in Mexico City, the public joined with the five ensembles of performers, sharing the space throughout a co-participatory unfolding performance event. The empty space was transformed into a dynamic archival-repertorial container of plurality, connecting Zapata with everyday lives in Tampico, Guadalajara, Mérida, Oaxaca and Mexico City. Semi-improvised, fully rehearsed and collective participatory scenes were held together in a palimpsest dramaturgical structure, enabling inclusivity, convivio and relajo. Incorporating deliberate interweaving and accumulation of stories, lives and experiences, the project engaged an open- and multi-layered structure of playfulness and community.

Figure 109.

For this project, remains encompassed a wide range of forms: everyday objects, songs, stones, sensory experiences and food; the iconic photo of Zapata's dead body; handfuls and sackfuls of earth and soil; a children's action song; a rebozo as a symbolic gendered container of life; a tortilla press and egg-boxes; and mangoes, mezcal and shrimp stew. Trans-temporal crossings tied profoundly impactful public national events with intimate private everyday lives. Remains of Zapata connected the Revolution of 1910 to the dirty war of 1960s and 70s, to sixteenth-century Spanish conquest and destruction, to the "now" of rights movements, transnational drug-traffickers and neo-liberal capitalism.

Using inclusive aesthetics, from everyday eating to extreme physicality, performers and spectators generated emotive responses and re-visions. As everybody knelt on the floor, writing names on stones and voicing personal stories around a prone body, they created re-visions of heroes through everyday lives. As four bodies constructed an entangled, electrified egg-box city of great fragility and executed rhythmic and nationalistic footwork of zapateado, they fabricated an immersive and poetic environment of contradictions. As an adult-child body was held high "in the arms of an assassin," repeating her rememory experience in the arms of the President, she performed resistance to official forgetting. As everybody joined in throwing darts at black balloons, hearing accounts of unjust land-use and drinking mezcal, they were embroiled in complicated practices of complicity. As a kneeling woman tried again and again to crush stones in a tortilla press she posed an uncomfortable reiteration of frustration. As everybody sang with hushed voices forming tiny houses in the space, they joined in a reflective action of contemplation. As three bodies moved in three freshly-formed mounds of earth, their galloping, twisting and rotating bodies were transformed by the earth and simultaneously transformed the earth. As individuals voiced stories of their everyday joys and struggles, marking their faces with wet earth and passing grains of soil from hand to hand, they created an interweaving fabric of intimate lives. As three bodies chatted and cooked a meal, they offered resistance to an environment of transnational drug-crime.

In the final scenario of *Zapata, Death Without End*, the co-mingling mass of multi-ensemble performers and spectators shared a freshly cooked meal on the theatre stage. Under the bright lights of the stage, the habitual and necessary everyday act of eating is transformed into a convivial collective action. Through remains of Zapata, in a corporeal sense, the past is a becoming (Figure 109).

3. *War in Paradise*

For three weeks, twenty-five practitioners generated deeply poetic embodied re-imaginings of frustration, duplicity, resistance and control through postmemory theatre experiments. They translated traces of rememory experiences of childhood play, school discipline, national allegiance, social environments and street protests to reactivate scenarios of precariousness and materiality. At the heart of the project was the body of history of Lucio Cabañas, the social activist and resistance leader who was assassinated in 1974 on government orders. In this documentary workshop project, the participants were seeking to explore creative processes through the intertextual novel of Montemayor. They experimented with compelling objects, movements, vocal repertoires and gestures—a balaclava, subverted national flags, marching, singing, balancing and fist raising. Creating temporal crossings they connected recent pasts with the Mexican Revolution, with sixteenth-century conquest, and with present-day social justice movements and increased militarization.

In the public performance of work-in-progress on stage in Mexico City, the twenty-five bodies articulated intensely moving and ethical reactivations of scenarios of repression and resistance. For the duration of the live event, as they marched, balanced, rotated, vocalized chants and sang songs, they performed an accumulation of trans-temporal remains. Merging

186

militarized, schooled, social and resisting bodies they unfixed and queered environments of control. One inverted body declared a call to action as "I, Lucio," balancing precariously yet firmly on her hands. Everybody proclaimed, "I am Lucio," generating a plurality of subjectivities in the "now" of the theatre action, simultaneously inhabiting and envisioning the "now" of complex, everyday lives. One body began to roll across the stage floor, her face layered and covered with a subverted and transgressive national flag. Her rolling, shrouded body came precariously close to the edge of the stage before gently shifting direction, creating multiple unpredictable journeys. twenty-five bodies sat on the front of the stage facing and applauding the public, confronting empty gestures of dishonesty. These same bodies stood with fists raised, repeating a trans-geopolitical gesture of power struggles and solidarity, uniting with countless bodies in resistance and executing possibilities. They wandered in curving paths, gently tapping naked skin in supportive encounters, performing acts of re-membering bodies tortured and disappeared. Through tender meandering movements and dynamic embodied reverberations, this transitory community of artists generated an unsettling of memories and resistance to official amnesia through performing palimpsest bodies (Figure 110).

Death and dying: What remains?
Of course, these theatre experiments with remains of bodies of history inherently contain dead bodies. Scenarios of death and scenarios of dying—material worked on incalculable times—are repeatedly reactivated and echoed. Significantly, though, these postmemory theatre processes translate remains of dead bodies into creative projections and potentiality.[14] Here, then, in a corporeal sense the past is a becoming. These bodies are archival sites for "critical reflection and contestation."[15] Through repetitions of traces in palimpsest bodies, trans-temporal remains of dead bodies offer possibilities for transformation.

Figure 110.

In *Mexican Trilogy* Nezahualcóyotl's death is formed with a tiny body-object, cradled in the arms of the trans-body, girl-deity-Diana, who voices death and wears the necklace of cempasuchil flowers—a collective ritual for those no-longer-living. Both bodies are enfolded in cloth and carried gently away. The death of Moctezuma is vocalized as a sensory account of the smell of burning flesh. Performers sit around the base of the grey-brick pyramid in the presence of the flickering blue flame, inviting the audience to meditate with them in real-time. La Malinche's death—of which little is known— is created from voiced questions spoken as seemingly disembodied phrases in the darkness — "Where are your bones?" "When did you die?" — performing knowledge as questions of history. In *Zapata, Death Without End*, Zapata's death is present through the real photo of his "real" dead body, apparently looking on as a body lies centre stage surrounded by an accumulation of stones re-visioning heroes of everyday life. In *War in Paradise* the death of Cabañas is re-formed as twenty-five bodies touch exposed flesh.

Coexistence

Through all the multiple performances of remains of bodies of history, dying and death always encompass forms of coexistence. Live bodies in performance are always palimpsest bodies containing traces of death. They encompass a doubleness and haunting which is present through the actual dying of the "live" performer. As Case and Blau observed, " 'live' performers move through 'real time toward their deaths as they perform."[16] According to Peggy Phelan, "the moving body is always fading from our eyes. Historical bodies and bodies moving on stage fascinate us because they fade. Our own duration is measured by our ability to witness this fading."[17] In the work of La Máquina, this fading is witnessed by the performers and spectators who are incorporated into these performance frames. Through strategies of convivio, these are performances with the audience, enabling dialogical, meditative and participatory audience-performer relationships. Drawing on

Figure 111.

Taylor again, these scenarios of deaths, lives, memories and histories are performed through "a politics of invitation, [and] a politics of community."[18] In *Mexican Trilogy* the direct contemplative and reiterated question "Do you remember?" is more about the future than the past. In *Zapata, Death Without End* spectators and performers co-participate as they throw darts, grasp grains of earth, smell oil and eat mangoes. Within an inclusive, invitational environment of community they gather around a table to share a freshly cooked meal that sustains their own bodies (Figure 111).

4. *Time of the Devil*

If postmemory is a traumatic relationship between present and past, mediated by imaginative creations for a future, then all humans encounter this form of memory in contemplating death. Here is a collective memory of the trauma of death and ever-present presences of living with the "end of living"— a universal, inescapable quality of humanness. In this study of postmemory theatre experiments playing with remains of bodies of history, *Time of the Devil* does not quite fit the mould. The body of history is inherently connected with dead bodies yet is not a dead body of history. The devil is, in essence, a conceptual no-body, an ephemeral body, a mythical body, deeply embodied in collective memories and histories, and in pasts and environments.

In this exquisite and playful solo trans performance, Malheiros guides herselves and her public on a corporeal pilgrimage through existential questions about living, life, dying, death and the materiality of bodies. Engaging a very direct politics of invitation and community, Malheiros performs an intensely convivial and open exploration of questions, with overt corporeal constructions and layering. Remains of this body/no-body of history are formed through words, clothes, spatialities, colours and iconic objects. Dialoguing with herselves and her audience, she verbalizes a continual thread of multiple texts, shifting and merging colloquial, scholarly and religious ideas as she criss-crosses two millennia. She amalgamates nineteenth-century dialogical words of Pessoa with fourth-century theological words of San Agustin with twenty-first century poetic words of dramaturge Lemus with her own colloquialisms and musings of her audience. She transforms her body and face in front of her spectators, layering her body with a nineteenth-century formal suit, overlaying facial hair, and assembling and constructing herselves as an accumulation of traces. She balances precariously on wooden sticks as she alters perspectives and generates potential paths, supporting a tiny, skeletal, headless body-form. She plays with destiny, walking around the auditorium and inviting her public to read their future on little pieces of paper inside fortune cookies. She poses, gestures and gesticulates in a space littered with death masks and little devil forms, re-imagining traumas of the unknown. She rehearses her finality, covering her face with life-size death masks. Inevitably and ultimately, she ends in a moving attitude of liminal provisionality (Figure 112).[19]

Figure 112.

Remaining differently through repetitions

Theatre to generate reflections: Face-to-face with ancestors

In a review of La Máquina, one theatre critic described how these performances, in effect, put "a giant mirror centre stage that requires audience members to come face-to-face with their ancestors."[20] Coming face-to-face is a strikingly corporeal practice of trans-temporal coexistence, juxtaposition and plurality—one body interfaces with another body and many bodies interface with many other bodies through palimpsest formations. A mirror generates obvious palimpsest bodies through waves of light energy and a solo object. Collectively seeking reflections in one giant mirror presents multiple selves and multiple bodies. Reflections are always plural and always transformed. Seeking one's own reflected body offers experiences of distortions, re-visions, erasures and multiplicities. These are ambiguous and plural, collective and individual, my "self" and not "my self."[21] Coming face-to-face with ancestors through performing palimpsest bodies involves multiple crossings. Drawing on Gloria Anzaldúa, these processes can "unflinchingly bring us [face to face] with our own historias," through in-betweenness and liminality.[22] As Laurietz Seda has described, these symbolic border crossings involve negotiation and exchange while in the act of performing.[23] Past and present are experienced through a palimpsest of remains and traces and as a confrontation of orders.[24]

On the subject of archives

In their work on the subject of archives, Taylor and Hirsch have combined their understandings of memory, postmemory and performance to ask: "What do we want or need from the past? How is the past put into the use of the present?"[25] In these performance projects of La Máquina "the past" is put into the use of the present through complex embodied inquiries. Their rigorous and playful transdisciplinary practices offer deeply

Figure 113.

corporeal and invitational environments for experiencing present contexts and for re-imagining possible futures. Their performances and workshops are forms of archives containing multifarious collections of traces, remains and ephemera.[26] Taylor and Hirsch suggest that the archive is "any accessible collection that potentially yields data, and a site for critical reflection and contestation of its social political, and historical construction."[27] It is also a "site of potentiality, provisionality, and contingency."[28] This is precisely the work of Malheiros, Faesler and their many collaborators and participants, as they engage with complex inquiries into official histories through these dynamic and playful performance projects. Crucially, through their embodied processes of inquiry, incorporating and juxtaposing multiple corporeal remains, they play with archival bodies and embodied archives as the very sites for generating productive tensions. Through their reiterations, repeats and reactivations, they unfix and destabilize problematic constructions. There is always a sense of provisionality and non-finality in these trans-temporal bodies.

Yet, as Taylor and Hirsch explain: "No one knows how any of these archives will end up—as dust, as free-floating data, as traces, or perhaps the memory of traces...dust, data, and traces that will be assembled and reassembled, each time, in different ways, for

Figure 114.

use in an ever-changing present."[29] As forms of feminist cultural activity, these complex embodied performance practices of La Máquina present the potential for remaining differently. Theatre scholar Elaine Aston has asked if it is possible for performance to "house" a culture resistant to and different from official, normative and prevalent cultures, expressing this as a central issue for feminist performance. She takes up Schneider's discussions of performing remains and remaining differently to describe the possibility of "feminist performance as archive."[30] In these projects of La Máquina, as the artists experiment with unsettled memories of postmemory and rememory through complex embodied practices and bodies as archives, the practitioners produce forms of feminist performance. Postmemory is ultimately about futures, incomplete pasts, pasts that are becoming and a plethora of bodies. Each repetition holds remains of other pasts, yet difference lies between the repetitions. In these repetitions the past is a becoming for "difference inhabits repetition."[31] Performing with remains of bodies of history through palimpsest bodies offers the potential to remain differently.

Unfolding accumulations of iterations

In moving this study to an ending, and as you sit holding this book-object (as paper or digital screen illuminated), with the multiplicities of bodies translated into words and photographs and contained in this pages, I close with an invitation for sharing in a performative palimpsest community through your palimpsest body. As humans we are aware of our bodies as palimpsests, always plural, multi-layered and trans-temporal, containing and diffusing remains of pasts in complicated presents as we generate possible futures. I end with a reiteration of a brief scenario from *Mexican Trilogy: Malinche/Malinches*. As you read, I invite you to move your body through these remains and traces, connecting with the sixteenth-century woman known as La Malinche and with myriad other lives, memories and histories.[32] This short scenario demonstrates the potential for palimpsest bodies in performance to reveal and unfold trans-temporal plurality, contradictions and complexity through repetitions of remains.

A person stands at table. She shakes out a tablecloth, places it carefully on the table, then she removes the cloth and folds it up, then she shakes it out and places it carefully on the table again, then she removes it and folds it up, then she shakes it out...all the time speaking to herselves and everybody who is listening, narrating micro I-stories of lives, procreation and experiences. (Figure 115).

Figure 115.

In this scenario of becoming, Malheiros' performs an accumulation of remains and traces as she gestures to the future: from Part 1, her yellow-painted body connects a contemporary woman with Alzheimer's, who is looking for her place of abode, and a deity of immortality; from Part 2, her dust-archival-labouring body queers history and excavates constructions; and from Part 3, her embroidering business-suited body generates a plurality of Malinches (carer, abuser, life partner, procreator, traitor, translator and guide). Her body is covered with an intricate knitted-painted tunic of ancient wisdom; of time immemorial; and of forgetting where home is. Her chest and heart (memory) are superimposed with a back-to-front waistcoat, inverting conventions of masculinity, conformity and institutional control. She embodies postmemory traumas that combine authoritarian control with misplacing home.[33] She embodies rememory experiences that merge extreme ferocity of corporeal rape with everyday violences of domesticity. In her public role, she is a plurality of women whose actions of translation and procreation bring retribution. In the private and intimate space of everyday living she performs ritual repetitions of (gendered) meal preparation, reactivating material already worked on immeasurable times before.

As she moves and speaks she reveals tensions of private hidden memories and public manifest histories. She inhabits her body as intimately part of passionate and violent pasts, even as her own actions generate environments that reform and transform. She exposes her innermost secrets, embedded within in her muscles, tendons, heart and lungs, as she vocalizes from the depths of her being. She performs a repertoire of ritual actions embodying expectations and preparations for eating and shared togetherness. She destabilizes the fixity of history through assembling and reassembling. Her tongue articulates a vocal-sonic palimpsest, interweaving multiple disparate lives. Her palimpsest body is an archival-repertorial holder, a conveyor of collective memories and home to many stories. Through performing remains as trans-temporal multiplicity, she unfolds poetic presences for future possibilities.

—*C stands at the table covered in a bright pink plastic cloth:*
    Slowly, she removes the cloth;
      And neatly folds it;

      Then suddenly unfolds it…and carefully re-places it on the table;
      Slowly, she removes the cloth;
      And neatly folds it;

      Then suddenly unfolds it…and carefully re-places it on the table…
      Slowly she removes the cloth;

      folds…
        and unfolds…

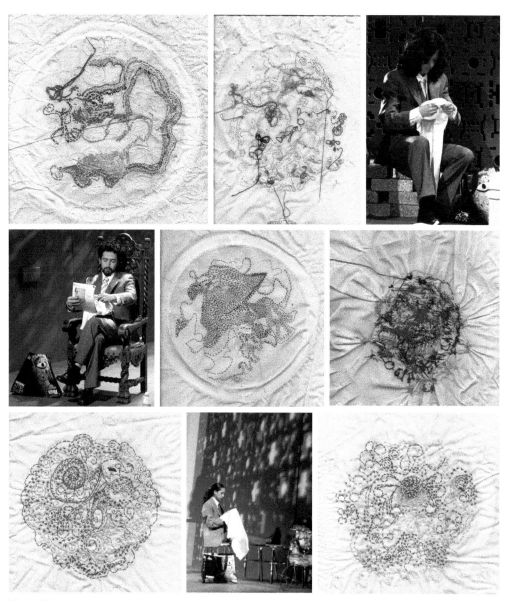

Figure 116.

References

Adame, Domingo. *Teatros y teatralidades en México: siglo XX*. AMIT: Universidad Veracruzana, 2004.

———. "La Facultad de Teatro: treinta y cinco años de formar teatristas universitarios." www.uv.mx/teatro/quienes-somos/historia-2/.

Adame, Domingo and Antonio Prieto Stambaugh, eds. *Jerzy Grotowski: miradas desde Latinoamérica*. Xalapa: Universidad Veracruzan, 2011.

Adler, Heidrun. "Prólogo." In *Un viaje sin fin. Teatro mexicano hoy*, edited by Heidrun Adler and Jaime Chabaud. Frankfurt am Main: Vervuert and Madrid: Iberoamericana, 9–12, 2004.

Adler, Heidrun and Jaime Chabaud, eds. *Un viaje sin fin. Teatro mexicano hoy*. Frankfurt am Main: Vervuert and Madrid: Iberoamericana, 2004.

Alcázar, Josefína and Fernando Fuentes, eds. *Performance y arte-acción en América Latina*. Mexico City: Ediciones Sin-Nombre, 2005.

Allain, Paul and Jen Harvie. *The Routledge Companion to Theatre and Performance*. London: Routledge, 2006.

Alzate, Gastón. *Teatro de cabaret: Imaginarios disidentes*. Irvine: Gestos, 2002.

———. "Paquita la del Barrio and Translocal Theatricality: Performing Counter(post)modernity." In *Trans/Acting: Latin American and Latino Performing Arts*, edited by Jacqueline Bixler and Laurietz Seda. Lewisburg, PA: Bucknell University Press, 160–77, 2009.

Anderson, Benedict. *Imagined Communities: Reflections on the Origin and Spread of Nationalism*. London: Verso, 1983.

Anzaldúa, Gloria E. *Borderlands/La Frontera: The New Mestiza*. San Francisco: Aunt Lute Books, 1987.

———, ed. *Haciendo Caras/Making Face, Making Soul*. San Francisco: Aunt Lute Books, 1990.

———. *Interviews/Entrevistas*. Edited by AnaLouise Keating. New York: Routledge, 2000.

Araujo, Raquel. "La simultaneidad en la construcción visual de *Calor*." In *Des/tejiendo escenas: desmontajes: procesos de investigación y creación*, edited by Ileana Diéguez. Mexico City: Universidad Iberoamericana y Instituto Nacional de Bellas Artes, 105–110, 2009.

———. "Aprendiendo a sembrar teatro." *Paso de Gato*, 59: 84–85, 2014.

Araujo, Raquel and Luis Castrillón. "Paisaje Meridiano del espacios para el arte." *Paso de Gato*, 57: 75–76, 2014.

Arce, B. Christine. *Troping Mexico's Historical No-bodies*. Doctoral thesis, ProQest, 2008.

———. *Mexico's Nobodies: The Cultural Legacy of the Soldadera and Afro-Mexican Women.* New York: SUNY Press, 2017.

Argudín, Yolanda. *Historia del teatro en México.* Mexico City: Panorama Editorial, 1985.

Arrizón, Alicia. "Soldaderas and the Staging of the Mexican Revolution." *TDR: The Drama Review* 42, no. 1: 90–112, 1998.

———. *Latina Performance: Traversing the Stage.* Bloomington: Indiana University Press, 1999.

———. *Queering Mestizaje: Transculturation and Performance.* Ann Arbor, MI: University of Michigan Press, 2006.

Arrizón, Alicia and Lillian Manzor. *Latinas on Stage.* Berkeley: Third Woman, 2000.

Artaud, Antonin. *The Theatre and Its Double.* Richmond: Oneworld Classics, 2010 [1964/1938].

Aston, Elaine. "Feminist Performance as Archive: Bobby Baker's 'Daily Life' and *Box Story.*" *Performance Research* 4, no. 7: 78–85, 2002.

Aston, Elaine and Geraldine Harris. *Performance Practice and Process: Contemporary [Women] Practitioners.* Basingstoke and New York: Palgrave Macmillan, 2008.

Auslander, Philip. *From Acting to Performance: Essays in Modernism and Postmodernism.* London and New York: Routledge, 1997.

———. *Liveness.* London: Routledge, 2008 [1999].

Azor, Ileana. "La mujer como sujeto corporal y reflexivo en el teatro mexicano actual. Dos experiencias, dos miradas, un nuevo síntoma." *Latin American Theatre Review* 36, no. 2: 63–72, 2003.

Baldwin, Jane, Jean-Marc Larrue and Christiane Page, eds. *Vie et mort de la creation collective/ The Lives and Deaths of Collective Creation.* Sherborn: Vox Teatri, 2008.

Baker, Christina. "Staging *Narcocorridos*: Las Reinas Chulas' Dissident Audio-Visual Performance." *Latin American Theatre Review* 48, no. 1: 93–113, 2014.

Barba, Eugenio. *The Paper Canoe: A Guide to Theatre Anthropology.* Translated by Richard Fowler. London: Routledge, 1995.

———. "La Danza del algebra y del fuego." In *Des/tejiendo escenas: desmontajes: procesos de investigación y creación,* edited by Ileana Diéguez. Mexico City: Universidad Iberoamericana y Instituto Nacional de Bellas Artes, 75–82, 2009.

Barthes, Roland. *S/Z. An Essay.* Translated by Richard Millar. New York: Hill and Wang, 1970.

Barton, Bruce. *Collective Creation, Collaboration and Devising.* Toronto: Playwrights Canada Press, 2008.

Beezley, William. "Cómo fue que el Negrito salvó a México de los franceses: Las fuentes populares de la identidad nacional." *Historia Mexicana* LVII, no. 2: 405–44, 2007.

———. *Mexican National Identity: Memory, Innuendo and Popular Culture.* Tucson: University of Arizona Press, 2008.

Benítez Dávila, Mónica Francisca. *Comunidades y contextos en las teorías y prácticas artísticas contemporáneas.* Mexico City: Universidad Autónoma Metropolitana, 2015.

Benjamin, Walter. *On the Concept of History.* Gesammelten Schriften I: 2, Translated by Dennis Redmond. Frankfurt am Main: Suhrkamp Verlag, 1974 [1940].

Berdan, Frances F. and Patricia Rieff Anawalt. *The Essential Codex Mendoza.* Berkeley: University of California Press, 1997.

Bergson, Henri. *Matter and Memory.* Translated by Nancy Margaret Paul and W. Scott Palmer. London: George Allen and Unwin, [1988] 1911.

Bigelow Dixon, Michael and Joel A. Smith. *Anne Bogart: Viewpoints*. Lyme: Smith and Kraus, 1995.

Bixler, Jacqueline. "The Postmodernization of History in the Theatre of Sabina Berman." *Latin American Theatre Review* 30, no. 2: 45–60, 1997.

———. *Convención y transgresión. El teatro de Emilio Carballido*. Xalapa: Universidad Veracruzana, 2001.

———. "Re-Membering the Past: Memory-Theatre and Tlatelolco." *Latin American Research Review* 37, no. 2: 119–35, 2002.

———. *Sediciosas seducciones: Sexo, poder y palabras en el teatro de Sabina Berman*. Mexico City: Escenología, 2004.

———. "The Politics of Tradaptation in the Theater of Sabina Berman." In *Trans/Acting: Latin American and Latino Performing Arts*, edited by Jacqueline Bixler and Laurietz Seda. Lewisburg, PA: Bucknell University Press, 2009, 72–90.

———. *Historias para ser contadas. El Teatro de Alejandro Ricaño*. Lawrence: Latin American Theatre Review Books, 2012.

Bixler, Jacqueline and Stuart Day, eds. *El Teatro de Rascón Banda: Voces en el umbral*. Mexico City: Escenología, 2005.

Bixler, Jacqueline and Claudia Gidi, eds. *Las mujeres y la dramaturgia mexicana del siglo XX*. Mexico City: Ediciones el Milagro, 2011.

Bixler, Jacqueline and Laurietz Seda, eds. *Trans/Acting: Latin American and Latino Performing Arts*. Lewisburg, PA: Bucknell University Press, 2009.

Blanco Cano, Rosana and Rita Urquijo-Ruiz. *Global Mexican Cultural Productions*. Basingstoke: Palgrave MacMillan, 2011.

Blau, Herbert. *Take Up the Bodies: Theater at the Vanishing Point*. Urbana: University of Illinois Press, 1982.

Blocker, Jane. "Repetition: A Skin which Unravels." In *Perform, Repeat, Record. Live Art in History*, edited by Amelia Jones and Adrian Heathfield. Bristol: Intellect, 199–208, 2012.

Bogart, Anne. *And Then, You Act: Making Art in an Unpredictable World*. London: Routledge, 2007.

Bogart, Anne and Tina Landau. *The Viewpoints Book: A Practical Guide to Viewpoints and Composition*. New York: Theatre Communications Group, 2005.

Borges, Jorge Luis. *El hacedor*. Buenos Aires: Emecé Editores, 1960.

Bourdieu, P. *The Logic of Practice*. Translated by R. Nice. Cambridge, UK: Polity Press, 1990 [1980].

Breining, Daniel. *Mexican Theater and Drama from the Conquest through the Seventeenth Century*. Lewiston, ME: Edwin Mellen Press, 2007.

Bremser, Martha and Lorna Sanders, eds. *Fifty Contemporary Choreographers*. Abingdon, UK: Routledge, 2011.

Britton, John. *Encountering Ensemble*. London and New York: Bloomsbury Methuen Drama, 2013.

———. "Introduction." In *Encountering Ensemble*, edited by John Britton. London and New York: Bloomsbury Methuen Drama, 3–47, 2013.

———. "Introduction (Part Three)." In *Encountering Ensemble*, edited by John Britton. London and New York: Bloomsbury Methuen Drama, 273–312, 2013.

Broadhurst, Susan. *Liminal Acts: A Critical Overview of Contemporary Performance and Theory.* New York and London: Cassell, 1999.

———. "Liminal Aesthetics." *Body, Space, Technology* 1, no. 1: 1–10, 2000.

Bruns, Gerald L. *Inventions, Writing, Textuality and Understanding in Literature History.* New Haven, CT: Yale University Press, 1982.

Buffington, Robert. "Theater." In *Mexico: An Encyclopedia of Contemporary Culture and History.* Santa Barbara, CA: ABC-CLIO, 494–99, 2004.

Burgess, Ronald. *The New Dramatists of Mexico, 1965–1987.* Lexington: University of Kentucky Press, 1991.

Burkhart, Louise M. *Aztecs on Stage: Religious Theater in Colonial Mexico.* Norman, OK: University of Oklahoma Press, 2011.

Bustamante, Maris. "Non-Objective Arts in Mexico 1963–83" (translated by Eduardo Aparicio). In *Corpus Delecti: Performance Art in the Americas*, edited by Coco Fusco. New York: Routledge, 225–39, 2000.

Bustamante Mouriño, Alicia. "Lorena Wolffer: Imágenes extremas del feminicidio." 19 March 2012. http://www.feminicidio.net/articulo/lorena-wolffer-imágenes-extremas-del-feminicidio [accessed 15 July 2015].

Butler, Judith. "Performative Acts and Gender Constitution: An Essay in Phenomenology and Feminist Theory." *Theatre Journal* 40, no. 4: 519–531, 1988.

———. *Gender Trouble: Feminism and the Subversion of Identity.* New York: Routledge, 1990.

Cameron, Derrick. "Tradaptation: Cultural Exchange and Black British Theatre." In *Moving Target: Theatre Translation and Cultural Relocation*, edited by Carole-Anne Upton. Abingdon and New York: Routledge, 17–24, 2014.

Carlson, Marvin. *Performance: A Critical Introduction.* Abingdon and New York: Routledge, 1996.

———. *The Haunted Stage: The Theatre as Memory Machine.* Ann Arbor: University of Michigan Press, 2001.

Campbell, Patrick. *Analysing Performance.* Manchester: Manchester University Press, 1996.

Carbonell, Dolores and Luis Javier Mier Vega. *Trés crónicas del teatro en México.* Mexico City: Universidad Nacional Autónoma de México, 2000.

Carrasco, Marilú. "La narración oral y el teatro, convergencias y divergencias." *Paso de Gato, no.* 56: 44–46, 2014.

Case, Sue-Ellen. *Feminism and Theatre.* New York: Methuen, 1988.

———, ed. *Performing Feminisms: Feminist Critical Theory and Theatre.* Baltimore, MD: Johns Hopkins University Press, 1990.

———. "Tracking the Vampire." *Differences* 3, no. 2: 1–20, 1991.

———. "Meditations on the Patriarchal Pythagorean Pratfall and the Lesbian Siamesian Two-Step." In *Choreographing History*, edited by Susan Leigh Foster. Bloomington: Indiana University Press, 1995, 195–99.

Ceballos, Edgar. *Diccionario mexicano de teatro. Siglo XX.* Mexico City: Escenología, 2010.

Chabaud, Jaime. "El teatro rural en México." In *Escenario de dos mundos. Inventario teatral de Iberoamérica Vol. 3*, edited by Moisés Perez Coterillo and Carlos Espinosa Domínguez. Madrid: Centro de Documentación Teatral, 149–51, 1988.

———. "Nota introductoria." In *Un viaje sin fin. Teatro mexicano hoy*, edited by Heidrun Adler and Jaime Chabaud. Frankfurt am Main: Vervuert and Madrid: Iberoamericana, 7, 2004.

———. "Teatro Comunitario ante la urgencia de humanidad." *Paso de Gato*, no. 58: 2–3, 2014.

———. "Un país en llamas y luto." *Paso de Gato*, no. 60: 2–3, 2015.

———. "La crítica: Teatro: Ecosistema teatro." *Milenio.com*. 1 January 2016.

Chamberlain, Franc and Ralph Zarrow, eds. *Jacques Lecoq and the British Theatre*. London: Routledge, 2002.

Chías, Edgar. *Benito antes de Juárez*. 2016. elfenixproducciones.com [accessed 16 December 2016].

Coerver, Don M., Suzanne B. Pasztor and Robert M. Buffington. *Mexico: An Encyclopedia of Contemporary Culture and History*. Santa Barbara, CA: ABC-CLIO, 2004.

Collins, John. "Elevator Repair Service and The Wooster Group: Ensembles Surviving Themselves." In *Encountering Ensemble*, edited by John Britton. London and New York: Bloomsbury Methuen Drama, 234–49, 2013.

Compton, Timothy G. "Mexico City's Spring 2008 Theatre Season." *Latin American Theatre Review* 42, no. 1: 107–118, 2008.

Connerton, Paul. *How Societies Remember*. Cambridge, UK: Cambridge University Press, 1989.

Cooper Alarcón, Daniel. *The Aztec Palimpsest: Mexico in the Modern Imagination*. Tucson: The University of Arizona Press. 1997.

Cordero Reiman, Karen and Alfredo López Austin. *Cuerpos desdoblados: Héctor Veláquez*. Mexico City: Terreno Baldío Arte, 2007.

Cortés, Eladio. *Dictionary of Mexican Literature*. Westport, CT: Greenwood Publishing Group, 1992.

Cortés, Eladio and Mirta Barrea-Marlys. *Encyclopedia of Latin American Theater*. Westport, CT: Greenwood Press, 2003.

Costantino, Roselyn. "Visibility as Strategy: Jesusa Rodríguez's Body in Play." In *Corpus Delecti: Performance Art of the Americas*, edited by Coco Fusco. London and New York: Routledge, 63–77, 2000.

———. "And She Wears It Well: Feminist and Cultural Debates in the Work of Astrid Hadad." In *Latinas on Stage*, edited by Alicia Arrizón and Lillian Manzor. Berkeley, CA: Third Woman. 368–421, 2000.

———. "Memoria colectiva y cuerpo individual: Política y performance de Astrid Hadad." *Conjunto* 121 (2001): 40–49.

———. "Politics and Culture in a Diva's Diversion: The Body of Astrid Hadad in Performance." In *Holy Terrors: Latin American Women Perform*, edited by Diana Taylor and Roselyn Costantino. Durham, NC and London: Duke University Press, 187–207, 2003.

———. "Mujeres inconvenientes: memoria, política y performance en México." In *La escena imposible ante el globo mundial*, edited by Laura Borrás Catanyer. Madrid: Fundación Autor, 83–93, 2003.

———. "Embodied Memory in Las Horas de Belén: A Book of Hours." *Theatre Journal* 53, no. 1:607–32, 2001.

CulturaUNAM Vértice: Experimentación y vanguardia. Mexico City: Centro Cultural Universitario, Universidad Nacional Autónoma de México, 2017. www.cultura.unam.mx [accessed 16 November 2017].

Cummings, Scott T. *Remaking American Theater: Charles Mee, Anne Bogart and the SITI Company.* Cambridge and New York: Cambridge University Press, 2006.

Cypess, Sandra M. "La dramaturgia femenina y su contexto socio-cultural." *Latin American Theater Review* 13, no. 2: 63–67, 1980.

———. "I, too, Speak: 'Female' Discourse in Carballido's Plays." *Latin American Theatre Review* 17, no. 1: 45–52, 1984.

———. *La Malinche in Mexican Literature: From History to Myth.* Austin: University of Texas Press, 1991.

Dauster, Frank. *Historia del teatro hispanoamericano: Siglos XIX y XX.* Mexico City: Ediciones de Andrea, 1966.

Daughtry, J. Martin. "Acoustic Palimpsests and the Politics of Listening." *Music and Politics* 7, no. 1: 1–34, 2013.

Day, Stuart. *Staging Politics in Mexico: The Road to Neoliberalism.* Lewisburg, PA: Bucknell University Press, 2004.

———. "Transposing Professions: Vicente Leñero and the Politics of the Press." In *Trans/Acting: Latin American and Latino Performing Arts*, edited by Jacqueline Bixler and Laurietz Seda. Lewisburg, PA: Bucknell University Press, 109–24, 2009.

de Beer, Gabriella. *Contemporary Mexican Women Writers: Five Voices.* Austin University of Texas Press, 1996.

De Marinis, Marco. "New Theatrology and Performance Studies: Starting Points towards a Dialogue." *TDR: The Drama Review* 55, no. 4 (T212): 64–74, 2011.

De Quincey, Thomas. "The Palimpsest of the Human Brain: Suspiria de profundis." *Blackwood's Magazine*, UK, 1845.

de Sahagún, Bernardino. *Historia general de la cosas de Nueva España.* Mexico City: Porrua, 1995.

Deleuze, Gilles. *Difference and Repetition*, trans. Paul Patton. New York: Columbia University Press, 1994 (1968).

Deleuze, Gilles and Félix Guatarri. *A Thousand Plateaus.* Minneapolis: University of Minnesota Press, 1987.

Delgado Martínez, César. *Waldeen. La Coronela de la danza mexicana.* Mexico City: Escenología y CONACULTA, 2000.

Díaz del Castillo, Bernal. *Historia verdadera de la conquista de la Nueva España.* Mexico City: Fernández Editores, 1961.

Díaz de León, Aida. "The Politics of the Past and the Fragmentary Present: Locating Memory in Spain and Latin America." In *Sites of Memory in Spain and America: Trauma, Politics and Resistance* edited by Aida Díaz de León, Mariana Llorente and Marcella Salvi. Lanham, MD: Lexington Books, 1–17, 2015.

Diéguez, Ileana. *Escenarios liminales: teatralidades, performances y política.* Buenos Aires: ATUEL, 2007.

———. *Des/tejiendo escenas: desmontajes: procesos de investigación y creación.* Mexico City: Universidad Iberoamericana y Instituto Nacional de Bellas Artes, 2009.

———. "Cuerpos ExPuestos. Prácticas de duelo (primeras aproximaciones)." *Cuaderno de Investigación* 3. Maestría Interdisciplinar en Teatro y Artes Vivas, Universidad Nacional de Colombia, 2009.

———. "El cuerpo roto / alegorías de lo informe." *Revista do LUME* November: 1–15, 2012.

———. *Cuerpos sin duelo. Iconografías y teatralidades del dolor.* Buenos Aires and Córdoba: DocumentA / Escénica, 2013.

Dillon, Sarah. *The Palimpsest: Literature, Criticism, Theory.* London: Bloomsbury Academic, 2007.

Doggart, Sebastian, ed. *Latin American Plays.* London: Nick Hern Books, 1996.

Dolan, Jill. *Utopia in Performance: Finding Hope at the Theater.* Ann Arbor: University of Michigan Press, 2005.

Doyle, Katy. "The Dawn of Mexico's Dirty War: Lucio Cabañas and the Party of the Poor." In The National Security Archive, George Washington University, December 2003. http://nsarchive.gwu.edu/NSAEBB/NSAEBB105/index2.htm [accessed 16 December 2016].

Dubatti, Jorge, ed. "Introducción." In *Flora y fauna de la Creación Macocal (Teatro deshecho I).* Los Macocos Banda de Teatro Buenos Aires: Atuel, 5–45, 2002.

———, ed. *Dramaturgia mexicana hoy.* México: Dirección General de Publicaciones (CONACULTA)/Centro Cultural Helénico/Atuel, 2005.

———. *Filosofía del teatro 1: convivio, experiencia, subjetividad.* Buenos Aires: Atuel, 2007.

Dunkelberg, Kermit. *Grotowski and North American Theatre: Translation, Transmission, Dissemination.* Doctoral Dissertation, Department of Performance Studies, New York University, 2008.

Eder, Rita. "Dos aspectos de la obra de arte total: experimentación y performatividad." In *Desafío de la estabilidad. Procesos artísticos en México 1952–1967*, edited by Rita Eder and Gabriela Álvarez. Mexico City: UNAM, Madrid: Turner, 1–5, 2014.

Fabião, Eleonora. "History and Precariousness: In Search of a Performative Historiography." In *Perform, Repeat, Record*, edited by Amelia Jones and Adrian Heathfield. Bristol: Intellect, 121–35, 2012.

Faesler, Juliana. "La Máquina de Teatro." In *Des/tejiendo escenas: desmontajes: procesos de investigación y creación*, edited by Ileana Diéguez. Mexico City: Universidad Iberoamericana and Instituto Nacional de Bellas Artes, 41–54, 2009.

Fediuk, Elka and Antonio Prieto Stambaugh, eds. *Corporalidades Escénicas. Representaciones del cuerpo en el teatro, la danza y el performance.* Buenos Aires: Editorial Argus-a Artes y Humanidades, 2016.

Flores, Alejandro. "Teatro para repensar la historia." *The Economist*, 17 March 2010. http://eleconomista.com.mx/entretenimiento/2010/03/17/teatro-repensar-historia.

Florescano, Enrique. *Memory, Myth and Time in Mexico: From the Aztecs to Independence.* Trans. Albert G. Bork. Austin: University of Texas Press, 1994.

Forsyth, Alison and Chris Megson, eds. *Get Real: Documentary Theatre Past and Present.* Basingstoke: Palgrave Macmillan, 2009.

Foster, Jonathan K. *Memory: A Very Short Introduction.* New York and Oxford: Oxford University Press, 2009.

Foster, Susan Leigh, ed. *Choreographing History.* Bloomington: Indiana University Press, 1995.

———. "Choreographing History." In *Choreographing History*, edited by Susan Leigh Foster. Bloomington: Indiana University Press, 3–21, 1995.

Foucault, Michel. *Language, Counter-memory, Practice: Selected Essays and Interviews by Michel Foucault.* Edited by Donald Bouchard. Ithaca: Cornell University Press, 1977.

Franco, Israel and Antonio Escobar Delgado. *El Teatro de ahora: un primer ensayo de teatro político en México*. Mexico City: Instituto Nacional de Bellas Artes, 2011.

Franco, Jean. *Plotting Women: Gender and Representation in Mexico*. New York: Columbia University Press, 1989.

———. "A Touch of Evil: Jesusa Rodríguez's Subversive Church." In *Negotiating Performance: Gender, Sexuality, and Theatricality in Latin/o America*, edited by Diana Taylor and Juan Villegas. Durham, NC and London: Duke University Press, 159–75, 1994,.

Frischmann, Donald. *El nuevo teatro popular en México*. Mexico City: Instituto Nacional de Bellas Artes, 1990.

———. "Desarrollo y Florecimiento del Teatro Mexicano: Siglo XX. *Teatro: Revista de Estudios Culturales/ A Journal of Cultural Studies*, 2: 53–59, 1992.

Fusco, Coco, ed. *Corpus Delecti: Performance Art of the Americas*. London and New York: Routledge, 2000.

———. "Introduction: Latin American Performance and the Reconquista of Civil Space." In *Corpus Delecti: Performance Art of the Americas*, edited by Coco Fusco. London and New York: Routledge, 1–20, 2000.

Gann, Myra S. "Masculine Space in the Plays of Estela Leñero." In *Latin American Women Dramatists: Theater, Texts, and Theories*, edited by Catherine Larson and Margarita Vargas. Bloomington: Indiana University Press, 234–42, 1998.

García Canclini, Néstor. "Anthropology: Eight Approaches to Latin Americanism." *Journal of Latin American Cultural Studies*, 11, no. 3: 265–78, 2002.

Garibay, Ángel María. *Posesía náhuatl*. Mexico City: Universidad Nacional Autónoma de México, 1965.

Garo, Elena. "La señora en su balcón." In *Teatro breve hispanoamericano contemporáneo*, edited by Carlos Solórzano. Madrid: Aguilar, 343–58, 1970.

Garzón Céspedes, Francisco. *El teatro de participación popular y el teatro de la comunidad: Un teatro de sus protagonistas*. Habana: Unión de Escritores y Artistas de Cuba, 1977.

———, ed. *Recopilación de textos sobre el teatro latinoamericano de creación colectiva*. Habana: Casa de las Américas, 1978.

Gladhart, Amalia. "Transference and Negotiation: Sabina Berman Plots Dora and Freud." In *Trans/Acting: Latin American and Latino Performing Arts*, edited by Jacqueline Bixler and Laurietz Seda. Lewisburg, PA: Bucknell University Press, 125–41, 2009.

Glantz, Margo. *La Malinche, sus padres y sus hijos*. Mexico City: UNAM/Mexico: Taurus, 2001 [1994].

Gómez-Peña, Guillermo. *El Mexterminator: antropología inversa de un performancero postmexicano*. Introd. y selec. de Josefina Alcázar. Mexico City: CONACULTA, INBA, Centro Nacional de Investigación y Documentación Teatral Rodolfo Usigli: Fideicomiso para la Cultura México/USA: Océano, 2002.

———. "Multiple Journeys: A Performance Chronology." In *Perform, Repeat, Record: Live Art in History*, edited by Amelia Jones and Adrian Heathfield. Bristol: Intellect, 315–32, 2012.

González-Cruz, Luis F. "XXVII Festival International de Teatro Hispano de Miami." *Latin American Theatre Review* 46, no. 2: 171–75, 2013.

Goodman, Lizbeth and Jane de Gay, eds. *Languages of Theatre Shaped by Women*. Bristol: Intellect, 2001.

Govan, Emma, Helen Nicholson and Katie Normington. *Making a Performance: Devising Histories and Contemporary Practices*. London: Routledge, 2007.

Grau, Andreé. "When the Landscape becomes Flesh: An investigation into Body Boundaries with Special Reference to Tiwi Dance and Western Classical Ballet." *Body and Society* 11, no. 4: 141–63, 2005.

Gutiérrez, Laura G. *Performing Mexicanidad: Vendidas y Cabareteras on the Transnational Stage*. Austin: University of Texas Press, 2010.

Gutiérrez Chong, Natividad, ed. *Women, Ethnicity and Nationalisms in Latin America*. London: Ashgate, 2007.

Gutiérrez, Sonia, ed. *Teatro popular y cambio social en América Latina: Panorama de una experiencia*. San Jose, Costa Rica: Editorial Universitaria Centro Americana, 1979.

Halbwachs, Maurice. *On Collective Memory*, edited translated by Lewis A. Coser. Chicago: University of Chicago Press, 1991.

Hall, Stuart. "Introduction: Who Needs 'Identity'?" In *Questions of Cultural Identity*, edited by Stuart Hall and Paul du Gay. London and Thousand Oaks, CA: Sage, 1–17, 1996.

Harrop, Peter and Evelyn Jamieson. "Collaboration, Ensemble, Devising." In *Encountering Ensemble*, edited by John Britton. London and New York: Bloomsbury Methuen Drama, 167–69, 2013.

Harvie, Jen. "Introduction: Contemporary Theatre in the Making." In *Making Contemporary Theatre: International Rehearsal Processes*, edited by Jen Harvie and Andy Lavender. Manchester, UK: Manchester University Press, 1–16, 2010.

Harvie, Jen and Andy Lavender, eds. *Making Contemporary Theatre: International Rehearsal Processes*. Manchester, UK: Manchester University Press, 2010.

Hayman, Ronald. *Theatre and Anti-Theatre: New Movements since Beckett*. Oxford, UK: Oxford University Press, 1979.

Heathfield, Adrian. "Then Again." In *Perform, Repeat, Record*, edited by Amelia Jones and Adrian Heathfield. Bristol: Intellect, 27–45, 2012.

———. "Introduction." *Perform, Repeat, Record*, edited by Amelia Jones and Adrian Heathfield. Bristol: Intellect, 435–40, 2012.

Heathfield, Adrian and Andrew Quick, guest eds. 2000. "On Memory." *Performance Research* 5:3.

Heddon, Deirdre. *Autobiography and Performance*. New York: Palgrave Macmillan, 2007.

Heddon, Deirdre and Jane Milling. *Devising Performance: A Critical History*. New York: Palgrave Macmillan, 2005.

Hellier-Tinoco, Ruth. *Removing the Mask: The Viejitos Dance as Ideological and Political Tool in Post-Revolution Mexico, 1920-1940*. Unpublished Doctoral Thesis, Birmingham City University, Birmingham Conservatoire, UK, 2002.

———. "Power Needs Names: Hegemony, Folklorisation and the *Viejitos* Dance of Michoacán, Mexico." In *Music, Power and Politics*, edited by Annie J. Randall. New York and London: Routledge, 47–64, 2004.

———. "Mexico, But Not Mariachi." *Classroom Music*. Rhinegold Publishing. Autumn Term 2, 2009.

———. "Dead Bodies/Live Bodies: Death, Memory and Resurrection in Contemporary Mexican Performance." In *Performance, Embodiment, & Cultural Memory*, edited by Colin Counsell and Roberta Mock. Newcastle, UK: Cambridge Scholars Press, 114–39, 2009.

———. "Corpo/Reality, Voyeurs and the Responsibility of Seeing: Night of the Dead on the Island of Janitzio, Mexico." *Performance Research* ("Memento Mori") 15, no. 1: 23–31, 2010.

———. "¡Saludos de México (el auténtico)!: Postales, anuncios espectaculares, turismo y cuerpos actuantes," *Fractal*, no. 47/48: 79–98, 2010.

———. *Embodying Mexico: Tourism, Nationalism and Performance.* New York: Oxford University Press, 2011.

———. *Women Singers in Global Contexts: Music, Biography, Identity.* Edited by Ruth Hellier. Champaign: University of Illinois Press, 2013.

———. "Vocal Herstories: Resonances of Singing, Individuals, and Authors." In *Women Singers in Global Contexts: Music, Biography, Identity,* edited by Ruth Hellier. Champaign: University of Illinois Press, 1–37, 2013.

———. "Staging Entrapment in Mexico City: La Máquina de Teatro's Reconstruction of the Massacres in Tenochtitlan and Tlatelolco." *Journal of the Society for Architectural Historians* 73, no. 4: 474–77, 2014.

———. "Embodying Touristic Mexico: Virtual and Erased Indigenous Bodies." In *Meet Me at the Fair: A World's Fair Reader,* edited by Laura Hollengreen, Celia Pearce, Rebecca Rouse & Bobby Schweizer. Pittsburgh, PA: ETC and Carnegie Mellon University Press, 71–80, 2014.

———. "Mexico." In *The Cambridge Encyclopedia of Actors and Acting,* edited by Simon Williams. Cambridge, UK: Cambridge University Press, 2015.

———. "Re-Moving Bodies in the USA/Mexico Drug/Border/Terror/Cold Wars." In *Choreographies of 21st Century Wars (Studies in Dance Theory),* edited by Gay Morris and Jens Giedersdorf. New York: Oxford University Press, 287–314, 2016.

———. "Reappropriating Choreographies of Authenticity in Mexico: Competitions and *The Dance of the Old Men.*" In *The Oxford Handbook of Dance and Competition,* edited by Sherril Dodds. New York: Oxford University Press, 139–166, 2018.

———. "Embodied Imagined Communities: Forging National Identity through The Viejitos Dance." In *The Oxford Handbook of Mexican History,* edited by William Beezley. New York: Oxford University Press, forthcoming.

Hern, Nicholas. *Peter Handke: Theatre and Anti-theatre.* London: Oswald Wolff, 1971.

Hernández, Mark A. "Restaging the Conquest of Michoacán in the 1990s: Víctor Castillo Bautista's *Nuño de Guzmán o la espada de Dios.*" *Latin American Theatre Review* 37, no. 1: 25–41 2003.

Hind, Emily. "Sor Juana, An Official Habit: Twentieth-Century Mexican Culture." *Approaches to Teaching the Works of Sor Juana Inés de la Cruz,* edited by Emilie L. Bergmann and Stacey Schlau. New York: Modern Language Association, 247–55, 2007.

Hirsch, Marianne. *Family Frames: Photography, Narrative, and Postmemory.* Cambridge, MA: Harvard University Press, 1997.

———. "The Generation of Postmemory." *Poetics Today* 29, no. 1, 103–28, 2008.

———. *The Generation of Postmemory: Writing and Visual Culture after the Holocaust.* New York: Columbia University Press, 2012.

———. "Connective Histories in Vulnerable Times." *PMLA* 129, no. 3: 330–348, 2014.

———. www.postmemory.net [accessed 15 May 2012].

Hirsch, Marianne, co-edited with Nancy K. Miller. *Rites of Return: Diaspora, Poetics and the Politics of Memory.* New York: Columbia University Press, 2011.

Hirsch, Marianne and Diana Taylor. "The Archive in Transit: Editorial Remarks." *é-misferica* "On the Subject of Archives." Summer 2012.

Hirsch, Marianne and Leo Spitzer. *Ghosts of Home: The Afterlife of Czernowitz in Jewish Memory.* Berkeley: University of California Press, 2011.

Hutcheon, Linda. *The Poetics of Postmodernism.* New York: Routledge, 1988.

———. "Historiographic Metafiction: Parody and the Intertextuality of History." In *Intertextuality and Contemporary American Fiction*, edited by P. O'Donnell and Robert Con David. Baltimore: Johns Hopkins University Press, 3–32, 1989.

———. *The Politics of Postmodernism.* New York: Routledge, 1989.

Huyssen, Andreas. *Present Pasts: Urban Palimpsests and the Politics of Memory.* Stanford, CA: Stanford University Press, 2003.

Ionesco, Eugène. *Present Past, Past Present*: *A Personal Memoir.* Translated by Helen R. Lane. Lebanon, IN: Da Capo Press, 1998.

Irazábal, Federico. "El teatro posdramático derivas de un concepto: Entrevista con Hans-Thies Lehmann." *Paso de Gato*, no. 57:78–81, 2014 [originally published in *Funámbulos* 2011].

Jameson, Frederic. "Marx's Purloined Letter." In *Ghostly Demarcations: A Symposium on Jaques Derrida's 'Spectres de Marx,'* edited by Michael Sprinkler. London: Verso, 26–67, 1996.

Jiménez, Sergio and Edgar Ceballos. *Teoría y praxis de teatro en México.* Mexico City: Grupo Editorial Garceta, 1982.

Jackson, Travis. "Culture, Commodity, Palimpsest: Locating Jazz in the World." In *Jazz Worlds/ World Jazz,* edited by Philip V. Bolhman and Goffredo Pastino. Chicago: University of Chicago Press, 381–401, 2016.

Jebelli, Jospeh. "We can cure Alzheimer's — if we stop ignoring it." *The Guardian*, 19 July 2017, https://www.theguardian.com/commentisfree/2017/jul/19/alzheimers-disease-death-old-people-science [accessed 15 August 2017].

Jeyasingh, Shobana. *Palimpsest*, Programme. Shobana Jeyasingh Dance Company. 1996.

———. "Palimpsest, 1996." www.vads.ac.uk [accessed 15 May 2014].

Jones, Amelia. "Foreword." In *Kinesthetic Empathy in Creative Practices*, edited by Dee Reynolds and Matthew Reason. Bristol: Intellect, 11–15, 2012.

———. "The Now and the Has Been: Paradoxes of Live Art in History." In *Perform, Repeat, Record*, edited by Amelia Jones and Adrian Heathfield. Bristol: Intellect, 9–22, 2012.

———. "Franko B. and Kamal Ackarie, Don't Leave Me This Way." In *Perform, Repeat, Record*, edited by Amelia Jones and Adrian Heathfield. Bristol: Intellect, 273–74, 2012.

———. "Santiago Sierra and the 'Contexts' of History." In *Perform, Repeat, Record*, edited by Amelia Jones and Adrian Heathfield. Bristol: Intellect, 363–66, 2012.

Jones, Amelia and Adrian Heathfield, eds. *Perform, Repeat, Record. Live Art in History.* Bristol: Intellect, 2012.

Joseph, Artur, Peter Handke and E. B. Ashton. "Nauseated by Language: From an Interview with Peter Handke." *TDR: The Drama Review* 15, no. 1: 57–61, 1970.

Jürs-Munby, Karen. "Introduction." In *Postdramatic Theatre*, edited by Hans-Thies Lehmann, translated by Karen Jürs-Munby. Abingdon and New York: Routledge, 1–15, 2006.

Kaye, Nick. *Site-Specific Art: Performance, Place, Documentation*. Milton Park, UK: Routledge, 2000.

Larson, Catherine and Margarita Vargas. *Latin American Women Dramatists: Theater, Texts, and Theories*. Bloomington: Indiana University Press, 1998.

Lecoq, Jacques. *Theatre of Movement and Gesture*. London: Routledge, 2006.

Lecoq, Jacques, Jean-Gabriel Carasso and Jean-Claude Lallias. *The Moving Body: Teaching Creative Theatre*. Translated from *Les corps poétique* by David Bradby. London: Methuen, 2000.

Lehmann, Hans-Thies. *Postdramatic Theatre*. Translated by Karen Jürs-Munby. Abingdon and New York: Routledge, 2006.

———. *Teatro posdramático*. Translated from German by Diana González. Mexico City: CENDEAC and Paso de Gato, 2013.

———. "Metamórfosis del teatro posdramático." Keynote lecture at conference *Hans-Thies Lehmann en la UNAM*, Universidad Nacional Autónoma de México, 28 October 2014.

Leñero Franco, Estela. "Pioneering Women in Mexican Theatre." *The Open Page*, no. 9: 15–18, 2004.

———. "Malinche, Malinches." *Revista Proceso*, 17 February 2011, http:// www.proceso.com.mx/ \?p=263157 [accessed 17 February, 2011].

Leñero, Vicente. *Vivir del teatro 2*. Mexico City: Joaquín Mortiz, 1990.

León-Portilla, Miguel. *La filosofía náhuatl estudiada en sus fuentes*. Doctoral thesis. Mexico City: Universidad Nacional Autónoma de México, 1956.

———. *Visión de los vencidos: Relaciones indígenas de la conquista*. Mexico City: Universidad Nacional Autónoma de México, 2007 [1959] (*The Broken Spears: The Aztec Account of the Conquest of Mexico* (Lysander Kemp, trans). Boston: Beacon Press, 1992).

———. *Cantares Mexicanos*. Mexico City: Universidad Nacional Autónoma de México, 2011.

Lepecki, André, ed. *Of the Presence of the Body: Essays on Dance and Performance Theory*. Middletown, CT: Wesleyan University Press, 2004.

———. "Introduction." In *Of the Presence of the Body: Essays on Dance and Performance Theory*, edited by André Lepecki. Middletown, CT: Wesleyan University Press, 1–2, 2004.

———. *Exhausting Dance: Performance and the Politics of Movement*. New York and London: Routledge, 2006.

———. "The Body as Archive: Will to Re-Enact and the Afterlives of Dances." *Dance Research Journal* 42, no. 2: 28–48, 2010.

Levinas, Emmanuel. *Ethics and Infinity: Conversations with Philippe Nemo*, trans. Richard Cohen. Pittsburgh, PA: Duquense University Press, 1985.

Lipsitz, George. "'Standing at the Crossroads': Why Race, State Violence and Radical Movements Matter Now." In *The Rising Tide of Color: Race, State Violence and Radical Movements*, edited by Moon-Ho Jung. Seattle: University of Washington Press, 36–70, 2014.

Lista, Marcella. "Play Dead: Dance, Museums, and the 'Time-Based Arts.'" *Dance Research Journal* 46, no. 3: 5–23, 2014.

López Austin, Alfredo, translator. *Cuerpo humano e ideología: las concepciones de los antiguos nahuas*. Mexico City: Universidad Nacional Autónoma de México, 1980.

Lyotard, Jean-François. *The Postmodern Explained: Correspondence 1982–1985*. Minneapolis: University of Minnesota Press, 1992.

Madrid, Arturo. "Foreword." In *Global Mexican Cultural Productions*, edited by Rosana Blanco Cano and Rita Urquijo-Ruiz. Basingstoke, UK: Palgrave MacMillan, xiii–xv, 2011.

Magaña Esquivel, Antonio. *Imagen y realidad del teatro en México (1533–1960)*. Mexico City: Instituto Nacional de Bellas Artes, 2000.

"'Malinche Malinches' inicia nueva temporada." *Informador,* www. informador.com.mx. May 7 2011.

Malkin, Jeanette R. *Memory-Theater and Postmodern Drama*. Ann Arbor: University of Michigan Press, 1999.

Malpede, Karen. "Theatre of Witness: Passage into a New Millennium." In *Performing Processes: Creating Live Performance*, edited by Roberta Mock. Bristol: Intellect, 122–38, 2000.

Maria y Campos, Armando de. *Teatro del nuevo México: Recuerdos y olvidos*. Mexico City: Escenología, 1999.

Marrero, Teresa. "Eso sí pasa aquí: Indigenous Women Performing Revolutions in Mayan Chiapas." In *Holy Terrors: Latin American Women Perform*, edited by Diana Taylor and Roselyn Costantino. Durham, NC and London: Duke University Press, 311–30, 2003.

———. "Theatre as a Wild Weed." *Theatre Journal* 56, no. 3: 454–56, 2004.

Mayer, Mónica. *Rosa Chillante: Mujeres y performance en México*. Mexico City: CONACULTA, 2005.

———. "Macular Degenerations: Some Peculiar Aspects of Performance Art Documentation." In *Perform, Repeat, Record*, edited by Amelia Jones and Adrian Heathfield. Bristol: Intellect, 105–20, 2012.

McCaughan, Edward J. "Navigating the Labyrinth of Silence: Feminist Artists in Mexico." *Social Justice* 34 (2007): 44–62.

———. *Art and Social Movements: Cultural Politics in Mexico and Aztlán*. Durham, NC: Duke University Press, 2012.

McEwan, Colin and Leonardo López Luján, eds. *Moctezuma: Aztec Ruler*. London and Mexico City: The British Museum Press with the Consejo Nacional para la Cultura y las Artes (CONACULTA) and the Instituto Nacional de Antropología e Historia (INAH), 2008.

Medina, Cuauhtémoc. "History Repeats Itself…Otherwise, It Wouldn't Be History." REDCAT, 24 June 2014.

Megson, Chris and Dan Rebellato. "Theatre and Anti-theatre." In *The Cambridge Guide to David Hare*, edited by Richard Boon. Cambridge, UK: Cambridge University Press, 236–49, 2007.

Merlín, Socorro. "Presencia de los rituales antiguos en el teatro mexicano contemporáneo: Los conjuros en *La hebra de oro* de Emilio Carballido." *Latin American Theatre Review* 38, no. 1: 61–71, 2004.

———. "La otra cara del teatro joven en México: *El amor de las luciérnagas de Alejandro Ricaño*." *GESTOS* 57: 53–63, 2014.

Mermikides, Alex. "Forced Entertainment—The Travels (2002): The Anti Theatrical Director." In *Making Contemporary Theatre: International Rehearsal Processes,* edited by Jen Harvie and Andy Lavender. Manchester, UK: Manchester University Press, 101–20, 2010.

Mermikides, Alex and Jackie Smart. *Devising in Process*. London: Palgrave Macmillan, 2010.

Meyran, Daniel. "Representar el pasado es repasar el presente o Las recuperaciones del mundo precolombino y colonial en el teatro mexicano contemporáneo." In *Un viaje sin fin. Teatro mexicano hoy*, edited by Heidrun Adler and Jaime Chabaud. Frankfurt am Main, Vervuert and Madrid: Iberoamericana, 43–55, 2004.

Middleton, Deborah K. "At Play in the Cosmos: The Theatre and Ritual of Nicolás Núñez." *TDR: The Drama Review* 45, no. 4: 42–63, 2001.

———. "Secular Sacredness in the Ritual Theatre of Nicolás Núñez." *Performance Research* 13, no. 3: 41–54, 2008.

Mijares, Enrique. *La realidad virtual del teatro Mexicano*. San Juan de los Lagos: Casa San Juan Pablos; Durango: Instituto Municipal del Arte y la Cultura, 1999.

———. "Pancho Villa, un héroe multifacético que cuenta cuentos a los niños." *Más allá del héroe. Antología crítica de teatro histórico hispanoamericano*, edited by María Mercedes Jaramillo and Juanamaría Cordones-Cook. Medellín, Columbia: Universidad de Antioquia, 321–327, 2008.

Millán Carranza, Jovita. *El Centro de Experimentación Teatral del INBA y sus propuestas escénicas*. Mexico City: Instituto Nacional de Bellas Artes y Literatura, 2014.

Miller, Greg. "How Our Brains Make Memories." *Smithsonian Magazine*, May 2010. http://www.smithsonianmag.com/science-nature/How-Our-Brains-Make-Memories [accessed 16 December 2017].

Milleret, Margo. *Latin American Women on Stages*. Albany: State University of New York, 2004.

Miralles, Juan. *Hernán Cortés: Inventor de México*. Mexico City and Barcelona: Tusquets, 2001.

Misemer, Sarah. *Secular Saints: Performing Frida Kahlo, Carlos Gardel, Eva Perón and Selena*. Martlesham: Tamesis Books, 2008.

Mock, Roberta. *Performing Processes: Creating Live Performance*. Bristol: Intellect, 2000.

Moncada Gil, Luis Mario. "Introducción." In *Dramaturgia mexicana hoy*, edited by Jorge Dubatti. Mexico City Dirección General de Publicaciones (CONACULTA)/Centro Cultural Helénico/Atuel, 1–5, 2005.

———. *Así pasan…efemérides teatrales 1900–2000*. Mexico City: Escenología e INBA, 2007.

Morrison, Toni. *Beloved*. New York: Random House, 1987.

Mukařovský, Jan. *Kapitel aus der Ästhetik*. Frankfurt am Main: Suhrkamp, 1970.

Múñoz, José Esteban. "Ephemera as Evidence: Introductory Notes to Queer Acts." *Women and Performance: A Journal of Feminist Theory* 8, no. 2: 5–16, 1996.

Muñoz, Sandra. "Diversidad en escena: una muestra de nuestro territorio teatral." *Paso de Gato*, no. 59:75.

Negus, Keith and Michael Pickering. *Creativity, Communication and Cultural Value*. London: Sage Publications, 2004.

Nelson, Robin. "Set Map Slip = Palimpsest (working title)." *Performance Research* 6, no. 2: 20–29, 2001.

Nemser, Daniel. "Triangulating Blackness: Mexico City, 1612." *Mexican Studies/Estudios Mexicanos* 33, no. 3: 344–66, 2017.

Nielsen, Lara and Patricia Ybarra. *Neoliberalism and Global Theatres: Performance Permutations*. Basingstoke, UK: Palgrave Macmillan, 2012.

Niggli, Josefina. *The Plays of Josefina Niggli: Recovered Landmarks of Latino Literature*, edited by William Orchard and Yolanda Padilla. Madison, WI: University of Wisconsin Press, 2007.

Nigro, Kirsten F. "Twentieth Century Theater." In *Mexican Literature: A History,* edited by David Williams Foster. Austin: University of Texas Press, 213–42, 1994.

———. "Inventions and Transgressions: A Fractured Narrative on Feminist Theatre in Mexico." In *Negotiating Performance: Gender, Sexuality, and Theatricality in Latin/o America*, edited by Diana Taylor and Juan Villegas. Durham, NC and London: Duke University Press, 137–58, 1994.

———. "¿Qué ha pasado aquí? Realidad e hiperrealidad en *Nadie sabe nada* de Vicente Leñero." In *Essays in Honor of Frank Dauster*, edited by Kirsten Nigro and Sandra M. Cypess. Newark, NJ: Juan de la Cuesta, 15–24, 1995.

———. "Hacidendo historia, haciendo teatro en La noche de *Hernán Cortés.*" In *Un viaje sin fin. Teatro mexicano hoy*, edited by Heidrun Adler and Jaime Chabaud. Frankfurt am Main, Vervuert and Madrid: Iberoamericana, 57–63, 2004.

———. "Algunas meditaciones sobre la representación de la violencia contra las mujeres: El caso de las mujeres asesinadas de Ciudad Juárez." *Latin American Theatre Review* 46, no. 1: 37–57, 2012.

Nora, Pierre. "Between Memory and History: Les Lieux de Mémoire." *Representations* 26: 7–25, 1989.

———. *Realms of Memory: Rethinking the French Past*. New York: Columbia University Press, 1996.

Núñez, Nicolás. *Anthropocosmic Theatre: Rite in the Dynamics of Theatre*. Translated by Ronan J. Fitzsimons, edited by Deborah Middleton. Amsterdam: Harwood Academic Publishers, 1996.

Nyong'o, Tavia. *The Amalgamation Waltz: Race, Performance, and the Ruses of Memory*. Minneapolis: University of Minnesota Press, 2009.

Obregón, Rodolfo. "Prólogo." In *Prácticas de lo real en la escena contemporánea*, edited by José A. Sánchez. Mexico City: Paso de Gato, 11–14, 2013.

———. "El ciclo de la dirección en escena." *Un viaje sin fin. Teatro mexicano hoy*, edited by Heidrun Adler and Jaime Chabaud. Frankfurt am Main, Vervuert and Madrid: Iberoamericana, 29–40, 2004.

Oddey, Alison. *Devising Theatre: A Practical and Theoretical Handbook*. London: Routledge, 1994.

Oddey, Alison and Christine White, eds. *The Potentials of Space: The Theory and Practice of Scenography and Performance*. Bristol: Intellect, 2006.

Olguín, David, coord. *Un siglo de teatro en México*. Mexico City: Consejo Nacional para la Cultura y las Artes, 2011.

Olsen, Christopher. "Transformation, Identity, and Deconstruction Part of the Survival Kit of Collective Theatres in 2007." In *Vie et mort de la creation collective (The Lives and Deaths of Collective Creation)*, edited by Jane Baldwin, Jean-Marc Larrue and Christiane Page. Sherborn, MA: Vox Teatri, 162–78, 2008.

Oropesa, Salvador A. *The Contemporáneos Group: Rewriting Mexico in the Thirties and Forties*. Austin: University of Texas Press, 2010.

Ortega, Ulises. "Tres obras que hablan de México." *Revista fusión 14*, 14 February 2012. http://www. fusion14.com/artes-escenicas/tres-obras-que-hablan-de-mexico/ [accessed 14 February 2012].

Ortiz Bullé Goyri, Alejandro. "El teatro indigenista de los años veinte: ¿Orígenes del teatro popular mexicano actual?" *Latin American Theater Review* 37, no. 1: 75–93, 2003.

———. *Teatro y vanguardia en el México posrevolucionario (1920-1940)*. Mexico City: Universidad Autónoma Metropolitana, 2005.

Osberg, Deborah. "Knowledge Is not Made for Understanding; It Is Made for Cutting." *Complicity: An International Journal of Complexity and Education* 7, no. 2: iii–viii, 2010.

Palimpsest: A Journal on Women, Gender, and the Black International. New York: State University of New York Press.

Partida, Armando. "La dramaturgía Mexicana de los noventa." *Latin American Theatre Review* 34, no. 1 :143–60, 2000.

Patán, Federico. "*Mejor desaparece* de Carmen Boullosa: La fragmentación como estructura." *Unomásuno*, 22 August 1989.

Paz, Octavio. *El laberinto de la soledad*. Mexico City: Fondo de Cultura Económica, 2004 [1950].

Pensado, Indira. "Desmontaje en tres intentos. La voz de *Autoconfesión*, espectáculo unipersonal de Gerardo Trejoluna." In *Des/tejiendo escenas: desmontajes: procesos de investigación y creación*, edited by Ileana Diéguez. Mexico City: Universidad Iberoamericana y Instituto Nacional de Bellas Artes, 205–216, 2009.

Pessoa, Fernando. *La hora del Diablo*. Mexico City: Verdehalgo, 2005.

Phelan, Peggy. *Unmarked: The Politics of Performance*. London: Routledge, 1993.

———. "Thirteen Ways of Looking at Choreographing Writing." In *Choreographing History*, edited by Susan Leigh Foster. Bloomington: Indiana University Press, 200–10, 1995.

———. *Mourning Sex: Performing Public Memories*. London and New York: Routledge, 1997.

———. "Marina Abramović: Witnessing shadows." *Theatre Journal* 56, no. 4: 569–77, 2004.

Poniatowska, Elena. *Fuerte es el silencio*. Mexico City: Ediciones Era, 1982.

———. *La noche de Tlatelolco: Testimonios de historia oral*. Mexico City: Ediciones Era, 1998 (*Massacre in Mexico* (Helen R. Lane, trans). Columbia: University of Missouri, 1991).

Popova, Elvira. *La dramaturgia Mexicana de los años 90 del Siglo XX desde la perspectiva de la postmodernidad*. Monterrey, Nuevo León: Universidad Autónoma de Nuevo León, 2010.

Portilla, Jorge. *La fenomenología del relajo*. Mexico City: Fondo de Cultura Económica, 1992 [1966].

Prieto Stambaugh, Antonio. "Camp, *Carpa* and Cross-Dressing in the Theater of Tito Vasconcelos." In *Corpus Delecti*, edited by Coco Fusco. New York: Routledge, 83–95, 2000.

———. "Wrestling the Phallus, Resisting Amnesia: The Body Politic of Chilanga Performance Artists." In *Holy Terrors: Latin American Women Perform*, edited by Diana Taylor and Roselyn Costantino. Durham, NC and London: Duke University Press, 245–74, 2003.

———. "Corporalidades: Política y representación en el performance Mexicano." *Teatro al Sur* 25, October: 7–15, 2003.

———. "Ileana Diéguez Caballero's *Escenarios liminales*." *E-misférica* 6, no. 1: n.p., 2009.

———. "'RepresentaXión' de un *muxe*: la identidad performática de Lukas Avendaño." *Latin American Theatre Review* 48, no. 1: 31–53, 2014.

———. "Memorias inquietas: testimonio y confesión en el teatro performativo de México y Brasil." In *Corporalidades Escénicas. Representaciones del cuerpo en el teatro, la danza y el performance*, edited by Elka Fediuk and Antonio Prieto Stambaugh. Buenos Aires: Editorial Argus-a Artes y Humanidades, 216–52, 2016.

Prieto Stambaugh, Antonio and Roldán Ahtziri Molina. *Investigaciones artísticas: Poéticas, políticas y proceses*. Xalapa, Mexico: Universidad Veracruzana, 2013.

Primavesi, Patrick. "The Performance of Translation: Benjamin and Brecht on the Loss of Small Details." *TDR: The Drama Review* 43, no. 4: 53–59, 1999.

Proudfit, Scott and Kathryn Mederos Syssoyeva. "Preface: From Margin to Center." In *Collective Creation in Contemporary Performance*, edited by Kathryn Mederos Syssoyeva and Scott Proudfit. Basingstoke, UK: Palgrave Macmillan, 13–38, 2013.

Radosavljevi, Duška. *Theatre-Making: Interplay between Text and Performance in the 21st Century*. Basingstoke, UK: Palgrave Macmillan, 2013a.

——. *The Contemporary Ensemble: Interviews with Theatre-Makers*. London: Routledge, 2013b.

Rashkin, Elissa J. *The Stridentist Movement in Mexico: The Avant-Garde and Cultural Change in the 1920s*. Lanham, MD: Lexington Books, 2009.

Reyes de la Maza, Luis. *El teatro en México durante la Revolución (1911–1913)*. Mexico City: Escenología, 2005.

Ribas-Casassayas, Alberto and Amanda L. Petersen, eds. *Espectros: Ghostly Hauntings in Contemporary Transhispanic Narratives*. Lewisburg, WV: Bucknell University Press, 2015.

Rich, Adrienne. "When We Dead Awaken: Writing as Re-Vision." *College English (Issue: Women, Writing and Teaching)* 34, no. 1: 18–30, 1972.

——. *On Lies, Secrets and Silence: Selected Prose, 1966–1978*. New York: W.W. Norton and Company, 1979.

Richter, Falk. *Siete Segundos: In God We Trust*. Mexico City: Paso de Gato, Edición realizada con la colaboración del Goethe-Institut Mexiko, 2008.

Rizk, Beatriz J. *El Nuevo Teatro Latinoamericano: una lectura histórica*. Minneapolis: Prisma Institute, 1987.

——. "Hacia una teoría de la traducción: adaptaciones, versiones y variaciones de un tema, otra manera de ejercer el oficio de autor en la obra de Enrique Buenaventura." In *Reflexiones sobre teatro latinoamericano del siglo veinte*. Buenos Aires: Editorial Galerna; Kiel: Lemcke Verlag, 41–48, 1989.

——. *Posmodernismo y teatro en América Latina: Teorías y prácticas en el umbral del siglo XXI*. Madrid, Iberoamericana, 2001.

——. "Imagining a Continent: Recent Research on Latin American Theater and the Performing Arts." *Latin American Research Review* 42, no. 1: 196–214, 2007.

——. *Imaginando un continente: utopía, democracia y neoliberalismo en el teatro latinoamericano. Tomo 1 (México)*. Lawrence, KS: LATR Books, 2011.

Roach, Joseph. "Culture and Performance in the Circum-Atlantic World." In *Performativity and Performance,* edited by Eve Kosofsky Sedgwick and Andrew Parker. New York: Routledge, 45–63, 1995.

——. "Bodies of Doctrine: Headshots, Jane Austen, and the Black Indians of Mardi Gras." In *Choreographing History,* edited by Susan Leigh Foster. Bloomington: Indiana University Press, 149–61, 1995.

———. *Cities of the Dead: Circum-Atlantic Performance*. New York: Columbia University Press, 1996.

Rodriguez, Jeanette and Ted Fortier. *Cultural Memory: Resistance, Faith & Identity*. Austin: University of Texas Press, 2007.

Rodríguez del Pino, Salvador, trans. *Five Plays in Translation from Contemporary Mexican Theater: A New Golden Age*. Lewiston, ME: Edwin Mellen Press, 2001.

Roesner, David and Matthias Rebstock, eds. *Composed Theatre: Aesthetics, Practices, Processes*. Bristol: Intellect, 2012.

Rokem, Freddie. *Performing History: Theatrical Representation of the Past in Contemporary Theatre*. Iowa City: University of Iowa Press, 2002.

Rubin, Don and Carlo Solórzano. *The World Encyclopedia of Contemporary Theatre: The Americas*. London and New York: Routledge, 2013.

Rubio, Miguel. *Notas sobre teatro*. Lima: Grupo Cultural Yuyachkani; Minneapolis: University of Minnesota, 2001.

Sánchez, José A. *Prácticas de lo real en la escena contemporánea*. Mexico City: Paso de Gato, 2013.

———. *Practising the Real on the Contemporary Stage*. Translated by Charlie Allwood. Bristol: Intellect, 2014.

Sánchez Moreno, Daimary. "40 años de investigación teatral en México: Del teatro de representación al teatro participativo, un acercamiento a la labor del Taller de Investigación Teatral/UNAM (Parte I)." *Frontal Gaceta*, gacetafrontal.wordpress.com [accessed 16 December 2016].

Sanchis Sinisterra, José. *Narraturgia. Dramaturgia de textos narrativos*. Mexico City: Paso de Gato, 2012.

———. "Un lapsus conceptual." *Paso de Gato*, no. 26: 27–30, 2006.

Schechner, Richard. *Between Theatre and Anthropology*. Chicago: University of Chicago Press, 1985.

———. *Performance Studies: An Introduction*. New York: Routledge, 2002.

Schlau, Stacey. "Sor Juana oversees the subversion of gendered state power: Feminist gestures in *De noche vienes, Esmeralda*." *Cuadernos de música, artes visuales y artes escénicas (Journal of Music, Visual, and Performing Arts)* 4, no. 1–2: 235–62, 2008/9.

Schmidhuber, Guillermo. *El teatro mexicano en cierne 1922–1938*. New York: Peter Lang Publishers, 1992.

Schneider, Luis Mario. *Fragua y gesta del teatro experimental en México. Teatro de Ulises. Esolares del Teatro. Teatro de Orientación*. Mexico City: UNAM, Equilibrista. 1995.

Schneider, Rebecca. "Performance Remains." *Performance Research* 6, no. 2: 100–108, 2001.

———. "Solo Solo Solo." In *After Criticism: New Responses to Art and Performance*, edited by Gavin Butt. Malden and Oxford, UK: Blackwell Publishing, 23–47, 2005.

———. *Performing Remains: Art and War in Times of Theatrical Reenactment*. New York: Routledge, 2011.

———. "Performance Remains." In *Perform, Repeat, Record: Live Art in History*, edited by Amelia Jones and Adrian Heathfield. Bristol: Intellect, 137–150, 2012.

Scolieri, Paul A. *Dancing the New World: Aztecs, Spaniards, and the Choreography of Conquest*. Austin: University of Texas Press, 2013.

Seda, Laurietz. "Etnia y clase social en el contexto de los procesos de la globalización en *La Malinche* de Víctor Hugo Rascón Banda." In *El Teatro de Rascón Banda: Voces en el umbral*, edited by Jacqueline Bixler and Stuart Day. Mexico City: Escenología, 91–102, 2005.

——. "Trans/Acting: The Art of Living 'In-Between.'" In *Trans/Acting: Latin American and Latino Performing Arts*, edited by Jacqueline Bixler and Laurietz Seda. Lewisburg, PA: Bucknell University Press, 13–23, 2009.

——. "Trans/Acting Bodies: Guillermo Gómez-Peña's Search for a Singular Plural Community." In *Trans/Acting: Latin American and Latino Performing Arts*, edited by Jacqueline Bixler and Laurietz Seda. Lewisburg, PA: Bucknell University Press, 227–37, 2009.

——. "Trans/Acciones de la memoria: *Proyecto 1980/2000: El tiempo que heredé.*" GESTOS, 57: 65–80, 2014.

Seed, Patricia, ed. *José Limón and La Malinche: The Dancer and the Dance.* Austin: University of Texas Press, 2008.

Seligson, Esther. *El teatro, festín, efímero. Reflexiones y testimonios.* Mexico City: Dirección de Difusión Cultural, 1989.

Serrano, Daniel. *El cazador de gringos.* Hermosillo, Mexico: Paso de Gato, Edición realizada en colaboración con el Instituto Municipal de Cultura y Arte de Hermosillo, 2007.

Serret, Estela. "Modernidad reflexiva y posmodernidad: apuntes sobre las identidades." *Revista Sociológica UAM,* 53: 213–22, 2003.

Silverman, Maxim. *Palimpsestic Memory: The Holocaust and Colonialism in French Francophone Fiction and Film.* New York: Berghahn Books, 2013.

Solórzano, Carlo. "Mexico." In *The World Encyclopedia of Contemporary Theatre: The Americas,* edited by Don Rubin and Carlo Solórzano. London and New York: Routledge, 310–30, 2000.

Southerland, Stacey. "Elusive Dreams, Shattered Illusions: The Theater of Elena Garro." In *Latin American Women Dramatists: Theater, Texts, and Theories*, edited by Catherine Larson and Margarita Vargas. Bloomington: Indiana University Press, 243–62, 1998.

Spackman, Helen. "Minding the Matter of Representation: Staging the Body (Politic)." In *The Body in Performance*, edited by Patrick Campbell. New York: Routledge, 5–22, 2001.

Steedman, Carolyn. *Dust: The Archive and Cultural History.* New Brunswick, NJ: Rutgers University Press, 2002.

Syssoyeva, Kathryn Mederos. "Introduction." In *A History of Collective Creation*, edited by Kathryn Mederos Syssoyeva and Scott Proudfit. Basingstoke, UK: Palgrave Macmillan, 1–11, 2013.

——. "Introduction." In *Collective Creation in Contemporary Performance*, edited by Kathryn Mederos Syssoyeva and Scott Proudfit. Basingstoke: Palgrave Macmillan, 1–11, 2013.

Syssoyeva, Kathryn Mederos and Scott Proudfit, eds. *A History of Collective Creation.* Basingstoke, UK: Palgrave Macmillan, 2013a.

——, eds. *Collective Creation in Contemporary Performance.* Basingstoke, UK: Palgrave Macmillan, 2013b.

Taylor, Diana. *Theatre of Crisis: Drama and Politics in Latin America.* Lexington, KT: University Press of Kentucky, 1991.

———. "Opening Remarks." In *Negotiating Performance: Gender, Sexuality, and Theatricality in Latin/o America*, edited by Diana Taylor and Juan Villegas. Durham, NC and London: Duke University Press, 14–16, 1994.

———. *Disappearing Acts: Spectacles of Gender and Nationality in Argentina's Dirty War*. Durham, NC and London: Duke University Press, 1997.

———. *The Archive and the Repertoire: Performing Cultural Memory in the Americas*. Durham, NC and London: Duke University Press, 2003.

———. "Performance and/as History." *TDR: The Drama Review* 50, no. 1 (T189): 67–86, 2006.

———. *Performance*. Buenos Aires: Asuntos Impresos Ediciones, 2012.

———. *Performance*. Translated from Spanish by Abigail Levine. Translated into English by Diana Taylor. Durham, NC and London: Duke University Press, 2016.

Taylor, Diana and Juan Villegas, eds. *Negotiating Performance: Gender, Sexuality, and Theatricality in Latin/o America*. Durham, NC and London: Duke University Press, 1994.

Taylor, Diana and Lorie Novak, eds. *Dancing with the Zapatistas: Twenty Years Later*. Durham, NC and New York: Duke University Press in collaboration with the Hemispheric Institute of Performance and Politics at New York University and HemiPress, 2015.

Taylor, Diana and Roselyn Costantino, eds. *Holy Terrors: Latin American Women Perform*. Durham, NC: Duke University Press, 2003.

———. "Unimagined Communities." In *Holy Terrors: Latin American Women Perform*, edited by Diana Taylor and Roselyn Costantino. Durham, NC: Duke University Press, 1–24, 2003.

Taylor, Diana and Sarah J. Townsend, eds. *Stages of Conflict: A Critical Anthology of Latin American Theater and Performance*. Ann Arbor: University of Michigan Press, 2008.

Thompson, Susan. "Freedom and Constraints: Jacques Lecoq and the Theater of Ensemble Creation." In *Encountering Ensemble*, edited by John Britton. London and New York: Bloomsbury Methuen Drama, 389–404, 2013.

Threadgold, Terry. *Feminist Poetics: Poiesis, Performance, Histories*. London and New York: Routledge, 1997.

Toriz Proenza, Martha. "Teatro en Coapa: Una experiencia educativa en la ciudad de México." *Educación y Humanidades* 1, no. 1: 27–44, 2010.

Toro, Alfonso de. "Los caminos del teatro actual: hacia la plurimedialidad espectacular postmoderna o ¿el fin del teatro mimético referencial? (Con especial atención al teatro y la 'performance' latinoamericanos)." In *Estrategias postmodernas y postcoloniales en el teatro latinoamericano actual. Hibridez-Medialidad-Cuerpo*, edited by Alfonso de Toro. Frankfurt am Main: Vervuert, 21–72, 2004.

Tortajada Quiroz, Margarita. "Branches and Roots: Two Generations of Female Mexican Choreographers Building Their Identity." Talk: *Body, Performance and Dance Research Platform*, 11 October 2010, University of California Riverside, Department of Dance.

Townsend, Sarah J. *The Unfinished Art of Theater: Avant-Garde Intellectuals in Mexico and Brazil*. Evanston, IL: Northwestern University Press, 2018.

Turner, Cathy. "Palimpsest or Potential Space? Finding a Vocabulary for Site-Specific Performance." *NTQ* 20(4): 373–390. 2004.

Turner, Victor. *From Ritual to Theater: The Human Seriousness of Play*. New York: PAJ Publications, 1982.

——. "Liminality and Performative Genres." In *Rite, Drama, Festival, Spectacle: Rehearsals toward a Theory of Cultural Performance*, edited by J. J. MacAloon. Philadelphia: Institute for the Study of Human Issues, 19–41, 1984.

——. "Are There Universals of Performance in Myth, Ritual, and Drama?" In *On the Edge of the Bush: Anthropology as Experience*, edited by E. Turner. Tucson: University of Arizona Press, 291–301, 1985.

——. "Are There Universals of Performance in Myth, Ritual, and Drama?" In *By Means of Performance: Intercultural Studies of Theatre and Ritual*, edited by Richard Schechner and Willa Appel. Cambridge, UK: Cambridge University Press, 8–18, 1990.

Underberg, Natalie. "Sor Juana's Villancicos: Context, Gender, and Genre." *Western Folklore* 60, no. 4: 297–316, 2001.

Underiner, Tamara L. *Contemporary Theatre in Mayan Mexico: Death-Defying Acts*. Austin: University of Texas Press, 2004.

Unger, Roni. *Poesía en Voz Alta in the Theater of Mexico*. Columbia, SC and London: University of Missouri Press, 1981.

Valdés Kuri, Claudio. "El proceso de creación de ¿*Dónde estaré esta noche?* de Teatro de Ciertos Habitantes." In *Des/tejiendo escenas: desmontajes: procesos de investigación y creación*, edited by Ileana Diéguez. Mexico City: Universidad Iberoamericana and Instituto Nacional de Bellas Artes, 151–160, 2009.

Valdés Kuri, Claudio and Analola Santana. "Entre la pluma y el sudor. Recuento de una experiencia entre un director y una dramaturgista." *GESTOS*, 59: 133–45, 2015.

Valdés Medellín, Gonzalo. "La estética de Juliana Faesler." *Revista Siempre*, May 25 2013.

Valdez, Mark. "Network of Ensemble Theatres." In *Encountering Ensemble*, edited by John Britton. London and New York: Bloomsbury Methuen Drama, 209–11, 2013.

van Delden, Maarten. "Past and Present in Víctor Hugo Rascón Banda's 'La Malinche' and Marisol Martín del Campo's 'Amor y conquista.'" *South Central Review: Memory and Nation in Contemporary Mexico* 21, no. 3: 8–23, 2004.

Varona, Alfonso. "Entrevista a Estela Leñero." *Latin American Theatre Review* 47, no. 2: 81–89, 2014.

——. "Entrevista a Ximena Escalante." *Latin American Theatre Review* 48, no. 1: 131–42, 2014.

Vaughan, Mary Kay and Stephen Lewis. *The Eagle and the Virgin: Nation and Cultural Revolution in Mexico, 1920–1940*. Durham, NC and London: Duke University Press, 2006.

Vázquez Touriño, Daniel. "Frustración magnífica y drama puro: el teatro de Legom." *Latin American Theatre Review* 47, no. 2: 63–79, 2014.

Verma, Jatinder. "The Challenge of Binglish: Analysing Multi-Cultural Performance." *Analysing Performance: A Critical Reader*, edited by Patrick Campbell. Manchester, UK: Manchester University Press, 193–202, 1996.

Versényi, Adam. *Theatre in Latin America: Religion, Politics, and Culture from Cortés to the 1980s*. Cambridge, UK: Cambridge University Press, 1993.

Verwoert, Jan. "The Crisis of Time in Times of Crisis." In *Experience, Memory, Re-enactment*, edited by Anke Bangma, Steve Rushton and Florian Wüst. Rotterdam: Piet Zwart Institute and Revolver, 37–40, 2005.

Villegas, Juan. "Closing Remarks." In *Negotiating Performance: Gender, Sexuality, and Theatricality in Latin/o America*, edited by Diana Taylor and Juan Villegas. Durham, NC and London: Duke University Press, 306–20, 1994.

———. *Historia multicultural del teatro y las teatralidades en América Latina*. Buenos Aires: Galerna, 2005.

———. *Historia del teatro y de las teatralidades en América Latina: Desde el period prehispánico a las tendencias contemporáneas*. Irvine, CA: Gestos, 2011.

———. "En los escenarios del mundo hispánico, 2013." *GESTOS,* 57: 10–12, 2014.

Ward, Julie. "Staging Postmemory: Self-representation and Parental Biographying in Lagartijas Tiradas al Sol's *El rumor del incendio*." *Latin American Theatre Review* 47, no. 2: 25–43, 2014.

Weinberg, Mark. *Challenging the Hierarchy: Collective Theatre in the United States*. Westport, CT: Greenwood Press, 1992.

Weldt-Basson, Helene Carol. *Subversive Silences: Nonverbal Expression and Implicit Narrative Strategies in the Works of Latin American Women Writers*. Madison, WI: Fairleigh Dickinson University Press, 2009.

Werth, Brenda. *Theatre, Performance, and Memory Politics in Argentina*. Basingstoke, UK: Palgrave Macmillan, 2010.

———. "Cuerpos desaparecidos y memoria corporizada en el teatro de la posdictadura argentina." In *Los Desaparecidos en la Argentina. Memorias, representaciones e ideas (1983–2008)*, coordinated by Emilio Crenzel. Buenos Aires: Biblos, 113–35, 2010.

White, Gareth. "Devising and Advocacy: The Red Room's Unstated." In *Devising in Process*, edited by A. Mermikides and J. Smart. London: Palgrave Macmillan, 93–109, 2010.

Wilkie, Fiona. *Out of Place: The Negotiation of Space in Site-Specific Performance*. Unpublished doctoral thesis, University of Surrey, 2004.

Wolffer, Lorena. "Cada performance es una historia." In *Des/tejiendo escenas: desmontajes: procesos de investigación y creación*, edited by Ileana Diéguez. Mexico City: Universidad Iberoamericana and Instituto Nacional de Bellas Artes, 147–150, 2009.

Wood, Silviana. *Barrio Dreams: Selected Plays by Silviana Wood,* edited by Norma Cantú and Rita Urquijo-Ruiz. Tucson: The University of Arizona Press, 2016.

Woodyard, George. "Prólogo." In *La realidad virtual del teatro mexicano*, edited by Enrique Mijares. Mexico City: Casa San Juan Pablos; Durango: Instituto Municipal del Arte y la Cultura, 15–18, 1997.

———. "Tres damas históricas de Víctor Hugo Rascón Banda." In *Un viaje sin fin. Teatro mexicano hoy*, edited by Heidrun Adler and Jaime Chabaud. Frankfurt am Main: Vervuert, Madrid: Iberoamericana, 65–79, 2004.

Ybarra, Patricia A. *Performing Conquest: Five Centuries of Theater, History, and Identity in Tlaxcala, Mexico*. Ann Arbor: University of Michigan Press, 2009.

———. *Latinx Theater in the Times of Neoliberalism*. Evanston, IL: Northwestern University Press. 2017.

Yépez, Gabriel. "Encuentro Internacional de Escena Contemporánea Transversales." *Paso de Gato,* no. 58: 92–94, 2014.

———. "Bitácora *Transversales*." Mexico City: Teatro Línea de Sombra and the Autonomous University, Mexico State, 2014.

———. "El ejercicio de la singularidad." In *Corporalidades Escénicas. Representaciones del cuerpo en el teatro, la danza y el performance,* coordinated by Elka Fediuk and Antonio Prieto Stambaugh. Buenos Aires: Editorial Argus-*a* Artes y Humanidades, 197–215, 2016.

Zúñiga Vázquez, Araceli. "Review of *Rosa Chillante: Mujeres y performance en México* by Mónica Mayer." Escaner, no. 76: September 2005, n.p. http://www.escaner.cl/escaner76/mutaciones. html [accessed 16 December 2017].

Notes

Introduction, pages 3–22

1 Epigraphs: www.lamáquinadeteatro; Taylor, *The Archive and the Repertoire*, 82; Schneider, *Performing Remains*, 33; Yépez, "Encuentro International," 93.
   All translations from Spanish are my own, unless otherwise stated.
2 Captions and credits are included in the "List of illustrations."
3 In Mexico, borders between creative artists, scholars and spectators are more fluid. The term "teatristas" refers to those involved with performance, theater, dance and scenic arts, encompassing scholars, creators and audiences.
4 Heathfield, "Then Again," 30.
5 Heathfield, ibid. Heathfield was reiterating ideas of Jan Verwoert in "The Crisis of Time in Times of Crisis."
6 For archives and repertoires see Taylor, ibid; for bodies as archives see Lepecki, "The Body as Archive"; for performing archives see Schneider, "Performance Remains," and Aston, "Feminist Performance as Archive."
7 Taylor, ibid., 35.
8 Lipsitz, "Standing at the Crossroads," 62–3.
9 Schneider, *Performing Remains*, 2.
10 Hirsch, www.postmemory.net.
11 Morrison, *Beloved*. Notably, Morrison's novel engages magical realism, a genre deeply relevant to Mexican sensibilities.
12 Rich, "When We Dead Awaken."
   The concepts of postmemory, rememory and re-vision were developed in contexts other than performance, but all three encompass creative and generative processes that are particularly helpful for analysing and creating theatre and performance seeking to investigate histories and memories.
   As my study relates to performances created by women who seek to challenge and rework accepted histories of embodied power relations, it is significant that the three concepts of postmemory, rememory and re-vision were developed by three women who were themselves engaged with matters of historical restraints (gendered and racial), and who drew on personal experiences embedded in these prejudices: Marianne Hirsch developed her notion of postmemory as a Jewish scholar in the United States, aiming to understand the nature of family

photographs in terms of bodies contained by and through photos, and as the ghosts of bodies and histories, particularly in relation to the Holocaust; Toni Morrison, distinguished author, explored personal and collective embodied racial histories of slavery and the Civil War in the United States in her novel *Beloved*, creating the moving concept of rememory to express the double-ness and haunting of the presence/body of the protagonist's dead daughter Beloved; and Adrienne Rich, a poet and feminist theorist whose gendered and embodied domestic roles and actions as wife and mother led her to sense that she was losing aspects of her self, developed her notion of re-vision of texts as a necessary form of empowerment and action.

13 Taylor, drawing on Roland Barthes' *Mythologies* (110), described "scenarios consisting of 'material which has already been worked on'…," ibid., 28.
It is worth noting that the Spanish word "escenario" means the stage (see, for example, Ileana Diéguez' study *Escenarios Liminales*).

14 Taylor, ibid.

15 I am drawing on Taylor's reiteration of Elin Diamond in her discussion of performance: "Elin Diamond defines performance in the broadest sense: a DOING/something DONE. This DOING/DONE lens allows us to understand performance across temporalities—present and past. DOING captures the *now* of performance…in this sense, performance can be understood as *process*—as enactment, exertion, intervention, and expenditure. […] [I]t is ALSO a thing DONE, an *object* or *product* or accomplishment. […] [T]he tension between the DOING and DONE—present and past—is very productive" (Taylor, *Performance*, 7–8, upper case and emphasis in original, translation from Spanish by Abigail Levine). Taylor's short book *Performance*, published in Spanish in Buenos Aires, contains many abbreviated translations of previous iterations of discussions on archives, embodied knowledge and performance from her own repertoire of publications and talks.

16 For this study, I am indebted to and in conversation with many scholars and artists in the areas of theatre, performance studies, dance and scenic arts. As well as the work of Taylor and Schneider, I particularly acknowledge the work of: Antonio Prieto Stambaugh (performance in Mexico, unsettled memories, scenic corporeality); Ileana Diéguez (performance in Mexico, liminality, bodies and memories); Gabriel Yépez (transversal performance in Mexico); Jane Blocker, Eleanora Fabião, Adrian Heathfield, Amelia Jones (corporeal temporality, repetition); José Esteban Múñoz (ephemera); André Lepecki (body as archive); Freddie Rokem (performing history); Joseph Roach, George Lipsitz, Jeanette Malkin, Karen Malpede (performing memory); Domingo Adame, Heidrun Adler, Raquel Araujo, Christina Baker, Jacqueline Bixler, Maris Bustamante, Jaime Chabaud, Roselyn Costantino, Stuart Day, Jorge Dubatti, Elka Fediuk, Jean Franco, Amalia Gladhart, Laura Gutiérrez, Antonio Magaña Esquivel, Kirsten Nigro, Laurietz Seda, Rodolfo Obregón, Alejandro Ortiz Bullé Goyri, Julie Ward, Patricia Ybarra (theatre, performance and dance in Mexico); Beatriz Rizk and Brenda Werth (performing history, temporality, archives, memory in Latin America); Juan Villegas (Latin American theatre); Susan Broadhurst (liminal performance); Hans-Thies Lehmann (liminal performance and postdramatic theatre); Susan Foster (choreographing history); Victor Turner (liminality); Richard Schechner (performance studies); Elaine Aston and Gerraldine Harris (feminist theatre and women practitioners); Paul Allain, John Britton, Emma Govan, Jen Harvie, Deidre Heddon, Peter Harrop, Evelyn Jamieson, Ian Lavender,

Alex Mermikides, Jane Milling, Roberta Mock, Helen Nicholson, Katie Normington, Alison Oddey, Scott Proudfit, Duška Radosavljevi, Jackie Smart and Kathryn Mederos Syssoyeva (ensemble, collective creation and devising).

17 I have listed many of Taylor's most relevant publications in the bibliography.

18 Schneider, "Solo Solo Solo," 40–1.

19 Ibid.

20 Schneider, *Performing Remains*, 33. "Performing the Archive: When we approach performance not as that which disappears (as the archive expects), but as both the *act* of remaining and a means of reappearance [...] we almost immediately are forced to admit that remains do not have to be isolated to the document, to the object, to bone versus flesh [...]. In this sense performance becomes itself through messy and eruptive reappearance, challenging, via the performative trace, any neat antinomy between appearance and disappearance, or presence and absence—the ritual repetitions that mark performance as simultaneously indiscreet, non-original, relentlessly citational, and remaining" "Performance Remains," 103 [2001].

21 Valdés Medellín, "La estética de Juliana Faesler," n.p. Gonzalo Valdés Medellín is a prominent theatre critic, playwright and author in Mexico.

22 I shorten La Máquina de Teatro to La Máquina when appropriate.

23 See Broadhurst, *Liminal Acts* and Lehmann, *Postdramatic Theatre* and *Teatro posdramático* (the latter is the Spanish translation from German, which, unlike the English translation, comprises the full text).

24 I draw on my personal interviews with Juliana Faesler and Clarissa Malheiros throughout this book, and also on published company materials. Interviews were carried out between 2009 and 2016.

25 See Chapter 2 and individual analysis chapters for the original and full titles of each of these projects.

26 In addition to directors Juliana Faesler and Clarissa Malheiros, I interviewed: Berenice Alcántara, Diana Fidelia, Natyeli Flores, Sandra Garibaldi, Horacio González García Rojas, Elizabeth Múñoz, Roldán, Ramírez, Edyta Rzewuska and Vladimir Bojórquez (various dates, 2010).

27 *pre/now/post: una trilogía*, Nitery Theatre, Stanford University, USA, 2013.

28 My experiences include careers as a professional actor, dancer, musician, puppeteer, composer, choir director, community arts facilitator, teacher and professor of performing arts, performance studies, music (particularly ethnomusicology), dance and drama. I particularly draw on foundational experiences which include: a BA in music, drama, dance, incorporating experimental interdisciplinary practices (Birmingham University, 1983); training in drama in education using techniques of Boal and Heathcote (Postgraduate Certificate of Education, City of Birmingham University, 1991); performance training in dance (European Contemporary [Jooss Leeder], Laban, ballet, tap); music (piano and violin [Guildhall School of Music and Drama, London], opera and voice [Birmingham Conservatoire]); and physical theatre (Meyerholdian techniques of biomechanics with Dr. Robert Leach). I have participated in many workshops over the decades, and have been particularly influenced by practitioners Bobby Baker and Su Andi (see Aston and Harris, *Performance Practice and Process*).

The strategies I describe in this study cohere with those that I have used during my 30-year career as a performer/creator; a facilitator in community-based performance projects; a teacher of drama-in-education; a lecturer in Contemporary Performance and Applied Theatre (University of Winchester); founder-director of Inter-Act Theatre Workshop (UK); and in my current position as Professor at the University of California, Santa Barbara (UCSB). At UCSB I am honoured to teach undergraduate students in courses that include: "Creating Experimental Performance: memories/histories, processes/practices" and "Theater & Performance in Mexico: embodying, resisting and subverting stereotypes."

29 My long-term research in Mexico began life with the theatre project *Aztec* in Britain (see description in this Introduction). I then initiated a doctoral project involving many years of research, which is still ongoing, in the state of Michoacán and in Mexico City. My study focuses on performative representations of two iconic sets of bodies: Indigenous P'urhépecha dancing old men in the *Viejitos Dance* of the Island of Jarácuaro, and kneeling Indigenous women celebrating the ceremony of Night of the Dead on the Island of Janitzio, Lake Pátzcuaro. As scenarios of material already worked on, and as remains and traces of pre-conquest peoples, civilizations and environments, these iconic bodies were used, and continue to be used, as stereotypes of Indigeneity, connecting matters of temporality, historicity and collective memory in contexts of nationalism and tourism. Both corporeal representations were appropriated in the 1920s postrevolutionary period for processes of nation building (creating an imagined community of Mexicanness (*mexicanidad*)). This was a time when theatricalization, exhibition and stage performance intersected and drew upon avant-garde theatre from Europe and Russia. These two practices were staged for audiences in costumbrista performances of the "everyday lives" of Indigenous peoples, with multiple reiterations over the ensuing decades in live practice (theatre stages, resort stages, museums, festivals), video (world's fair exhibitions), film (Disney), photos (tourist brochures and postcards), narrative description (folkloric and tourist literature) and objects (souvenirs). These representative and symbolic bodies are, in effect, palimpsests, containing traces and remains of previous centuries, and corporeal postmemory of invasion, domination, destruction and revolution. For my publications see Hellier-Tinoco, *Removing the Mask*, "Power Needs Names," "Dead Bodies/Live Bodies," "Corpo/Reality, Voyeurs and the Responsibility of Seeing," *Embodying Mexico*, "Embodying Touristic Mexico," and "Embodied Imagined Communities."

30 See www.msem.ucpress.edu.

31 Barba, *The Paper Canoe*, 12, cited in De Marinis, "New Theatrology," 67.

32 Villegas, "Closing Remarks," 306.

33 Gutiérrez, *Performing Mexicanidad*, 209 n2.

34 These ranged through community theatre, television, physical theatre and puppet theatre, for example: *In the World: A Revolutionary Tale* by Maxim Gorky, Proteus Theatre Company, Haymarket Theatre, Basingstoke; *Nice Work* by David Lodge, BBC TV; *The Gun* by Alan Hancock, Nigel Stewart, director, Claire Russ choreographer; and *Treasure Island* directed by John Blundell, Cannon Hill Puppet Theatre, Midlands Arts Centre, Birmingham.

35 Leicestershire Theatre in Education Company, directed by Maurice Gilroy, OBE, with actor-creators Paul Waring, Jane Perkins and Simon Cuckson.

36   In a very different dynamic from the effects of colonization in Mexico, a deep awareness of British colonization and domination in many global contexts was experienced in late twentieth-century Britain through migrations of people from formerly colonized countries.

37   I am referencing Taylor, ibid., 11–12: "The West has forgotten about many parts of world that elude its explanatory grasp. Yet, it remembers the need to cement the centrality of its position as the West by creating and freezing the non-West as always other, 'foreign,' and unknowable. Domination by culture, by 'definition,' claims to originality and authenticity have functioned in tandem with military and economic supremacy." I return to Taylor's important observation presently.

38   As I write I am aware of this environment as a complex palimpsest of histories, memories and temporalities: as Indigenous land colonized by Spanish explorers in the eighteenth century; part of Mexico after Independence in 1821; and then invaded by and incorporated into the United States in 1846.

39   As Daniel Nemser describes: "Every translation, however apt, will necessarily alter the source text, whether by flattening the ambiguities of textual meaning or by grafting on new associations from the target language. [...] As such, we should consider the politics of every act of translation," Nemser "Triangulating Blackness: Mexico City, 1612," 344. As editor of the journal *Mexican Studies / Estudios Mexicanos*, I recently had the privilege of bringing to publication Nemser's article on the social construction of blackness and racialization of Black bodies in colonial Mexico.

40   Phelan, "Thirteen Ways of Looking," 200.

41   Foster, "Choreographing History," 9.

42   Lepecki, "Introduction," 3.

43   Negus and Pickering, *Creativity*, 5.

44   Primavesi, "The Performance of Translation," 54–55.

45   Barthes, *S/Z. An Essay*. Although Barthes was specifically making distinctions in the realm of novels, his concepts still offer some perspectives on my own choices for translating live transdisciplinary performance into writing. Curiously, his temporal ideas do not necessarily cohere with my uses of palimpsests and the past as a becoming: thus, "The writerly text is a perpetual present, upon which no consequent language [...] can be superimposed," ibid., 5.

46   I am aware the some readers will find my writing awkward to read. I make unconventional shifts and combine seemingly ungrammatical conventions. Some sentences comprise multiple clauses, whereas others are brief and singular.

47   Taylor, ibid., 25–26.

48   Taylor, ibid., 35.

49   Villegas, ibid., 307.

50   Taylor, ibid., 11–12.

51   Villegas, ibid.

52   I am reiterating the performative use of square brackets by Elaine Aston and Geraldine Harris in title of their book *Performance Practice and Process: Contemporary [Women] Practitioners*. Through their performative [ ], Aston and Harris indicate that these expert practitioners are indeed women and are "gender aware," but it is the diversity and richness of their practices and processes that are under discussion. As a participant in the "Women's

Writing for Performance Project," organized by Aston and Harris (Lancaster University, 2003–6, Arts and Humanities Research Council) on which their book is based, I here acknowledge the profoundly important work of both Aston and Harris and all the artists involved with that project.

53 Costantino, "Politics and Culture in a Diva's Diversion," 205.

54 De Marinis, "New Theatrology," 68.

55 Threadgold, *Feminist Poetics*, 1. She goes on to note, "In feminist theories and practices what has been at issue is the rewriting of patriarchal knowledges," ibid.

56 https://www.themagdalenaproject.org.

57 See also my chapter "Re-Moving Bodies in the USA/Mexico Drug/Border/Terror/Cold Wars," in *Choreographies of 21ˢᵗ Century Wars*.

58 Readers will notice obvious repetitions of key quotations and concepts in more than one chapter. In this era of fragmenting books and selecting discrete chapters, particularly for use in university classrooms, I hope that this strategy may facilitate the potential usefulness of smaller sections with student groups.

Chapter 1, pages 23–40

1 Epigraphs: Jeyasingh, *Palimpsest* and "Palimpsest, 1996" n.p.; Taylor, *The Archive and the Repertoire*, 82; Cypress, La Malinche in Mexican Literature, 1; Bustamante, "Non-Objective Arts in Mexico," 225 (The English version was published in translation and I have switched two words to create what may be a better flow: original "which processes have been extended"); Foster, "Choreographing History," 10.

2 Fabião, "History and Precariousness," 122.

3 Fabião, ibid.

4 Schneider, *Performing Remains*, 104. Schneider has reiterated this idea in three published venues, with slight alterations. In "Performance Remains" [2001] she wrote: "To read 'history' as a set of sedimented acts that are not the historical acts themselves but the act of securing any incident backward—the repeated act of securing memory—is the rethink the site of history in ritual repetition. This is not to say that we have reached the 'end of history,' neither is it to say that past events didn't happen, nor that to access the past is impossible. It is rather to resituate the site of any knowing of history as body-to-body transmission," 105.

5 Lista, "Play Dead," 9. Conversely, Mexican art critic and curator Cuauhtémoc Medina, in a talk titled "History Repeats Itself...Otherwise, It Wouldn't Be History," has suggested that "History has stopped being about historical memory, and has become occupied by short-term memory [in which] things are only historical if we can experience them, only ancient if we can wear them on the weekend," n.p.

Although these four performance projects of La Máquina were initiated with concepts of bodies of history, they are not history plays or history performances. My aim here is not to compare these four performance projects of La Máquina with other works but to discuss performance strategies dealing with transdisciplinary postmemory re-imaginings and rememory experiences. In Mexico, many playwrights and scenic artists use history to investigate the present (see the following chapter for details). In his insightful work *Performing History*, Freddie Rokem discusses play scripts developed by a single writer focusing on the French Revolution and the Shoah. In his study, Rokem examines "Strategies employed in the theatre, through which events and figures from these particular pasts (which in different ways are situated in the heart of the national consciousness of these places) have been 'resurrected' in the *here* and the *now* of theatrical performances," 2, emphasis in original. Although there are obviously connections to Rokem's notion of performing history in theatrical performances, there are also distinct differences, particularly in terms of working with personal experiences of participants in devising processes.

6   *Palimpsest* was choreographed by Shobana Jeyasingh and performed by the Shobana Jeyasingh Dance Company (1996–97). Jeyasingh was born in Madras, India in 1957, and began taking Bharata Natyam classes as a young child. She particularly developed her career in Britain. Significantly, relating to my notion of performing palimpsest bodies, many of the poses of Bharata Natyam are embodiments of poses depicted in stone sculptures. See www.shobanajeyasingh.co.uk and Bremser and Sanders, *Fifty Contemporary Choreographers*.

7   Palimpsest and "Palimpsest," n.p. See also Robin Nelson's discussion of Jeyasingh's work in relation to palimpsest in "Set Map Slip = Palimpsest (working title)."

8   Taylor, ibid., 82.

9   Taylor also specifically references Paul Connerton's study *How Societies Remember*.

10 Taylor, ibid.

11 See, particularly, Taylor, *The Archive and the Repertoire*, 79–109. In this chapter, Taylor encompasses a discussion of *I, Too, Speak of the Rose* (*Yo también hablo de la rosa*) by renowned Mexican playwright Emilio Carballido, focusing on the character of the Intermediary. The Intermediary is an individual trans-temporal woman whose body contains and connects multiple individual and collective memories and histories—in other words, a palimpsest.

12 In the field of theatre and performance scholarship, Cathy Turner has engaged the term palimpsest specifically in relation to site-specific theatre and space, describing how "space is often envisaged as an aggregation of layered writings — a palimpsest" (373). She discusses Mike Pearson's theatre/archaeology and his uses of co-existent host (host site) and ghost (created by the theatre-makers), whereby the host can be seen through the ghost, with these performances relying on the complex superimposition and coexistence of a number of historical and contemporary narratives and architectures. She describes how, "The event of the performance is seen as the rewriting of space through a new occupation of space in tension with what precedes it," referring to the "palimpsest-like layering of 'host' and 'ghost' spaces" (374 and 376). She references a vocabulary of strata, fragments, ruins, narratives, traces, monuments, past, absence, transgression, negotiating boundaries, remaking and rewriting. Turner also presents many other notions that I engage in my current analyses, notably ideas of play, experience, inter-subjectivity, potential space, simultaneity, and liminality, Turner "Palimpsest or Potential Space?"

In another use of palimpsest connected with notions of performance and location, Fiona Wilkie has referred to processes of configuring and manipulating space in relation to site-specific performance, specifically encompassing an erasure: "Site-specific performance's act of writing on a space might simultaneously be an act of erasing what has previously been written, as in the palimpsestic image employed by Nick Kaye: 'the palimpsest, a paper "which has been written upon twice, the original having been rubbed out" (Onions 1973) or "prepared for writing on and wiping out again" (Onions 1973), not only provides a model for the relationship of non-place to place, but, in the context of a transitive definition of site, of site-specificity itself,"' Wilkie, *Out of Place*, 87. Notably, her own usage is a form of palimpsest through layering and reiteration as she cites Nick Kaye, "Performing the City," in *Site-Specific Art*, who in turn was citing the entry of Onions in *The Shorter Oxford English Dictionary* 1973.

13 Schneider, "Solo Solo Solo," 41.

14 Schneider, ibid.

15 De Quincey, "The Palimpsest of the Human Brain," n.p.

16 See Taylor, ibid., 96: "Mestizaje (unlike hybridity) refers to the *both/and* rather than the neither/nor, the double-coded as opposed to the fragmentary sense of subjectivity." In the following chapter, I return to discuss these environments and contexts in relation to the strategies of La Máquina.

17 Etymologically the term palimpsest combines "palin"—"again"—with "psêstos"—"rubbed smooth."

18 Notably, footprints are used as an iconographic device in the codices, the painted books, of the pre- and immediate post-invasion peoples of Mesoamerica. For example, in the *Codex Mendoza* several sets of multiple footprints appear, indicating the direction of people's physical movement. La Máquina draws on these "remains" of bodies through ideas of journeys and migrations in *Mexican Trilogy* (Chapter 3).
Schneider also refers to concepts of footprints in relation to bodily memory (particularly referencing C.S. Peirce's notion of an indexical remain), *Performing Remains*, 11.

19 In a recent volume titled *Sites of Memory in Spain and Latin America: Trauma, Politics, Resistance*, editor Aida Díaz de León invokes the idea of "the palimpsest of memory" and draws on Taylor's concepts of archive and repertoire, "The Palimpsest of Memory," 4 and 12. In "The Palimpsest of Memory: Reconstructing Race, Culture and Religion from Colonial Times to the Present in Peru, Mexico and the Dominican Republic," Díaz de León describes erasure and the "archeological approach to memory [...] delv[ing] into the layers of the past to reveal something that should have remained concealed," referring also to methodologies and the investigation of overlapping layers of discursive forms as a "palimpsest-like structure," ibid., 12.
Other useful examples of "palimpsest" in recent scholarship include: *Present Pasts: Urban Palimpsests and the Politics of Memory*, in which Andreas Huyssen invokes notions of palimpsest to discuss collective identity, memory and history, considering how they interrelate to create public identity, and how memory of historical trauma has a unique power to generate works of art; *Palimpsest: A Journal on Women, Gender, and the Black International*, which is "by and about women of the African Diaspora and their communities in the Atlantic and Indian Ocean worlds," therefore encompassing notions of collective histories/memories, journeys, and racial and gendered politics; Tavia Nyong'o's description of the palimpsest of racial politics as sedimented in debates about history and memory, in *The Amalgamation Waltz*; "Acoustic Palimpsests" by J. Martin Daughtry; "Culture,

Commodity, Palimpsest" by Travis Jackson; *Palimpsestic Memory* by Maxim Silverman; and *The Palimpsest* by Sarah Dillon; and *Palimpsesto*, a journal of Iberoamerican social studies.

20 Bergson's philosophical discussions around questions of body, perception, mind and memory offer some fascinating descriptions that suggest notions of performing palimpsest bodies through postmemory and rememory, *Matter and Memory*.

21 Bergson, ibid., 298.

22 Heathfield, "Then Again," 28; ibid.; Schneider, ibid., 10.

23 Bustamante, "Non-Objective Arts," 225.

24 Five hundred years ago English had a highly developed subjunctive mood. Today the mood has practically vanished. Contemporary speakers tend to use the conditional forms of "could" or "would" to indicate statements contrary to reality: "If I were a butterfly, I would have wings."

25 Turner, "Are There Universals," 295 and 12. The ideas of metamorphosis and transfiguration may seem to be applicable here, particularly in terms of processes of transformation. However, the key to palimpsest bodies lies in the plurality and trans-temporal traces. With metamorphosis and transformation, remains and traces of a previous body or existence are usually gone. Taylor's discussions comparing mestizaje and hybridity are also useful: mestizaje refers to and entails *both/and* and hybridity entails neither/nor or either/or, see Taylor, ibid., 96–102.
Susan Broadhurst, in her discussion of liminal aesthetics and liminal acts, explains that "Turner was ingenious in linking performance to this marginalized space which holds a possibility of potential forms, structures, conjectures, and desires," "Liminal Aesthetics," 1.

26 Diéguez, *Escenarios liminales*, 60. In this study, Diéguez particularly draws on Turner to discuss performance in Mexico.

27 Phelan, "Thirteen Ways," 208. Joseph Roach and Sue-Ellen Case also provide useful insights: "To speak of *the* body, as if it were only one, effaces the particularity of bodies…Just to begin to make the list of the diversity and reciprocity of bodies is to question the totality of the body," Roach, "Bodies of Doctrine," 150, emphasis in original; and Sue-Ellen Case famously described how "The lesbian body, defined by its desire, is always two bodies," "Meditations," 198.

28 Hall, "Introduction: Who Needs 'Identity'?" Jaime Chabaud, Mexican theatre scholar and playwright, observed that "we cannot understand ourselves as an 'I' but rather many 'I's' interacting with a 'reality' that is much more complex," Chabaud, "Nota introductoria," 7.

29 Lepecki, "Introduction," 3. In "El cuerpo roto," which translates as "the broken body," Ileana Diéguez writes of remains and absences, referencing the interrelationship between a singular body of a broken person—*cuerpo roto*—and a collective of broken people—*corpus roto*, 9. In her analysis of "absent" and "disappeared" bodies in relation to art, violence and mourning, Diéguez discusses bodies transformed by violent interruptions to life where the artwork is a memory of the pain, see Diéguez, *Cuerpos ExPuestos*, "El cuerpo roto," and *Cuerpos sin duelo*. See also Phelan's *Mourning Sex* for an analysis of different instances of injured bodies; and Coco Fusco's seminal volume *Corpus Delicti* on performance art in the Americas that addressed "the illegitimately violent exercise of power over bodies," Fusco, "Introduction," 2–3.

30 Spackman, "Minding the Matter of Representation," 12.
31 Many scholars have analysed aspects of theatre, performance and memory. One of the most influential is Jeanette Malkin, who, in *Memory-Theater and Postmodern Drama*, examines the theme of memory in plays written by US and European playwrights since the 1970s. She describes how, in these plays, the past is "no longer grounded [but is] a past which floats within the collective unconscious, in a place of fragmented collective identity. These plays 'remember' in ways parallel to the theories of knowledge that inform them and thus become paradigms for a vision of the world," 3.
For discussions of memory, history, theatre and performance in Mexico see, for example, William Beezley, Jacqueline Bixler, Roselyn Costantino, Stuart Day, Ileana Diéguez, Elka Fediuk, Jean Franco, Laura Gutiérrez, Mark Hernández, Daniel Meyran, Enrique Mijares, Kirsten Nigro, Elvira Popova, Antonio Prieto Stambaugh, Beatriz Rizk, Laurietz Seda, Diana Taylor, Claudio Valdés Kuri, Maarten van Delden, Julie Ward, Patricia Ybarra and Gabriel Yépez.
32 Hirsch, http://www.postmemory.net, *Family Frames*, *The Generation of Postmemory*, "The Generation of Postmemory." Hirsch developed her concept of postmemory in relation to the Holocaust.
33 See Julie Ward's excellent analysis of a recent theatre work by renowned company Largatijas tiradas al sol engaging the concept of postmemory, Ward, "Staging Postmemory."
34 Drawing on Jean-François Lyotard: "The 'post-' of 'postmodern' does not signify a movement of comeback, flashback or feedback, that is, not a movement of repetition but a procedure in 'ana-': a procedure of analysis, anamnesis, anagogy, and anamorphosis that elaborates an 'initial forgetting,'" Lyotard, *The Postmodern Explained*, 80. Significantly for this study of performance engaging many of the aesthetics of postdramatic theatre (Lehmann), scholar Karen Jürs-Munby, in her "Introduction" to the English translation of Lehmann's work, references Lyotard and draws attention to this aspect of the "post" of postdramatic, noting that it is "not an 'epochal category' or chronological 'after' or a 'forgetting' of the past but 'a rupture and a beyond that continue to entertain relationships with [drama] and are in many ways an analysis and 'anamnesis' of [drama],'" "Introduction," 188, fn3.
35 "Sethe gathered hair from the comb and leaning back tossed it into the fire. It exploded into stars and the smell infuriated them. 'Oh, my Jesus,' she said and stood up so suddenly the comb she had parked in Denver's hair fell to the floor [...] She had to do something with her hands because she was remembering something she had forgotten she knew," Morrison, *Beloved*, 73.
36 In recent writings on archives as and in bodies, authors draw on previous theorizations from Foucault, Derrida, Deleuze and Guatarri. In "Repetition: A Skin which Unravels," Jane Blocker offers a repetition of Derrida's definition of archives as that which preserves and remembers, alters and forgets, and "is empowered to create origins, as the place from which things commence, the site where history begins [...]. That is, the archive stands as a monument to forgetting," 204–5. See also: Adrian Heathfield and Amelia Jones, *Perform, Repeat, Record*; André Lepecki, *Of the Presence of the Body*; and Rebecca Schneider and Diana Taylor, ibid. In *Dust: The Archive and Cultural History*, historian Carolyn Steedman describes archives as "stories caught half way through: the middle of things; discontinuities," i. Taylor describes a body as a "receptor, storehouse and transmitter of knowledge," ibid., 81–2.

37 Taylor, ibid., 82.

38 Malpede, "Theatre of Witness," 136–37.

39 Costantino, "Embodied Memory," n.p. Costantino discusses performances by Mexican performance artist Jesusa Rodríguez, and particularly the performance *Las Horas de Belén*, in relation to which she writes of "battles for interpretive power that occur on the body's surface flesh and its interior universe, struggles [that are] as much part of the colonial experience as of contemporary globalization and neo-liberalism," ibid.

40 Lines described this in an after-show talk back with the artist: 8 October 2016, Granada Theater, Santa Barbara, USA.

41 Pensado is discussing Butoh in Mexico, "Desmontaje en tres intentos," 208, n5 ("Cuerpo contenedor de vivencias"; "Todas las experiencias que graban los huesos, más que la piel"). Andreé Grau makes a fascinating observation that Tiwi dancers of northern Australia "have an extensive vocabulary for body parts, but no word for 'body' as a bounded entity, comparable to the 'body' conceptualized by ballet dancers," "When the Landscape Becomes Flesh," 141.

42 See, for example, Phelan, *Unmarked*; Auslander, *Liveness*; Múñoz, "Ephemera as Evidence"; Schneider, "Solo Solo Solo"; and Jones, "Foreword," "The Now and the Has Been" and "Franko B. and Kamal Ackarie." In this study I do not specifically analyse concepts of liveness, deadness and ephemerality, and I am not dealing with concepts of the phenomenology of the body as discussed by Merleau Ponty (see, for example, Phelan, *Unmarked* and Auslander, *Liveness*). Taylor considers issues of hauntology, drawing on Jameson (drawing on Jacques Derrida, who coined the term *hauntologie* (*Spectres de Marx* 1993)) to describe how "the living present is scarcely as self-sufficient as it claims to be; [...] we would do well not to count on its density and solidity, which might under exceptional circumstances betray us," Taylor, ibid., 133, citing Jameson, "Marx's Purloined Letter," 39.

A widely celebrated death-life concept in Mexico involves the collective performative ritual event of Day/Night of the Dead, which offers a framework of celebratory commemoration and reflection. People eat sugar skulls marked with the name of living loved-one as they concurrently spend time at the graves of dead loved-ones, providing food for the loved-one. The recent animated film *Coco* explores aspects of bodily materiality in relation to Night of the Dead.

Artist Frida Kahlo repeatedly depicted her own body in her paintings as palimpsest bodies in coexistent states of liveness/deadness (see Sarah Misemer's discussion in *Secular Saints*). Issues of the spectral and of haunting have a strong presence in Latin American and Spanish literatures and cultures. "Haunting, the spectral, and the effect of the unseen [...] carry a special weight in contemporary Latin American and Spanish cultures [...] due to the ominous legacy of authoritarian governments and civil wars, as well as the imposition of the unseen yet tangible effects of global economics and neoliberal policies," Ribas-Casassayas and Petersen, *Espectros*, 2.

There is a rich literature on notions of physicality/virtuality in relation to bodies, memory and disembodiment. See, for example, Brejzek 2006. See also my own analysis of *Timboctou* by Alejandro Ricaño, directed by Martín Acosta, produced by CalArts and the University of Guadalajara, in Hellier-Tinoco, "Re–moving bodies." As the case study projects of La Máquina de Teatro only tangentially engage with virtual reality and video technologies, I do not encompass these wider discussions in this book.

43 Rich, "When We Dead Awaken."

44 Rich, *On Lies, Secrets and Silence*, 3.

45 Ibid. Significantly, Rich initially developed her concept in relation to a theatrical framework, taking the title of her piece "When We Dead Awaken: Writing as Re-Vision" from a play by Henrik Ibsen, titled *When We Dead Awaken (The Resurrection Day)*.
The notion of counter-memories posited by Michel Foucault is also apt, as residual or resistant forms of knowledge that withstand the official versions of history, in *Language, Counter-memory, Practice*.

46 Seda, "Trans/Acting," 14. In relation to palimpsests, I particularly connect Seda's notion of rearticulating the interstitial spaces with the idea of writing/working between the lines: Gerald Bruns has described how, "to write is to intervene in what has already been written; it is to work 'between the lines' of antecedent texts, there to gloss, to embellish, to build invention upon invention. All writing is essentially amplifications of discourse: it consists of doing something to (or with) other texts," *Inventions, Writing*, 53.

47 Ybarra, *Performing Conquest*, 22; Rizk, *Posmodernismo y teatro*, 68, 88, 61–92.

48 Malkin, *Memory-Theatre and Postmodern Drama*, 1, 3.

49 Schneider, *Performing Remains*, 6–7, emphasis in original. Although Butler was dealing with performativity and gender, such that "the body becomes its gender through a series of acts which are renewed, revised, and consolidated through time," these embodied reiterations and sedimented acts are applicable to constructing all forms of identity, in specific temporal moments, see Butler, "Performative Acts," 523.

50 Schneider, ibid., 10; Schechner, *Between Theatre and Anthropology*, 36; Jones, "Foreword," 12. Jones describes how, "The performative [is] loosely understood here via theorists from J.L. Austin to Roland Barthes, Jacques Derrida, and Judith Butler as the reiterative enactment across time of meaning (including that of the 'self' or subject) through embodied gestures, language and/or other modes of signification," ibid.

51 Taylor, ibid., 28, quoting Roland Barthes' *Mythologies*.

52 Bourdieu, *The Logic of Practice*, 72.

53 Hutcheon has described how "echoes of the texts and contexts of the past [are] known to us today through [...] texturalized traces," making the writing of history "inherently intertextual," "Historiographic Metafiction, 3; *The Poetics of Postmodernism*, 81.
Múñoz, "Ephemera as Evidence," 10. As Múñoz was discussing queer acts, his ideas are eminently useful for conceptualizing performing palimpsest bodies through notions of blurring of boundaries, border crossings and trans issues, generated through the performativity of embodied traces, and particularly in terms of re-visions of bodies of history.

54 Taylor, ibid.

55 Taylor, ibid.

56 Threadgold discusses Bourdieu's conceptualization of the habitus of the body as re-vision, in *Feminist Poetics*, 101, emphasis in original. She goes onto describe processes of "re-placing the body" not "reactivating them to function mimetically" but creating and reconstructing them as different, ibid.

57 Threadgold, ibid., 99.

58   Taylor refers to transmission and transformations in terms of multiplication and simultaneity, performance shift, doubling and preserving rather than erasing antecedents, ibid., 46–49.
59   Seda, ibid., 17.
60   Jones, "Foreword," 14, quoting Lepecki, "Introduction."
61   Ibid. Seda discusses performance aesthetics involving "ceaseless process[es] of reinventing and redefining the art of living 'in-between,'" ibid.
62   A Nahuatl word meaning "in the middle of it," nepantla was used 500 years ago by Mexica peoples as they were being colonized by the Spaniards. Miguel León-Portilla describes how Indigenous people who were conquered by the Spanish created their own "in-between" culture—the new world that they inhabited was made up of parts of both cultures and offered a limited but real sense of resistance, since at least part of their own culture was kept, see *La filosofía náhuatl*.
63   See Anzaldúa, *Interviews/Entrevistas*, 176.
64   Convivio, which literally means to coexist or to co-live, is the concept of the Argentinian theatre scholar, Jorge Dubatti, see *Filosofía del teatro 1: convivio, experiencia, subjetividad*. In her discussions in *Escenarios liminales*, Diéguez specifically draws on Dubatti's work, 33. (see also Chapter 2, note 59).
65   Notably, Taylor develops "scenario" as an extension of Bourdieu's habitus, ibid.
66   Each of these phrases and concepts connects with the many performance and theatre concepts presented in this book, and particularly those of Aston, Costantino, Diéguez, Fabião, Hirsch, Morrison, Prieto Stambaugh, Rich, Schneider, Seda, Taylor, Yépez and the artistic directors of La Máquina de Teatro, Faesler and Malheiros.

Chapter 2, pages 41–65

1   Taylor, *The Archive and The Repertoire*, 82.
2   It is important to note that this is not a comparative study or survey. My focus is specifically on four discrete projects of La Máquina. I refer readers to useful studies of theatre and performance in Mexico: see final note in this chapter.
3   For more information on La Máquina de Teatro see, for example, the company's website http://lamaquinadeteatro.org); their Facebook page; Ceballos, *Diccionario mexicano de teatro*: Faesler, "La Máquina de Teatro"; Obregón, "Prólogo," 13; and Rizk, *Imaginando un continente*.
     Since 1994, Faesler and Malheiros, as La Máquina de Teatro, have undertaken a wide range of performance projects that have won awards and have been critically acclaimed. They have participated in major festivals such as the International Cervantino Festival, Guanajuato and the Miami Festival, USA. Complementing their projects with La Máquina, both Malheiros and Faesler are prominent artists who are engaged to direct and collaborate with other major scenic arts projects in Mexico. Malheiros is an eminent physical theatre actor, performer, director and teacher. Faesler is a renowned director and designer, with multiple productions to her credit as a theatre and opera director, a creative collaborator with dancers and visual artists, and a scenographic and lighting designer. Both Malheiros and

Faesler teach and run labs and workshops, with performers and students testifying to their inspirational methodologies and practices. Many performers name Faesler and Malheiros in their professional biographies as highly influential in their own careers.

The following is a brief summary of performance projects by La Máquina de Teatro undertaken between 1994 and 2017: *Respública; Anarquía. 2° Congreso del Partido Liberal Mexicano; Galileo. Una tragicomedia cósmica; Tríptico de Encarnaciones: Pessoa/La Hora del Diablo, Kafka/Dónde estás están todos los mundos; Proyecto Ruelas; Zapato busca sapato* (International Cervantino Festival, Guanajuato, 2016); *El futuro abandonado; La Traviata* (Giuseppe Verdi); *La mujer quien mató a los peces; El Pequeño Salvaje; Sueño de una noche de verano* (International Cervantino Festival, Guanajuato, 2014) *El Inspector V.01: Los impecables* (J.B. Priestley); *Antígona; Alma* (José Miguel Delgado); *La Violación de Lucrecia* (Benjamin Britten); *El Rey se muere* (Eugène Ionesco); *Fuenteovejuna - Acción colectiva* (Félix Lope de Vega) Laboratorio de arte alameda, San Luis Potosí; *Laboratorio de Investigaciones escénicas 5.0/Teatro Análogo/Texto; Laboratorio de Investigaciones escénicas/ Teatro Análogo 4.0/Asuntos familiares; Orfeo y Eurídice, Cuatro Variaciones para Tres Bailarines y un Adolescente sobre la Ópera de Cristoph W. Gluck; La maizada* (David Olguín); *Niño de Octubre* (Maribel Carrasco); *Laboratorio de Investigaciones escénicas 2.0/Teatro Análogo/Trolebús Escénico; Mientras más se grita menos se mata; Matericaloopovera; Devenir Homúnculo; Laboratorio de Investigaciones escénicas 1.0/Hecho en México, Tierra, Patria; Madera* (Tania Solomonoff); *Sueño de una noche de verano* (William Shakespeare, Félix Mendelssohn); *La Tempestad* (William Shakespeare) in collaboration with Natsu Nakajima, Rubén Ortiz and Gerardo TrejoLuna; *¿Qué oyes Orestes?* in collaboration with Quiatora Monorriel (Evoé Sotelo and Benito Gonzáles); *El cazador de gringos* (Daniel Serrano); *Siete segundos (In God we trust)* (Falk Richter); *El otro* (Enzo Cormann); *Divina Justicia, Apuntes escénicos a partir de "La Tragedia Española" de Thomas Kyd; la Eva Futura* (Villiers D'Isle Adam); *Frankenstein o el moderno Prometeo* (Mary Shelley); *Alicia en la cama* (Susan Sontag); *La gran magia* (Eduardo de Filippo); *Rosencrantz y Guildenstern han muerto* (Tom Stoppard).

4 Valdés Medellín, "La estética de Juliana Faesler," n.p.
5 Tortajada Quiroz, "Branches and Roots," n.p.
6 Tortajada Quiroz, ibid.
7 See, for example, Collins, "Elevator Repair Service and The Wooster Group," 242.
8 Tradaptation combines translation-adaptation to convey the sense of annexing old texts to new cultural forms and involves "a wholesale re-working and re-thinking of the original text, as well as its translation and/or translocation into a new, non-European context," Cameron, "Tradaptation," 17, citing Verma, "The Challenge of Binglish," 201 n1. Although the four projects under discussion in this study do not use pre-existing theatre scripts, La Máquina do work with conventional scripts (including by William Shakespeare, Félix Lope de Vega, Thomas Kyd, Eugène Ionesco, Tom Stoppard and J.B. Priestly). However, even when using play scripts the company engages collective exploratory processes to thoroughly re-work and re-conceptualize each play through processes of tradaptation. La Máquina's processes of tradaptation involve experimental translation and adaptation to a new context, each time undertaking radical re-workings to explore localized issues and generating thorough and complex re-visions. They also

work with scripts and novels of Mexican playwrights and authors (such as *La maizada* by David Olguín, *Niño de Octubre* by Maribel Carrasco, and *El cazador de gringos* by Daniel Serrano).

9   For my own conceptions of palimpsest bodies as plural and layered, the work of Frida Kahlo is significant for her recurring creations of her own inside-outside, traumatized, doubled palimpsest body, some painted from her reflection as she lay on her back immobile, looking up at the mirror on her ceiling. She paints herself as two bodies, sitting side by side, holding hands, connected through body parts. For a fascinating theatricalization of Kahlo's body as a palimpsest body see *Las dos Fridas*, by Mexican actors/writers Bárbara Córcega, María del Carmen Farías and Abraham Oceransky (1998) as discussed by Misemer, *Secular Saints*, 21–27. Notably, Mexican self-identifying feminist artist, activist and author Mónica Mayer suggests that Kahlo was a performance artist and a precedent for French-born performance artist Orlan's work in her body-cutting, Mayer, "Macular Degenerations," 107. La Máquina generate embodied intertexts with Frida Kahlo's suited body in their *Mexican Trilogy, Malinche/Malinches*. Through trans-temporal remains, five business-suited bodies perform re-visions of gendered violation and control, connecting La Malinche with Frida Kahlo with contemporary women (see the following chapter).

10   "'Malinche Malinches,' inicia nueva temporada," *Informador*, n.p.

11   Lehmann, *Postdramatic Theatre*.

12   Broadhurst, *Liminal Acts*, 1.

13   See Govan, Nicholson and Normington, *Making a Performance*, 7. For recent discussions on collective creation, devising and ensemble practices, see also: Barton, *Collective Creation*; Benítez Dávila, *Comunidades y contextos*; Britton, *Encountering Ensemble*; Diéguez, *Des/tejiendo escenas*; Garzón Céspedes, *El teatro de participación*; Harvie and Lavender, *Making Contemporary Theatre*; Heddon and Milling, *Devising Performance*; Mermikides and Smart, *Devising in Process*; Mock, *Performing Processes*; Oddey, *Devising Theatre*; Radosavljevi, *Theatre-Making* and *The Contemporary Ensemble*; Syssoyeva and Proudfit, *A History of Collective Creation* and *Collective Creation in Contemporary Performance*; Valdés Kuri, "El proceso de creación"; and Weinberg, *Challenging the Hierarchy*.

14   I have discussed the choice of descriptor for the work of La Máquina de Teatro with Faesler and Malheiros. Many terms such as alternative, physical, body-based, contemporary, interdisciplinary and experimental are relevant, although each carries its own baggage. The term "teatro experimental" and the idea of experimentation is currently used in Mexico, see, for example, *Vértice: Experimentación y vanguardia*.

     For teatro personal and técnicas corporales see, for example, Fediuk and Prieto Stambaugh, *Corporalidades Escénicas*; Yépez, "El ejercicio"; and Araujo, "Aprendiendo."

     For liminal performance see Broadhurst, *Liminal Acts* and "Liminal Aesthetics"; and for postdramatic theatre see Hans-Thies Lehmann, *Postdramtic Theatre* and *Teatro posdramático*. It is important to note that both liminal performance and postdramatic theatre as analytical frameworks are pertinent to Mexican contexts: Ileana Diéguez, one of Mexico's pre-eminent theatre and performance scholars, engages the concept of liminal performance as a key element of her research (see *Escenarios liminales*). Lehmann's study on postdramatic theatre was translated from the original German into Spanish as *Teatro posdramático* and published in Mexico in 2013. Notably, this is the full version, unlike the English translation, which comprises only part of the original text. In Mexico, Lehmann has been an invited speaker at theatre events: see Irazábal, "El teatro posdramático"; and Lehmann, "Metamórfosis".

15 This is stated by Collins, ibid. 235, within his discussion of experimental and devised performance.

16 See Taylor, *The Archive and the Repertoire*. See also Lipsitz, who finds a problem with vanguardism describing the "misguided, destructive results of leftist vanguards in the United States and around the world," "Standing at the Crossroads," 67–8, n. 25.

17 As Prieto Stambaugh has noted, the term "feminist" can be regarded as ideologically loaded and even colonialist, "Wrestling the Phallus, Resisting Amnesia," 249. The term "feminism"—"feminismo"—has been used in Mexico for well over one hundred years (for example, political-satirical caricaturist Jesús Martínez Carrión used this term in his publication *El Colmillo Público* in the early 1900s). As the directors of La Máquina themselves engage the term, I therefore apply it to interpret their work. For other discussions on feminism and performance in Mexico see, for example, Azor, "La mujer"; Bixler and Gidi, *Las mujeres*; Costantino, "And She Wears It Well"; Cypess, "La dramaturgia femenina"; de Beer, *Contemporary Mexican Women Writers*; Franco, *Plotting Women*; Fusco, *Corpus Delecti*; Mayer, *Rosa Chillante*; Nigro, "Inventions and Transgressions"; Rizk, *Posmodernismo y teatro*; Rodríguez del Pino, *Five Plays*; Schlau, "Sor Juana"; Taylor and Villegas, *Negotiating Performance*; and Taylor and Costantino, *Holy Terrors*. See also feminist periodical publications such as *Debate Feminista*, *Fem*, *La Revuelta* and *Cihuat* (see, for example, www.unamenlinea.unam.mx/recuros and http://archivos-feministas.cieg.unam.mx/publicaciones).

For readers unfamiliar with the seventeenth-century playwright Sor Juana Inés de la Cruz, I mention her briefly here in order to note her extraordinary role in initiating a trajectory of feminist theatre practices in Mexico. Known as one of the world's greatest women playwrights and as a nun writing from within a patriarchal system (literally writing in her convent cell in Mexico City), she crafted plays that were subversive, political, ideological, witty and humorous, and which questioned gender norms and patriarchal power using deliberately embodied provocations and interventions. In the *Loa for The Divine Narcissus*, she reactivates the "scenario of encounter" by staging a confrontation between two Indigenous citizens and two Spanish military and religious colonizers, embodying a relationship through corporeal practices of embodied repertoires, as the Spanish characters dance an Indigenous Mexica dance—the Ritual of the Seeds to the Great God of the Seeds. She offers a gendered re-vision of official narratives, in the form of the two protagonists as women (Indigenous and Spanish), who embody status and power in relation to the two men (see Taylor and Townsend, *Stages of Conflict*). Significantly, the iconic body of Sor Juana herself (which also circulates in everyday life on the 200 peso banknote in Mexico) has been re-activated in performance, by Jesusa Rodríguez, as a palimpsest body to explore contemporary issues, (see Taylor and Costantino, *Holy Terrors*).

18 This connects with the concept of anti-theatre, an idea which Faesler is particularly interested in and a term used by author and critic Gonzalo Valdés Medellín to describe La Máquina's work: "If there is a way to define Faesler's scenic proposal with *Malinche/Malinches,* it would be 'anti-theatre,'" "La estética," n.p. Of course, Austrian playwright Peter Handke himself used the term anti-theatre (see Joseph, Handke and Ashton, "Nauseated by Language"), as did Ionesco to refer to his plays and the works of playwrights such as Stoppard, Albee, Pinter,

and Shepard (see Hayman, *Theatre and Anti-Theatre*). It is not coincidental, therefore, that the directors of La Máquina have generated inspirational tradaptations of plays by Ionesco and Stoppard, as well as using Handke's anti-theatre strategies in devising processes.

19 Aston and Harris, *Performance Practice and Process*.

20 Broadhurst, *Liminal Acts*, 14; Lipsitz, "Standing at the Crossroads," 62–63.

21 Chabaud, "Un país en llamas y luto," 3. I have already drawn attention to the research of scholar Ileana Diéguez and here note her study *Cuerpos sin duelo* (*Bodies without mourning*). In this work she analyses ways in which violence penetrates aesthetic and artistic representations, discussing connections between body, art, violence, grief, sorrow and mourning (*duelo*), focusing on artists and social actions, particularly examining how art can be connected to mourning on stages when, even for the funeral rites, the bodies are absent.

22 Lipsitz, ibid., 61–2 (citing Felice Blake and Paula Ioanide).

23 Relajo is an idea developed by late Mexican philosopher Jorge Portilla, *La fenomenología del relajo*.

24 Rodríguez in Costantino, "Visibility as Strategy," 67, citing Seligson, *El teatro, festín*, 158–159.

25 Chabaud, "Nota introductoria," 7.

26 Notably, the prominence of visual arts created a focus on multi-temporality and bodies in art. Using my framework of palimpsest bodies, the muralism of Diego Rivera, José Clemente Orozco and David Alfaro Siqueiros reactivates fragments of historical scenarios depicting iconic bodies from multiple time periods, which are juxtaposed and layered to generate a sense of precariousness and haunting.
In the postrevolutionary years, prominent experimental artistic groups included: Ulysses Theatre, the Stridentist movement, the Contemporaries, Orientation Theatre, Universal Theatre and the Theatre of Now.
In the 1920s to 40s, in an atmosphere of global exchange, artists from Europe, Russia, the USA and South America migrated to Mexico and Mexican artists spent time abroad. Notably, Antonin Artaud gained a visa to visit Mexico after the failure of one of his theatre productions in 1936 in Paris and, in a symbiotic relationship, he influenced, and was influenced by his experiences in Mexico. From the 1940s onward, Meyerhold's biomechanics and the practices of Stanislavksi and Vakhtangov were disseminated in Mexico by migrant Japanese director Seki Sano.

27 Examples include: Poetry Out Loud (see Unger, *Poesia*), the so-called Rupture generation, Alejandro Jodorowsky and Miguel Sabido. The work of Jerzy Grotowski and the Polish Laboratory Theatre, The Living Theatre and Eugenio Barba and Odin Theatre have all been influential in Mexico (see, for example, Adame and Prieto Stambaugh, *Jerzy Grotowski*; Barba, "La danza"; and Dunkelberg, *Grotowski*). Grotowski's *Towards a poor theatre* circulated in Mexico from the 1970s. A student of Grotowski, Nicolás Núñez, founded the Theatre Research Workshop of the National Autonomous University of Mexico (UNAM) in 1975 (see Sánchez Moreno, "40 años").

28 Yépez, "Encuentro Internacional," 92. See, for example, the National Centre for Arts (CENART) which offers a "methodology based in sets of 'variable' and 'flexible practices,

with transversal educational practices which enable common paths in diverse disciplines: body, space, time and memory," www.CENART.mx [accessed 15 July 2016].

29   A few major ensembles include: el Teatro de Ciertos Habitantes, Teatro Ojo, Teatro Línea de Sombra, La Rueca, La Rendija, La Comedia Humana, Lagartijas tiradas al sol.
I should note that given my focus on the four performance projects of La Máquina, my intention is not to gloss over the complexity and diversity of the trajectories. Some artists work with official institutions, others deliberately generate their own spaces of resistance, and others (in the case of La Máquina) engage both/and strategies. I draw attention to Taylor and Costantino's evocative descriptions of the experiences of resistant women performance artists, Hadad, Rodríguez and Felipe, who were "repulsed by the male-run and artistically limited and limiting nature of Mexico's theatrical and cultural institutions," Taylor and Costantino, "Unimagined Communities," 6. After the 2006 election, Rodríguez's creative resistance movement (resistencia creativa) took place on the streets in the centre of Mexico City. The participants used "decontextualized gestures" to increase contexts of no collaboration and produce ungovernability, Diéguez, *Escenarios liminales*, 177–85.

30   Jones, "The Now and the Has Been," 14.

31   It is striking that the influence of Lecoq and Bogart is repeatedly documented and discussed in many recent studies on devising, collective creation and ensemble theatre, see, for example, Britton, ibid., Collins, ibid., Govan et al, ibid., and Syssoyeva and Proudfit, ibid.

32   Malheiros was selected to complete the full three-year training with Lecoq. For details of Lecoq's techniques see Lecoq, *Theatre of Movement and Gesture*; Lecoq et al, *The Moving Body*; and Thompson, "Freedom and Constraints."

33   This is the training method of the SITI Company, following Bogart's on-going collaboration with choreographer and movement theorist Mary Overlie, see Bogart, *And Then, You Act*; Bogart and Landau, *The Viewpoints Book*; and Cummings, *Remaking American Theater*. It is, of course, relevant that viewpoints specifically incorporates concepts of in-betweenness, connecting to the Mexica concept of Nepantla, and Gloria Anzaldúa's use of nepantla as seeing from two or more perspectives simultaneously, *Interviews/Entrevistas* and *Borderlands/La frontera*. Notably, director Faesler is influenced by Jorge Luis Borges' notion of body as journeys through time and, drawing on the short story "Borges and I," she notes, "[i]f you could take a photo of your life, of your movements, and you make a drawing of where you've come from, there is a whole geography there, there's a whole map that's been created." Borges has described a sense of doubleness of self and persona, of walking the streets, of footprints, journeys and ephemeral traces, see *El hacedor*.

34   Faesler studied in London, at Central St Martin's School of Art, and in Mexico City with Julio Castillo, Ludwik Margules and Hector Mendoza. She is a founding member of the Academy of Theatre Art and has been nominated for, and has won, many prizes, including the prestigious Premio Villanueva.

35   These artists are influenced by many theatrical forms prevalent from nineteenth century into the twentieth centuries, joining body-based characterizations of topical and political material with the art of improvisation in forms which included revue (*revista*); travelling tent (*carpa*) theatre; and a form of zarzuela known as *género chico*.

Using my interpretive concept of palimpsest bodies, Hadad specifically reactivates remains and traces of iconic bodies of history, performing them through costume, movement, vocal, musical and textual iterations, with poses, facial expressions and literal layering of costume elements rendering her body as always multiple, liminal and trans. Traces of bodies are transformed and re-visioned through juxtapositions, interweavings and superimpositions. In *Heavy Nopal* she embodies an iconic stone sculpture of the deity Coatlicue, creating a costume reiterating elements of the stone sculpture body, simultaneously layering and interweaving trans-temporal remains and traces: a pre-invasion Mexica skull rack; the sacred heart of Jesus; a stereotypical nationalistic folkloric charro hat; and a gas mask, to "denounce[s] pollution, unequal north/south relations, oppressive gender and sexual relations, and anything else that occurs to [her]" Taylor ibid., 5 (see the following chapter for La Máquina's re-vision of Coatlicue in *Mexican Trilogy*).

36 Costantino is describing Jesusa Rodríguez: see "Visibility as Strategy," 64. See, for example, Gastón Alzate's discussion of Paquita la del Barrio in which he describes Paquita's body as "the site of her text," in "Paquita la del Barrio and Translocal Theatricality," 168.

37 A few performers include: Mónica Mayer and Maris Bustamante (who founded the feminist collective Polvo de Gallina Negra in 1983), Elvira Santamaría, Eugenia Vargas, Hortensia Ramírez, Lorena Orozco, Doris Steinbichler, Mirna Manrique, Rocio Boliver, Ema Villanuevas, Katia Tirado, and Lukas Avendaño.

38 Prieto Stambaugh, "Wrestling the Phallus," 247. See, for example, Lorena Wolffer's work, *Mientras dormíamos (el caso Juárez)* reactivating scenarios of violence done to women's bodies and forms of impunity. She performs remains of multiple bodies, drawing on her body "the wounds inflicted upon some of the hundreds of women who have been murdered in Ciudad Juárez since the 1990s," Mayer, "Macular Degenerations," 111. Little by little, her body is altered into a map of abuse and ill treatment (see Bustamante Mouriño, "Lorena Wolffer," n.p.). Engaging my interpretive ideas, Wolffer is performing palimpsest bodies, opening up questions about complicity and power as her skin is the container and embodied archive of individual named women's bodies, collected together as one body. However, Mónica Mayer has questioned the aesthetics of hyperreality, writing of "Scary Scars" and of "women artists who turn their bodies into archives of violence, marked by the crimes of political power and the most ferocious misogyny," asking "[h]ow do we keep the balance between making violence visible and making a permanent backup copy of it in our bodies? When are these types of works politically effective and when do they become a spectacle or a stereotype?" Mayer, ibid.
In *Mexican Trilogy, Malinche/Malinches*, for one brief scene of rape and violation, when "Cortés" rapes "La Malinche," the ensemble use a hyperreal aesthetic which was developed in the processes of collective creation (see the following chapter, Scenario of violation (1)).

39 In what may seem to be an incongruous leap, I include here a very brief description of theatre practices enacted in Mexico City almost five hundred years ago—"America's First Theatre," Burkhart, *Aztecs on Stage*, 2. Although the politics and intent of these performative practices is poles apart from the goals of La Máquina, nevertheless, they encompass overt forms of bodies as palimpsests, "doubleness" and embodied repertoires. As I am

interested in body-to-body transmission, elements of these practices persist in influencing performative aesthetics. The aim of these staged practices after colonization was to teach historical and religious knowledge and concepts in order to subjugate and convert the Indigenous colonized peoples. Combining spoken dialogue, dance and music, these multi-disciplinary, large-scale enactments encompassed embodied syncretic praxes layering and juxtaposing Indigenous and European practices. Spanish colonizers and priests recycled Indigenous performance practices, using the native language of Nahuatl, superimposing new "identities" over the previously existing Mexica practices and bodies. The Indigenous bodies of the participants were essentially performing palimpsest bodies, holding remains of their ancestors in their bodies, and always incorporating a plurality of being themselves and a "role" at the same time (a form of Nepantla). Therefore, these performative processes of subjugation included corporeal resistance through being "themselves" and "Jesus" or "the Devil" simultaneously. Each body functioned as both subversive and resistant, as the participants "became" Jesus, Mary, saints, angels, devils, Jews, Romans, soldiers, and priests right in the centers of their own communities, while also remaining themselves—looking and talking like ordinary native people, see Burkhart, ibid., 3–27. Actors also embodied concepts such as "Time," "Penance," and "Death" (see *Final Judgment* (1533) in Burkhart, ibid. 59–78, and in Taylor and Townsend, *Stages of Conflict*). Significantly, many of these practices continue in the twenty-first century, particularly as dance-dramas performed in local socio-religious celebrations (see Hellier-Tinoco, *Embodying Mexico*).

40 All the specific figures of history and the episodes explored through these four projects of La Máquina have been the subject of many and varied prior theatre, performance and scenic arts projects ranging through plays, performance art, ensemble creations and choreographic works. My objective in this book is not to compare the performance projects of La Máquina with these other scenic explorations of connected material. I have, therefore, made the decision not to include a list of other work. For performing history and memory in Mexico see, for example, Bixler, Costantino, Cypess, Day, Diéguez, Fediuk, Franco, Gutiérrez, Mijares, Nigro, Popova, Prieto Stambaugh, Rizk, Seda, Seed, Taylor, Valdés Kuri, van Delden, Ward and Ybarra.

41 Taylor, ibid., 96. This is in contrast to ideas of absenting and surrogation, as developed by Joseph Roach to think about ways that transmission occurs through forgetting and erasure, see *Cities of the Dead*. As noted in the previous chapter, see Taylor, ibid., 79–109 for a detailed discussion of mestizaje. See also Arrizón's insightful study, *Queering Mestizaje*.
In Mexico, the three principal "groupings" are Indigenous, African and European peoples. In colonial New Spain (1521 to 1821) a porous racial classification or caste system was in place that ordered racial groups hierarchically according to their proportion of Spanish blood. In Mexico, racial politics are notably different in comparison with the USA and Europe, due to the different histories and classification of bodies, specifically in terms of the phrase "of colour," see Lipsitz, "'Standing at the Crossroads.'"
Particularly apt for my study is a description of the palimpsest of racial politics as sedimented in debates about history and memory, see Nyong'o, *The Amalgamation Waltz*.

42 See Serret, "Modernidad reflexiva" for a discussion of the theory that argues that Mexican womanhood is based on two opposing images: the mestiza Virgin of Guadalupe and the

Indigenous Malinche. For readers who are unfamiliar with the Virgin of Guadalupe, I briefly mention this fundamental and ubiquitous body, even though La Máquina do not reactivate her specifically. She is Mexico's most replicated and revered body, a syncretic body, generated within and for processes of conquest and domination. Taylor describes how the Mesoamerican goddess, the mother of gods, Tonantzin was folded into the brown-skinned Christian Virgin of Guadalupe through "innumerable transformations [...] a form of multiplication and simultaneity [...] [a] strategy of doubling and staying the same, of moving and remaining, of multiplying outward. The performance shift and doubling [...] preserved rather than erased the antecedents [...]. Had the pre-Conquest goddess been successfully surrogated by the Virgin, or did she [...] live on in the Christian deity?" Taylor, ibid., 46–49. (As a palimpsest citation, Taylor [44] quotes the sixteenth century Florentine Codex by Bernardino de Sahagún, *Historia general de las cosas de Nueva España*, as quoted by twentieth century historian Enrique Florescano, originally published in Spanish, but translated to become *Memory, Myth and Time in Mexico*. This account also documents the palimpsest process of a church being built on the site of the temple to Tonantzin). Taylor's deeply poetic description incorporates core characteristics of my concept of palimpsest bodies: the Virgin of Guadalupe's body is plural, phantasmagorical and yet wholly tangible. Significantly, this specific body-form of the Virgin of Guadalupe exists on a cloth held in the Basilica in Mexico City, where the cloth is both the remains of her body and also *is* her body as material entity.

43 Paz, *El laberinto de la soledad*, 86 ("un país cuya herencia mestiza ha dejado a todos sus habitantes como herederos de las tradiciones tanto conquistadoras como conquistadas de sus antepasados. Por lo tanto, en cada momento el mexicano debe escoger entre 'chingar o ser chingado'"). Paz's study, *El laberinto de la soledad (The Labyrinth of Solitude)* is one the most famous and controversial examinations of Mexican identity.

44 Cypess, *La Malinche in Mexican Literature*, 2. In her detailed and insightful study, Cypess analyses various novels and plays. Although these plays connect with my own study of La Máquina's theatrical exploration of La Malinche, as I am specifically interested in transdisciplinary aesthetics and collective creation, I have not made cross-references here.

45 Bustamante, "Non-Objective Arts in Mexico," 225.

46 Obviously, my intention is not to offer a survey of historical matters, but rather to provide a few examples for readers unfamiliar with some key events: the US invaded in 1846, resulting in a loss of huge territories, a loss that remains as a wound and trauma and that has been described as a "rupture that created two Mexicos: a Political Mexico and a Cultural Mexico," Madrid, "Foreword," xiii–xiv; during the Reform period of 1861, multiple transformations for liberalizing the state included the re-purposing of religious buildings, convents, and churches; in 1864 French powers invaded resulting in the imposition of a foreign ruler (Emperor Maximilian) and the occupation of the country until 1867. In the twentieth century, the Mexican Revolution (1910–1920) involved chaotic movements of peoples throughout the territory, in struggles for rights of land and liberty. The postrevolutionary processes of forging a nation in the 1920s and 30s involved various strategies for creating a single united body (corpus). The great diversity and multiplicity of peoples was to be unified through "Mexicanness" (*mexicanidad*) and through the performativity of a shared authentic national identity (see, for example, Gutiérrez *Performing Mexicanidad*; Hellier-Tinoco, *Embodying Mexico*; and Vaughan and Lewis, *The Eagle and the Virgin*).

47 Cooper Alarcón, *The Aztec Palimpsest: Mexico in the Modern Imagination*.

48 It is important to note that the domination of the Mexica peoples was only the first of many subsequent acts of colonization of Indigenous peoples. Each has its own histories of power struggles and transformations.

49 Miguel León-Portilla describes how Indigenous people who were conquered by the Spanish created their own "in between" culture—see *La filosofía náhuatl* (for more details see Chapter 1, note 62).

50 Heidrun Adler describes how the "circular thinking of Mexicans …is shown in reiterations—with historic clothes, in classic themes, like a vicious circle, in compulsive retrospectives of the past—like an infinite journey, *a journey without end*, in time, like an introspection into who I am, like a journey on the path of transformation and death," "Prólogo" 12 (emphasis in original), in Adler and Chabaud, *A Journey Without End. Mexican Theater Today*.

51 Forms of documentary and testimonial theatre and performance have been prevalent in Mexico, as in many other countries (see, for example, Prieto Stambaugh, "Memorias inquietas").

52 Faesler, interview with author, quoting Benjamin, *On the Concept of History*, Thesis VI. Faesler and Malheiros quote Benjamin in the public programme for *Mexican Trilogy*.

53 Faesler, ibid.; Benjamin, ibid., Thesis II. Faesler describes how she uses "history" as a portal to access the present. "History" therefore exists as a form of liminality, always and inherently containing trans-temporal plurality.

54 "Raymond Williams notes that the term 'fiction' embodies a duality of meaning in which two clear but contradictory ideas are acknowledged […] imaginative literature and also 'pure (and sometimes deliberately deceptive) invention," Govan et al, *Making a Performance*, 55.

55 See discussion of renowned Mexican director Rodolfo Obregón, "Prólogo."
In his Prologue, Obregón specifically mentions Juliana Faesler (13). In his opening remarks, he opens up questions of tensions between the opposition of real and fictitious, and between exercises of imagination and what we label as reality. He then generates a fascinating citational palimpsest, repeating Lehmann, who was, in turn, repeating Jan Mukařovský: "This ambiguity […] reaches labyrinthine levels of course in the theatre, a practice and a social situation that—according the influential contemporary theorist Hans-Thies Lehmann—'as nothing else, forces us to realize "that there is no clear boundary between the aesthetic and the extra-aesthetic realm." [That] to varying degrees art always contains extra-artistic admixtures from the real—just as, inversely, there are aesthetic factors in the extra-artistic realm," Obregón, "Prólogo," 11, (Obregón quoted Lehmann, *Postdramatic Theatre*, 101, who was quoting Jan Mukařovský, *Kapitel aus der Ästhetik*, 12. Various linguistic translations were also involved (German, English, Spanish and my own reiteration is from Spanish to English).

56 Govan et al, ibid., 60, drawing on postmodern critic Louis Renza. See also, for example, Forsyth and Megson, *Get Real*; Jones and Heathfield, *Perform, Repeat, Record*; Magaña Esquival, *Imagen y realidad del teatro en México*; Mijares, *La realidad virtual del teatro mexicano*; Nigro, "¿Qué ha pasado aquí? Realidad e hiperrealidad"; and Sánchez, *Prácticas de lo real / Practising the Real*.

57 As I noted in the previous chapter, Taylor describes how "the scenario forces us to situate ourselves in relationship to it, as participants, spectators, or witnesses," ibid., 32.

58 Harvie, "Introduction: Contemporary Theatre in the Making," 14.

59 As noted in the previous chapter, convivio—to coexist or to co-live—is the concept of Argentinian theatre scholar, Jorge Dubatti, *Filosofía del teatro 1*. In her discussions of liminal stages and scenarios, Ileana Diéguez draws on Dubatti, *Escenarios liminales*, 33. As Antonio Prieto Stambaugh observes "convivio […] is the dialogical process that occurs when theatre practitioners engage with the audience. For Diéguez, *convivio* allows for a range of practices that may lead to a shared aesthetic experience, but also, and for her more importantly, to a collective politics," Prieto Stambaugh, "Ileana Diéguez Caballeros' *Escenarios liminales*," n.p.

60 Arce, *Troping Mexico's Historical No-bodies*, n.p. See also Arce, *Mexico's Nobodies*.

61 See Benedict Anderson's classic study, *Imagined Communities*. For interpretations in Mexican contexts see, for example, Taylor and Costantino, "Unimagined Communities" and Hellier-Tinoco, *Embodying Mexico* and "Embodied Imagined Communities."

62 Two "sets" of bodies are used to re-member Independence and the Revolution: for Independence, José Maria Morelos and Father Hidalgo; and the Revolution, Emiliano Zapata, Pancho Villa and *las soldaderas* or women soldiers. In a striking gendered difference, "women soldiers" are essentialized as a mass, see Arce, *Mexico's Nobodies* and Arrizón, "Soldaderas" and *Latina Performance*.
As an indication of contradictory positionality, Faesler and Malheiros both participated in official performative events in the 2010 bicentennial and centennial commemorations of Independence and the Revolution.

63 Rizk, *Posmodernismo y teatro en América Latina*, 68–75, 88; and Nigro, "Inventions and Transgressions, 138. See also Gladhart, "Transference and Negotiation," 125; and Adler, ibid., 11. Analysing the work of performance artist Emma Villanueva, Prieto Stambaugh writes: "Unsettled memories call attention to the mechanisms of institutional amnesia, the way power deploys silence and absence to control a population and keep it from demanding justice," "Wrestling the Phallus, Resisting Amnesia," 259.

64 Villegas, *Historia del teatro*, 177; and Rizk, *Posmodernismo y teatro*, 69, discussing the work of prolific feminist author, Elena Garro. In a recent example, *Benito antes de Juárez*, by playwright Edgar Chías, uses the past to examine the present through the body of history of Benito Juárez, one of Mexico's most commemorated Presidents, and significant as an Indigenous man of Zapotec origin. As Chías describes: "[This is] a historical fiction [which] re-creates a definite moment in the life of Juárez at the age of 28, […] something that happened in 1834, a fictionalized time, of a distant 'then' and paradoxically present. It deals with something that happened yesterday, today, and, sadly, will not stop happening soon," Chías, *Benito antes de Juárez*. Benito Juárez is performed as a statue, as the performer, covered in gold paint, moves into the iconic corporeal pose by which the man Juárez is commemorated, a live body performing a sculpted, metal, archival, memorialized body of history who asks the audience, "[w]hat do you think happened?" ibid.

65 Nigro, "Inventions and Transgressions," 142. Nigro notes that *El eterno feminino* (1976) by Rosario Castellanos "can be considered a liminal text, a non-narrative theatre piece that allows women to tell their own stories, and reveals constructedness of Woman," ibid., 140. Notably, La Malinche is one of the women in Castellanos' play. Nigro explains that it was not "simply a question of making a his into a her story, but rather of understanding

how stories come to be in the first place, and how they work to make themselves seem transparent," ibid.,138. See also, for example, works by playwright Carmen Boullosa, which use fragmentation and simultaneous trans-temporality to examine notions of truth (Nigro ibid., Patán "*Mejor desaparece*," and Taylor & Costantino, *Holy Terrors*, 181).

66 For analysis, see, for example, Adler and Chabaud, *Un viaje sin fin;* and Popova, *La dramaturgia Mexicana*.

67 See, for example, discussions by Costantino, Gutiérrez and Taylor.

68 Taylor, ibid., 82.

69 Ibid.

During the writing of this book, in September 2017, two earthquakes in Mexico ruptured bodies, lives, lands and buildings. Significantly, the second of these, which specifically impacted Mexico City, was reported through understandings of this metropolis having been formed on shifting foundations, with references to the origin narrative of a settlement created on an island in a lake.

70 To the north of Mexico City, the vast ceremonial location of Teotihuacan contains pyramids, grand plazas and ball courts, partially reconstructed in the twentieth century, offering the possibility of walking through a "lost universe." In many locations throughout Mexico, remains of stone structures are also interwoven into vegetation. In Chiapas, for example, thick jungles continue to conceal intricate and substantial buildings.

71 The carving is a depiction of the dismembered body of the goddess Coyolxauhqui (daughter of Coatlicue).

72 The concept and word "reforma"—literally to form again in a different way—is part of common consciousness. In Mexico City, the street Paseo de la Reforma runs through the heart of the city. This street was originally created for and named after the imposed Austrian Empress Carlota, wife of the "figurehead" Emperor Maximilian during the Second Empire (1864–67).

73 Designed by architect and urbanist Mario Pani, this was envisioned as an urban utopia for a positive future.

74 For narration in Mexican theatre, see, for example, Carrasco, "La narración oral y el teatro"; and Sanchis Sinisterra, *Narraturgia*.

75 I refer readers to useful studies of theatre, performance and scenic arts in Mexico, published in English and Spanish (given as two lists). For the sake of brevity I include the author's name rather than the title. Full bibliographic details are given in the References. **English:** Domingo Adame, Gastón Alzate, Alicia Arrizón, Christina Baker, Jacqueline Bixler, Daniel Breining, Robert Buffington, Ronald Burgess, Louise Burkhart, Maris Bustamante, Don Coerver, Eladio Cortés, Roselyn Costantino, Sandra M. Cypess, Stuart Day, Gabriela de Beer, Sebastian Doggart, Myra S. Gann, Amalia Gladhart, Guillermo Gómez-Peña, Laura Gutiérrez, Mark Hernández, Estela Leñero Franco, Teresa Marrero, Mónica Mayer, Edward McCaughan, Deborah Middleton, Margo Milleret, Sarah Misemer, Josefina Niggli, Kirsten F. Nigro, Nicolás Núñez, Salvador Oropesa, Antonio Prieto Stambaugh, Elissa Rashkin, Beatriz Rizk, Salvador Rodríguez del Pino, José A. Sánchez, Laurietz Seda, Carlo Solórzano, Stacey Southerland, Diana Taylor, Sarah J. Townsend, Tamara Underiner, Roni Unger, Alfonso Varona, Maarten van Delden, Adam Versényi, Juan Villegas, Julia Ward, Patricia Ybarra.

Spanish: Domingo Adame, Heidrun Adler, Josefina Alcázar, Gastón Alzate, Yolanda Argudín, Ileana Azor, Mónica Francisca Benítez Dávila, Jacqueline Bixler, Alicia Bustamante Mouriño, Dolores Carbonell, Edgar Ceballos, Jaime Chabaud, Roselyn Costantino, Sandra M. Cypess, Frank Dauster, César Delgado Martínez, Ileana Diéguez, Jorge Dubatti, Rita Eder, Elka Fediuk, Israel Franco, Donald Frischmann, Fernando Fuentes, Sonia Gutiérrez, Sergio Jiménez, Antonio Magaña Esquivel, Armando de Maria y Campos, Mónica Mayer, Socorro Merlín, Enrique Mijares, Jovita Millán Carranza, Luis Mario Moncada Gil, Sandra Múñoz, Kirsten F. Nigro, Rodolfo Obregón, David Olguín, Alejandro Ortiz Bullé Goyri, Armando Partida, Federico Patán, Indira Pensado, Elvira Popova, Antonio Prieto Stambaugh, Hugo Hernán Ramírez, Luis Reyes de la Maza, Beatriz Rizk, José A. Sánchez, Daimary Sánchez Moreno, José Sanchis Sinisterra, Guillermo Schmidhuber, Luis Mario Schneider, Laurietz Seda, Martha Toriz Proenza, Alfonso de Toro, Claudio Valdés Kuri, Daniel Vázquez Touriño, Lorena Wolffer, Gabriel Yépez, Araceli Zúñiga Vázquez.
For journals see, for example, *Latin American Theatre Review*, *GESTOS* and *Paso de Gato*.

Chapter 3, pages 69–125

1   La Máquina de Teatro, *Trilogía Mexicana* literature.
2   *Trilogía Mexicana: Nezahualcóyotl/Ecuación escénica de memoria y tiempos; Moctezuma II/La Guerra sucia; Malinche/Malinches*. Created 2006–2009. Direction, set design and lighting: Juliana Faesler; performers: Clarissa Malheiros, Diana Fidelia, Roldán Ramírez, Natyeli Flores, Alam Sarmiento, Horacio González García Rojas and Juliana Faesler; creative team: Edyta Rzewuska, Sebastián Romo, Vladimir Bojórquez and Quetzal Calixto León; original music: Liliana Felipe; sound design: Bishop; dramaturge and history advisor: Berenice Alcántara (Ph.D.); production: José Juan Cabello and Sandra Garibaldi; executive producer and project management: Elizabeth Muñoz. It was a production of: la Dirección de Teatro de la Universidad Nacional Autónoma de México, La Coordinación Nacional de Teatro, del Instituto Nacional de Bellas Artes, El Sistema de Teatros de la Ciudad de México and El Festival de México, 2010.
    Performances have taken places in Mexico (Mexico City, Nuevo León, Guanajuato, Toluca, San Luis Potosí), Cuba, Colombia and the United States.
    The first iteration of Part 2, *Moctezuma II* by La Máquina was based on the operatic work *Montezuma* by Carl Heinrich Graun (composed in 1754). This was performed at the Teatro de la Ciudad in 2009, in collaboration with Verónica Alexanderson and Karla Múñoz, and directed by José Areán. From the opera production, the company reconstructed the piece as a more experimental theatre work. Some musical elements were retained and the musical score was developed and treated through computer programs. Two musicians were present at the back of stage throughout, although they do not appear in the photos. I do not include a discussion of the music in this study, because my focus is on palimpsest bodies.
3   Over the past few years I have generated extensive writing and practice-as-research performances as forms of analyzing *Mexican Trilogy*. This brief chapter is a palimpsest containing traces of those iterations.

4   There are variations in the spelling of Nezahualcóyotl's name. During Part 1, the ensemble perform a scenario specifically questioning notions of historiographical accuracy and truth by debating meanings and spellings of his name.
    The intricacies of the terms Nahua, Mexica, Aztec and other Mesoamerican delineations are complex. Here I use the term "Mexica" to refer to the peoples and Nahuatl to refer to the language. Mesoamerica was home to complex and ever-transforming societies of peoples with diverse ways of living and hundreds of languages. Famously, the Mexica peoples created their floating city of Tenochtitlan (now Mexico City) on an island in Lake Texcoco.

5   For example, a bronze casting by Jesús Fructuoso Contreras in the historic centre portrays Nezahualcóyotl pointing and seemingly reaching out of the sculpture into the space around. The icon for the Nezahualcóyotl metro stop is the head of a coyote, as a representation of the translation of the name as "hungry coyote."

6   As Faesler described: "The irony is that Neza City is located in/on the same Lake Texcoco where Neza was emperor. It was built on the (drained) water of Lake Texcoco. After 1560, when the colonizers removed the water, this land was not suitable for farming or cattle. It was just salt. It was like a lost land."

7   In twenty-first century Mexico, names and attributes of gods of the Mexica cosmogony are still part of a shared understanding.

8   The colonial era codices also contain Classical Nahuatl (in the Latin alphabet), Spanish and also occasionally Latin. For biographies and poems by Nezahualcóyotl and other Nahuatl poetry, the company drew on scholarly work by Ángel María Garibay K. and Miguel León-Portilla, under the supervision of scholar Dr Berenice Alcántara, who also taught the history classes during the devising processes. For descriptions of Nahua concepts of human bodies the ensemble used the sixteenth-century document, *The Human Body and Ideology: Ancient Nahuatl Conceptions* (*Cuerpo humano e ideología: las concepciones de los antiguos nahuas*) translated into Spanish from Nahuatl by Alfredo López Austin.

9   As Faesler explains: "We said: 'We want to see the gods,' as a way of recovering them, renaming them, reviving them, re-membering them. The question was how do you bring them to the stage? What is that world like? How do we not get caught up in representation? How do we not become absurd? We were working with codices and sculptures—all Mexica. We find square lines; and with the codices, flat surfaces. How could we translate that iconography into the contemporary body, into movement?—that was one of the strongest routes of exploration. With those beings we were attempting to re-adapt ourselves, especially through those sculptures. There is always a corporal memory there that you begin to embody [imprimir] or to work with. That's how we began to work on the part of the physical expression in the body—the incarnation/in-the-body/embodiment of this world, so that it would be a work about memory, how we used to be, and how we are now."

10 Notably, various performers and performance artists have used body paint as an integral part of their work: see, for example, Jesusa Rodríguez, *El Maíz* (yellow body-paint) and *Barbie: The Revenge of the Devil* (red body paint), see Taylor and Costantino, *Holy Terrors*; and Ema Villanueva *Ausencia* (black body paint) and *Pasionaria, caminata por la dignidad* (half red and half black body paint), see Prieto Stambaugh, "Wrestling the Phallus."

11 For example, the *Codex Mendoza* depicts sets of multiple footprints, see Berdan and Rieff, *The Essential Codex Mendoza*.

12 See quotation from the *Nezahualcóyotl* programme in this chapter.

13 The headdresses were created by conceptual plastic artist, Sebastian Romo: Huehuetéotl, the elder god of gods and god of fire—a brazier-headdress; Huitzilopochtli, god of sun, war, human sacrifice, the patron of the city of Tenochtitlán (Mexico City), and guide—a headdress comprising many long multi-coloured balloons; Tezcatlipoca, a deceitful game-playing god, associated with enmity, discord, temptation, war, strife and the jaguar—a headdress of a skull-like face and bones, and rough cloak covered with metal bottle caps; Quetzalcóatl, the plumed or feathered serpent god—a headdress of wooden struts and cloak of straw; Tlaloc, god of rain, fertility and water—a painted form of a much-replicated statue.

14 Coatlicue holds significance in Mexico and for Chicana communities in the United States. Performance artists Jesusa Rodríguez and Astrid Hadad have both created performances through de-construction and re-membering of Coatlicue: Rodríguez explores issues of genetically modified maize; and Hadad produced what she calls her "postmodern Coatlicue," see Gutiérrez, *Performing Mexicanidad,* 67–68.

15 At the opening of the following scene, N again foreshadows her role as La Malinche. With her black-painted body, black-yellow-painted face and wearing a skull mask, she speaks about the Mexica concept of bodies, quoting directly from the sixteenth-century text *The Human Body* (*Cuerpo humano,* López Austin trans.): *"Our navel is the centre, the perforation,…Our lips and mouth are the border, the edge of all things…Our tongue, with her we speak."*

16 The recent film *Coco* (Disney 2017) plays with imaginaries of the celebration of Night of the Dead and the familiarity of skeletons as body-forms continuing with everyday lives after death. The narrative also sets up the concept of two different states of dead bodies.

17 Cempasuchil flowers (from the Nahuatl word *cempohualxóchitl*), known as flowers of the dead/of death, are used throughout Mexico between 31 October and 2 November to celebrate All Souls Day, Night of the Dead and Day of the Dead.

18 Problematically, some very personal ritual remains of Moctezuma II are contained in European locations. Notably, Moctezuma's green feathered headdress is in Vienna and his turquoise mask is in London, in the British Museum. This mask was used as the iconic marketing face for the 2010 exhibition "Moctezuma: Aztec Ruler," see McEwan and López Luján, *Moctezuma: Aztec Ruler.* Reiterations of Moctezuma's mask appeared on a range of merchandise, including grocery bags in the supermarket Sainsbury's. These bags were used by La Máquina in *Mexican Trilogy: Malinche/Malinches* as containers of the conch shells (remains of Moctezuma) (Figures 63–65).

19 Faesler says: "Moctezuma is one of the figures, from my point of view, who is the most intriguing, most romantic, and the most tragic in universal history, because his destiny was to be the last ruler of a world that was going to end. Ever since I was young I always thought: What a thing to be born and then know you'll be the one who is going to hand-over power to the foreigner."

20 The phrase "the Dirty War"—*la Guerra Sucia*—is mostly frequently applied to periods of state terrorism in Chile, Guatemala, El Salvador and Argentina, but is also used for the period of 1960s and 1970s in Mexico (see also Chapter 5, note 3). La Máquina specifically

engage events of this era in *Zapata, Death Without End* (Chapter 4) and *War in Paradise* (Chapter 5). For other theatre and performance studies discussions on performance and the dirty war in the Americas, see, for example, Taylor, *Disappearing Acts*; Werth, *Theatre, Performance, and Memory* and "Cuerpos desaparecidos"; and Diéguez, *Escenarios liminales*.

21 Accounts included: *The True History of the Conquest of New Spain (Historia verdadera)* by Bernal Díaz del Castillo; and *Vision of the Defeated: Indigenous Accounts of the Conquest (Visión de los vencidos)* a translation from Nahuatl by Miguel León-Portilla.

22 The accounts included *The Night of Tlatelolco: Testimonies of Oral History (La noche de Tlatelolco)* by Elena Poniatowksa.

23 In one scene, R declaims "The Sixth Declaration of the Lacandon Jungle," a manifesto issued by the Zapatista Army of National Liberation (EZLN) on 28 June 2005. He stands at the front of the stage, off the front of the platform, and engages direct declamation to generate the most overt scene of anti-theatre in the trilogy.

24 It is a fairly normal occurrence in Mexico City that a chance digging reveals another part of the destroyed civilization. As I noted in the previous chapter, in 1978, electrical workers uncovered the large sculpture of the dismembered body of the goddess of the moon, Coyolxauhqui. This subsequently led to a search for, and discovery of, the Great Temple (el Templo Mayor), the physical and spiritual centre of the Mexica universe.

25 One 2D head takes the multiplicity further, reconstructing the iconic Mexica jaguar warrior mask, comprising a human head covered by a jaguar mask. The performer embraces three faces with one body: two "painted" faces and a living face: a veritable palimpsest face. (See also the logo for Aeroméxico, the national airline of Mexico, which uses the eagle-warrior palimpsest head.)

26 Notably, the concept of political deconstructions and reconstructions was a key element when the ensemble created this work in 2010, coinciding with the bicentennial of Independence (1810) and the centennial of the Revolution (1910). As Faesler noted: "What we wanted to do was build a pyramid throughout the course of *Moctezuma*, as an action that was both symbolic and political—it seemed very interesting to me as an action, to take the time to create and to reconstruct a pyramid in that moment of 2010 in which we were living—and then destroy it."

27 This aesthetic offers connections with the outdoor spectacles of the first American theatre in the immediate post-conquest period (see Chapter 2, note 39 and Burkhart, *Aztecs on Stage*) and the large-scale theatricalization in the postrevolutionary era, including performances of Aztec narratives at the Pyramids of Teotihuacán in 1925 and the presentation of Mayan culture in Oaxaca in 1929 (see Ortiz Bullé Goyri, *Teatro y vanguardia*).

28 This concept is drawn directly from Nahuatl language, in which an idea is stated and repeated and restated again with a different term for the same idea.

29 There are over sixty Indigenous languages in Mexico in the twenty-first century, so the list is long: "*Nahua, Maya, Zapoteca, Mixteco, Totonaco, Tzotzil, Tzetzal, Mazahua, Mazateco….*"

30 As the conch shell is sounded each day in Mexico City in a socio-political ritual dance, this archival-repertorial sonic object is deeply embedded in continued actions of resistance.

31 *Historia general de las cosas de la Nueva España* (de Sahagún, 1995 [1576/1585]). This work is a bilingual collection (Nahuatl and Spanish), in which de Sahagún used what might be regarded as ethnographic and anthropological methods to gather information from within the culture.

32 In 1520, thousands of Mexica nobles were executed by Spanish invaders. The killings took place during a religious celebration being held in the Great Temple. On 2 October 1968, just ten days before the opening ceremonies of the Olympic Games in Mexico City, soldiers— acting under orders of the Mexican government—opened fire on a demonstration of some 10,000 students in the Plaza of the Three Cultures, Tlatelolco. At least forty-four people were killed (the actual number has never been determined) and hundreds wounded. Thousands were detained and over 1,200 arrested.

Faesler has described her own embodied and creative responses to the two events: "Immediately it was clear to me that we could weave together those two great wounds that the city has. […] It brought together those two experiences: of the Mexica warriors and the students. They were both in the same celebration, or rather in political meetings demanding action for certain things, which is like a religious ceremony but at the same time it's a reaffirmation of identity. They were already surrounded: the entrances were closed; the story is the same. As I began to read both, what started happening to me—I remember it perfectly—the impact on my body […] that the two were absolutely the same […] the lightning—the signals—the gunshots—how they closed the doors, they didn't let anybody get out. […] So then we decided to put them together. The thing about history is that it is not one, it's many—it repeats itself, it alters, it continues happening."

33 This is one of the "Songs of Sorrow" (titled "The last days of the siege of Tenochtitlán"), translated into Spanish by Ángel María Garibay (see *Posesía náhuatl*) and by Miguel León-Portilla (see *Cantares Mexicanos*).

34 The ensemble also used twentieth-century academic and philosophical publications, including: "The Sons of La Malinche" in *The Labyrinth of Solitude* (*El laberinto*) by Octavio Paz; *La Malinche, Her Parents and Her Children* (*La Malinche*) by Margo Glantz; *Hernán Cortés. Inventor of Mexico* (*Hernán Cortés*) by Juan Miralles; and *Borderlands/ La Frontera: The New Mestiza* by Gloria Anzaldúa. Verbatim reiterations of words written by all these authors are included in the performance, spoken by La Malinche as forms of re-contextualization, challenge, ownership and resistance.

35 Somewhat puzzlingly, in a review of a performance of *Malinche/Malinches* that took place in Miami, the reviewer suggests that the performers "tell or stage, in pieces, the true history of the real La Malinche," González-Cruz, "XXVII Festival International," 173.

36 A description by Brazilian performer/scholar Eleonora Fabião is particularly apposite: "*língua* means both language and tongue; its double meaning relates word and flesh, writing and muscle, speech and taste…It is about *língua*, about searching, saying, listening, reading, inventing, copying, copyrighting, writing the necessary words to formulate a momentary answer for the recurrent question: what are the relationships between language and body?," "History and Precariousness," 121.

37 Notably, Antonio Prieto Stambaugh describes how performance artists aim "not only to expose the construction of the body in culture, but also the metaphorical and physical

destruction of bodies in society. Working in a cultural environment that reproduces the ideal image of women as silent and passive, they aggressively create 'noise' within silence, a disturbance not necessarily dependent on speech, for they may resort to the performance of silence as a way of unsettling their audiences into another way of seeing the body politic," "Wrestling the Phallus," 248.

In *Subversive Silences,* Weldt-Basson observes that many twentieth-century Latin American and Latina women writers employ "thematic and stylistic silences in their narratives [...]to situate a reader within feminist perspectives, to subvert silence's patriarchal meaning and invest it with a combative dimension," 17. Significantly, through a double citation, she also engages the term "palimpsest": "...women's writing is a 'double-voiced discourse' that always embodies the social, literary, and cultural heritages of both the muted and the dominant. [...] One implication of this model is that women's fiction can be read as a double-voiced discourse, containing a 'dominant' and a 'muted' story, which [Sandra] Gilbert and [Susan] Gubar call a 'palimpsest,'" 23–24 [Gilbert and Gubar 1985, 263–66, in *New Feminist Criticism,* E. Showalter, ed.]).

38   As Faesler describes: "Of course I know Frida's work: she always dressed like a man, like George Sand and like many other women who also adopted that strategy" (interview with author). Known for her need for agency, for creating new identities and roles for herself, and for playing with sexuality and gender, Kahlo used her body as living art for challenging sexual stereotypes, positioning her [woman's] body as subject in direct opposition to patriarchal texts. She was very aware of her own identity construction through embodied performativity, particularly with her hair and clothes.

In the postrevolutionary epoch of the 1920s, Kahlo dressed in a suit and painted herself dressed in a suit. For example, Kahlo painted *Self-Portrait with Cropped Hair* after her betrayal by her husband, Diego Rivera. She painted herself sitting on a chair, wearing a suit (ill-fitting, with no shirt and tie [probably Rivera's suit]), looking at the viewer, with open scissors in her right hand. She painted another iteration in 1940, just after her divorce from Diego was finalized. She cut her hair after she discovered the affair between her sister Christina and Diego, and after her divorce, see Misemer 2008. See the frontispiece of Jean Franco's *Plotting Women: Gender Representation in Mexico* for Kahlo's painting of herself.

39   Faesler describes how this is "a completely urban connotation, of a period in México City when they built all the housing developments with this socialist utopia of generating this perfect way of life for the proletariat. So in the 1960s in Mexico they built a few of these developments: one of them is at Tlatelolco, where the massacre took place. And these things like latticework are reminiscent of the Mesoamerican borders—those borders that were important in 1960s Mexican design that were an appropriation of everything Aztec (*aztequismo*). But they also have a super contemporary style of the architects Mario Pani and González de León. You can see some metro stations where everything is like that."

40   Octavio Paz, in "The Sons of Malinche" (*El laberinto*), wrote of "a country whose mixed heritage has left the inhabitants as inheritors of traditions of conquesters or conquested by the predecessors. That is why in every moment a Mexican must choose between 'fucking or being fucked' ('chingar o ser chingado')," 86 (see Chapter 2, note 43 for Spanish original). Paz analyses the concept of La Chingada and presents La Malinche as a violated woman

(part victim) and also part traitor to her nation. The offspring of the Spanish man and the Native woman is identified as "the son of la Chingada" ("hijo de la Chingada"), one of the strongest insults in Mexico. In Paz's words, "the Mexican people (the sons of Malinche) have not forgiven La Malinche for her betrayal."

41 There is a play in Spanish with *border*—to sew—and *adorner*—to embellish truth, facts or a story. As an interesting side note, Govan et al., in their discussion of autobiographical performance, describe how "the human memory acts as a filter […] What is remembered may not be the truth but an embroidered version of the real," *Making a Performance,* 63. During the performances of *Mexican Trilogy,* the five performers generated embroidery that remains as material traces of the live performances (see Figure 116 for photos of these remains).

42 As another layer of corporeal remains, on the side of each bag containing the conch shell is a photographic life-size replication of the real turquoise mask of Moctezuma, with the words "Moctezuma: Aztec Ruler," "British Museum" and "Sainsburys'" (see note 18).

43 Faesler describes this scenario as a sequence of emptiness: "You no longer know who you are. You fold the tablecloth and you put it on again. That horrible emptiness of identity—an emptiness between Alzheimer's and old age, remembrance, memory…You lose your sense of being. You don't know who you are. If you don't have a conscience, if you don't have a memory, it's absolutely abysmal. So the moment comes that relates to this, because we don't know anything about La Malinche. Nothing…There is an action of putting stories very close together and creating a monologue—the same discourse in the same moment—it's the same person, with multiple personalities or who has fallen into this limbo. All of a sudden you turn around and you say: 'Where are the keys?' You had them in your hand, and then you don't know—they're seconds those moments that create unsteadiness. Sometimes, all of a sudden, I get scared, since I'm so prone to getting lost. I get to the corner near my house and I say: 'Where am I?' As a human being this is a petrifying fear because you lose your sense of being."

44 Karen Malpede has written: "If inside the play itself there is no one capable of bearing witness, no one who hears, sees, and takes into the body the truth of the other's story, the audience is let off the hook, so to speak, since it can then perceive no possibility of witnessing, and hence no real resistance to violence," "Theatre of Witness," 132.

45 See endnote 40: "a son of a bitch" is *"un hijo de la chingada."*

46 Firstly, *Hernán Cortés: Inventor of Mexico* by Juan Miralles; and secondly, an extract from "The Sons of Malinche," in *The Labyrinth* by Paz (see note 40).

47 This scene creates a striking intertext with a scene in the play *Árbol de Esperanza* by Enrique Mijares (1995), dealing with Frida Kahlo and Diego Rivera. Frida bathes Diego, and each refers explicitly to body parts of the other as a form of struggle and power play: Diego: "I don't understand why you had to shave off your Zapata-moustache that I liked so much. Shave your head when you want to, but don't shave your moustache again!" Frida: "However, if we talk about your chest, if you had disembarked on the island governed by Sappho, the women warriors wouldn't have executed you. Your extraordinary breasts would have given you the right of admission!"

48 Diéguez writes of "presence as texture" ("la presencia como textura"), *Escenarios liminales,* 188.

49 See Schneider, "Performance Remains," (2001), 106 ("To the degree that [performance] remains, but remains differently, or in difference, the past performed and made explicit as performance can function as the kind of bodily transmission conventional archivists dread, a counter-memory— almost in the sense of an echo…")." See also Blocker, "Repetition: A Skin which Unravels," who repeats Schneider's discussion and references Gilles Deleuze, "who insists that 'difference inhabits repetition,'" 201. For Deleuze, "In every way, material or bare repetition, so-called repetition of the same, is like a skin which unravels, the husk of a kernel of difference and more complicated internal repetitions. Difference lies between two repetitions," Deleuze, *Difference and Repetition*, 76 (see also Epilogue, note 31).

Chapter 4, pages 127–153

1 *Zapata, muerte sin fin*. March 2014 to March 2015. Residency el Foro del Dinosaurio del Museo Universitario del Chopo, Universidad Nacional Autónoma de México, Mexico City. Concept and direction: Juliana Faesler; Production: Moisés Enríquez and Sandra Garibaldi. Details of the five participating companies are as follows:

    i. La Máquina (Mexico City) is the company at the core of this study, directed by Faesler and Malheiros. For this project, Faesler and three other participants formed the ensemble. Two were particularly experienced in experimental devising and one was more familiar with dance and the folklórico repertoire. Participants: Juliana Faesler (director), Sandra Garibaldi, Carmen Ramos, Isacc López. (Vicenta Peruric participated in the workshops but not in the final performance);

    ii. A la Deriva Teatro (from Guadalajara, Jalisco) is a professional community and schools theatre company, creating theatre work to enable students and children to think about their current lives. For this project, this company used a flexible framework of participation, engaging a few young professional actors to take part in the workshops and performances. Participants: Susana Romo and Fausto Ramírez (directors [Ramírez is a renowned director with a long career with University of Guadalajara]), Horacio Quezada, Alejandro Rodríguez and Viridiana Gómez Piña. Susana and Fausto's 2-year-old daughter Juliana (named for Juliana Faesler) was present on stage during most of the public performances;

    iii. Teatro de la Rendija (from Mérida, Yucatán) is a professional experimental, body-based and conceptual company, who have their own theatre space in Mérida, where they perform and host other companies. For this project, three professional physical theatre performers participated. Participants: Raquel Araujo (director), Katenka Ángeles, Rafael Hernández and Alejo Medina. (For discussion of work by La Rendija, see Araujo, "Aprendiendo a sembrar Teatro"; Araujo and Castrillón, "Paisaje Meridiano"; and Prieto Stambaugh, "Memorias Inquietas");

    iv. Colectivo Escénico Oaxaca, from Oaxaca City, Oaxaca, is a community-based collective that specifically engages with Indigenous communities in the surrounding regions, and works with teachers and professors (for example, one professor of environmental science at the Polytechnic College uses theatre to work with K-12 children). The collective is based in a house in Oaxaca, and is a location for arts activities and community activities. Participants: Rosario Sampablo (director), Olga Herrera, Itandehui Méndez and 3-year old daughter Luna, Palemón Ortega, Ángeles Olivares, Federico Ramírez, Manuel Rubio, Jesús Loaeza, Omar Castellanos, Marycarmen Olivares.

v.   A-tar, from Tampico, Tamaulipas, is a loose ensemble of three performers. Participants: Sandra Edith Muñoz Cruz (director), Víctor de Jesús Zavala Vargas and Sergio Enrique Aguirre Flores. Muñoz is full-time professional director of theatre for the municipal government, directing a youth theatre group. She is also involved with the Artistic Direction of the National Theatre Showcase, see Muñoz "Diversidad en escena."

Distances and directions from Mexico City: Guadalajara, Jalisco, 300 miles west; Mérida, Yucatán, 1,000 miles north east; Oaxaca city, Oaxaca, 230 miles east; Tampico, Tamaulipas is 300 miles north.

I use first names to identify performers throughout this chapter.

2   Between 1876 and 1911, dictator Porfirio Díaz served seven terms as president, ruling through repression and promoting elitism (and so-called "high" arts of Europe). The Mexican Revolution (1910–1920) was fought to change this, through struggles for land and liberty. Zapata was born in a rural village in the state of Morelos, and grew up in an environment where peasant communities experienced the pressure of the landowning classes as they monopolized land and water resources. Elected to become an organizer in the peasant actions for land and rights, he was a leading figure in the Mexican Revolution. He coordinated large movements of people, known as the Zapatistas, with demands for "Reform, Freedom, Law, and Justice."

3   See photos of the performance. The face on the dartboard is a reproduction of the iconic photo of Zapata's dead body.

On 10 April 1919, Zapata was assassinated by an opposing nationalist faction. Zapata's dead body was photographed. The man who ordered his assassination, Pablo González, wanted the body photographed so that there could be no doubt that Zapata was dead.

4   2010 marked the centenary of the Revolution, so governmentally orchestrated ceremonies, high-profile theatricalized public parades, exhibitions, displays and large-scale public spectacles re-memorialized Zapata.

Significantly, 2010 also marked the bicentennial of Independence; therefore, troped bodies of Independence (Father Hidalgo and Morelos) were amalgamated with the troped bodies of the Revolution (Zapata, Villa and the soldaderas), as overt palimpsest bodies tracing remains of Mexican histories.

5   El Ejercito Zapatista de Liberación Nacional, EZLN.

6   The axiom "Land and Liberty" ("Tierra y libertad") is attributed to noted anarchist, social reform activist and important figure in the social movement that sparked the Mexican Revolution, Ricardo Flores Magón. Significantly for my study dealing with remains of bodies, a request was denied for the return of Flores Magón's body to Mexico from the United States. Flores Magón died in a penitentiary in Kansas (he had particularly opposed the vast US presence in Mexico and the appropriation of peasant lands; he had fled to the

United States and was arrested three times). In 1922, Mexican authorities made the request "That there be brought to rest in the soil of his native land […] the mortal remains of Ricardo Flores Magón," "Mexico's Martyr," *The Nation* (18 December 1922), Vol. CV No. 2998: 702. The US authorities denied the request and Magón was buried in Los Angeles. His "remains" were finally brought to rest in his native soil in 1945.

7   This is the title of a poem written in 1939 by José Gorostiza, an educator, diplomat and poet, who, between 1928 and 1931, was part of the vanguard literary and theatre movement known as The Contemporaries (los Contemporáneos); see, for example, Oropesa, *Los Contemporáneos Group* and Ortiz Bullé Goyri, *Teatro y vanguardia*. I urge readers to seek out Gorostiza's poem through the Internet. In his long, metaphysical and deeply corporeal text, he captures the circular, repetitive movement of life—the idea that "life is death without end." Through the poetic reference, the framework of aesthetic playfulness is combined with ideas of journeys and ephemerality. The poem (in translation) opens: "Full in myself, besieged in my skin/ by an intangible god that suffocates me,/ falsely announced perhaps/ by a radiant atmosphere of lights/ that hides my spilled consciousness,/ my shattered wings into shards of air,/ my blind and graceless plodding through the mud;/ full in myself—glutted—I discover myself/ in the bewildered image of water,/ nothing but an unwithering stagger,/ a collapse of fallen angels/ into the intact delight of their own weight/ that has nothing/ but a blank face/ half sunken already, like an agonizing...."

8   Zapata was known as a horse-rider, who wore his charro suit with pride. Horses were crucial to the outcome of the sixteenth-century Spanish conquest and to the processes of the 1910 Mexican Revolution.

9   It is owned by the National Autonomous University of Mexico (UNAM).

10   These clothes are global signifiers of authentic Mexicanness and most often associated with mariachi music, constructed as "the music of Mexico," see Hellier-Tinoco, "Mexico, But Not Mariachi."

11   As an iconic repeat of "Zapata," stick-on moustaches are used during annual celebrations of the Revolution. Various playwrights and artists have experimented with the moustache as a provocative performative item, see, for example, Astrid Hadad's "La Virgencita," (Gutiérrez, *Performing Mexicanidad*) and Sabina Berman's play "The Mustache" (see Taylor and Costantino, *Holy Terrors*, 279–89).

12   Fabião references Deleuze's description of a scar as a "present fact of having been wounded," "History and Precariousness," 124.

13   Zapateado simply refers to "footwork" from "zapato" meaning shoe. The similarities between Zapata and zapato are purely coincidental.

14   On 10 June 1971, a protest march by students and teachers, seeking educational reform, was brutally contained by an elite group of paramilitary soldiers known as los Halcones (the Hawks), with over 120 deaths, and many terrible injuries. This was just three years after the 1968 student massacre in the Plaza of the Three Cultures, Tlatelolco. Although the involvement and order of Echeverría was suppressed, in 2006 he pleaded guilty, but was exonerated.

15   Mexican theatre scholar Antonio Prieto Stambaugh, drawing on Mary Douglas, notes that "Unsettled memories call attention to the mechanisms of institutional amnesia, the way

power deploys silence and absence to control a population and keep it from demanding justice," "Wrestling the Phallus," 259.

16 See Diéguez, "El cuerpo roto," 4, drawing on Jean-Luc Nancy.

17 For my discussion of the crafting of the iconic image of "the kneeling Indigenous woman," see Hellier-Tinoco, *Embodying Mexico*. This corporeal imagery is still used in tourist literature in the twenty-first century.

18 In some musical practices in Mexico (particularly música jarocha), an animal jawbone is used as a percussive instrument. These practices are forms of embodied repertoires and traces of bodies of enslaved West Africans transported across the Atlantic Ocean to Mexico in the sixteenth century.

19 There are some similarities to work of British performance artist Bobby Baker, particularly her *Kitchen Show* and *Kitchen Demo* (Daily Life series), in which Baker uses her own palimpsest body through scenarios of everyday food and cooking to examine issues of domesticity, controlled bodies and acts of violence (albeit a less visible form of violence) in provocatively playful, performative processes. I am deeply grateful to Bobby Baker for her inspirational performances. See Epilogue for further connections to Baker's work.

Chapter 5, pages 155–166

1 *Taller de montaje: Guerra en el paraíso de Carlos Montemayor.* Director: Juliana Faesler. El Museo Universitario del Chopo, UNAM, Mexico City, 2–20 March 2015. Director of the Residency at el Chopo: Mariana Gándara. Participants: Alaide Ibarra, Alan España, Alejandra Hinojosa, Arely Pérez, Carlos Felipe López, Carlos Casanova, Carol Borka, Diana Luna, Elisa, Emiliano Vázquez Massimini, Gabriela Martínez, Gisel Casas, Irving Guevara, Isacc López, Jorge Becerril, Juliana Faesler, Laura Vega, Marcela Gallardo, Marisol Zepeda, Moammar González, Moises Enríquez, Oscar Serrano Cotán, Paulina Elias, Pavel Akindag, Rita Maria Nieto, Roberto Cabral, Roberto Campos, Selene Islas, Viridiana Narud, Vladimir Zecua, Yadhira Velázquez, Zeltzin Alonso (alphabetically by first name).

2 *Guerra en el Paraíso* 2009, Carlos Montemayor, México: Debolsillo.

3 In Mexico, as elsewhere in the world in the 1960s, there was an increase in challenges to norms of patriarchy, with counters to privileging of wealth over education and through citizen movements for social justice, rights, freedom and equality, with a particular focus on Indigenous rights. It was an era of deep societal and political unrest, with increased militarization. The government crushed insurgencies with violent strategies, particularly through tactics of a counterinsurgency campaign against rural guerrillas. President Luis Echeverría used the military to suppress and repress the insurgence of challenges to the status quo. This was the era of Mexico's "dirty war." Dirty war is most often used in relation to events in Chile, Guatemala, Argentina and El Salvador; however, as previously secret documents are being declassified, and as bodies are found, the evidence for disappearances and torture demonstrates that Mexico's dirty war was indeed brutal, see, for example, Doyle, "The Dawn of Mexico's Dirty War." This was therefore a period of disappearances and

concealment, of brutalized and disappeared bodies. Two of the most extreme events were the 1968 Tlatelolco massacre and the 1971 Halconazo, both involving government-ordered killings of protestors by military agents. See Chapter 3, *Mexican Trilogy, Moctezuma II/ The Dirty War* and Chapter 4, *Zapata, Death Without End* for other performances of these events in the work of La Máquina (see Chapter 3, note 20).

4 Cabañas launched his rebellion in the mountains of Guerrero. He was known to the US State Department as "the most important single leader" of the Mexican armed opposition, see Doyle, ibid., n.p.

5 The lack of knowledge of Cabañas' figure and name stands in obvious contrast to the troped and iconic figure of Emiliano Zapata, leader of the Mexican Revolution.

6 The raised fist dates back to ancient Assyria as a symbol of resistance.

7 A national flag is obviously an archival and iconic object of intense symbolic power. For uses of flags in performance protest, see "washing the flag" in Peru, Buenos Aires and Mexico, Diéguez, *Escenarios liminales*, 93–97, 175–85.
As in most nations, the national flag of Mexico is a protected object, with lawful uses requiring embodied respect. Daily flag ceremonies are held in schools and public plazas. Individuals carry the flag and collectively everybody salutes the flag in civic ceremonies with rituals of patriotism and allegiance that are intimately linked with collective embodied knowledge. The Civil Salute to the National Flag (*El saludo civil a la Bandera Nacional*) is a specific and fixed choreography: "Raise the right arm and place right hand across the chest, in front of the heart; the hand is flat and the palm of the hand is facing the ground."
In Mexico, the national flag is explicitly coupled with martyrdom, heroism and bravery. As material already worked on, an iconic scenario of national heroism and bravery engages a performative body-wrapping action. In 1847, during the US-Mexican War, six cadets, who were subsequently named as "the Boy Heroes"—los Niños Héroes—were defending the fort of Chapultepec against the US Marines. As William Beezley describes, "When the battle was clearly lost, the last six cadets, rather than surrender, took the flag and went to the highest parapet, where Juan Escutía wrapped himself in the banner and the six plunged to their deaths," Beezley, "Cómo fue que el Negrito," 424 and *Mexican National Identity*, 14–15.
In the *War in Paradise* project, the participants also used flags referencing the Popular Revolutionary Union Emiliano Zapata. (Unión Popular Revolucionaria Emiliano Zapata (UPREZ)) which includes the iconic face of Zapata. The UPREZ was formed in 1987 as a convergence of many urban organizations campaigning for social justice.

8 This resistant use is in stark contrast with skiers, mountaineers and hikers, who wear this item for leisure-time activities.

9 This major movement for Indigenous rights, land and education was launched in 1994, with high-profile strategies of global presence. This iconic head covering has been worn by women and men of the EZLN since the commencement in 1994, and, as a form of trans-clothing in resistance, is combined with unique clothes of each local Indigenous community (defying pan-indigeneity). Leader Subcomandante Marcos wore a balaclava in 1994 when launching the EZLN as means to conceal his "real" identity, always provoking the question: Whose body is this? It is worth noting that the presence of the (non-Indigenous) body of Subcomandante Marcos was used to engender multiplicity and simultaneity. Notions of

queering and multiplicity were particularly in evidence because Marcos promoted the idea of manifold identities to fit many contexts— as Rashkin describes: "Subcomandante Marcos [...] encouraged a queer reading of his own persona, and included gays and lesbians in his vision of 'a world where everyone fits.' [...] In response to media speculation about his 'true' identity, Marcos famously wrote: 'Marcos is gay in San Francisco, Black in South Africa, an Asian in Europe, Chicano in San Ysidro, an anarchist in Spain, a Palestinian in Israel [...] In other words, Marcos is a human being in this world,'" 150, 153, fn. 60.

When women in "traditional" Maya clothes wear the balaclava, they subvert their own gendered identity (see Marrero "Eso sí pasa aquí.") For discussions of the work of the collective Empowering Maya Women (FOMMA, Fortaleza de la Mujer Maya) and playwrights Petrona de la Cruz and Isabel Juárez Espinosa, see Taylor and Townsend, *Stages of Conflict*; Taylor and Costantino, *Holy Terrors*; and Underiner, *Contemporary Theatre in Mayan Mexico*.

10 There are similarities to the "camp" marching in *Monty Python's Flying Circus* (1972) performing Marching Drill.

11 Naming themselves as Lucio Cabañas is an act that counteracts the fear of anonymity and being forgotten in death, see Diéguez, "El cuerpo roto."

Chapter 6, pages 167–177

1 *La hora del Diablo* (full title: *Tríptico de Encarnaciones: Pessoa/La Hora del Diablo*) was conceived and performed by Clarissa Malheiros and created by Malheiros and Juliana Faesler, working through their lab-based devising processes. The piece is based on texts by Fernando Pessoa, San Agustín, Cecilia Lemus and Vilém Flusser. Other production details include: artistic collaboration, Toztli Godínez de Dios; musical organization, Ricardo Lomenitz; violinist: Ladron de Guevara; and heads, Salomé Tovar. *La hora del Diablo* premiered in El Museo Universitario del Chopo, UNAM, March 2015 and was selected as the Mexico City representative for the *11th Festival of Monologues: Theatre of a Solo Voice 2015*, organized by the governmental offices of the Secretary of Public Education, National Office of Arts and Culture and the National Institute of Fine Arts (Teatro en una Sola Voz—Festival de Monólogos, SEP, CONACULTA, INBA, 8 July–3 August 2015), with performances in diverse Mexican cities.

2 As noted, Hirsch's original concept is specifically connected with the Holocaust (see *The Generation of Postmemory*).

3 Within Mexican environments, the Devil has a temporal history of 500 years, introduced as a fundamental belief within the Christian Catholic Church by Spanish missionaries and conquesters. This concept was given bodily form in theatricalized spectacles of the first American theatre of 1531 in Tlatelolco. These performances were designed to instil fear and inculcate belief, through theatricalized and embodied (gendered) concepts of "sin" and "hell." The bodies of Indigenous actors were superimposed with costumes produced from designs in European religious art (woodcuts, paintings and statues), in which the Devil had horns, hooves and a tail. In *Final Judgement*, a morality play spoken in the Indigenous Nahuatl language, "the cast acted out Judgment Day, when the world would come to an end and the

souls of the dead would return to their bodies," Burkhart, *Aztecs on Stage*, 3. Lucia, a woman who has had sex outside marriage, is offered the chance to repent, as she witnesses the work of the Devil, see Burkhart, ibid., 59–78. In the twenty-first century, the Devil is embodied and performed throughout Mexico in socio-religious dance-dramas and in Passion Plays: see, for example, videos of the Passion Play in Iztapalapa and the discussion by Hellier-Tinoco of La Danza de los Catrines on the Island of Urandén, Lake Pátzcuaro, in which "devils" wearing sequined suits and masks are the mischief-makers who aim to disrupt the order by interrupting the "ordered" choreography and the dialogue, *Embodying Mexico*.

4 Believers eat a small wafer—the host—as an embodied sacrament to ensure futurity. Through the belief in transubstantiation, the wafer is the body of Christ; consuming Christ's body—the host—therefore promises futurity through life after death. This is an embedded and embodied cultural practice in Mexico.

5 *La hora del Diablo (Ficciones del Interludio)* by Fernando Pessoa (1888–1935). Significantly, Pessoa was a prolific writer who used approximately 75 names for his publications, which he did not call *pseudonyms* but *heteronyms,* in order to reflect his understanding of his own multiple and diverse selves.

6 San Agustín's writings influenced the development of western Christianity and western philosophy. Flusser was a philosopher and journalist (known as a dialogic thinker), interested in existentialism and phenomenology (Czech-born, he lost all his family of Jewish intellectuals in the World War II German concentration camps. He lived in London, then São Paulo and Rio de Janeiro). Cecilia Lemus Navarro has an extensive career as a dramaturge and theatre artist in Mexico City.

7 This may seem similar to the Brechtian technique of creating a character on stage in view of audience by putting on/taking off clothes. I suggest that Malheiros's performance is more complex, because she is not creating a character but accumulating layers and sediments to perform plurality and in-betweenness throughout.

8 See my discussion on gendering, identity and vocality, Hellier-Tinoco, "Vocal Herstories," 3–7.

9 In medieval theatres in Mexico (originating in European practices) a *tablado*—a wooden platform or stage—was constructed outside and inside churches for the performance of religious and morality plays. Spatiality was an essential element, with specific locations for earth, heaven and hell. Bodies moved to these places by means of ropes and pulleys. "Hell" was located under the main platform and a raised platform was "heaven." The principal platform was moved up and down with ropes. "Angels" came down from heaven, spoke their lines and went back up. "Jesus" and "Mary" ascended to heaven either with ropes or walking up the rungs of a ladder, climbing up to enter heaven. These proxemic relations of bodies in motion and being moved were engaged for conversion, not just for the sake of staging, see Burkhart, ibid.

10 These small hollow crisp cookies, each containing a tiny piece of paper inside with a single phrase, were invented in the United States but are connected with China.

11 See Díeguez, "Cuerpos ExPuestos," for an insightful discussion on the use of heads in performances of power, including: the theatre of horror; a de-constructed body (*el cuerpo des/montado*); a head separated from body as the image/remains of supreme

exercise of power; and the linking of tzompantli to the decapitated head displayed on the dance floor in Uruápan, Michoacán. She draws on Benjamin to describe the emblematic dismemberment of martyred Baroque bodies and references other contexts in Mexico (such as the decapitation and display of the insurgents in Guanajuato in the struggle for Independence). She describes a broken body as an exhibition of a body visibly fragmented, mutilated, un-made, deconstructed and removed from its traditional anatomy, ibid., 5. Concepts of disconnected heads in Mexico also explicitly reference remains of pre-Hispanic civilizations, particularly in the form of the huge, stone, sculptural Olmec heads.

Epilogue, pages 179–194

1 Fabião, "History and Precariousness," 124; Costantino, "Politics and Culture in a Diva's Diversion," 205; Jebelli, "We can cure Alzheimer's," n.p. and Foster, *Memory*, 2.
2 Yépez,. "Encuentro Internacional," 93. See also ideas of unfolding bodies created by Mexican sculptor Héctor Veláquez, who has explored the idea of the human body with new and old "skins" and in relation to contours and layers (see *Cuerpos desdoblados,* literally "unfolded bodies," by Karen Cordero and Alfredo López Austin).
3 Fabião, ibid.
4 Taylor ibid., 35.
5 Again, I am repeating Schneider, "Performance remains" (2001 and 2012) and *Performing Remains*.
6 As Schneider notes, "[w]e must be careful to avoid the habit of approaching performative remains as a metaphysic of presence that privileges an original or singular authenticity. Indeed it has been the significant contributions of performance theorists such as Blau and Phelan that have enabled us to interrupt this habit," "Performance Remains," 103–4.
7 Schneider, ibid.
8 Prieto Stambaugh, "Wresting the Phallus," and "Memorias inquietas," 216.
9 Jeyasingh, *Palimpsest* and "Palimpsest 1996," n.p.
10 Phelan, "Marina Abramović: Witnessing shadows," 574.
11 "Theater and performance offer a place to scrutinize public meanings, but also to embody and […] enact the affective possibilities of 'doings' that gesture toward a much better world," Dolan, *Utopia in Performance*, 5.
12 Taylor, "Opening Remarks," 15.
13 I am again referring to Schneider's ideas of performing remains: "If the past is never over, or never completed, 'remains' might be understood not solely as object or document material, but also as the immaterial labor of bodies engaged in and with that incomplete past: bodies striking poses, making gestures, voicing calls, reading words, singing songs, or standing witness," *Performing Remains*, 33.
14 Foster wrote of the challenge to use "dead bodies to lend a hand in deciphering […] present predicaments and in staging some future possibilities," Foster, "Choreographing History," 4, 6.

See Schneider's discussion of death in "Performance Remains," 104–5: "Death appears to result in the paradoxical production of both disappearance *and* remains. Disappearance, that citational practice, that after-the-factness, clings to remains—absent flesh ghosts bones," 104.

15 Taylor and Hirsch, "The Archive in Transit," n.p.

16 Case, "Meditations on the Patriarchal," 195, citing Blau, *Take Up the Bodies,* 83.

17 Phelan, 1995, 200.

18 Taylor, "Opening Remarks," 15.

19 See Taylor and Hirsch, "The Archive in Transit," n.p., for archives and provisionality.

20 "[This is] a project that deeply penetrates the labyrinthine passageways of our history, delves into the vestiges of the myths, removes the dust of forgetfulness and puts a giant mirror centre stage that requires audience members to come face to face with their ancestors," Ortega, 2012. In her discussion of live performance, Phelan notes that Emmanuel Levinas has argued that it is in the face-to-face encounter that ethics is distilled, Phelan, ibid. citing Levinas, *Ethics and Infinity*. However, as I described, particularly in Chapter 3, the Scenario of encounter in which Moctezuma and Cortés come "face-to-face" is, perhaps, one of the most traumatic scenarios of postmemory in the history of Mexico.

21 I am reminded again of Frida Kahlo's processes as she created re-imaginings of her own body. Confined to lie on her back in bed, looking at a mirror on the ceiling above her, she created her multiple selves from her reflection.

22 Gloria Anzaldúa, *Haciendo Caras/Making Face, Making Soul*, iv.

23 Seda, "Trans/Acting: The Art of Living 'In-Between,'" 17: "trans/acting [...] calls attention to the transgressive and performative nature of territorial and symbolic border crossings [...] [and] connotes negotiation and/or exchange while in the act of performing."

24 Bustamante, "Non-Objective Arts in Mexico."

25 Taylor and Hirsch, "The Archive in Transit," n.p. This is their introduction to the double issue of *E-misférica*, On the Subject of Archives. "More than a repository of objects or texts, the archive is also the process of selecting, ordering and preserving the past. It is simultaneously any accessible collection that potentially yields data, and a site for critical reflection and contestation of its social political, and historical construction [...] What do we want or need from the past? How is the past put into the use of the present? [...] [W]e look at the archive as the site of potentiality, provisionality, and contingency."

26 Lipsitz has explained how communities can be called into being through performance, particularly connecting past and present, describing expressive cultural works as "archives of collective struggle, [and] as repositories of collective memory," 62–3.

27 Taylor and Hirsch, ibid.

28 Taylor and Hirsch, ibid. As Carolyn Steedman describes in *Dust: The Archive and Cultural History*, "You find nothing in the Archive but stories caught half way through: the middle of things; discontinuities," i.

29 Taylor and Hirsch, ibid.

30 Aston, "Feminist Performance as Archive." Significantly for me, in her discussion Aston analyses the work of British artist Bobby Baker, who specifically generates performances dealing with food, home, gender roles and domesticity. I am grateful to Bobby Baker for her deeply insightful workshop at Lancaster University, organized by Aston and Geraldine Harris

(Women's Writing for Performance Project, AHRC, 2003–6). Each year at the University of California, Santa Barbara I use Baker's video of her performance *Kitchen Show* to initiate my course on "Creating Experimental Performance: memories/histories, processes/practices."

31   For Gilles Deleuze, "In every way, material or bare repetition, so-called repetition of the same, is like a skin which unravels, the husk of a kernel of difference and more complicated internal repetitions. Difference lies between two repetitions," Deleuze, *Difference and Repetition*, 76. In her discussion titled "Repetition: A Skin which Unravels," Jane Blocker repeats Schneider's use of palimpsest: "any action [...] 'is already a palimpsest of other actions, a motion set in motion by precedent motion or anticipating future motion or lateral motion.' For her, a beginning, 'by virtue of its "again-ness," is never for the first time and never for the only time—beginning again and again in an entirely haunted domain of repetition: image, text, and gesture'" Blocker, 201, citing Schneider, "Solo Solo Solo," 41. I return again to Schneider's ideas concerning performance, archives and repetition as articulated in "Performance Remains" (2001 and 2012). Her own reiteration of her 2001 writing, repeated in 2012, is a palimpsest with small yet significant alterations. Marking the differences between the two traces, I quote both iterations, but use the convention bold/ for the 2012 alteration, followed by the prior 2001 rendering underlined: "To the degree that it [performance] remains, but remains differently or **in difference**/*in difference,* the past performed and made explicit as **(live)** performance can function as the kind of bodily transmission conventional archivists dread, a counter-memory—almost in the sense of an echo [...]. If echoes [...] resound off of lived experience, such as performance, then we are challenged to think beyond the ways in which performance seems, according to our habituation to the archive, to disappear. We are also and simultaneously encouraged to articulate the ways in which performance, less bound to the ocular, **'sounds'**/'enters' (or begins again and again, as Stein would **have it**)/write, differently, via itself as repetition — like a copy or perhaps more like a ritual — as an echo in the ears of a **confidence keeper**/a confidante, an audience member, **a witness**/a *witness*" ("Performance Remains" 2012, 146/2001, 106).

32   This scenario and palimpsest body in *Malinche/Malinches* coheres with The Intermediary in Emilio Carballido's play *I, Too, Speak of the Rose (Yo también hablo de la rosa)*, see Taylor, ibid., 79–86 (and Chapter 1, note 11).

33   As I described in Chapter 3, this scenario was developed through Juliana Faesler's own fears and experiences of forgetting, performed as rememory through Malheiros: "You no longer know who you are. You fold the tablecloth and you put it on again. That horrible emptiness of identity—an emptiness between Alzheimer's and old age, remembrance, memory…you lose your sense of being." As a re-vision of Faesler's "emptiness," I propose these embodied experiences and questions about "knowledge" as trans-temporal, plural accumulations of multiplicity, possibility, potentiality and contingency through palimpsest bodies.

Index

Note: Page numbers in **bold** indicate an image.